THE SHA'DAA SERIES

I0659669

SHA'DAA™ Inked

Copyright ©2016 Copper Dog Publishing, LLC

Published by Moondream Press, an imprint of Copper Dog Publishing, LLC
537 Leader Circle
Louisville, CO 80027

Visit our Web site: www.copperdogpublishing.com

Credits:
Cover and Interior Design: Helen Harrison
Edited by Edward F. McKeown
Sha'Daa™: Inked created by Michael H. Hanson

Library of Congress Control Number: 2016910277

ISBN: 978-1-943690-11-4

First Edition: July 2016

Printed in the United States of America

SHA'DAA
INKED

CREATED BY:

MICHAEL H. HANSON

EDITED BY

EDWARD F. MCKEOWN

FOREWORD BY:

HALO JANKOWSKI

INTRODUCTION BY:

TRENT ZELAZNY

MoonDream PRESS

AN IMPRINT OF COPPER DOG PUBLISHING, LLC

Contents

DEDICATION

*To all the ones who love us and gave us the time,
space and support to create The Sha'Daa.*

– Team Sha'Daa

For the strength of the Pack is the Wolf, and the strength of the Wolf is the Pack.
— Rudyard Kipling

In union there is strength.
— Aesop

I'd like to take this opportunity to thank the small army of individuals responsible for this shared-universe series making it into print:

All of the many wonderful and talented authors who have come on board this exciting and ongoing project.

C.J. Henderson (Novelist) who generously spent a good portion of the last year of his life mentoring me in the ways of writing, editing, and running a small press, as well as co-writing the final chapter of this anthology.

Edward F. McKeown (Editor) whose fierce drive and professionalism have kept this project on track through some very tough times.

Halo Jankowski (Tattoo Artist) for writing the Foreword.

Trent Zelazny (Novelist) for being gracious enough to give us his words for the Introduction.

Catherine van Sciver (Proofreader) for reviewing the manuscript in record time.

Helen Harrison (Graphic Artist) for creating yet another one of her awesome book covers for The Sha'Daa.

From the depth of my heart, I thank you all.

Michael H. Hanson
Sha'Daa Creator/Co-Author
Piscataway, NJ
2016

FOREWORD

by Halo

SKIN WAS ONE OF THE VERY FIRST CANVASES for art. Sticks and stones rubbed and sharpened at points were amongst some of the first paintbrushes. Tattooing was initially a form of scarring the body that involved wounding oneself and packing dirt or ashes into the injury to mark and discolor it permanently. Our prehistoric ancestors cut holes into their skin, charred sticks in the fire, let them cool, and then applied the black substance to the manmade lesion to create tribal markings showing their ferocity and status.

As tattooing involved pain, blood, and fire, the primitive man believed the process released sacred life forces, just as the flowing of blood was also associated with a sacrifice to the gods. This link between our pain, tattoo symbols, and the supernatural is not just a good premise for this book series, but a *very* serious spiritual practice that happened in our history.

I've been tattooing for eleven years now. As a tattoo artist I specialize in portrait tattoos and realistic tattooing. Due to the nature of what I tattoo, I am constantly exposed to some of the deepest and most profound real-life stories it is possible to hear in my field. These tattoos represent family members lost, new family members joining, and even those that are dying. Sometimes this can be a way to commemorate a new happiness, represent a new point in your life, or symbolize a turning point. Alternatively these symbols, portraits, and artwork are a coping mechanism. They help people and encourage them to be happy about the times that they've had together, as both a memorial to a past time or individual.

Tattoos are like a photo album or even like a time capsule. When someone looks at me, they can see a skull, zebra stripes, and stars around my eyes, just as anyone can see an illustration.

When I look at my arm I see a tattoo of a nurse. I remember that my mother was a nurse and came to me in the hospital during a time when the dark gloom of death hovered over me. The tattoo represents the care that she provided to me.

When I look at my dragon tattoo I remember being young, in a chair trying to learn more about art and desperately yearning to become a better artist by receiving the tattoo.

When I see my tattoos, I can remember a point in my life and who was my friend at that time. I can look at these works of art and recollect why I got them and perfectly picture an important point in my life. There aren't many things that always stay with you until you die, reminding you of where you've been and who you were and hopefully, allow you to be proud of where you've come.

Just as the dark shadow of SHA'DAA impends its doom over this book, these supernatural tattoos manifest ways for the character to battle it. This premise is relatable as my battle with cancer has taught me a lot about the preciousness of life and family. It revealed to me my mortality and what I was actually capable of. I have many tattoos representing this time in my life, during and after, to give me strength and wisdom to endure and thankfully, beat my cancer.

Although a placebo effect, since obviously tattoos aren't a cure for cancer, what they can represent and remind you of is indisputable. What they mean to us is no different than how a familiar melody might give us the strength to work out a little bit longer. A child in danger might not mean much to anyone else, but the same situation would give the mother the almost superhuman strength to lift a car to save her young.

Life is such a precious and inestimable prize. There is nothing that can compare to it, and in the face of our demise we hold onto not the physical things we own, but the things that remind us of what it *is* to be *alive*.

I'm not much of a writer, but as an artist I am in constant awe of how wonderful a gift tattooing is to my life. The people's lives I've been able to touch and help just by creating art is nothing more than extraordinary and I'll know that they will always remember our interaction when they look at their body 60 years from now. This time capsule of artistic branding is the closest thing to Magic and the Supernatural I've had the pleasure to express with my life.

When THE SHA'DAA rears its ugly calamity, be sure that I'll be working at "Mom's Bane" helping prevent the apocalypse one Supernatural Tattoo at a time.

Halo Jankowski, Tattoo Artist
Black Lotus Tattoo Gallery
Hanover, Maryland
July 2016
www.blacklotustattoos.com
blacklotustattooremoval.com
http://www.tattoosbyhalo.com/home.html

INTRODUCTION

by Trent Zelazny

'D POSTED A PICTURE OF MY NEW TATTOO ON Facebook with the caption: "Finally covered the main scars from my suicide attempt in 2010, thus closing that chapter on my life…"

Ed McKeown saw my post, and was kind enough to ask me if I would like to write a short introduction for SHA'DAA: INKED, to which I responded with a blunt, monosyllabic yes (actually I said I'd love to).

It'll be short, I promise.

Since I was 16 I'd wanted a tattoo, though I didn't get my first until I was 38, only a year ago. And now I have this one.

Sometimes I'd wonder why I was waiting so long, but now I understand.

For me, the two tattoos I have, each, in its own way—sorry to use a cliché—is a badge of honor. On my upper right arm I have Daryl Dixon's wings. Some may find that silly and too fanboy, but I don't. Anyone who knows me know what a huge fan I am of *The Walking Dead*, both the comics and the TV show, but that is a miniscule piece of a puzzle that finally came together in the form of those wings after thirty-eight years.

Quite simply put, they say that I am a survivor. Even if I die tomorrow, that I've somehow managed to cheat Death as long as I have is truly astounding. So I am a survivor, and fucking proud of it.

There is an overfilled Rolodex inside me, jammed with card after card of WTH?, WTF?, and Whu-?&%$&*^!&^!?/?!*$#@??!?!?!!, many of them laminated with thick layers of trauma. That's the nut-shelled version.

The tattoo I posted on Facebook is that of a thunderbird across my left forearm. Solid black. Like all else, my reasons for this particular piece are numerous and diverse, but I shall abridge myself as best as possible.…

Before my amazing wife Laurel, I'd been engaged to a woman in Tallahassee, Florida. It was indeed a rocky situation, as she was bipolar and refused to take medication, and I was quickly blossoming into a one-foot-in-the-grave alcoholic.

In April, 2010, she went up to southern Georgia, put a gun to her head, and pulled the trigger. A couple of hikers found her body. Two-plus months of drunken agony later, I took a serrated steak knife and slashed myself down to the bone, and in seconds wore a dripping crimson evening glove.

A last-minute happenstance saved my life. If you are curious, I've written about it at length elsewhere online.

That was on July 4th.

And now, six years later, here I am, alive, sober, reasonably healthy; but most important of all, I'm happy. I'm married to the most amazing (and compatible) woman in the world, got a couple of cute dogs, two brand new kittens, more than a couple good friends, and in real life I get paid to play make-believe. I may not be rich, but I think that's pretty cool.

But to go from who I was in Florida to who I am now, back here in New Mexico, has been an awful lot of arduous, heart-wrenching, and terrifying strolls down deep, dark, dank, dismal corridors, where I've opened doors upon things I never wanted to see, or see again. It was a lot of processing, this thing and that, then this one again, process after process, over, under, in and out, through mind, heart, soul—which sometimes sync up and sometimes diverge—and I'm not done yet; I'll never be done. The difference now is my life actually feels worth living. I'm still here somehow, and now I have others to consider, and after everything, I see life now as a precious gift, something very much worth working for, and fighting for.

I carried this scar with me, this reminder, for almost six years. It will be with me forever, of course, but for me this has been an intense year, one of transition, and of transformation.

Born and raised in the southwest, the cultures have been a part of my life in one way or another for as long as I can remember. The thunderbird's origin, I believe, is Aztec, though it is also American Indian, a symbol of power, strength, and, for the Aztecs at least, a warrior symbol. It is also a variation of the Greek Phoenix, the long-lived bird that is cyclically regenerated, or reborn. In addition, for me personally, it is also a reminder to always sing, and to remember the strength and power of music.

I feel I have been reborn. Not in any creepy way, but hindsight shows you things through a different lens and with a different filter. Time and again, hindsight has projected the entire story, frame by frame, on the backs of my eyes. It shows my life slip away from me, numerous terrors and personal flaws, getting in too deep and still going too far; it makes me watch myself break, crumble, crash, burn, and fall. Conversely, it also shows me who I am now, and for the first time in my life, I don't utterly despise the face I see in the mirror. Instead I see a guy who's not perfect by any means, but who's a survivor, and he'll do just fine for now.

The thunderbird, the Phoenix I put on my arm, tells this story from beginning to end, in great detail if you look closely. It also serves as protection, and I can feel its power.

While I may or may not be any kind of actual warrior, I do know that I'm a survivor, and, to reiterate, life is a precious gift—the most precious of all—and it's very much worth working for and fighting for.

Mom's Bane

THE FIRST TWO HOURS OF THE CURRENT summer solstice passed in a frenzy of activity. Already Haumea had tattooed ten walk-in clients here at Mom's Bane, the longest running and most infamous of underground tattoo parlors ever to grace Planet Earth. It was an eclectic mix of ink jobs representing every style from tribal, Japanese, graffiti, and new school to trash polka, American traditional, portraits, and Celtic, and all of them, of course, bearing Haumea's very special eldritch imprint.

Ironically enough each one of these recent clients had insisted on, and paid premiums for "rapid delivery," a very special Mom's Bane service that required the use of one of the parlor's quick-rooms, temporally accelerated suites where one hour passed for every second in the main shop, or real world. In the quick-rooms you could tattoo for twelve hours straight, sleep an entire eight-hour shift, shower, and eat a meal or three, and still enter the main tattoo shop with only seconds passing. There were major drawbacks to extended stays in these paradoxical rooms for the unwary. None of this mattered to Haumea, shop owner and head tattoo artist, as she never slept and never aged, a gift, or curse depending on how you looked at it, acquired millennia ago, along with ownership of this transdimensional establishment.

A glance at the shop's seventeenth-century, French, rolling-ball clock, a magical device that told more than time, indicated that Mom's Bane now stood in the heart of Harlem and would be translocating every few hours between there, Gorky Park in Moscow, New Orleans, Temple Bar in Dublin, and the Liaoning Street Night Market in Taipei.

All five of her night-shift crew had their hands full and the reception area had already filled with ten more potential clients, with the same number out in the dark alley, vaping and trading texting addresses on their smartphones. Haumea yanked a can of Red Bull from her station's little fridge, cracked it, and downed it in a single swig.

She glanced for a moment in her wall mirror and considered herself. Just shy of five foot eleven, her slender but strong form filled out a black vest and dark blue jeans well. A small, ebony top hat rested comfortably on long raven locks, all which accentuated her most striking feature, her face, that of a beautiful young woman who'd had a traditional Calavera artwork, popularly known as a sugar skull, painted over her face, ears, and upper neck. Closer examination would show it was no mere make-up application, but the result of many painful hours under a tattoo needle wielded by a true master.

Haumea took a long yawn, stripped off her black latex gloves and replaced them with a bright pink pair.

"Oh, now those are cute. But they really don't go with the turquoise wrist band."

Haumea's eyes opened wide as she spun around and looked upward into the piercing ebony eyes of a tall man dressed in an expensive looking black suit and wearing a matching trench coat and fedora. The oppressive heat outside seemed to have had no effect on him. His features were striking, clean-shaven with a square jaw, aquiline nose, and high forehead, all possessing sharp angles that caught a multitude of shadows in the well-lit tattoo shop, a powerful and mysterious face.

"Benedict," Haumea gasped, "by Lono it is you. But wait. I heard you started calling yourself *Johnny* some time back. Sweet outfit. Quite a change from the old duster. It's been decades. In fact, almost…"

"…two centuries," Johnny finished.

"I was at that auction," Haumea whispered, "at the Luminous Museum in Syracuse. I left just hours before the big fire… and the rest. I remember watching the news videos Johnny. I knew it was you fighting that hell god. Word was you got sucked into another universe. Is that where you've been all these years since?"

"Oh I was gone far longer than that, my dear," Johnny said with some weariness, "and the distance from there to here is very nearly inconceivable… but my station here is a most holy responsibility, and no one and nothing may bar me from it. Surely you of all beings that crawl, walk, swim, and fly upon the planet know this."

"Look, things are a bit crazy right now," Haumea said, leaning to the side and looking at fresh customers piling into the shop behind Johnny, "take me out for breakfast later? We can catch up."

Johnny smiled, splitting his face with the grin Haumea remembered and still dreamed about, whether she wanted to or not. His teeth were perfect, shiny white, with the single exception of a gold left lateral incisor that flashed for a moment, reflecting an overhead lamp.

"Whoa," Haumea said, "that bling in your teeth is throwing me for a loop. You *have* changed."

"Ku'u Lei, I'm here on business," Johnny said. "Weren't you suspicious about your unusual number of surprise clientele since midnight? The darkness has finally arrived. Surely you feel the difference in the touch of the wind, the kiss of rain, and the rising fever in your blood. It is time."

Before Haumea could deny the truth of it, she sensed the tendrils of an ancient sea change enter her heart, and spark a lighthouse-like awareness in her soul.

"No," she said, "not..."

"*Sha'Daa*," Johnny whispered.

Haumea shuddered.

Debbie Does New Orleans

by Edward F. McKeown

"IT'S NOT LIKE I'M A MEAN DRUNK," DEBBIE Middleton said downing her fourth Hurricane and leaned her impressive rack on the dark wood and gold trim of the bar.

"I'm sure that's right," the bartender replied, wiping down a glass with his bar towel. The moon beamed in through the street level windows, reflecting off his black eyes and the short dark horns that curved from his forehead. Despite the late hour, he and Debbie had The French Casket to themselves. The other night denizens had fled into the shadowed streets when Debbie wandered in, her helmet of bright blond hair shining, rhinestones on her denim jacket and wearing thousand-dollar cowboy boots. She'd looked more like a country singer slumming than a vampire on a bender.

"Yep. Most people like me, goddamn it. I give them the night of their lives in exchange for some blood. All they need is a day or two of Gatorade and vitamins afterwards. Haven't killed a lousy human in eighty years. Well, unless they were trying to kill me." She tipped back her drink, almost falling off the barstool. "Another."

"Careful now," he said, starting to fix another hurricane. "It's a long way to the floor even for a short gal."

"Who you calling short?"

"Now, now, no offense meant."

"See this ring?" Debbie said, showing a gold ring mounted with a milky white crystal.

The bartender, a minor demon, raised a hand to ward her off. "Yep, keep that back, honey child. Not good for me to touch that there. Didn't think it would be good for you either."

"Like I was saying, I'm special," she slurred. "I'm so damn popular that a Knight Templar gave me this ring, a White Pass. He's pretty, the boy that gave me this. Pretty, young, and naïve. Damn," Debbie sniffled.

"Sounds like boyfriend trouble," the demon said, sliding the drink in front of her.

"Hell yes, I'm a two-hundred-year-old monster that used to kill people. He wants to go on dates. So I'm here trying to shake him out of my blood. Well whoever's blood I got in me." She raised her glass as if in a toast. "Damn you, Jeremy Leclerc."

The bartender scratched his chin. "Heard of him. He's bad news to our side."

"I'm a vamp," she said, "got no side but my own. Anyway quit interrupting. Here I am, broken hearted, just trying to have a couple of drinks and this witchy woman tries to drive me out of New Orleans in my first vacation in years. 'Taint fair I tell you."

"Still," he said. "It would have been better if you hadn't killed her. She was Baron Samedi's woman."

"Too bad, so sad. Would have been better if she hadn't driven pins into that doll she made of me. She'd have lived if she hadn't driven that one pin… well let's just say in a very delicate spot."

The bartender shook his head. "The Baron's going to be pissed. The French Casket is neutral ground. Everybody can come here. Once you leave, you're on your own."

Debbie picked up the Hurricane and drained most of it. "Honey, I been on my own since I was born in a Charlestown whorehouse."

"One hears many sad tales here," the bartender intoned.

Debbie laughed and finished her drink. She slid off the stool, hanging up the heel of her cowboy boot on the stool and nearly pitching over on her nose. As soon as she caught her balance, she gathered her remaining dignity and turned to the bartender. "What do I owe you?"

"Tonight is on the house," he said with a shrug and a toothy grin. "The French Casket will remember your visit. You'd best be heading underground soon. Sun comes up early in these parts."

Debbie nodded her thanks and staggered out the door into the warmth of the June evening. There streets were still full of revelers wandering about the never-ending party of the French Quarter. She reflexively eyed some of them but felt no need for new blood. She was still full of the life force of Rascatal; Witch Queen of New Orleans, and likely wouldn't need to feed for a week. But as she scanned the crowd, she noticed a tall, lean man standing just beyond the pool of light cast by an ornate street lamp, watching her.

Her eyes glimmered a warning as she met his stare, but this merely drew a sardonic smile in which a gold tooth winked at her. Despite the heat, he wore a dark trench coat and a fedora that cast his eyes in shadow.

Debbie squared her shoulders and marched right up to the gaunt stranger, who watched her approach with no sign of concern. She stopped a pace away looking up at him; he overtopped her five foot two inches by a foot and more.

"Hello, little girl," he said in a deep resonant voice. Then, eyeing her, added, "Well maybe not so little."

"Who you with?" she demanded. "Baron Samedi?"

He chuckled and something about that made the hair on her head stiffen and rise. "No, I know him though, the Death Loa of Haiti. He considers himself among the bad and the dangerous."

"Isn't he?" she said, cocking her head.

"Not so much," he replied.

"Oh. Are you bad and dangerous?" she asked coyly.

His eyes widened into huge inky pools and the gold tooth shone with a light of its own. As if a veil had been ripped way, Debbie now saw what he was: ancient, powerful, and infinitely deadly. She froze. Then the veil dropped and he was just a tall man on a city street. She tried to slow her breathing and thought about running.

"You're a young lady with a problem," he said, the sardonic grin fixed on his face. "You're in love."

"Am not," she returned, startled into speech.

"Are too," he returned and laughed. The laugh seemed to clear the street around them as if it had a physical force of its own. "Worse yet, he's a young living human, a Knight Templar you've been helping fight the forces of darkness. Is that a sensible thing for a vampire to do?"

"How the hell do you know all that?" she shot back, too angry to be wise. "And who the hell are you?"

"I'm just Johnny the Salesman," he replied.

Debbie's face couldn't turn any paler, which was good but the last remnants of her drunk fled in terror. "No. You're… you're a myth, a boogeyman to frighten little imps and demons with."

"Hee-hee," Johnny said and danced a soft show move in front of her. "Here's Johnny. But enough about me— we were talking about you."

"What do you want?" she asked softly, knowing escape and defense were both futile.

"What do I always want?" he returned mischief and madness in the dark eyes, "to trade and to play the Great Game of the Sha'Daa."

"It's coming?"

"Oh, Darling, it's already here. It's going to be a busy forty-eight hours."

"Jeremy," she snapped. "Jeremy Leclerc—"

"You were about to ask me if he is safe?"

"Yes, dammit!"

The sardonic smile relented some. "Oh dear, you have it worse than I thought. Well, he's young, strong, and not as dumb as you fear. The Sha'Daa will be worse in some places than in others, in some it won't even be noticed. Who can say?"

"Damn," she swore. "Ain't you got better things to do with your time than chat up a little old country girl?"

"Time, time, time, never ask what's become of it," he quoted. "Yes, I and Santa Claus whip through little holes in time, in the pauses that refresh. But for all of that, I have time for you Debbie Middleton. You have something I need."

"What?" she asked trying not to shiver.

"Your pretty white-stoned ring, a gift from your boyfriend to the vampire with a heart of gold. The White Pass has greater virtues then those who gave it to you know."

"Can't say I like the thought of giving it up. A woman my age doesn't get that many offers with a ring. Those old bastards Jeremy forced into it weren't that happy, even though I'd helped destroy a Bain-Sidhe terrorizing rich bitches at the mall. I might not get another. "

"Well the Sha'Daa will be breaking out here in a number of particularly New Orleans ways, but I understand Baron Samedi has put all his plans on hold until he deals with the insult you did him, draining his current main squeeze dry."

"I'm entitled to defend myself, even from humans, under the White Pass."

"Which may cut some ice with the Templars, but will do nothing for you with the Baron. What I have to offer may allow you to see another moonrise." He snapped his fingers and a card appeared in them. It held the picture of a girl. Her face was covered with a tattoo of a human skull and she wore a top hat. Dark hair and eyes completed the picture. The effect of it all was equal parts horrible and beautiful.

"This is Haumea; she runs a very special tattoo parlor called Mom's Bane. It appears various places, various times, and time is various when you are in it. This card entitles you to her services."

"A tattoo on my lily-white skin? I don't think so. Tattoos are a long-term commitment for a vamp."

"Might make the difference between seeing the future or not. You fancy yourself a time-tourist. Be sad if the future happened without you there to see it. Then there's your beau, Jeremy. You could get back in time to help him. If you're alive."

Debbie considered. "So where do I find this tattoo-vixen?"

"The card will take you there," he said. "Just follow where it points."

She looked at the card and the image on it looked back and her and winked. It raised a hand to give a cheery wave.

"Dammit," Debbie said, slipping the ring off her finger and handing it to him. "I know I'm going to regret this."

"That's optimistic," Johnny said, "after all, only the living have regrets." His smile widened as his image became blurry and indistinct. Finally, there was only the smile hanging in the air with its gold tooth winking. Then it too was gone. Debbie caught the card as it fluttered in the air.

"God damn Cheshire Cat," she muttered. Then, looking down at the card said, "Ok, Haumea, which way are we going?"

The skull-faced girl on the card gave a wicked grin and pointed left. Debbie walked on for fifteen minutes following the card's finger, like a demonic Siri down the back alleys of the French Quarter. The very air rippled for a moment and a short wave of nausea washed through Debbie. Instinctively she realized she'd crossed through some kind of portal, but to where she was not sure. Debbie finally stepped into a particularly disreputable looking alleyway where a red light glowed in the window of a sagging two-story building.

She looked down at the card, and the figure on it gave her a cheesy grin and a theatrical double thumbs up.

Debbie marched forward. Muggers and rapists didn't concern her except as occasional snacks and her preternatural senses disclosed no other threat. She walked up to the door next to the window with its fringed red lamp and knocked. The door swung open, though by what means she could not tell.

Debbie entered a foyer that could have been to a well-maintained Victorian home. It had red damask wallpaper, dark wood accents, and drapery everywhere. Old paintings hung in dim alcoves with long gone faces gazing down on her. A few well-upholstered chairs and love seats dotted the floor. At the far end and somewhat incongruously, was a large counter at waist height, holding an old style cash register.

The curtain behind the counter stirred and the young woman from the card appeared. She was prettier in person and with a greater dignity. She towered over Debbie, and the top hat accentuated this. Her dark shirt and jeans showed off her petite figure. She smelled and felt wrong to Debbie's senses; this was something that had once been human but was no longer so.

"Welcome to Mom's Bane," she said in a voice which held the rich green tones of the far Pacific.

"I'm Debbie Middelton. Johnny sent me."

"I'm Haumea. That Johnny has been keeping me busy. Lucky for all that time takes strange turns in Mom's Bane. Come with me." She turned and raised the brocaded curtain. Debbie entered and Haumea took her arm and guided her to a room to the right. This room held a bed and a chair along with some machinery she assumed was for tattooing.

"So, you going to show me some work?" Debbie said, looking around. Surprisingly there were no tattoo designs on the walls.

Haumea smiled. "No. Every tattoo here is unique and I know what you will need."

Debbie arched an eyebrow. "That's a little presumptuous isn't it, Missy? I think I'd like some input into something so permanent."

Haumea didn't look offended. "I'm the greatest tattoo artist in the history of the world. What I do is more than art, more than beauty, its necessity. Or did you think Johnny sent you here for a tramp stamp? Now please take off all your clothes. I need to see what I'm working with."

Debbie grumbled, but slid out of her clothes to stand naked before the other woman, her pale body shining in the unnatural perfection of the undead. Haumea walked around her and then began running her hands over Debbie's body.

"Well plenty to work with here."

"Yeah," Debbie said. "I'm kinda over-upholstered, especially up top. I've always envied a small lithe figure."

Haumea nodded and placed her hands on Debbie's breasts lifting and examining each one.

After a few seconds Debbie raised an eyebrow. "Well either pop one in your mouth or turn loose of them."

"Yes, yes," Haumea said. "These will do nicely."

"So have said thousands of men and hundreds of women," Debbie shot back, miffed at the casual fondling.

"But not both," Haumea said. "I think the left one. And even better, you'll heal instantly, so no time in the quick-rooms." The skull-tattooed woman pointed to a wall where two framed tattoos adorned the wall. Debbie knew they hadn't been there a minute ago. On one plaque shone a Crusader cross on a shield, a symbol of the Knights Templar. The other held a stylized storm cloud, but it was not a dull gray, it rippled as if with inner lightening.

Debbie shot Haumea a dirty look. "Honey, you tattoo a Templar cross on me and I will burn."

"No," Haumea said with complete confidence, "if *I* do it, you will not burn."

"So what then," Debbie asked, "one on each boob?"

"No. The cloud will cover the Templar Cross."

"What the hell sense does that make?" Debbie demanded.

Haumea smiled. "Perhaps it only makes sense in Hell, or the Sha'Daa, but it was for this you were sent here."

Debbie crossed her arms, glaring at the cross and shield. "Damnation, I came to New Orleans to forget about Templars and all their crap. Now I'm going to be tattooed with the mark of one?"

"Seems to me that one has a left a mark on you already." Haumea said. "I force this on no one. But I have much to do. You must decide now."

Debbie sighed, knowing she had chanced on the battlefield of powers far greater than a vampire. She wanted to get back to Jeremy in Charlotte, but would Samedi let her slink off if she wanted to? She could hope the Sha'Daa wouldn't strike with full fury in a town so dull that Sherman hadn't bothered to burn it, but it was too much to hope for.

"OK, Spooky-girl. My boobs are in your hands....again."

Debbie slipped out of Mom's Bane and retraced her route. Long habit made her check the sky in her first few steps away from the shop and she froze in her tracks. The moon was exactly where she left it when she entered. There were still hours to dawn.

For lack of a better plan, she headed back toward her hotel. Her pink VW with its tinted UV-resistant glass was there. With it she could dare running through the daylight to get home. There were no buses this early and she simply jogged. Debbie might not be built like a marathoner, but she simply didn't tire. She stuck to shadows and reluctantly slowed if she saw people in the street, a busty woman running in cowboy boots, attracted attention even in New Orleans.

The motel she'd picked had ironically been named Knight's Rest, but it backed up to woods that made for easy entry and exit for a woman unfazed by mosquitoes, snakes, or spiders. She'd gained a position only a dozen yards from her pink VW when an impact from behind threw her to the ground. A hood that smelled of garlic and other herbs noxious to vampires slipped over her head. She clawed and struck and sent bodies flying but her senses swam and faded as she was borne to the ground by still more.

Debbie came to in a damp-smelling basement, her hands and feet tied and the hood still on her head though it was pulled off a moment later. She lay in a large room with a huge pot boiling in its center over a propane stove. Around the room stood a rank of zombies, not the ravening ghouls of TV but the revived dead, servants of the death Loa. They stared emptily at whatever they were facing.

Baron Samedi sat on a chair made of bones and glared down at her. He wore a tuxedo and top hat and a similar tattoo to Haumea, the skull over the face; maybe it was a New Orleans thing. Glasses without lenses perched on his nose and he clutched a glass of rum in one hand and a thick cigar in the other. While he appeared to be a black male, she knew the thing before her had never been human. Two lesser and skinnier versions of himself tittered obscenely and stirred the large pot.

"I do not like you," Baron Samedi said, in a high, nasal voice, "and I like most women. But you, you come to my town. You kill my woman. Drink her dry without so much as a by your leave. You disgrace me in front of the other demons. All my plans are on hold as no one will follow me. No, de Baron does not like you."

His assistants shouted encouragement. Debbie remembered that they were Baron La Croix and Baron Cemitiere, both of whom might just be manifestations of Samedi himself.

"How does Maman Brigette feel about it?" she shot back.

Samedi cringed and looked around at the mention of his wife. "Nary you mind that girl, you should be thinking about your own self."

"So what can I do to make it up to you?" she said mock-sweetly.

Now he smiled. "Ah yes, we come to it. You will bargain with me, yes?"

"I might."

"Oh, I think you will." His gaze drifted to the boiling pot.

"Or what? I go in the pot? Wouldn't that be a waste of a truly magnificent pair?"

The Baron laughed. "Sorry no, breasts are for babies. De Baron likes de booty."

"So sorry I ain't a Kardashian."

"The pot isn't for soup, vampire. It's a special solution that can shrink anything to the size I want." He jingled a necklace of tiny human and demon skulls. "Wouldn't affect your kind anyways."

"But as to you. Too many have heard of how you have disgraced me. You, who work with the Templars to thwart our own kind. Many know of you. Having you serve me will give me great face," he said, spreading his big hands. "So you will swear an unholy oath to me, slave your will to mine, just as these do." He gestured with his cigar at the cordon of zombies. "Then you will kill the Templar, Jeremy Leclerc, and bring me his head. I will shrink it and wear it for a pendant."

Debbie expressively and exhaustively told Samedi where he could insert his own head in a location that it would be forever safe from daylight. He listened visibly impressed. "Now dat some fine cursing," he said, sipping his rum. "But enough of your sass, girl. You join my crew or you burn, vampire."

"Go to Hell," she said.

"Been there," he replied. He looked at his lesser incarnations. "Ok boys, take her outside." Zombies lurched into motion behind the lesser barons. Debbie kicked and struck as best she could with her limbs bound, the ropes that bound her were bespelled or she would have snapped or stretched them. But despite her struggles she was borne out, mercifully still in full darkness and down to the shoreline. There she was chained between metal poles and spread eagled on the ground.

"Ah," the Baron said, "so much to do this night. Can't even take time to enjoy a woman. The Sha'Daa is a harsh mistress. But you will not have long to wait. The sun rises soon. Come boys, we have potions to brew and invocations to make before we leave for the front."

He drew a deep lungful of cigar smoke and blew it out. "Last chance to reconsider."

Debbie ignored him. He shrugged and gestured to his followers. "Have fun working on your tan. It gonna be a cloudless day."

The Baron and his followers, little fonder of the sun then most night creatures, headed back to the cellar they'd emerged from.

Debbie threw herself at the chains but they were heavy and sound. She might wrench the poles out of the ground in time but already the sky was growing pink. The rosy fingered child of Dawn reached over the horizon with a hand that would take her out of this existence. She sighed as the rim of the sun appeared. "Well, well, so this is the end. Two hundred and seven years. Not a bad run. Some loving, some hating, seen a lot of life and too much of death."

Hot tears spilled down her face, surprising her. "I didn't think," she said to herself, "it would hurt this much to go. It ain't the pain, though that will be bad enough. It's all that future I ain't gonna get to see."

The first rays of the sun struck her, with the warning of the agony to come. Suddenly she felt something a stirring in her body, almost sexual in nature. The tattoo on her breast was glowing; its gray lit more each second from within. Then it was gone, in its place was the shining whiteness of the shield with its red templar cross.

Debbie wondered how she was seeing anything and then realized that she lay in the shade. Above her was a thick cloud, not covering the horizon but it threw a deep shade in every direction for a thousand yards. Beyond it the sun slanted down its golden rays into the world.

"Well I'll be damned." She looked back down at her breast and the Templar shield was also gone. Then she realized that the shield was lying next to her, on the chain that held her right arm. The chain was softening, glowing as if under great heat. She pulled her arm free as the chain melted. This shifted the shield to reveal a sword under it, similar to the one Jeremy bore, but without its magic gem in the hilt. She placed the shield on the other chain and in minutes was free.

Debbie stood in the shade of her own personal cloud and hefted sword and shield. Step by booted step, she stalked toward Samedi's cellar.

Maman Brigette rose from her rocker and opened the door to her big old house in the swamp to an imperious knock. She looked down at the small, busty woman with her bright blond hair who held a rum cask under one arm. Her aura was that of the undead.

"What is a vampire doing in daylight on my porch?" she demanded, then glanced up at the sky. "Where has the sun gone?"

"You Maman Brigette, wife of Baron Samedi?" the blond asked.

"Wife," she replied bitterly. "Yes, of that no good, womanizing, cheating, damn…" she went on for a minute.

"Yes," the woman said, "that's the one. Well good or bad news, depending on how you feel about it. I'm Debbie Middleton, vampire, sometime good girl. I drank his mistress dry, he came after me. That put me in a pickle." She offered the cask to Maman. "So anyway, I dumped him in a vat of head-shrinking super potion and then pickled him. He's too hard to kill but he's out of it for now."

From inside the cask a tinny, voice cursed furiously. Debbie shook the cask and it subsided.

Maman stared at Debbie. "How did you find me?"

"I gave his two minions a choice of a 10-second head start if they told me. It worked out for one of them."

"Which one?"

"Damned if I could tell them apart."

"I like you, little girl," Maman said. She tucked the cask under one beefy arm. The high-pitched voice began again. She struck the top of it with a resounding thump. "You shush now."

Maman turned back to Debbie. "How about you come in for some nice iced tea?"

"Sorry," Debbie said. "I have a hot date in Charlotte, North Carolina."

"You be safe then. Roads not good just now." She looked back up the one vast cloud on the otherwise sunny day. "Damndest thing."

"Ain't that the truth," Debbie said, with a bright smile as she turned for her little pink VW.

Pounding Skin

AUMEA WAS THIRTEEN YEARS OF AGE IN
403 A.D. and the third daughter of the King of the Menehuni. She
knew she would soon be bartered off in marriage to the first born
son of a great sea trader from the Marquesas Islands, so it was as great a shock
to her when the sleeping mountain god Kohala stirred to life, and the Island's
Kahuna said that a royal sacrifice was needed to create a sleeping spell for the
waking volcano deity.

Haumea begged her father but to no avail. The people were terrified of
the minor earthquakes, and she was eventually laid across the main altar at the
highest and most sacred Heiau, temple to the gods.

The Kahuna, a large, vicious, and petty man whose face and arms were
covered with thick scarification marks, raised a sharp obsidian dagger in anticipation of harvesting Haumea's heart. Twice he had tried to win her favors in
private, and having been denied and humiliated both times, he'd singled her
out in revenge, demanding publicly that only her royal virgin blood would
save them all.

Angry at her father and her people for cowering to the fear mongering
of the corrupt Kahuna, Haumea refused to play the dutiful sacrifice, spitting defiance at all those who came too near to her, and glaring hatefully at
the Kahuna.

Just as the head priest began lowering the dagger, the worst tremor yet
struck the island, and the ground split open on the highest slope next to Kohala's main peak. All of the priests, including the Kahuna, fell screaming into the
maw of the steaming chasm. Haumea's father and the rest of the people ran
off in terror.

Haumea, her hands and feet tied and weighed down, lay poised on the
lip of the newly born pit of death. Her heart pounded painfully in her chest,
but she would not give in to despair. She was the daughter of a king, and would
face her death with dignity.

Haumea, a voice spoke in her mind, *truly you are a worthy sacrifice.*

She knew she was hearing the voice of the god, Kohala.

But my hunger has been appeased, Kohala continued, *and I need no
further blood force. You may live the rest of your mortal life as you will, or, if*

you choose of your own free will right this moment, I will shall sing to you the blessing of Kumulipo for the honor of your bravery this day.

"And what would I do then," Haumea whispered, "for I no longer wish to be the daughter of a king."

Your life will be long, Haumea, Kohala spoke with a voice like thunder, *I only demand that you choose a following that honors your heritage, and your beliefs. Decide now, for the sleep of many millennia is upon me.*

"Great Kohala," she whispered, "I accept your blessing. I will become my tribe's Tufugu, and I will scribe the history of our people on the flesh of thousands."

So be it, Kohala said, and the ground shook harder than before. Intense pain flooded Haumea's entire body, and it felt as if hot lava poured through her veins and arteries. She screamed and fell into unconsciousness.

"The Sha'Daa," Haumea shouted, "is going to start today?"

"Actually, my dear," Johnny said, leaning forward in a confidential manner and lowering his voice, "it started two hours ago. And just between you and me, it has been a rather exhilarating one hundred and twenty minutes… so far."

Haumea bit her lower lip and growled. A dozen different thoughts flew through her mind at once.

"Our plan is still in effect," Johnny said.

"Of course," Haumea said with enough anger in her voice to raise the eyebrows on her coworkers. She waved them back to their work, "thousands of tattoos for way over a century, but still, we need a lot more to make your plan work."

"You've got less than two days," Johnny said, turning toward the door.

"Looks like I'll be spending a lot of time in the quick-rooms," Haumea smirked, "lucky I had fresh food stocks and all other supplies replenished this past week. So, you think we've got a real shot at surviving this holocaust?"

"Oh," Johnny shouted over his shoulder, "maybe a snowball's chance in Hell."

"Listen up everyone," Haumea yelled to her staff, "triple-overtime pay for the next two days."

This spurred a cheer from the gang, but a frown from Haumea shut them up just as quick.

"Right now, phone and text your backups and any artists you've ever wanted to give a break in the biz," Haumea added, "we're about to get swamped

and we'll need all the help we can get. Next walk-in, drag your ass over here. Stat!"

An unknown twenty-something client strode up to Haumea and quickly pulled off his Steve Austin Six Million Dollar Man t-shirt to expose his pale, hairless, unimpressive torso.

"I want Xena the Warrior Princess's Chakram tattooed on my chest," he said, "but there's a catch."

"What's that?" Haumea asked.

"I want it composed of an equal proportion of fractal dotwork, radiant lines, three-dimensional octagons, and Celtic circles."

Haumea sighed. It was definitely turning into one of those days.

CHAPTER TWO

Pipelines

By Beth W. Patterson

T HOSE WHO DANCE MUST PAY THE PIPER, he thought for the umpteenth time, kicking an empty cigarette carton into a gutter. *Or is the fiddler?* In any case, he knew that paying the musician meant accepting consequences, and once again, those daft tourists seemed to think that trad music inconsequentially grew on trees. Diarmaid fancied himself a musical martyr, bravely taking one for the team time and time again, wondering when he would see his real glory. He glanced over his shoulder at the cheery three-story building that was The Oliver St. John Gogarty, where he played regularly. He stared into the abyss of the impassive windows, but they had no answers for him.

A streak of silent lightning overhead threatened to crack the sky. The whiskey he'd consumed earlier in the night suddenly gave him hot razors in his heart.

Diarmaid Mac Aodha was a compact man, with stern gunmetal-blue eyes but a gentle mouth. His curly red-brown hair gave him the deceptively cuddly appearance of a wooly fox. His habitual crooked grin was fading, though. He had once loved the sessions at Gogarty's, loved the smell of leather and wood when he opened his case and took out his pipes, strapped the bellows to his elbow and around his waist, and adjusted his reed for a strong back "D". The tuning of his drones, the testing of his regulators in cascading intervals … it was as sacred a ritual as an entire orchestra tuning up. The fiddlers and box players were always intense or sanguine in their playing, but his was a Zen-like process: the unconscious control of the airbag under his left arm and the pumping of air with his right, like a second set of lungs working while his fingers danced over the chanter. The uilleann pipes were what gave traditional Irish music its distinctive sound.

But now he was very burned out. The tourists drove him crazy with their requests for Riverdance in its entirety, "Danny Boy," or worst of all "Amazing Grace," not even knowing the difference between the sweet Irish bellow-blown uilleann pipes and their obnoxious Scottish highland counterpart. Even the Willie Clancy festival in Miltown Malbay had become a cesspool for debauchery and the musicians couldn't even hear each other in the pubs. Here it was already summertime, and he'd decided not to go this year.

It had been a strange night overall. The crowd had been subdued. And then his best friend Seamus had been acting strangely, not joking about Morris dancers or anything, just murmuring some word in Irish that even Diarmaid couldn't place—not even after years of learning Irish Gaelic in school, including translating *Peig Sayers*. Seamus had just kept sipping his pint and saying, "*Seádá. Tá Seádá orm.*" What was that word? Nest? Shed? He couldn't recall. "Shah-daah," he sounded it out, but nothing came to mind.

A distant low groan—like mechanical brakes, but heavier—punctured the dome of the night sky. It was too late for rubbish collection to be making the rounds, and Diarmaid shivered but shrugged it off.

He'd known that being a full-time musician was going to be challenging, but nothing had prepared him for this changing world. And now he had to forever face the disappointment of his mum, who had wanted him to be a farmer like his Da. No matter what successes might await him in the future, she was dead now and he could never prove his worth to her.

His younger brother Lorcan had gotten all the praise in the family. After their Da had died, Lorcan had valiantly stepped up to take over the family dairy business. Back in their native Ballymore Eustace, right on the Kildare-Wicklow border, his brother had not only carried on the farming enterprise, but had also somehow developed a subspecies of cow that was the paragon of milk production, with an extra large udder and six teats instead of four. Lorcan had attributed it to ingenious breeding. But Diarmaid harbored some sort of suspicion that it was a genetic mutation, and a bad omen to boot. *Such crimes against nature could open the doorways to nefarious things,* he'd often said. But then again, he was sensitive to anything unusual.

He had always been fascinated with legends of the faeries, and there were so many names for them: the *Sidhe,* the fey, the Good Folk, the Shining Ones, even the Tuatha Dé Danann, the original race of people in Ireland. But he was torn between the unseen world and pragmatism. The eldest son, he felt it his incumbent duty to protect his family and still somehow live his dreams, all the while trying to live with the embarrassment that was his mother. She had been a *seanachie,* a storyteller, which was unacceptable in society. Although nowadays, when women could finally drink full pints of Guinness instead of from dainty half-pint glasses without too many disapproving stares, female storytellers were still considered unseemly. They were "crowing hens," meddling in men's affairs where they didn't belong.

But all who knew his mum had come to respect her, for she was one of the few remaining people who had actually heard a banshee. By the way she had described it, it must have sounded like an air raid siren screaming its bereavement from the depths of Hell. He certainly didn't want to think of what he'd have done in her shoes, and reluctantly admired her courage.

And now she was dead, and he was without structure. Forever a *culchie*—a country bumpkin—among the Dubs, he had taken care of her for the last decade, commuting weekly from Dublin to Glendalough on the bus. He still had mixed feelings about her; he adored her, despised her, and feared her, and it had affected everything in his life: his music, his obsession with the supernatural, and his social interactions. He found that he couldn't sustain relationships because no woman could ever measure up to his mother. He had wanted to protect his family from intruding ladies—or was it the other way around?

He'd just dumped that nubile American girl tonight after his gig at Gogarty's. He was positive that she would accept his excuse that he had come to think of her as a sister. He couldn't understand her rage. Perhaps he shouldn't have tried to further explain why that was a caveat, but with her being from Louisiana and all she might not have understood. He hoped that she wouldn't try to put some sort of a voodoo hex on him.

His mother would have known about the subject, but she would have been suspicious of his affiliation with magic if he'd asked her. She had been paranoid of everything that might have invoked the fairies.

Which is why he practically froze with one foot in the air at the sight of the brand new tattoo parlor, called Mom's Bane. The name was both ominous and enticing. Yes, he'd wanted a tattoo for years, but getting so much as a single earring would have broken his mother's heart.

A tattoo would be liberating . . .

He blinked at the sight of the figure across the way. With the broad-brimmed hat, at first he thought it was his hero Paddy Keenan, arguably the greatest living uilleann piper. But as the figure stepped into the light, he could see that the face was much younger . . . and yet infinitely old, like a well-guarded icon. The glint of gold in the front tooth shone like a beacon.

"Lovely piping tonight, there," the stranger addressed him in a heavy traveler's accent. *Where could he be from? Ballyfermot?* He thought he knew all of the travelers in the music scene, and wondered how far and wide this fellow got around.

Like every polite Irishman, Diarmaid offered a cigarette to the shadowy figure. It was good protocol to share your fags with everyone else before lighting up yourself. American tourists had never caught on to that, or the importance of buying rounds of drinks for others.

The man's smile was unsettling, but not unpleasant. "My name's Johnny. I will offer you a trade, lad: your fag for a bit of advice. In a world about to change—if it continues to exist, that is—you need some permanent ink on your skin. I strongly suggest that you go into that tattoo parlor and ask for Haumea. Tell her to use her better judgment."

The pungent smell of antiseptic and intrusive buzz of needles set his nerves on edge. A few clients were smiling in the mirrors at their still-bleeding designs, and the owner of the shop materialized out of the shadows like a bat.

He never swore. The strongest expletives he ever uttered were along the lines of "Judas priest!" and "Crumbs!" But the floral skull-faced woman was more than he was prepared to wrap his brain around.

"*Fuck!*" He hadn't even realized that it was he who had uttered it until the eyes staring from their black sockets twinkled in sympathy. He could now see that it was not a bare skull adorned in flowers, but an impressive tattoo that covered her entire face instead. It reminded him of a piece of folk art he'd seen in a Mexican restaurant in Cork City; that was as close as he got to knowing anything about Mexican lore. The morbid ink-mask belied her outrageous attire, from her oversized top hat to her t-shirt that read NEVER PLAY LEAPFROG WITH A UNICORN. The law of inevitable death clashed with the shocking absurdity. It was like looking at the Grim Reaper in a tutu, and he was even more unnerved.

"Em." He cleared his throat. "Em. Are you Haumea?" he asked, chagrined at his own timorousness.

She smiled, the giant teeth etched into her full lips stretching, all the better to eat him with, he thought. "You must be Diarmaid. Johnny told me that you'd be giving us a shout." She led him to the nearest chair already set up as if he'd made an appointment.

"But…" The rest of the words evaporated in his throat. The stranger with the gold tooth had never asked his name, and surely couldn't have made arrangements with this terrifying woman in so little time. Senses dulled, he felt the way his friend Seamus was acting at the pub earlier that night as he allowed himself to be led to the chair like a farm animal. To be shorn, to be milked, to be slaughtered, to be adorned, he no longer cared. What difference did it make?

She hiked up his sleeve so quickly with such authority, he was certain that there was some mistake.

"Who's Johnny?" he said, and smiled in that special way as she shaved his left bicep with a touch that was almost caressing. He was suddenly self-conscious of his blue-white, freckled Irish skin. The snap of a rubber glove onto her hand made him compulsively tighten his buttocks.

She stood with one hand on her hip, head tilted to one side, holding the bright silver tattoo gun in the other like a weapon from outer space. "You're a nervous client, aren't you?" she remarked. "Johnny would be the bloke that you shared your smokes with. As far as *who* he really is, well, that's none of your business. Now you have a job to do. So be a big boy and make yer mum proud."

He recoiled at the mention of his mother. "That's quite a gun you're got there," he tried to joke, desperate for a subject change.

Her eyes glittered from their oversized sockets. "We don't like that word, young man. This is not a gun, and we are not in America. Call it an 'iron.' That should comfort you, as iron is repellant to those fey that have kept you so equally entranced and terrified all these years. But as soon as we're done here, the iron gets hidden. We need the *Sidhe* tonight."

He was so distraught by her apparent ability to read his thoughts, he didn't even notice the iron aiming at his unblemished skin. He jumped slightly at the first touch of the needles, more in surprise than pain. "Don't be such a wimpy little *haole*," she chided him. He didn't know what a "howley" was, but he got the distinct feeling that it was a slur. But what was he going to do while this skull-faced woman was injecting ink into his skin? He tried to relax and breathe. It wasn't all that bad really . . . it was like someone pinching the skin of his bicep hard and shaking vigorously. There was something narcotic in the ink, he thought. Even the discordant buzz of the iron held something of a drone. Otherworldly scenes were playing on the ceiling—bucolic portraits of animals capering with tiny insect-winged people—and he allowed himself to be drawn into the visions for...minutes? Hours? Where had the time gone?

He glanced at his watch and blanched. *It's like being in a fairy mound, only in reverse,* he thought. In the realm of fairy, you might party all night long and emerge the next morning to discover that a hundred years had passed and all of your loved ones were long dead. In this case, he'd been inside for hours, but according to his watch less than a minute had passed. It was unnerving, to say the least. But the curiosity to see his new mark overrode any fear, and he caught his breath when Haumea held up the mirror.

An old medieval image of a pig playing the pipes shone on his angry pink skin. Surrounding the outline was a swirling dark purple spiral like a tiny slice of the world beyond, dotted with tiny stars—or perhaps glowing eyes. Perhaps it was a trick of the light, but he could have sworn that he saw them twinkle and wink.

Even as the tattoo was still weeping fresh blood, he couldn't resist touching the bandage. A distant reedy sound called from somewhere far away. He touched it again, and the drones kicked on.

"Judas priest!" he gasped. He brushed the entire length of the tiny chanter with a feather-light touch, and a few strains of "Brian Ború's March" began to sound. And as the music started, the rest of the mortal world began to crinkle.

"You have to get out of here, Diarmaid. You have a job to do." Haumea's voice was stern, and he cringed at once again being bossed around by a woman. He was about to deny her the satisfaction, but shrank at her bone-faced glare. Now was not the time for issues.

As he stepped over the threshold of the shop, she planted a quick kiss on his cheek. Beneath the ink that cast the illusion of hard teeth, her lips were petal soft, and fierce heat crept up his cheeks.

That kiss sent a shockwave, flinging his body into the street. When he regained his composure, Haumea was gone and he was no longer in the Temple Bar area. As he pushed himself to his feet, his hands had a hard time finding traction. The ground was now a blanket of glistening crumbled rocks, slick with dew.

The pervasive thick haze made it hard to identify his location, although the setting looked familiar. The squatting monoliths gaped from the ground like jagged teeth, and the perimeter was perfectly round. He could be any of the ancient sites he'd read about in school: stone circles all across Ireland were certainly not uncommon. The looming shapes that surrounded him were indiscernible in the mist. But something was wrong. There was no scent of earth, no grass, no distant lowing of cattle. He was in a graveyard of crushed dreams and forgotten tunes. The monoliths might have been tombstones commemorating long-dead ideals.

It was as if he were at the hub of some sort of wheel, and could see infinite spokes stretching out beyond, and concentric wheels beyond the rim. He suddenly felt impossibly small. His world was not the only one, and it most definitely was the weakest.

And these stones began to move. Slow undulations, barely discernible in the fog gave way to violent rocking as limbs unfolded from their sides. The surrounding shadows grew taller as the specters rose to their feet, warriors all, eyes like glowing embers. These were beyond anything he'd seen in story-books. Some of them had insect wings, but they also had horns, hooves, tails, and extra limbs. They were all prepared for battle, the *sidhe*. They began to pulse a low murmur like a rhythmic chant, a steady heartbeat in the midst of all that lacked form.

And impossibly Diarmaid's best friend Seamus was standing among them, still acting as strangely as he was in the pub, eyes fixed on some distant invisible point.

"Seamus, what are you doing here?" he demanded.

His mate's reply was thick and expressionless. "*Tá Seádá orm, á Dhiarmaid.* The Sha'Daa is upon me, Diarmaid. The death of time and space. It is upon everyone. The veils between realms—ours, the *Sidhe,* and beyond—are thin."

A screech forced both young men to double over and clap their hands over their ears, as the wail tore the veil between worlds even wider. It was the embodiment of grief and insanity, bringing to mind a siren with a thousand teeth and a bottomless stomach. The banshee heralded this Sha'Daa, and the opening of new worlds, terrifying worlds. If this was what his mother had heard, then no wonder she'd been touched in the head. But something even more frightening lay beyond through the rent of time-space fabric. He looked, and thought his heart would stop.

Haumea was no longer the strangest thing he'd ever seen.

This was no land of faery. This was chaos. A rent in the sky reflected and duplicated, like an image caught between two mirrors infinitely reflected, a terrifying world that made no sense: fire, inverted mountains, and an infinitesimal sea of eyes.

It was a non-place where nothing could be remembered or predicted. It was rent with holes in space and time, gaping like empty eye sockets in a metaphysical skull, spanning eternally inward where thought once transpired. And the creatures that emerged terrified him so badly, the breath was sucked from his body in a vacuum.

Fey could be mischievous, but they had their roles in the shared world, for boon or for bane. But the . . . *things* that inhabited this dimension were almost inconceivable. They were the Others—this was the only name that formed in Diarmaid's mind. They lacked form. Only vibrations held them together, and those that he could hear struck such a panic into his heart, he was almost completely paralyzed.

Music was his entire reason for existence, and now destruction had assumed dictatorship over the world of sound. These Others used frequency oscillations that collided and tore each other apart. The waveforms slammed into his body like a typhoon, knocking him to the ground and creating confusion among his eldritch allies.

His eyes unscrambled one visual. It may have been a sentient being, but he had no way of telling. It was something round and legless, a featureless face that shrieked a buzzer, announcing the end. *Time is up.* He could not make eye contact with a blank mask, and the fact that it could somehow still see him turned his paralysis into uncontrollable tremors.

Another creature glided silently into view like a fast-moving glacier. Shaped like a giant pyramid with a pair of undead eyes at its pinnacle. A shaggy, white devourer of life force, it could only bellow a great drone. The long, low note was unchanging, maddening. A drone could be creation; in fact, it was the very foundation of Celtic music. But without a melody to cause tension and release, it would level out everything into *sameness.* Sounds were vibration. Sounds could create and destroy.

A second pyramid slid alongside the first, sounded a dissonant tritone, instilling terror. Soon the life force of his world began to ebb with the droning of the Others.

"Play it, Diarmaid." The voice in his mind may have belonged to Johnny or Haumea, or even Seamus—he wasn't sure, but it didn't matter.

His cold, stiff hand reached up and touched the tiny pipes, fingers smearing the tattoo with fresh blood. He didn't quite know how he would operate such a tiny replica of his instrument—and with one hand, to boot— but somehow his fingers instinctively knew where to go, and he didn't even question why. The sound was not emanating from the skin on his arm, but instead it was resonating everywhere. From the Mountains of Pomeroy to the Plains of Kildare to the Cliffs of Moher and beyond, something was waking for every tune he called. Even faraway Newgrange was yawning its solstice secrets. He played his tiny piece of flesh art for dear life as the *Sidhe* began to open the gates between mortal, fey, and something darker and more terrifying beyond. He played even as it fell upon deaf ears of the world he loved.

The music of his tiny tattoo brought strength back into his body, and he regained his footing. The assembled fey drew sanity from his playing and reassembled their ranks. It was to be a standoff. The fairies light and dark versus the Others. Diarmaid secretly thought that he and the fey didn't stand a chance, but he played O'Neill's March with a bravado that he didn't feel. Terrified as he was, he offered his challenge on behalf of the Good Folk that he'd come to love, and his mortal world that he loved most of all.

Once the call to battle had sounded, he instinctively opened his pipes case and strapped on the bellows. He perched on the edge of his case, his favorite makeshift chair. The leather strap just under his fresh ink felt hot and thick. His fingers, now slick with blood, skittered across his chanter, adrenaline pumping into his mind as he automatically pumped air into the bag. It was breathing, unconscious, and essential. His wrist flicked out and hit the regulators, strengthening the melody in intermittent little harmony intervals. As the battle raged, he willed all of his mental power into the music that fueled his army. He played every tune he knew that was associated with the fey. *"The Gold Ring, The Ivy Leaf, Sí Beag Sí Mór, The Strayaway Child ..."*

The agonized screaming of a *Sidhe* warrior ripped his concentration to shreds, scattering notes like dry leaves in the wind. Diarmaid made the mistake of looking in the direction of the sound and froze at the sight. One of the Others had bitten the fey man completely in two and was noisily chewing the lower half while the *Sidhe*, still alive, was vainly trying to pull his remaining torso away on a pair of bloodless arms. The droning pyramid beast, mindless eyes frozen wide, suddenly stopped. Dropping the mass of carnage from its maw, it fixed Diarmaid in its gaze and launched a note at him. The terrified piper fell into a frozen paralysis. The legless pyramid slowly glided toward him.

A new sound rent the chaos. Discordant and toneless, it was brassy as sunshine, and warmth flowed back into his extremities. It was the sound of a crowing hen. The bird was as plain as a solid piece of ground, but he would have recognized the soul that lived inside it anywhere.

Mum! he cried inwardly.

He did not know how his mother had become caught between two worlds, but he was so grateful to see her, he nearly dropped his chanter. She had tormented him his entire life, but she was still his mum, and he'd missed her. Yet in the thick of the battle he could not call out to her, this spirit in bird form giving power to the Good Folk. But the brazen crowing turned the battle around. Bright and shining, the fey began to drive back the enemy.

One of the Others bore down on the modest little chicken but suddenly seized up in obvious pain. It bent itself into a backward arc, howling. A fairy wielding a pendulum like a tiny bolas had leapt onto it, drilling time and structure into its entropic form. Diarmaid shook himself hard and resumed playing, ignoring a second shriek from the monster. As long as he kept the music up, life force was being given to the world, and the ragged hole that was a portal to other worlds could not widen.

A swamp of tiny men riding the backs of sheep and pigs charged into the fray. Many were crushed under the broad bases of Others, but a few managed to throw the abominations off their course. *"Widdershins!"* one called, and the others urged their mounts into a counterclockwise path around the gargantuan creatures. Diarmaid picked up the pace of a reel and found that the whirling ring of fey and farm animals was drawing strength from the increased tempo. He thought of the speed of Finbar Furey's playing, went into the wildest piping he knew, and his allies great and small finally held their nemeses at bay. He wasn't sure if the pyramids were sentient, but he could have sworn that their bellowing drones sounded frustrated as they became rooted into place.

For a fraction of an instant everything was stock still: the *sidhe*, the *Tuatha Dé Dannan,* the Others, and the flickering tear between worlds momentarily frozen into a bright beam. Then the flashing recommenced. An odd vacuum rush momentarily sucked all of the air backwards through the hole, and the wailing of the banshee mingled with deflated groans of Others.

The gap began to close as one by one the Others retreated, chased by the fey, bright and dark. One by one, they all disappeared through the portal into their respective worlds beyond. Other things chased the enemy too: a genetically modified cow, a woman with an hourglass, and a crowing hen. *The crowing hen!*

He called out to the humble little bird, words of love that he had never been able to tell his mother while she was alive. Just before following the specters into the hidden world, the plain little creature turned and looked at him.

She might have recognized him just then. He chose to believe that the creature that bore the soul of his mum cocked a feathered head and clucked approval of him at long last before fading into the dawn.

He hoped that she was finally proud of him. She had driven him mental, but she had been a great lady.

Something began to shake the ground, back and forth like a massive overstuffed washing machine, only ten times as violently. Diarmaid was nearly unseated from his case and had to brace himself with one arm to protect his precious pipes.

With a colossal clang, some sort of portal swung shut. He was standing back in front of Gogarty's, the loud, obnoxious tourists inside oblivious to the near destruction. Seamus, who appeared to be passed out drunk on the pavement, was the only thing different from when Diarmaid had left the pub hours—or minutes—ago. In the momentary stillness, he tried to sort everything that had just happened into his brain, but only one important factor kept surfacing. *Mum is proud of me,* he told himself in a rush of incredulous joy.

He stole a concerned glance at his friend, but a young man with subtly pointed ears was already attending to him, removing his shoes, covering him in a soft blanket and slipping a folded towel beneath his head. "Don't worry there, Diarmaid. We're going to give him a lift home. When he wakes, he remember meeting a traveling piper at Bewley's after the late night session for sausages, eggs, and chips. He'll recall having crashed on his couch, and return to his flat with fond memories."

It was the best that Diarmaid could hope for, and he wasn't sure whether or not he'd erase the memory of tonight's horrors if he could. He bid the unusual man goodbye and walked out without looking back.

He straightened his shoulders like a warrior, a champion among the commoners. No piper in the history of Ireland had undergone a rite of passage like this. Ten earthly minutes had passed, and Dublin seemed to have slept through it all. A stray Jack Russell terrier trotted purposefully towards the Ha'Penny Bridge. A drunken teenage couple was snogging in the doorway of a chip shop, oblivious to the world—and the next world, and the one after that, and so forth.

He had helped to stave off a near-apocalypse and seen a dimension of Hell that could never be described in words. In light of these true horrors, he somehow knew that he no longer had a reason to fear the *Sidhe*. They were his allies for all time, even the dark fey. But he would leave a bowl of milk outside his front door as an offering, just in case. The pipes beneath his sleeve purred in accordance with his thoughts. He couldn't wait to show his new tattoo to his mates. He suspected that he alone would be able to hear its music, but like so many things that had happened tonight, it was a secret he was satisfied with keeping.

It did not matter what was defined in this mortal world as success. He no longer cared if he was Esau to Lorcan's Jacob. *For it is I, Diarmaid MacAodha, who has wrestled with the immortal and won,* he crowed to himself.

And then the unexpected note belled out, and he was undone. The deep sustained blast of a faraway barge threatened to snap him in half like a dry sapling.

Some trace of the cataclysmic war had adhered to the droning he heard in everything: engine brakes, electric lights, the flow of the Liffey, or the monotone of his neighbor's endless platitudes. Something had leaked into his world. It would follow him all the days of his life and ambush him when he least expected it, and It would kill him someday.

Was he still a noble martyr when every moment was terrifying?

It stalked him with infinitesimal patience. It knew his every move, like a spurned lover obsessed or a diabolical government strategy. He could not see It, but he had no choice but to watch It back, and to play the tunes that held back the madness. He was the last remaining pipeline into his world. Only his eventual death would ensure that the mortal realm was safe at last.

Those who dance must kill the piper, was his last thought, and the faraway crowing of a hen concurred.

Slinging Ink

AUMEA ALWAYS ENJOYED NEW CUSTOMERS arriving in Mom's Bane. Most had never heard of her establishment, or at best, had thought it was an old wives tale, told to impress kids. As tattoo parlors went, its pedigree was lost in the mists of time. Many folks now elderly clearly remembered going to it when they came of age, but even back then it had a veneer of history that belied the young, albeit tattooed, visage of its proprietress, Haumea.

Three quarters of her customers over the centuries were drunk when they arrived, and often were never able to find their way back to the shop after sobering up and trying to return the next day. Mom's Bane did not like to sit in one place. The parlor had a foot in every major city on the face of the Earth.

There is always an alley, or a dark and avoided street, in every city on this planet, and each one is a nexus for that city's darkness, angst, and fear. In ancient times such locales were often the sites of temples, or worse. Haumea, with the help of a shadowy and very powerful fedora-wearing salesman as payment for a very special gift, had managed to permanently anchor Mom's Bane to every one of these nexus points. Their inherent power, added to what was already trapped and contained in Mom's Bane's very foundations, allowed the shop the blessing and curse of instant and often constant mobility, a blessing for avoiding tax collectors, city inspectors, and landlords, and a curse for trying to recruit return customers.

Haumea had never received a quality complaint from any of her tattooed clients, those that did make their way back to Mom's Bane, though the occasional trickle of angry spouses, put-off BFFs, and upset parents was one of her occupation's few drawbacks. Unlike the majority of tattoos that fade over the decades, and in recent years can be removed with Q-switching lasers, Haumea's eldritch handiwork, like a tempestuous but committed marriage, was permanently welded to a person's skin, for better or worse.

Always Faithful

by Arthur Sánchez

RAYMOND DELGADO WAS DYING AND HE knew it. The thirty-five-year-old science teacher forced himself to sit up so that he could lean back against an overturned steel worktable. The room around him was in shambles. Laboratory equipment lay broken at his feet. Shattered glass and spilled chemicals covered the floor. Small fires were burning in the corners. All around him the bodies of the dead, both human and . . . monster lay in heaps.

Supported by the hard surface of the table, Ray propped the shotgun he was holding against his hip. The last monster had been fast—too fast. And though Ray had managed to blow the creature's head off, it still succeeded in slamming into him with claws like pruning shears. At first the pain was such that he couldn't even scream. But now, in the aftermath of the attack, all he could tell was that he was lying in a puddle of blood unable to feel his legs.

Movement out of the corner of his eye made him spin the barrel of the shotgun around and start to squeeze the trigger. He pulled up only when he saw that it wasn't another monster. It was just Shorty scrambling out from behind a pile of propane tanks. The gang-banger was battered and bloodied but otherwise unscathed. He'd done well with the AK-47 he was carrying. He'd made the monsters pay for all the "soldiers" he'd lost.

"Hey man," Shorty said as he arrived at Ray's side, "you ok?" But the look on the teen's face told Ray it was just a polite question.

"Get out while you can," Ray told him. "I'll cover you. When you get outside tell the police, or the National Guard, or whoever you find that they don't need anything fancy to fight these things. They're delicate. They pop like balloons. Just don't let one get near you." He held up a bloodied left hand as evidence that he knew what he was talking about.

Shorty nodded. "Sorry it played out this way. You did real good — for a busted up old Marine." Shorty grinned at his not so funny jab.

Ray ignored it. What mattered right now were the students. Thankfully the official school year had ended a couple of weeks ago so the classrooms weren't packed with hundreds of bored teenagers, but there were still dozens of students in the building doing their summer classes. That was the reason Ray was even here—to teach remedial chemistry. He could only hope the administrators had followed the protocol for an active shooter and had gotten everyone out the back door. He didn't want his kids anywhere near this place when the real fighting started.

"Tell whomever you find," he said, struggling against a wave of nausea that was hitting him. "Tell them to hold the line. These things are scouts. They're just testing our defenses. The real engagement is still coming. Don't let anything in or out of the hole and we might make them reconsider their plans."

Shorty's pug-like face frowned. "The what?"

Ray pointed out the broken windows of the ruined classroom at the glowing yellow disk that hung suspended between his school and what had been, until just a few hours ago, the local clubhouse of one of the city's most notorious street gangs. It was about ten feet around and glowing like a miniature sun but without any heat or light. "That's where they came from. That's the breach in the perimeter."

Shorty shook his head. "Dude, you're not in Kandahar any more. This is L.A."

Ray didn't argue the point. He knew where he was and he knew an invasion force when he saw one. "Get going," he said, "before they regroup."

Shorty didn't fight him on it. Instead, he gripped his weapon, gave Ray a firm nod, and sprinted for the door. Ray didn't bother to watch him go. Instead he looked down at the hand that held the shotgun. The tattoo on his wrist was tingling slightly and Ray wondered if that meant his grip was going to fail him. Then he read the simple block letters that were inscribed into his skin and remembered that his grip would never fail him. "Semper Fi" was the Marine motto. It had been how Ray had tried to live his life and it was how he planned to die. People were depending on him. He wouldn't let them down.

"But you've already let people down," a familiar voice said to him. Ray's head shot up to see Maria standing a short way in front of him. Her jet-black hair glistened in the sunlight and she had on that tank-top and shorts combo that used to drive him crazy. She had the longest, tannest, legs of any woman he'd ever known. *"But that wasn't enough for you,"* she said accusingly. *"You had to go off and play soldier."*

"Maria?" He struggled to speak. "How? . . . Where?" But he knew it couldn't be her. The girl in front of him was still eighteen. Maria, today, lived in Phoenix with her husband and a two year-old son.

"It could have been your son," she said as she approached him. *"It should have been your son."* The hatred in her eyes was unmistakable.

Ray's tattoo was burning now as if it were being drawn on him for the first time. The pain helped sharpen his thoughts. If it couldn't be Maria then it had to be . . . Ray swung the shotgun around and pulled the trigger. The image of Maria faded as the slugs tore through the monster and it was thrown back against a wall. The long-legged pink-skinned creature that lay battered there reminded Ray of a hairless cat. He found it disgusting. "Serves you right you motherless son of a —"

Shorty's AK-47 erupted from somewhere behind him. Ray tried to lift himself up so he could see over the table but couldn't manage to do it. He legs still wouldn't work. There was a second burst of machinegun fire followed by the scramble of claws and a muffled cry. Then the room fell silent.

Ray waited to see if anything else would happen but when nothing did felt compelled to call out: "Shorty? Shorty, you all right?"

Silence.

Then someone tossed an object over the side of the table so that it landed at his feet with a dull thud. It took Ray a second to realize it was Shorty's head. They'd never been friends but Ray felt a pang of regret for Shorty's death. The teen had deserved better than that. Then he pushed the emotion aside knowing that while Shorty's troubles were over his were just beginning. Tossing Shorty's head at him was a message. The monsters wanted him to know that he was on his own. Nobody outside the building was getting any word on what was happening inside the building.

"Hey Ray, you ready for this or do you need me to come over there and help you lace up your boots?"

Ray looked up to see that he was now standing in a dusty street in the shadow of some rust-colored buildings. "Seriously?" he thought. "If I have to be hallucinating why can't I be hallucinating about Vegas? Why this shithole?" But Ray knew exactly where he was and, more importantly, *when* he was.

Turning to look down the line of Marines who were waiting to launch the raid, he could see Jackson standing at the door to the house. A warlord was supposed to be hiding in that house and Jackson was anxious to bag the bastard and get out of there. *"Dude, I need the latch key,"* he said. *"You wanna get up here and use it?"*

Ray looked down at the shotgun in his hand. It was the one from the lab—a top of the line 20 gauge semi-automatic Remington. Shorty's gang hadn't scrimped on the hardware when they'd moved into the neighborhood.

Ray had tried to call the cops on them but without a legitimate complaint the law couldn't do anything. So Ray opted for an understanding. Nobody from Shorty's gang would cross the street to the school and nobody from the school would cross the street to the clubhouse. Which is why when Ray ran there needing a gun it was a small miracle the gang members didn't shoot him. Of course, having one of the monsters crashing through the front window of the house had sort of clarified the situation. The amazing part was that they not only gave him a gun but they loaded up and followed him into battle.

No, the shotgun Ray had carried in Afghanistan was a basic double-barrel model that might have been new 50 years ago. Not much in a firefight but perfect for blowing the locks off of front doors. That was the reason why they called it the "latchkey" and it was Ray's job to use it. But they'd gotten some new recruits that morning and he'd wanted to make sure everyone knew their job. At least, that's what he told himself. All day he'd had a bad feeling about this mission and for some reason Jackson had spent the day itching for a fight. He didn't have any patience on the best of days but today the man was in a mood.

Despite knowing what was about to happen, Ray started down the street and tried to shout out a warning. "Bobby, don't —"

"*Screw this,*" Jackson said as he kicked in the door. "*I ain't waiting any longer.*" Time seemed to slow down as Ray watched as the explosion set off by the I.E.D. strip the flesh off of Bobby's skull. The entire event only took an instant but Ray remembered screaming for an eternity.

The hallucination should have ended there but it didn't. Ray now found himself wandering down a dark alley with his service pistol in one hand and a half drunk bottle of Jack Daniels in the other. Oh yeah, he recalled, then *this* happened. He never did figure out how he'd ended up outside the wire that night. Jackson's death wasn't his fault. Jackson was an idiot who should have waited. But on some level Ray felt it *was* his fault. It was his job to clear the way. He should have been the one standing there and not Jackson. He'd failed to do his job and someone else had paid the price. Ray placed his hand against the wall to steady himself and felt the rough brick under his palm. God it felt real.

There were some streets in Kandahar where a U.S. Marine was told never to go. The odds of getting out alive are worse than fighting insurgents up in the hills. But there were other streets where you could go—where a soldier was actually welcomed regardless of what side he's on. On those streets the very same people who would slit your throat a few blocks over will now gladly offer you all the booze, drugs, and under-aged girls you could afford. This was one of *those* streets.

Ray remembered thinking he should find a bar—that there had to be a bar somewhere down this street. But instead he ended up in front of a lonely-looking storefront with a bright blue door and a crazy neon sign over it that wasn't even in Arabic. The sign in the window said "Mom's Bane, Tattoo Parlor" in English. That's when Ray decided that what he wanted was a tattoo. A lot of the guys had them. Some had incredibly complex tattoos of girls on bikes or screaming eagles with wings outstretched and talons at the ready. It's a sin in Islam to have a tattoo so some guys got them to stick it to the fundamentalists they were fighting. Of course, it's a sin to get a tattoo if you're a Christian or a Jew too. *"Ye shall not make any cuttings in your flesh ... nor print any marks upon you"* (Leviticus 19:28). Ray's grandmother had quoted that verse to him all through high school in the hopes he wouldn't ever get one.

Sorry grandma.

Ray holstered his gun and pushed open the door to the shop. He wouldn't need it in there. A tattoo parlor in one of the most dangerous places in the world wouldn't be run by the Taliban. Besides, the people running this place would have to be crazy as hell to be here so he wasn't going to scare them with a semi-automatic and a bottle of Jack Daniels.

At first Ray thought he'd wandered into an old-fashioned barber shop. There was a waiting area with weather-beaten chairs lining the wall. That was separated from the actual tattooing area by a low carved railing. Inside the working part of the shop there were six ancient barber chairs—all currently unoccupied. Mirrors lined the walls and then he noticed the artwork. There were drawings everywhere of every type of tattoo you could possibly imagine. Some of them were so detailed they looked like miniature paintings. Ray didn't think he'd want anything as complicated as that. Actually, as his brain started to clear from his alcohol-induced haze, he wasn't sure he really wanted a tattoo at all. It seemed to him for a moment that what he was looking at blurred and looked different. He had the oddest feeling that the parlor might not look the same to different people.

A bell had gone off when he entered the parlor and now someone was coming to answer it. A figure emerged from the shadows of a doorway at the far end of the room and the dude was huge—like sumo wrestler huge. He was Japanese and had on a coarse cotton shirt and pants. The outfit reminded Ray of what you'd wear in a martial arts class

As the big man approached Ray his shirt fell open and Ray saw what had to be the most impressive koi and water lilies design he'd ever seen. The flowers were a radiant pink and the fish's scales appeared iridescent. But the weird thing was that in Ray's drunken stupor he could have sworn that the fish turned its head to look at him before giving him a wink. Ray stared at that fish right up to the point that the man was standing in front of him.

The big man placed massive fists on his hips and looked at Ray as if evaluating him. "Hmmm, you're a soldier, you want Angus." Then with a dismissive wave he turned and stepped over to one of the tattooing stations and began arranging his equipment.

Standing in the shadow of where the big man had been was a small, red-haired, half-naked madman. Ray could tell he was mad from the fact that he was wearing a kilt—in Afghanistan. All of the man's exposed skin was covered in tattoos—his face, neck, chest, arms, hands, and legs were covered in Celtic runes and strange stylized animals.

Ray definitely didn't want any part of that. "Ah, thanks, no, I'm thinking I should just—" Angus saw his hesitation and immediately took offense. He gave Ray a grimace worthy of Scottish Highlander and slapped his chest with the flat of his palms. It was a challenge as primal as combat itself. Ray actually found himself squaring off to face the man before he realized what he was doing. "Hey, you know what? We're starting off all wrong. I was thinking of something . . . Well, I came in looking for . . ." Ray wasn't sure what he wanted to say.

"Yes," a female voice cut in. "What is it that you are looking for?"

Both of the tattoo artists and Ray turned to the speaker at the other end of the room. The woman who was standing there was exotic, beautiful, and repellant all at the same time. Ray was dumbfounded. She was a slender, dark-haired girl wearing a bikini top and cut-off denim jeans — which, in the land of Burkhas, was like walking around naked. But it was her face that stopped him. She'd had her face tattooed with a sugar-skull design from the Mexican Day of the Dead celebration. It was beautifully ornate, and delicate, and reminded you of the one thing we're all certain to find—death.

She began walking toward him with a casual confidence. "I ask you again: What are you looking for?"

Ray was suddenly sober. Any trace of the buzz he'd had was gone. "Miss, do you realize how much danger you're in? If the locals find out that there's a tattooed woman in here they'll burn the place down."

The girl smiled. "Yes, I believe they'd send some representatives to speak to us." She glanced over at the left wall and Ray followed her gaze. On a shelf were four human skulls. They were bleached white and had been inscribed with delicate vines and floral designs—like sugar skulls. "But we won't be here much longer so you needn't worry about me." This time she glanced to the right at a large round clock that hung on the wall. Ray looked over to see that it was ten to midnight. He was going to going to catch hell for wandering off like this. "But you were about to tell me what it is that you wanted."

Ray wanted to escort her to the nearest airport and get her ass out of here but that wasn't any of his business and something told him this girl knew her business far better than he did. "Ah, sorry, this was a mistake. I should never have come in here."

"Angus is one of the best," she assured him, "and the perfect artist for a warrior. He can give you a tattoo that will make you invincible to your enemy's weapons or another that will make sure you never lose courage." Angus, who was standing behind her, beamed at the compliments and pointed proudly at two different tattoos on his chest. Apparently he was also his own catalog.

Ray shook his head. "Look, it's been a lousy day and I was feeling crazy. Maybe the best thing for me to do is go back to my bunk and sleep it off." He put the bottle of Jack Daniels down on the railing. The booze was just one more bad decision in a day full of bad decisions.

The girl knew instantly what he was talking about. "A memorial tattoo then — in honor of your fallen friend." She swung open the gate to the railing and invited him into the tattooing area.

Ray hesitated. "No," he said, "not a memorial tattoo." He'd never liked Jackson that much anyway. "I think," he fumbled, "I think I was looking for something that would serve more as a reminder."

The girl looked at him with large dark eyes that sparkled with curiosity. "An interesting distinction. Not a memorial but a reminder. A reminder of what, may I ask?"

Ray shrugged. "I'm not sure. I guess I was thinking of a reminder of 'Why?' Why do we do this? Why do we fight? Why risk our lives killing or getting killed?"

For the first time since he'd met her it was the girl who seemed at a loss. "And what sort of tattoo would serve as such a reminder?"

Ray didn't know where any of this was coming from yet he knew his answer. "Marine's like to say: 'Semper Fi.' I think I'd those words tattooed somewhere I can see them."

"Always Faithful." The girl seemed impressed. "Powerful words." Her eyes then took on a faraway look as she imagined the shape and form of the tattoo.

Ray, however, didn't want her getting any cute ideas. "That's all I want," he said, hurriedly. "Just the words. Simple block letters. No flowers, no guns, no nothing—just the words."

The girl gave him a knowing smile. "Just the words? Something simple and to the point?" Her smile turned into a full grin. "You are a man of rare intelligence and wisdom Sergeant. And you don't even know it." Ray didn't know why she said that about him, but before he could ask the sumo wrestler appeared over her shoulder.

"Tick tock, Haumea," the big man said as he indicated the clock on the wall. It was now five of midnight.

Haumea acknowledged him with a nod. "Right. We have work to do but I think we can do it in the time allotted. Simple design. Nothing fancy. Powerful words to serve as a powerful reminder." She picked up the bottle of Jack Daniels Ray had put down on the railing and Ray watched as much of the good whiskey disappeared down her throat. She wiped her mouth with the back of her hand and looked him straight in the eye. "Commission accepted."

What happened after that was sort of fuzzy but the next thing Ray knew he was back in the alley with a brand new tattoo and no whiskey.

Something screamed in his head and Ray looked up to see that he was back in the lab. There was smoke in the air and it was making it hard to breath. From his left he saw one of the monsters charging him. Ray swung the shotgun in its direction and blew it away. He then swung the shotgun around and killed the monster that was trying to sneak up on him from the right. They were getting creative and he knew it was only a matter of time before they got to him.

Someone began clapping. "Impressive," a man's voice said, "most impressive. You realized the first creature was only a distraction and anticipated the real attack."

A man emerged from the far end of the aisle. He wore a fedora pulled low over his eyes and a long trench coat. Ray didn't recognize him. He had no memory of having ever met "Sam Spade."

"That's because I'm not a hallucination," the man told him. "I'm real."

Ray grimaced. "Everything real today has tried to kill me. So, you'll forgive me if I'm hesitant to believe you."

The man had a big expressive smile and a gold tooth that sparkled in the firelight. "Belief is not a prerequisite. The name is Johnny and I'm here to do a little business with you Sergeant Delgado."

Ray blinked several times just to see if the man would disappear. He didn't. "Look, Johnny, if you're a hallucination I don't remember you so you're wasting your time. And if you're real, you picked a hell of a day to make a sales call. You need to get out of here and warn the National Guard, the cops, whomever, the monsters are coming."

Johnny, who was taking in the extent of Ray's wounds, shook his head sadly. "The monsters are always coming," he said. "That's how the universe works. And the police already know. They've set up a perimeter and the National Guard is arriving to reinforce them as we speak. By the way, the school has been evacuated. You bought them the time they needed to move the students to a place of safety."

Ray let out a sigh of relief. "Thank god." Then he looked at Johnny more critically. "You a detective? Is that why you're dressed like that?"

Johnny shook his head. "I'm more of an independent contractor. But more to the point, you were reliving an experience just now, weren't you? Kandahar. Afghanistan. A dark alley and a strange little tattoo shop?"

Ray stared at the man. "How did you know?"

Johnny ignored the question. "I believe you met a friend of mine there. Brunette, slender, awesome sugar-skull tattoo on her face, green eyes?"

Ray recognized the description. Was this guy at the tattoo parlor? "Yeah, I met her. Don't remember any green eyes, though."

Johnny shrugged. "It depends on the light. Anyway, my friend gave you a gift."

Ray glanced down at his tattoo. "I went back a couple of times to settle up my account but I never found the place again."

"That's how she works," Johnny assured him. "One and done. There are no second chances with her and I should know." The look in Johnny's eye implied that he was talking about more than just tattoos. "Anyway, you must have impressed her because she gave you a very special tattoo. May I see it?"

Ray tried to shake the cobwebs from his mind. The blood loss was starting to affect his thinking. His hallucination was getting pushy. "See what?"

"The tattoo," Johnny explained.

Ray frowned. "Why? It's just two words. Nothing special."

Johnny smiled and tilted his head so that Ray could see his eyes. They were burning bright with an unnatural intensity. "It's funny that you should say it's nothing special when clearly it is. There was a time," he said softly, "when tattoos were more than fashion statements worn by movie stars and professional athletes. There was a time when tattoos were always . . . special. Every drop of ink had meaning. Every line was drawn with a purpose." He indicated Ray's right hand. "That's why I'd like to see yours."

Ray shifted the shotgun to his left hand and extended his arm. He didn't know why he was doing this. He was a way better shot with his right hand and the enemy was lurking just beyond his line of sight. But for some reason he felt it important to indulge his hallucination.

Johnny took Ray's hand and gently turned it over to expose the wrist and the simple lettering that adorned it. He whistled appreciatively. "It's not often that she does one of these. It's a great honor."

Ray's frown deepened. "Words? You mean your girl doesn't do words very often?"

Johnny was careful not to touch the tattoo but he examined it closely. "These aren't just any words," he explained. "These are words of power. This is old magic—*very* old magic. It dates back to a time when people understood how much power words have. To tattoo yourself with them is to draw upon that power and," he added with emphasis, "to feed it — to keep it alive. The bearer of a tattoo like this has to preserve the magic. That's where most people fail. They're just not that interested in doing what it takes to keep the magic going. You're obviously different. From what I can see you've not only fed the magic, you've made it grow."

Ray pulled his arm back and transferred the shotgun back into his good hand. His hallucination was annoying. "Don't know about any magic. Can't even do card tricks so I'm not sure what you think this tattoo is doing for me. And how, exactly, do you *feed* magic?"

Johnny swept back his trench coat and sat down on his heels to be at Ray's eye level. He spread his hands like a magician trying to show that he had nothing to hide. "Generally by being true to your purpose. In your case: being faithful to your mission, your cause, the people you serve and protect."

Ray glared at him. "You know. As imaginary friends go you are one —" Something in Johnny's body language caught Ray's attention and suddenly his tattoo began to tingle.

Johnny watched him with those intense eyes and without looking away said: "Check your six."

But Ray was on it. He didn't know if he heard the scrambling of its claws or, on a level he wasn't even aware of, sensed the movement but he knew the monster was there. Bracing the butt of the shotgun on the floor he pivoted the barrel up and fired straight up, without looking. There was a moment of silence followed by the sound of something heavy sliding off the top of the table and hitting the floor behind him. There was also a fine mist of bright green ichor descending on them. Ray noticed two things about the blood. First, it was cold—freezing cold as if it had been refrigerated. Second, none of it was landing on Johnny. The mist seemed to part and go around him.

Johnny cocked an eyebrow. "What about now? Anything magical in what you just did?"

Ray started to deny that anything more than good training was involved in him taking out an enemy combatant without looking but then the improbability of the situation hit him. He wasn't an action hero in some movie. Real people have to aim. "I, I don't know."

Johnny's grin returned. "That's it. Think about it. Did life change after you got the tattoo?"

Ray would have laughed if he wasn't having enough trouble drawing a breath. "Hell no, I served another two years and got shot twice."

Johnny watched him. "How long does it take to recover from a gunshot wound?"

Ray shrugged. "Not long. Neither was all that serious. They just grazed —" Ray caught on to his logic. "That doesn't prove anything."

Johnny tried not to appear smug. "Sure it does. It proves you're not as certain as you pretend. But regardless of whether you believe me or not, I'd like to trade you for your tattoo."

Ray wondered if Johnny wasn't just another monster trying to get close enough to attack him. He wondered if he shouldn't shoot him.

"Please don't," Johnny said. "You're going to need the ammunition."

Ray glared at him. "Now I know you're just in my head."

"Cause I can read your mind?" Johnny asked.

"Cause you want to trade for a tattoo," Ray answered. "Kind of hard to trade away something that's drawn on you."

Johnny nodded his head. "Ordinarily, yes, but this isn't an ordinary situation and I'm not an ordinary person. Listen, the invasion is about to begin and I have just what you need to stop it. But I need something in return. I need your tattoo."

Even though it was insane Ray knew what Johnny really wanted. "What you want is to steal my magic."

Johnny avoided eye contact. "Hmm, well, yeah, steal is a strong word. I want to trade you for it. I don't want all of it — just what you've stored in the words." He indicated the tattoo.

Ray shook his head. "Like this day couldn't have gotten any weirder. Can we do Vegas now? There are a couple of showgirls I'd really like to see again."

Johnny was confused. "Sorry? Oh, ah no, still not a hallucination. This is reality."

"Doesn't feel like it."

"Doesn't matter. Monsters are here. World's in danger. You're dying. You have one hope of winning the battle and I'm here to offer it to you." Johnny held out a battered old Zippo lighter with the Marine emblem on it. He flicked it open to show that it still worked. "Do you know what an I.E.D. is?"

This time Ray did laugh. "There isn't a Marine alive who doesn't know what an Improvised Explosive Device is." He didn't bother to mention that there were plenty of dead men and women who also knew what an I.E.D. was. Then he looked around the room at its spilled chemicals, ruined hardware, and stacks of propane tanks. His lab had been completely self-contained. Everything in it had been donated so that he kids could work on science fair projects and lab experiments. "You want me to blow myself up?"

"Actually," Johnny said, a little embarrassed. "I'd rather you blew them up, but I acknowledge that you can't have one without the other. Price of victory. Sorry."

Ray noted the fires that were burning hotter and brighter all around him. "It's going to happen anyway. No need to trade me for it."

"Tick toc," Johnny said.

For a second Ray almost felt like he was back in a stuffy tattoo parlor in a forgotten corner of the world. "What did you say?"

"Tick toc," Johnny repeated. "Time is not on our side. You are right that this place is going to blow, but by my estimate you'll have been dead fifteen minutes when it does. And the invasion will have begun five minutes before that. So you see you must remain faithful to your cause if you are to win."

Ray glared at him. "I see what you did there. Cute."

Jonny nodded his head. "Good, keeps anyone from saying that I tricked you. And in the interest of full disclosure there's one more thing that you need to know. This isn't going to be easy. Your tattoo has helped you remain faithful ever since you got it. It didn't give you anything you didn't already have but it made what you had all that much stronger—easier to access. When I take it from you it'll hurt. It'll hurt in your body and it'll hurt in your soul. Doubt will try to cloud your sense of certainty. Fear will try to drain you of courage. You will have to try harder than you have had to in years to remain true to who you are and the cause you serve."

Interestingly, Ray understood what his hallucination was trying to tell him. "What you're saying is that when stripped of the magic I may discover I'm not the man I thought I was."

Johnny nodded his head. "Life is a series of discoveries. Sometimes, what we find out about ourselves is disappointing."

Ray understood that too. "Been there, done that. Not going to be a problem. But you're telling me that blowing up the school *will* stop the monsters?"

Johnny did an impressive imitation of Ray when he answered: "They're delicate. They pop like balloons."

Ray nodded. It was probably due to the blood loss, but where his conscious brain couldn't help him his subconscious mind had created a hallucination that was giving him the answer to his problems. "And a big enough explosion will create a shockwave that will make them *all* pop," he reasoned for himself. It was a no brainer. He was a dead man anyway. "Alright, I'm in. I'll trade you my tattoo for the lighter. What do I have to do?" Not that Ray believed there was anyone there with whom to trade, but if this was how his mind was working out the problem of defeating the monsters then he was fine with letting it run its course.

"Doesn't matter. Monsters are here. World's in danger. You're dying. You have one hope of winning the battle and I'm here to offer it to you." Johnny held out a battered old lighter with a distinctive unit insignia and the words: *69th US Infantry, The Fighting Irish* emblazoned on it. He flicked it open to show that it still worked. "Do you know what an I.E.D. is?"

This time Ray did laugh. "There isn't a Marine alive who doesn't know what an Improvised Explosive Device is." He didn't bother to mention that there were plenty of dead men and women who also knew what an I.E.D. was. Then he looked around the room at its spilled chemicals, ruined hardware, and stacks of propane tanks. His lab had been completely self-contained. Everything in it had been donated so that he kids could work on science fair projects and lab experiments. "You want me to blow myself up?"

"Actually," Johnny said, a little embarrassed. "I'd rather you blew them up but I acknowledge that you can't have one without the other. Price of victory. Sorry."

Ray noted the fires that were burning hotter and brighter all around him. "It's going to happen anyway. No need to trade me for it."

"Tick toc," Johnny said.

For a second Ray almost felt like he was back in a stuffy tattoo parlor in a forgotten corner of the world. "What did you say?"

"Tick toc," Johnny repeated. "Time is not on our side. You are right that this place is going to blow but by my estimate you'll have been dead 15 minutes when it does. And the invasion will have begun five minutes before that. So you see you must remain faithful to your cause if you are to win."

Ray glared at him. "I see what you did there. Cute."

Jonny nodded his head. "Good, keeps anyone from saying that I tricked you. And in the interest of full disclosure there's one more thing that you need to know. This isn't going to be easy. Your tattoo has helped you remain faithful ever since you got it. It didn't give you anything you didn't already have but it made what you had all that much stronger—easier to access. When I take it from you it'll hurt. It'll hurt in your body and it'll hurt in your soul. Doubt will try to cloud your sense of certainty. Fear will try to drain you of courage. You will have to try harder than you have had to in years to remain true to who you are and the cause you serve."

Ray understood what his hallucination was trying to tell him. "What you're saying is that when stripped of the magic I may discover I'm not the man I thought I was."

Johnny nodded his head. "Life is a series of discoveries. Sometimes, what we find out about ourselves is disappointing."

Ray understood that too. "Been there, done that. Not going to be a problem. But you're telling me that blowing up the school *will* stop the monsters?"

Johnny did an impressive imitation of Ray when he answered: "They're delicate. They pop like balloons."

Ray nodded. It was probably due to the blood loss but where his conscious brain couldn't help him his subconscious mind had created a hallucination that was giving him the answer to his problems. "And a big enough explosion will create a shockwave that will make them ALL pop," he reasoned for himself. It was a no brainer. He was a dead man anyway. "Alright, I'm in. I'll trade you my tattoo for the lighter. What do I have to do?" Not that Ray believed there was anyone there with whom to trade but if this was how his mind was working out the problem of defeating the monsters then he was fine with letting it run its course.

"You don't have to do anything," Johnny said. "I've got this part." He handed Ray a lighter which Ray took in his left hand.

Ray looked down at the scratched and battered lighter which bore the insignia of the 69th Fighting Irish. It had seen some action but then again so had the guys of the 69th. They'd been in every conflict since the Civil War. "This is an Army unit," he said, almost without thinking. "You don't happen to have a *Marine* lighter?"

Johnny shrugged. "Sorry, I only have what I've been given."

Ray shrugged in turn. "It's all good. 69th have done their part." Ray looked at the lighter again and felt an odd connection to a man he'd never met. "Don't suppose you'll tell me what the poor guy who gave you this got for *his* troubles?" he asked. Johnny smiled but didn't answer. Instead he produced a small empty glass vial and waved it over Ray's right wrist. Suddenly the vial was filled with black ink. Ray looked down and saw that his tattoo was gone. "Wow, neat trick. But I don't feel —" Searing pain slammed into Ray. It was so intense that he couldn't speak.

"And that would be the pain you weren't feeling." Johnny said, with a touch of sympathy. "It'll only get worse from here. But your task is simple— light a fire. This lab has always been an accident waiting to happen. Once it blows the concussive blast of the explosion will travel through the portal and kill 100,000 demons. They'll pop like balloons."

Ray's eyes were shut tight with pain but the statement made him open them again. "That many?"

Johnny stood up and pocketed the vial. "That's just the first wave. But they won't have enough time to organize the second wave once the destruction hits so your job will be done. Your kids will be saved. Your world will be safe. And no-one will know what you've done. It'll just look like an industrial accident." He began to turn away.

Ray was surprised that his subconscious wasn't having Johnny stick around. But then, he wasn't sure where his subconscious got a hold of a lighter. "It was never about medals or citations," Ray said to the departing stranger.

Johnny turned and smiled. "I know. Otherwise, the magic in the tattoo wouldn't have worked. It was always about keeping the faith." He gave Ray a nod and tipped his hat to him. "Semper Fi."

Ray returned the nod. "Semper Fi."

And then, as if he'd never even been there, Johnny was gone.

"Ay, Raymond, what have you done?" And older woman chided him. The voice was unmistakable.

"Abuela?" Ray instinctively tried to sit up straight but the movement caused him to nearly black out with pain. "Abuela, that you?"

A short, pudgy, gray-haired woman in a floral housecoat and pink slippers appeared to Ray's left. *"I warned you, Raymond,"* she said with obvious distress. *"I warned you what would happen if you didn't read the Bible. Every night, Raymond, every night!"* Her glare was a mix of anger and disappointment. It was an expression only a grandmother could create.

"Abuela, I did good. I didn't join a gang. I served with honor and now I'm a schoolteacher."

But his grandmother was unimpressed. *"But you did so many bad things, Ray-Ray. And you could have been so much more."*

"He could have been a husband and a father," said another voice. Maria appeared to his right. *"I loved you, Ray. I would always love you but that wasn't enough for you, was it? What we could have had together wasn't enough for you!"* Maria threw up her hands to cover her face as she began to weep.

"And when all was said and done you weren't even much of a Marine," Jackson said as he strolled down the aisle in front of Ray. *"You let others die because you were too much of a coward to do what needed to be done."*

Ray shut his eyes and tried to shake the haze from his mind. He was getting confused. Jackson is dead. Maria is married. His grandmother is —

"Waiting for an answer," she chided him. *"Raymond Delgado, what do you have to say for yourself!"*

The three of them were descending on him. Each was glaring at him — demanding answers that he would never be able to give. "I tried to do my best," he began. "I tried to . . ." Jackson is dead. Maria is married. His grandmother is in a nursing home.

"You sons of bitches," Raymond muttered. And the three ghosts before him faded to reveal three six-foot tall hairless cats balancing on their hind legs. The monsters all hissed at him in unison. There were all close enough to strike now and there was no way he'd get all three before one of them got to him. The monsters, recognizing that he understood his situation, all smiled at him as they prepared to pounce.

Ray lifted the barrel of his shotgun one last time. The monsters, well acquainted with his skill hesitated. That was all Ray needed to flick open the lighter. It was just a single bright flame illuminating the dark. The monsters, catching the sudden movement, all turned to look at the lighter. They didn't understand the purpose of such a small flame until Ray dropped it on an over-turned Bunsen burner, which ignited some sulfur, which led to a series of flames and fires around the room that eventually found its way to a ruptured propane gas tank.

Ray looked at the monsters as they followed the progression of flames with fascination. It wasn't until it was too late that the significance of what was happening became clear to them. They all turned to stare at Ray who gave them a nod and said: "Semper Fi."

The explosion, and its corresponding shockwave, leveled the building. On one side of the portal 100,000 monsters perished. On the other side, a single marine remained true to his mission of protecting his kids and saving the world. And most of that world remained blissfully ignorant of the bargain that had made it all possible.

Grinding and Carving

HAUMEA EXITED THE MAIN BATHROOM AND saw they were now six hours into the Sha'Daa. She clenched her teeth hard to keep in a groan. By her own subjective chronometer she had actually spent a solid week in the temporal boundaries of a quick-room, pumping out a good seventy-five tattoos with nary a break for food and water. Her eyes were starting to fry but she still had hundreds of more tattoos to create for the big plan.

The background noise had picked up dramatically in Mom's Bane, and the interior had starting looking like an outtake from the *Star Wars* cantina scene. Word had spread about the Sha'Daa, and magical beings, hybrid demons, extraterrestrial aliens, and a variety of uncommitted hostile sub terrestrials had started piling in to be inked with protection spells, power enhancers, and a wide variety of charms and alchemistic symbols.

Haumea gave the crowd the once over but didn't sweat it. She'd invested a small fortune in the ancient stones hidden on either side of the one and only entrance to Mom's Bane. Each Olmec head was over two-thousand five-hundred years old and contained some of the most powerful of bound spirits, chained by a series of ancient hexes that permanently compelled their obedience. Anyone or anything that bore her ill will would not be allowed inside this holy chamber.

"You're looking a bit tense," a familiar voice said behind her, "the bohemian lifestyle becoming a bit much for you?"

Haumea spun around and smiled up at Johnny.

"Not gonna happen, tall, dark, and handsome," Haumea said, batting her long eyelashes.

"And our tattoo quota?"

"Slave driver," Haumea frowned, "it's going to be tight… but we're on schedule."

Johnny leaned forward slightly, extended his hand forward, and quickly ran a long right index finger gently along the left side of Haumea's face. She could feel her skin blushing and prayed it didn't show through her ink.

"Do you ever regret this?"

"What?" she asked, "agreeing to your insane deal a millennia ago? Or, these tattoos you gave me?"

"Both, my dear."

Haumea reached up to grab Johnny's hand but he had already pulled it away.

"I have no regrets, Johnny," Haumea said, "except, well, not getting to see more of you over the years."

Johnny finally made eye contact with Haumea, and she felt her normally hypnotizing green eyes nearly overwhelmed by The Salesman's dark, bottomless pupils.

"My travels are at the whim of human destiny," Johnny said sadly, "you of all people know this Haumea."

A flash of anger crossed Haumea's face, but she bit down on it and let it stew. This was an old wound, and wouldn't be healed in a single conversation, not here, not now.

"Otherwise," Johnny continued, "your crew seems to be holding up okay."

"Some newbies are getting the mother of all apprenticeships, but hell, this is Mom's Bane. We're par for every course. Supplies are holding out so far, though we've had a hell of a run on chromium ink. Popular color today.

"I know your place has adequate defensive enhancements, but when you've got the time, keep an eye out for any, ummm, unusual fellows who come in."

Haumea glanced for a moment at four vampires, two golems, a Venusian/Martian couple, and two warlocks all being tattooed on the main floor.

"You're shitting me, right?" she asked.

"I think I'm being followed." Johnny said.

"Is anyone, or, uh, anything actually capable of that?" Haumea asked.

"Before today… no. But these are strange times indeed, and I have wares to market."

And on that note Johnny strode out the front door.

A seven-foot-tall albino manbat strode up to Haumea, its bright pink eyes twice the size of a human being's.

"What's your pleasure?" Haumea asked.

"An ancient curse is tattooed on my back," the manbat said with a surprisingly high-pitched voice, "I need a cover-up, something appropriately noble, and powerful, and, uhhh… frightening."

"What kind of curse?" Haumea asked walking around to look at the naked creature's backside.

"An ancient hex," it whined, "words that lessen my power among my followers… and enemies."

The inked script was elegant and sharp, and still quite legible.

"*My Little Pony Rules*," Haumea said, "yeah. I see your problem."

Blood Lines

by Diane Arrelle

THE ADVERTISEMENT BLEW AROUND EVANGE-line's feet. Skittering across the cracked sidewalk in the early morning sunlight, the damp hand bill seemed to beg for attention.

She shuddered and pulled her sweater tighter as the cold wind pushed the previous night's debris toward the gutters.

"Hey look," Bernadette said, picking up the grimy handbill. "Mom's Bane Tattoo Parlor. The best of the best," she read aloud. "A hell of a deal in any language."

She smiled at Evangeline and said in her most persuasive tone, "Do you remember that today's our birthday? I intend to celebrate with tats for both of us. We could get matching tattoos, won't that be fun?"

Evangeline groaned. "Don't tell me, you had matching tattoos all planned out for us and never bothered to mention it?"

Bernadette laughed, "Oh Vange, lighten up. It's my birthday present to you."

"Bernie, you can't be serious."

"Yo little sis, did you forget our deal? The one where you picked the location and I get to pick the itinerary?"

Evangeline frowned, "Some itinerary, let's get away from this section of Dublin before we get mugged in broad daylight."

Bernadette looked around and grinned at her sister. "Better go back to Florida, your Irish blood has become too diluted for Ireland."

She took in a deep breath of stale beer mixed with trash and urine, and nodded with nostalgia and satisfaction. Sure this place was disgusting, but it was the kind of disgusting she loved. Drunks sleeping in doorways, trash everywhere. Just the way she always liked it. She remembered waking up in many a doorway herself back when she was younger.

She looked over at Evangeline and saw the tiredness etched in the deep lines on her face. She'd been that exhausted half an hour ago, but being on the dirty streets of the Temple District was like a shot of adrenaline.

"Yer getting old, me little sister," she said to Evangeline and with a stab of guilt, and knew she was right. She studied her sister, taking in the steel gray curls and weathered face, and knew she looked every one of her sixty-five years. She often wondered why her own long red hair never faded to gray or why her face still looked forty.

Evangeline laughed and Bernadette smiled, the guilt dissipating as she saw Evangeline's crows-feet crinkle up into laugh lines. "Bernadette, according to our parents you are less than twenty-four hours older than me. Don't give me that little sister guff and drop the fake accent. We haven't lived in Ireland in fifty-eight years."

Evangeline stifled a large yawn and continued. "Remember we can't take all day with this whim of yours. Tattoos seem like a really bad idea to me. Seriously, all I really want is to catch a nap before we go meet Uncle Coyle."

Bernadette caught her eye and winked. "You'll love doing this once you remove that rod stuck up your proper, little ass. Now let's find Mom's Bane on my phone."

As they walked, Evangeline asked, "Now that we are back in the old country, do you wonder who your real parents were?"

Bernadette stopped and looked her in the eyes. "Mom and Dad are my real parents and you are my real sister. Blood doesn't make a family."

They resumed walking and the buildings got dingier. "Almost there," Bernadette said. "According to my phone and this flyer, it is just around the corner."

They turned the corner and both stopped short.

"Bernie, that is one long, dark, alley," Evangeline whispered.

Bernadette frowned and looked at the flyer in one hand and the phone in the other. "According to the GPS, the tattoo parlor should be right down there."

"Let's go back to the hotel, this place just gives me goose bumps." Evangeline urged. "This is a setup to get mugged and murdered. I did not survive teaching high school in Miami just to get killed in Dublin."

Bernadette stood her ground and said, "I'm sure I see colored lights down a ways. I'm going to check it out. Coming with me?"

Evangeline heaved a noisy sigh, "Bernie, someday you are going to be the death of me, I just pray it's not today."

Bernadette grabbed Evangeline's shaking hand and dragged her forward until they stood in front of Mom's Bane Tattoo Parlor. It was as narrow as the alley, barely wide enough for a door. No room for windows, the only sign of its existence was the buzzing neon over the wooden door.

Shrugging, Bernadette grasped the handle and said, "What the hell, it's birthday present time." As she pushed the door inward on squeaky hinges, she gripped Evangeline's hand tighter and pulled her inside.

The place was brightly lit with long hallways off to the sides. A woman, covered in tattoos from head to foot, smiled and said, "Welcome to Mom's Bane, we've been expecting you."

"What does she mean by that, expecting us?" Evangeline whispered to Bernadette.

"Just salesmanship, that's all."

"I've put you both down the end of the hall to the right. Don't be afraid, you'll love the results or your money back," the woman said and turned away.

The door she pointed to opened and a middle-aged man with thinning brown hair, wire rimmed glasses, khaki slacks, and a polo shirt waved to them to come. As they went into the room covered floor to ceiling with pictures of tattoo ideas, Evangeline whispered into Bernadette's ear, "This guy could be my dentist. Totally harmless, although he does have a unique tattoo of a winged unicorn on his hand."

"Hello, ladies, my name is Maury, glad to meet you at last. Got anything in mind here?" he asked.

They both shook their heads no.

"Come on a whim?"

Evangeline smiled and said, "It's our birthday today, and well, Bernie's correct, I've waited 60 years to do something really daring."

"Ah I see, birthday tattoos. Well a fine day to get them, actually a perfect day. Please, I'm an expert at this, let me surprise you both."

"You," he said to Bernadette, "Take off your shirt, your back is crying out to me."

Bernadette looked at Evangeline, shrugged, and took off her shirt. As she sat with her back exposed, Maury said, "You, my dear, are a wild spirit. Like venom, the blood of your father's ancestors runs fast in your veins."

The artist started the inking process.

Bernadette closed her eyes letting the exhaustion wash over her. She dozed lightly as the buzz of the coils driving the needles into her skin turned into a soothing background hum.

"All done," he said and turned Bernadette to a large mirror that reflected her back in the mirror in front of her.

Bernadette laughed like a small child being given a beautifully wrapped present as she studied the long green and yellow snake that crossed her back. It was a pleasant looking reptile, powerful and yet it seemed to be smiling like it had a secret it wasn't going to share.

"I just love it! It's absolutely perfect...it's so...so me!"

Bernadette stared in amazement when her sister rushed to the chair the second she'd gotten up.

Evangeline asked in an excited voice. "What do you see for me? Something absolutely wonderful?"

He looked at Evangeline, "You, I see, I see strength when the time is needed."

Both sisters burst out laughing, "Boy do you have that wrong!" Evangeline sputtered. "I'm always afraid of making the wrong choice. Look, I just have to ask, because you look and sound like an accountant from New York, what are you doing in Ireland at an out of the way tattoo parlor?"

Maury shrugged and said. "Looks are deceiving. I'm an artist and my palette happens to be human flesh. "

"Uh, not the nicest way of putting it."

Maury shrugged again. "Please relax and take off your slacks."

Evangeline sat upright, "Now, wait a minute!" she snapped.

"Oh, Vange, just take them off," Bernadette chided. "After all, I stripped down to my C cups. He's just gonna ink you."

A minute later with legs bare, Evangeline sat stiffly in the chair as Maury began her tattoo.

"Ow, I've changed my mind. This hurts!" she snapped.

Maury smiled and said in a soothing tone, "Don't panic, calm down. It's all right. The pain goes away after a few minutes, you just numb up a little and then it's actually enjoyable. Wait and see. I won't hurt you, I promise."

After an hour Maurry leaned back, wiped the sweat off his face and said in voice so soft it was almost a whisper, "This has got to be one of the best I've ever brought back."

Evangeline looked down at her leg and gasped, "Ohhh, it's so beautiful, so lifelike," she cooed at the pearlescent, winged unicorn with golden hooves and a golden spiraling horn. The horselike creature's snowy coat seemed to shimmer pink and then blue with an inner glow.

"Bernadette paid at the front desk then said, "Oops, I forgot to tip Maury. Be right back."

She ran back to the room they'd just left, rushed in, and stopped. There was no sign of Maury, but there was a tall, gaunt man covered from the top of his bald head down to the tops of his feet sticking out of a pair of sandals. "Oh", she said raising her hand to her face in a surprised gesture. "I... I was looking for Maury."

He smiled, a smile too wide for his face and said, "He's gone. Can I help you?"

She thought for a second then blurted, "I wanted to give him a tip."

The man held out his hand, the hand with the same tattoo Maury had on his and said. "I'll make sure he gets it."

She couldn't tell the ominous looking guy she didn't trust him so she handed him the money and rushed out to the front of the shop.

"Tip him?" Evangeline asked.

Shaking her head in the affirmative, Bernadette walked on without a word, feeling worried because she'd felt confused. *Must be the exhaustion*, she decided. "Come on, let's go find our hotel and force them to have the room ready for us."

She yawned and headed away from the Temple District. "I've had enough excitement for our first morning here."

Walking along, Evangeline nudged Bernie with her elbow, "Notice the guy standing in the shadows? I saw him earlier."

Bernie squinted in the sunlight. "I saw him earlier as well, by the Temple Bar. I'm sure it's the same guy, I mean how many men do you know who dress in a trench coat and wear a hat nowadays. Weird guy, think he's stalking us?"

"Don't know," Evangeline said and shuddered. "Let's pick up the pace."

They walked faster and as they turned the corner, Bernadette saw the sign of their hotel just a block down and let out the breath she'd hadn't realize she was holding. She knew she was abnormally fearless, but still, she and Evangeline were two older women in a foreign country. "Safety just ahead," she said and stopped short when Evangeline screamed.

Somehow the man in the hat and coat was standing right in front of them.

"Ladies," he said with a tip of his hat. He smiled and his gold tooth gleamed brightly in the late morning sun. "Please, don't be afraid. I'm an acquaintance of your Uncle Coyle who is waiting for you just inside the hotel lobby. My name is Johnny. You must be Bernadette," he said holding out his hand to her.

She didn't know why but she was compelled to grasp it and shake it.

"And you have to be Evangeline," he said extending his hand to her.

Evangeline glanced at her sister and held her hand out as well. "Our uncle knows you?"

"Most definitely."

She shrugged. "Well, ah, Johnny, why are you following us?"

He grinned, his mouth a straight line with the corners barely turning up. "I deal in trade and you both have something I need. Don't worry, I will trade you something you will both find valuable in the immediate future. The Sha'Daa is coming."

"Trade?" Bernadette asked ignoring the last crazy part of his sentence. She trusted this man but didn't understand why. She didn't really trust anyone very much.

And that made her jittery. "Why?" she asked, wanting to understand the feelings she had toward this odd stranger.

Evangeline bobbed her head to the left and pointed away from him. She stepped moved to the side and Bernadette followed. "What's going on here?" she whispered. "I don't know but I got this feeling that he's OK," Bernadette whispered back." I have mixed feelings, I trust him but I don't like him. In fact, I'm scared of him even though I know in my gut he means us no harm."

Bernadette turned back to him and asked again, "Why?"

"It's my business. I'm a trader."

Evangeline stepped into the conversation. "How do you know our uncle?"

"We've met on many occasions. I've even traded with him from time to time. Coyle has spoken of you and I just wanted to meet you both. I know we can help each other."

"How?" Evangeline asked.

"Well, Bernadette, I want you to trade your watch for this engraved Celtic snake bracelet."

Bernadette looked down at her watch. "It's just a cheap knock-off. Why do you want it?"

"It will help someone else in another trade. Is it a deal?"

Shrugging, she said, "Why not, I love things from Ireland, even though you know that I know there are no snakes here. Never were any, so it's got to be a cheap knock-off as well."

"Ah but you'd be surprised at how real it can be," Johnny said

She pretended to ignore him because somewhere deep in her subconscious something was warning her to take it. She slipped the metal reptile on her arm noting that it felt warm not cold as it touched her skin. She wrapped coil after coil up her wrist almost to her elbow. Looking up at him, she said, "I like how it's made to coil up my arm . So it's a deal."

He turned and looked at Evangeline. "I'd like to trade you this silver locket and chain."

She looked down at his extended hand and gasped. It was just like the locket her mother had worn. She knew immediately that she had to have it, at any cost. "Oh!"

"…In exchange for your engagement ring."

"Oh." she repeated looking at the small diamond set in gold."

"Do it," Bernadette encouraged her. "You know it means nothing to you anymore. The bastard cheated on you over four decades ago and you've never stopped wearing it."

"But it has been on my right hand. I keep it as a reminder that I didn't need him or any other man ever again." Evangeline displaying more spunk then her sister had seen in years. "That bastard cheated like a dog because he just couldn't wait for our wedding night. Damn right I'll trade it."

Bernadette smiled as Evangeline turned red and sputtered. "Sorry, I don't normally curse, you know," she said to Johnny and pulled the ring off her finger.

She dropped the diamond ring onto Johnny's open palm and picked up the locket. She held it out to her sister. "Look Bernie, isn't it beautiful?"

Bernadette gently fingered the filigree and the thin fine wire necklace that looped through the ring at the top of the locket at least eight or nine times. "Well you certainly got the better deal!" she said, feeling just the slightest ting of jealousy. She looked up to say something to Johnny, but he was gone with his new treasures; a ring of regret and a cheap watch.

"Oh well, that was a disconcerting experience, on a totally disconcerting day and it's not even noon yet. I hope that room's ready." Evangeline said sighing. She took one step toward the door when it opened and out walked Uncle Coyle, his red hair sparkling in the sunlight.

Bernadette squealed like a child and ran into his arms before Evangeline even reacted.

"Uncle Coyle!" Bernadette squealed.

"Ah Bernie, how are ya doin?" he asked giving her a bear hug. "And Vange, come here and hug yer old uncle. I've got a surprise for you both, I just cancelled your room. I'm taking my favorite nieces on a road trip."

Bernie suddenly feeling like a kid again clapped her hands and laughed. "Oh, to where? Someplace we've never visited?"

"Come on ladies, you're carriage awaits," he said pointing to a small car parked a few yards away. "Those redeyes are awful flights. Get in and relax, our trip will take a few hours and you girls can take a long nap. I guarantee you'll both feel like new women when you wake."

They got in, Bernie taking the entire back seat and Evangeline in the passenger seat. She didn't even remember closing her eyes, but when she opened them it was late afternoon and the car was stopped in front of an old stone castle with neon lights over the door advertising a pub.

Feeling rested, Bernadette became aware that it was more than a day since she'd eaten a good meal, airplane food not counting as nourishment of any kind. She was thinking about what she'd order first when she looked at Evangeline. "Hey Vange, you OK, you're looking pale."

Evangeline opened her eyes and sat up straight in her seat. "Not really, I—"

"Time to grab a bite, my girls," Uncle Coyle interrupted in a booming voice. "And make it hearty because I've got a really full night you know. Special night indeed, two birthday girls and the Summer Solstice."

"Girls! We're woman and well past big birthday celebrations," Bernie said with a laugh. "But a hearty meal sounds wonderful!"

Evangeline snapped at her, "Bernie, my leg is killing me. I wish we'd never gotten tattoos. I bet sweet little Maury used dirty needles and tainted ink."

"Come on. Move your slow ass already and let me out of this car. I'm starving!" Bernadette yelled, lightly smacking Evangeline in the head.

"Seriously, Bernie. I'm in real pain. Act your darned age."

"Well today, I turn sixty-five so I guess I'm acting my age. When did you decide to be a bitchy old lady?"

Evangeline grimaced. "Today, right after you made me get this tattoo."

"Seriously? It hurts? I can't even feel mine at all. We'll look at it right after we order some food."

Bernadette squeezed out and helped Evangeline hobble into the pub. "If it isn't oozing bodily fluids or something equally drastic, I'm giving you the drama queen award of the year."

"Bernie it really hurts, hurts like nothing I've ever experienced before."

They sat and Uncle Coyle yelled in his new, still booming voice, "Barkeep, my niece needs a shot to to ease her pain and my other niece needs one in sympathy."

"Great idea. But we've got really empty stomachs, so make it light on the hard stuff. Where's the menu?" Bernadette asked.

"Ah, well, I've ordered our meal already, a classic feast. We dine down in what was once the dungeon. Come eat with me my ladies."

Leaning heavily on Bernadette's shoulder, Evangeline slowly limped down the stairs.

"Bernie," Uncle Coyle said, as they slowly made their way down what appeared to be an endless flight of narrow stone steps. "Bernadette, it is time."

"Time for what?" she asked, bothered by the serious tone of her usually jovial uncle's voice.

"You are not just an orphan I handed to my brother. Bernadette you are my spawn."

"I'm what?" she asked feeling dizzy. "You're my father?"

"Yes, you are feeling the changes with each step we take. The closer you get to the portal, the stronger my genes become. I am one of the many sentinels for the Sha'Daa. Many years back, ten thousand to be exact, our side lost. With each generation that stayed on this realm, we diluted our bloodline. You can call me, or rather us, the children of what human's refer to as monsters. Even with a weakening bloodline, every so often a baby is born with enough evil blood to be worthy of the Sha'Daa. You, my daughter, are one. In fact, you ripped your real mother to shreds when you were born."

"Is this some kind of joke?" Bernadette asked, feeling woozy, nauseous and yet surprisingly strong.

"Bernadette, I am your father, I took you to a human family, convinced them I was the father's brother and they raised you. Now, tonight you are needed. The portal will open at midnight and the world must be ready."

Evangeline appeared to be in a trance and with each step she became a lighter load to support. Soon Bernadette was carrying her like a baby. "She looked down at her arms, they were longer, muscular and hairy. "This is nuts! Why me? What if I don't want to be a….a…monster?"

"You have no choice," her newfound father said. "You are what we are and you must obey. We are almost to the bottom, to the portal, put the human host down."

Bernadette looked at the frail old woman in her arms and felt a tear on her cheek. With anger bubbling up from her very being, Bernadette snapped. "This is not some tool for your take-over. This is my sister."

Before she knew what hit her, a fist smashed into her face and she crashed down the last few steps, her sister still in her arms. She gently put Evangeline down, stood up, and felt her cheek. The blow should have broken her bones, but it didn't do any damage at all. She glared at her father and was shocked by his appearance. Just as she had noticed changes to her arms, now her legs were covered in red fur, and she felt her strength growing. Coyle too had changed, growing bulkier, out of proportion. She took in his long, heavily muscled arms hanging from the tattered remains of the shirt he'd just been wearing. His fingers ended in talon-like claws. The hair on his head appeared to be blowing wildly although she could feel no wind.

Evangeline groaned and tried to sit up. She squinted at her sister and what had once been her uncle and cried out, "What's going on?" Moaning, she looked down at her leg and began to shake, tears streaming down her cheeks.

Bernadette saw that Evangeline's pant leg, now blood-soaked was stretched to the point that the seams were ripping apart. She watched her sister's blood overflow her shoe in a spreading pool. She tried to go to her, to help, but somehow Coyle wouldn't let her move. His will pushed her against the wall of what she now saw was a cave, a cave far below the pub they had been in. Then she looked around at her surrounding and realized that there were about twenty other half-human half-demon or monster or whatever they were surrounding her uncle and Evangeline who looked at Bernadette pleadingly. "Bernie… Bernie help me!" she mumbled. "Bernie I'm dying. Help me!"

Bernie didn't move and Evangeline slumped over unconscious.

Coyle walked over to her body and kicked her in the ribs. "Wake up human scum. You can't die yet. You have to give the unicorn its freedom."

Evangeline screamed and opened her eyes again. "Bernie? Where's my sister? Please don't hurt her. Please let my sister go."

"Oh the human, not only a virgin of high moral values, is a heroic selfless one at that." Coyle said with a snort.

Laughter filled the room and Evangeline closed her eyes again. With the laughter, the hold on Bernadette relaxed and she walked calmly to her sister.

Uncle Coyle called out, "Bernadette, my child, go to the human and tell her what is going on."

Bernadette sat on the floor next to her, "Vange we are not sisters. We are not even the same race. You are a human and like all humans tonight, you are going to die. The unicorn's freedom will kill you swiftly. A kind death."

"Of course we're sisters, sisters all our lives. Race, blood, it doesn't matter, I love you and you love me," Evangeline said softly through clenched teeth.

Bernadette wiped the tears from her cheeks. She looked at the salty liquid on her fingers. "A reminder of the human half of my blood." She looked at Evangeline and took her hand with her own hand that was elongating and growing talons and said. "Coyle is a minion of evil, sort of like a demon and not a full-blooded one either, but enough to father me.. He's not even your uncle, but Dad, I mean your dad, always thought they were brothers. Demon magic."

"But we are sisters. Nothing will ever change that." Evangeline whispered. "Nothing will... ever... change ...that."

Bernadette sighed. "Uncle Coy—, I mean Father, please leave us. Let me deal with the unicorn rebirth and my late sister. Let me put her down gently. Allow me that last little bit of humanity."

"As you wish daughter. We have work to do anyway. Do your duty and we will do ours. We will be back at midnight and together we will open the portal."

"Father, I understand why we were compelled to get tattoos. I understand that Evangeline is the human vessel giving the unicorn rebirth, but a unicorn? They represent purity."

Coyle smirked at her, "Yes, they represent pure evil."

"I see," she said, "and my snake? That's evil as well?"

"No, quite the opposite. Myth has changed the roll of creatures involved with the Sha'Daa over the centuries. Snakes hate us, they will die gladly defending the human world."

"So why do I wear a serpent?"

"To make sure you are with us. If that snake on your back moves off you to help the humans, you will die just like your human relation."

"Well, so far so good." Bernadette said. "Now, let me get to work here."

The monsters went out the mouth of the cave and the cavern became dark as night. Bernadette hadn't realized they had light that traveled with them. She concentrated and her talons tingled, glowed red, and a fireball shot out from her fingertips and hovered overhead. "Hmmm," she mumbled. "Strength and magic tricks. Maybe being half-monster isn't all bad."

The fireball lit up the cavern, and she sat beside her sister and wondered how she was going to get them out of this mess, save the world, and finally get dinner. "Vange? Vange wake up."

Evangeline eyes fluttered then closed.

Bernadette felt totally helpless for the first time in her life. She ripped Evangeline's pants off and watched the tattoo of the unicorn throb, then pulsate, and finally, in an explosion of blood and bone, break free. It stood for a moment then shook the gore off its incredible translucent coat. It grew to a seven-foot-tall beast in a matter of seconds and without giving either woman a second look, flew off.

Bernadette wanted to see where it went, but she couldn't leave her sister bleeding to death. "Vange, you probably can't hear me but I can't help you. I don't know how."

As if in answer, the metal bracelet came alive and slithered off her wrist, and formed a tourniquet around Evangeline's shattered leg. But, as Bernadette felt hope flutter, she realized that Evangeline wasn't breathing anymore.

Bernadette felt alone, abandoned, for the first time in her life. She always knew she'd have her sister by her side and now Evangeline was dead. She put her head on her dead sister's chest and wept.

A burning sensation began on her back and moved over her shoulder and she realized that her tattoo was moving. *Now, I'll bleed to death as well, Both of us killed by our tattoos. How fitting*, she thought,

She felt the blood rushing down her back and the pain growing more fierce. The green and yellow reptile slithered over her shoulder and down her right arm. Bernadette was paralyzed with fear, as she watched the snake reach her wrist and sink its fangs into her vein. She screamed and the metal snake unwound itself from Evangeline's body and sank it's fangs into Bernadette's other wrist. She screamed ever louder as she realized that the metal snake had to be composed of iron and, like silver, poisonous to her kind. The burning venom rushed through her blood and she knew she was dying too.

She couldn't take a breath, couldn't move, she just lay next to her sister and waited for the pain to end. Both snakes disconnected and slithered back to Evangeline's body and sank their bloodstained fangs into her shattered leg. Bernadette sat up and lit the fireball that had gone out. Evangeline had moved, she saw her leg jerk.

She looked at her bleeding wrists and figured the snakes knew what they were doing. She hugged Evangeline's leg with her bloody wrists and let their blood mix. She felt herself slipping away but just held on even tighter.

"Bernadette, Bernie, wake up."

Bernadette opened her eyes in a blackened cave. She created a feeble excuse for a fireball and discovered Evangeline sitting up, with both her legs intact.

"Wow, Bernie you saved my life!"

"Only in a way. I guess our blood mixed because I felt myself changing again, becoming human and you, you started to breath. I still have enough demon blood in me make a fireball and to heal fast and," she pointed to the healed leg, "now so do you. Do you remember what is going on here?"

Evangeline nodded her head. "The unicorn is free now, did it go away?"

They listened to the screams coming from the cliffs above them. Bernadette shuddered. "I can only assume that is the unicorn at work. That damned thing is evil, a demon beast."

The sisters got up and went outside on the small beach and looked at the carnage. The saw people being pushed from the tall cliffs overhead, then the unicorn would fly down and impale anyone who moved.

"We've got to stop it. I gave the damned thing life, I have to do something." Evangeline said jumping up. "What stops a demon creature, anyway?"

"Well, my newfound father told me to avoid cold iron, it hurts us, can stop us in our tracks. He also said silver has powers against us as well, just not as powerful as iron."

Evangeline looked at her sister and grinned. "I've got it." She said and took off her locket and undid the clasp of her necklace. She started to unwind the multi looped wire chain. "Bernie help me straighten this out, it looks like it could be a couple of yards long."

As they stretched out the wire, Evangeline asked, "How can we get the unicorn back down here?"

Bernadette looked thoughtful. "Why don't you call it? It thinks you died so that may piss it off."

Evangeline looked at the silver wire stretched on the rocky beach and asked, "Do you have a wire cutter?"

"Oh damn, I left it in my purse. No, I don't have a wire cutter, but I do have these." Bernadette stared down at her hands and her nails started to elongate into claws. She ripped off a fifteen-foot piece of wire.

Nodding, Evangeline called out as loudly as she could. "Oh unicorn? Oh unicorn come back because you didn't finish me off."

To Bernadette's surprise she saw the red glowing eyes first, rising above the cliffs, and she gasped at the size he'd grown. The wingspan was at least twelve to fifteen feet and the white coat and golden horn shimmered in the light of the almost full moon which had just broken out from behind a cloud bank.

She watched the beast swoop down toward her and hoped that silver could control it. She made a lariat of the wire and threw it over the beasts head and stopped it in midflight. The unicorn lunged toward Evangeline but Bernadette held firm to the silver leash that was burning into her hands.

Evangeline ran around the beast and grabbed the leash away. It was coated with her sister's blood. "What now? How are we going to tame him?"

Bernadette stared at her hands as they rapidly healed. "The locket. Blind him with the locket. I can't touch that much silver."

Evangeline looked at the locket she was still holding. "I hate to ask this, but take the wire."

Bernadette grabbed the leash.

Evangeline worked the hinge of the locket back and forth until it snapped. "Hold it tight," she called and ran at the beast in front of her, dodging to avoid the horn. In a rapid upward motion, Evangeline stabbed both halves of the silver locket in the unicorn's eyes.

The animal let out a bloodcurdling scream and collapsed on the beach. Bernadette held onto the wire, blood dripping from her hands that appeared to be cut to the bone. Evangeline took the silver leash and Bernadette created two small fireballs and willed them to fly into the beast's eyes melting it into silver pools that hardened into blinding shells.

The three of them sat on the beach as the moon rose higher making the cliffs a lighter gray across the starry black sky.

"Coyle said the minions of evil with him are only the front runners, they're planning to cause as much fear as possible before the main onslaught arrives through the cave at midnight. He called it the Sha'Daa," Bernadette said, then added, "Seems I gave away my watch, any idea what time it is?"

Evangeline reached into her sweater pocket and pulled out her phone. "It's ten-fifty. We have an hour to stop a horde of bloodthirsty monsters and do something with a deadly, blind unicorn."

"I think he likes me," Bernadette cooed and petted the horned creature. "See he's rubbing my hand."

Evangeline rolled her eyes.

They sat in silence, the unicorn nickering and butting Bernadette to keep petting him. Suddenly there was movement on the gravelly sand. Snakes! Hundreds of snakes were burrowing up from under the beach. The sisters sat perfectly still and watched the vile reptiles surround them. "Now what?" Bernadette asked softly. "Can this night get any worse?"

"It will, in about an hour for everyone else," Evangeline whispered.

The legless reptiles moved as one and slithered into the cave ignoring the two women.

"Why snakes? I'm mean there are no snakes in Ireland, so why are they here?" Evangeline asked. "I guess we ought to follow and see what they're going to do."

Tiptoeing, Evangeline grasped Bernadette's hand and they entered the cave. Bernadette threw out a fireball and they saw the snakes congregating around the opening to another realm. In front of all of them were the bracelet snake and the tattoo serpent.

"What are they doing?" Once again, as one, all the snakes moved, Evangeline stared in awe as they piled up blocking the entry completely with their bodies.

In answer, the metal snake slithered up to Bernadette and then slithered away. When she didn't move it repeated the movement.

"I think it wants you to follow." Evangeline prompted. "Do it."

The snake led them to a huge mass of twisted metal shoved behind some large rocks. . Bernadette threw up another fireball and they studied it.

"Oh my lord," Evangeline gasped. "It's made up of iron cover snake carcasses. I think the snakes died saving the world last time. I think the snake wants us to move it in front of that portal. I think they want us to pour molten iron over them and seal the door like it must have happened last time."

"And how are we going to do that in less than an hour?"

Evangeline looked back at the unicorn still resting on the beach. "Use your new pet. Have it drag that iron snake sarcophagus to the portal and then use you new fire trick to re-melt it."

Bernadette snorted. "That's a dumb idea, but what the hell, let's give it a try."

She got the unicorn to shove the metal mass back to where it must have stood 10,000 years ago. Once it was in place up against all the snakes, Bernadette shot fireball after fireball at it.

Evangeline stood by watching as the metal glowed red and melded onto the living serpent wall, creating a new blockade. "That ought to work, I hope," she muttered. "It looks great."

Bernadette took a shaky breath, feeling drained. "Let's block the cave entry and burn down the pub above us. Nothing we can do about those demons who are already loose but why don't you text everyone and post about silver and iron weapons. Maybe steel will work as well. Maybe we can get a bunch of them killed before they realize no one's coming to their party. Thank goodness for the internet."

"Sounds like a plan," Evangeline said and added, "I have to tell everyone not to harm the snakes. Who knew they were the good guys."

"Yeah," Bernadette said with a catch in her voice. "They are the real heroes here."

Back on the beach Evangeline worked on her cell as Bernadette mounted the flying unicorn and whispered into its ear. The beast rose up gracefully then kicked at the cliff until a rockslide covered the cave entrance.

Finished, Bernadette led the blind animal to Evangeline and said, "Climb aboard, he won't hurt you now. He's our only way up."

Evangeline mounted the creature and it ignored her, turning its head to rub it against Bernadette's thigh. As they flew, they searched for the pub, but the only thing in the right area was a castle in ruins. "I guess the pub was just demon magic. What do we do now?"

"Land," Bernadette said.

They dismounted and the entered the ruins. Bernadette looked around. Yes, it had been the pub, only now it was as it actually appeared, dirty and untouched for decades. They found the door that lead down to the cave and she called in her unicorn and let it playfully smash the wall with its hooves until the stones jarred loose and the stairs disappeared under the collapsing wall.

The sun was rising as they sat on the grass by the ruin. The unicorn munched on the dew soaked lawn as they waited and watched for any sign of the demons or their army. "I think you can go back to the hotel now." Bernadette said. "Uni and I will drop you off."

"What about you?"

"Well, I'm more demon than I want to be, so I'm going to stay here, buy this place, fix it up and call it home. You go back to Florida and handle my finances. I think I can live a couple of lifetimes here with my pension and savings."

"You can't be serious?" Evangeline wailed. "I can't go home alone. I don't know what I'd do without you. You're my sister!"

"Well not really, not by blood." Bernadette sighed.

"Fuck blood." Evangeline said, and smiled as she used the curse work. "We are sisters and will be forever."

Bernadette cleared her throat, "About forever. My father, my real father, Coyle, told me that demons have a much longer life span than humans so I guess I'll be here a really long time. I have to stay and make sure that those loose monsters never get the entry cleared. I've got my pet unicorn to protect me and keep me company."

Then she grinned and laid her hand on Evangeline's regrown leg. "Oh, and then there's the other part. You know how you always complain that I don't age like you, well that was because of my demon blood, and Vange, we now share that blood."

Evangeline hugged her sister. "Well, you better make this place habitable, because I'll be visiting you every year for the Solstice. You know we always celebrate our birthdays together and I don't see any reason to stop. Do you?"

"Nope," Bernadette agreed. "I expect we'll continue to celebrate together for at least the next century or two."

Apprentice

AFTER KOHALA BEGAN HIS SLUMBER OF centuries, Haumea's father the King, and his people, were surprised to find her alive and unbound, and walking into the main clearing before the King's bamboo palace.

They could tell she had been blessed by a great power, as her eyes had changed from black to green, and her feet did not leave impressions in the soil anymore.

One warrior thought she was a demon who had taken her dead body upon itself, wearing her skin like a Kapa Kihei. He screamed and ran at Haumea, swinging a vicious shark toothed club in a wide arc quickly intersecting with her head.

Haumea nimbly ducked under the strike, thrust a hand forward as quick as a snake striking, and ripped out the throat of Alika, one of her father's most prized Kao bodyguards, with a single clench of her fingers.

Afterwards she announced she would become the new Kako'o to Kapula, the aging and near blind Tufuga who lived in a small cave further inland. The King quickly gave his blessing, then turned away, striding back to the safety of his palace. Father and daughter never spoke again.

Haumea's tattooing apprenticeship had begun.

Cambion

by Kacey Ezell

I SLAMMED MY CAR DOOR WITH UNNECESSARY force and hitched my duffel bag up onto my shoulder. Overhead, the gunmetal sky rumbled with thunder, and I mumbled curse words under my breath as fat drops started to patter down on me. With a sigh, I hitched my bag up one more time and began the long walk across the parking lot toward the back door of the club.

Desires had seen better days, but it was still the best paying strip club in Albuquerque. Girls from all over this dust and tumbleweed-choked desert came here to dance. I, myself, regularly pulled in over a thousand dollars in tips on a good night. Not bad for a girl who never finished high school.

But tonight wasn't looking like a good night. I briefly considered sprinting to the door, but since the parking lot was a half-mile long, I decided that I'd just arrive wet and tired, instead of only wet. So I walked, keeping my dark hair down against the rising wind as fantastic lightning split the sky.

"Lola," a voice said. A male voice, older. I paused, looked up warily, the fingers of my right hand curling around the canister of pepper spray I kept on my keychain. Ordinarily, I wouldn't have stopped, but he'd said my real name.

The older man stood in front of me, his angular face pale in the dim light. He wore a black overcoat, and a hat, and as I met his eyes, he smiled, revealing a single gold incisor.

"Do I know you?" I asked, wondering what he wanted. That was unusual for me. Usually, I didn't have to wonder. It was a game I'd played since I was little. I would look at someone and guess at what they wanted. Over time, I'd gotten pretty good at it. Being able to guess at a person's deepest desires came in handy, in my line of work. But this guy was a mystery, which put me on edge. That, and him knowing my name.

"You wish to know what I want? What I always want. I want to make a trade, a sale."

"Look, buddy, I'm a dancer, not a hooker. Try Central in a few hours," I said, shifting my weight backwards, away from him.

The Salesman shook his head impatiently. "No, no," he said. "That is not what I seek from you. You have a new tattoo, yes?"

I blinked. How did this guy know so much? I flicked my eyes toward the club door, where Benny, one of the bouncers, stood waiting for me. He raised his eyebrows in a question, asking if I needed help. I shook my head briefly, but the knowledge that he was there made me feel marginally better. "Yes," I answered. "I got it last weekend."

"I want to see your tattoo, in return, I will give you information that may save your life."

I looked at him for a long moment, but in the end it seemed harmless enough. I was, after all, a stripper. Showing people my body was kind of my job. I dropped my bag to the ground and turned to the side. I crossed my arms over my stomach and lifted my shirt high enough to reveal the plain black push-up bra that I'd put on to drive to work. My frillier stuff was in the bag, because it wasn't nearly as comfortable. I saved that for the stage.

My ribs were still sore, but the redness had gone down. I thought the tat was healing nicely. It was a beautiful depiction of a fallen angel, her wings spread, her head down, her arms drawn inward. The tips of her wings were an inky black, fading through all the various shades of gray to reach a snowy white where they touched her shoulders. I liked the effect, even though the shading had been pure torture. But the artists at Mom's Bane knew their stuff. Every time I looked at her in the mirror, I was struck again by the powerful emotion contained in her pose.

"Ahhh, yes," the Salesman said. "The fallen angel, cast out for her wickedness. Her agony resonates. I am saddened for her."

"It was her own doing," I said, surprising myself. "She made her choices."

He lifted his eyes from my tattoo to my face. "So she did," he said. "And so must you. Tonight will not be a regular night for you, Lola. The Sha'Daa has come. Evil stalks you, haunts this place. For ten thousand years, evil has waited, and tonight they will try to come through. You must stop them."

"How?" I asked, mesmerized.

"You must choose. That is all I will tell you, unless you wish to make another trade?" He smiled again, wider. "Your lipstick is beautiful."

I blinked, the momentary spell broken. "My lipstick?" I asked, letting my shirt fall back into place. "Okay, nutbag. Look, I'm not giving you my MAC Rebel. It costs fourteen dollars a tube! I've gotta go," I said. I picked up my bag and brushed past him as lighting sliced the sky again, followed by the deafening crack of thunder.

"Could you believe that guy?" I asked Benny as he held the door open for me.

"What guy?" he asked. "Better get inside before you get all wet, Angel-Eyes." I looked quizzically at him, but his smile was genuine. Benny was one of the good guys. He was also, it turned out, a big Clint Eastwood fan, and he'd told me once that my eyes were the exact color of fine whiskey. "Angel-Eyes" became his nickname for me. All he wanted was to earn an honest wage doing something he was good at. He wanted to look out for us girls, it made him feel like a man. It didn't seem like him to be screwing with me, but I supposed anything was possible.

"Yeah, whatever," I said, my bad mood returning as I pushed inside and headed for the cramped dump of a dressing room.

Despite my feeling that tonight would be a bust, we ended up with a packed house before I even went on. Some of the newer girls came back for their breaks giddy with excitement. I watched them squeal about the tips they'd gotten and the number of dances they'd sold. I was only twenty-two, but I felt ancient and cynical around them. I'd learned early on not to say anything to the younger girls... that way lies madness. They were young and pretty enough now, but I knew how to read what they wanted, and they weren't going to find it here.

Here, all they'd find would be the illusion of affection, and eventually, reality would set in. When that happened, the lucky ones quit. The not-so-lucky ones stayed, but they chased that illusion, that rush through other means, usually chemical in nature. The club management said that they had a strict policy about drugs on the premises, but more than one dancer used her break to do a quick bump in the dressing room or the bathroom. And that was before the clients started offering it. Turning down a client's offer was frowned upon in this establishment.

The voice of the DJ cut through my reverie, bringing me back to myself. "Please welcome to the main stage, the lovely Lady Diamond!" he announced, and the grinding beat of Di's music started to thump through the floorboards. My set was immediately following Di's, so I took one last look in the mirror and slicked on another coat of Rebel before tucking it, and my bag, into my locker.

Cesar, the club manager, came to the door of the dressing room. "Angel, you're up next," he said. I gave him a look, since I was already lining up behind the door to the main stage. "And there's someone here asking for you. Older guy, black coat. He's sitting at nine. Find him afterward. Ladies, you're not making money in here. If you're on a break, it's done. Get back out there." He left amid groans and giggles, and several of the girls followed him out onto the floor.

A smattering of applause accompanied the last beat of Di's song. I took a deep breath and closed my eyes for a moment, concentrating on my routine. The DJ's voice came over the system again. "Give it up for Diamond! Thank you, sweetie. All right, gentlemen. Prepare yourselves. Coming right now, to the main stage, Desires gives you… Aaaaaaaangellllllllll!"

I slipped through the door and waited behind the black velvet curtain. The sounds of breathing replaced the DJ's voice, followed by a haunting melody that wove in and out of the breath cadence. I slipped through the curtain.

I want you now.

Tomorrow won't do…

The lights flashed around me as I twirled slowly, feeling the eyes on me, feeling the desires of the crowd as I undulated to the old Depeche Mode song. I reached out, my hand finding the cool hardness of the pole. With a quick kick, I pulled myself up, inverted, and anchored myself in place with my legs.

I could feel their desires pulsing through me as I peeled my top off slowly, leaving my flesh bare to the swirling lights and the needy eyes. A muscle contraction allowed me to twist around the pole as I descended, catching myself with my arms. I extended first one leg, and then the other, holding myself in a split while the music built. When it dropped, I dropped, in a release move that slid me down to a point six inches above the stage floor. I caught myself with my hands, and then slowly curled my legs, one by one, back around the pole until I sat with the heels of my shoes touching, the pole between my legs.

The want intensified as the song wound on, the singer's aching voice reverberating through the club's speakers. Fueled by the need of the crowd, I lowered my back slowly to the stage floor, and then arched my hips up, transitioning to a backward roll that landed me in another slow split. For the first time in the routine, my eyes met the eyes of one of the club's patrons. He was sitting in the front row, his eyes glassy, his mouth open just a bit. I tilted my head just a little and curved my lips upward, and his shaking hands couldn't put his money on the stage fast enough. I leaned slowly forward and gathered up the bills with a whispered, "thank you, baby," before moving on to the next patron, and the next.

When the song ended, I had a pile of money in my hands, and another in my garter and in my g-string. I gathered up my top with a practiced move and exited the stage toward the DJ booth, riding on the rush that performance always seemed to provide. I couldn't understand these girls who got hooked on coke, for desire was a much more powerful drug.

"Let's give it up for Angel!" the DJ said into the microphone, over the cheers and applause that competed with the thunder outside. I smiled up at him, and the DJ, his eyes as hot as anyone in the crowd, smiled back at me. He covered the microphone for a minute while I arranged the money into a neat stack and logged the amount in the proper book. "You're amazing," he said.

"Thanks, Hon," I replied, trying not to notice that he wanted to lick the tiny droplets of sweat off of my collarbone. For just one more second, I let his desire surge through me like lightning under my skin, and then I gave him a quick smile and ducked behind the curtain to go freshen up.

Back in the dressing room, I gave one of the newer girls a Look, and she quickly moved aside, affording me a spot at the mirror so that I could replace my clothing and repair my makeup. Desires was a bit of a dump, perhaps, but it was my dump. Since I brought in the most cash for tips and private dances, I was undisputed queen of the hill. Many of our clients came just to see me, and everyone knew it.

I pulled a brush through my night-dark hair and used a q-tip to clean up where my eyeliner had smudged. One more coat of mascara on my dark lashes, and I was set. I generally tried to play up my eyes, since they were my most striking feature. After my breasts, of course. And my ass.

"Angel! Client's waiting for you!" Cesar snapped at me. I met his eyes coolly in the glass of the mirror and finished sliding the tube of lipstick over my lips. While he fumed, I capped the tube, stored my bag, and then blew him a kiss in the mirror. "Coming, Cesar," I said in a simpering voice. He glowered at me, his lip curved in a sneer, but we both knew that he wasn't going to do anything to his prize moneymaker.

"Listen, Cesar," I said as I walked out of the dressing room, hooking my arm through his as was protocol when the manager "delivered" one of us to a client. "If this is the same guy that stopped me in the parking lot, I'm out. Guy was a wierdo, kept trying to steal my lipstick."

"I don't give a fuck how much of a wierdo he is, this dude spent a thousand dollars in the champagne room," Cesar growled, managing to do so through his "club manager" smile. "You'll keep him happy or you really are out, Angel. You hear me? I'm not fucking around on this one."

I would have protested more, but as we moved out into the main part of the club, I could see that the point was moot. There was a gentleman sitting at table nine with a hat and a dark coat, but it wasn't the creep from the parking lot. So I inhaled slightly and gave a pouty little smile as we approached.

"Mr. Cambion," Cesar said, inclining his head respectfully. I kept my smile in place, though watching Cesar kiss ass made me want to gag. "May I introduce…" Overdone pause for dramatic effect, "Angel?"

I stepped forward, offered my hand, palm down, for the client to take. He wrapped his own long fingers around my fingers and brought my knuckles to his lips. My smile didn't slip, but I did raise an eyebrow as Cesar stepped away.

"Good evening, Mr. Cambion," I said, easing into the chair next to his. "I hope you enjoyed my set."

"Good evening, Ms. Angel," he replied, leaning back in his own chair and removing the half-shaded sunglasses he'd been wearing. I blinked in surprise. His eyes were the same color as mine. I'd never seen anyone else who had the same yellow-gold iris, but he did. His smile deepened, indicating that he'd noticed me noticing. "You have a lovely tattoo on your side," he said. "May I see it?"

I continued to meet his eyes as my hands rose to unbutton the sheer black blouse that was all I wore over the g-string. I worked slowly, and then turned to let the material slide down my shoulder and arm. With a sweep of my hand, I pulled the shirt away and twisted so that he could get a good look at my fallen angel. I glanced down, and then back up at him. Something about him unsettled me, and in that moment, I figured it out. Like the guy in the parking lot earlier, I couldn't read this guy, didn't know what he wanted. And what was with everyone wanting to look at my tattoo today?

The wall just behind Mr. Cambion was mirrored. Though the club was as dim as ever, there was just enough light for me to get a look at my tattoo. I blinked again, and shifted so more of the light fell on her, and then I nearly gasped out loud.

Her wings were entirely black, rather than the beautiful fade effect of before. Her head was lifted, and where her eyes should be, two flames burned with orange and reds so intense, I almost felt as if my skin were scorching.

"Yes," Cambion said. "She is changing, coming into her power, as are you, my dear Angel." His voice slid over me like a caress, and I looked back at him in confusion.

"I don't know what you're talking about," I said, fighting to keep the tremor out of my voice.

"I know," he said, soothingly, "It is tragic. You should not have been kept innocent of your heritage and power. But it is no matter. The tattoo called to me, and I have found you just in time. The Sha'daa is upon us, and tonight we will come into our true power."

That did it. The creepy Salesman guy had talked about the Sha'daa, too. I felt anger building inside me, burning away the confusion. It felt good, and I let it rise.

"Listen, buddy," I said lowly, leaning forward. "I don't know what you're talking about, and I don't care. I'm not giving you my lipstick or anything else, except for maybe a dance, and that's only if you pay double." I fully expected him to turn me down. Copping that kind of aggressive attitude with a client took them out of the fantasy. They came here to believe that beautiful women wanted their company, wanted their attention. They didn't come here to be bossed around. They got enough of that at home.

Cambion just shook his head. "No, my darling," he said. "I do not want you to dance for me. I want you to dance for these people. Raise their lust, just as you have been doing. Feed from them fully, for tonight you can. The barrier between the worlds is thin, reach for your demonic heritage, little succubus, and drink their life energy. The stronger you become, the stronger I shall become, and together we will usher in a new age."

I just stared at him, not moving.

He leaned toward me, capturing my fingers with his own. "You can feel it, can't you?" he whispered. "So can I. You feel how much they want you, want to touch you, drink you in. You feel that need and you *take* it. You drink *them* in, and they fill you with power. Every time you dance, every time you move, you get stronger. Because you *know*. You know what they want, and how to make them want it more."

I shook my head, my heart pounding. His smile only grew.

I surged to my feet, pulling my hand back abruptly and nearly knocking over the little cocktail table between us. "I don't know what you're talking about," I said, coldly. *Cesar be damned,* I thought as I pivoted on my platform heels and walked away.

The night just got weirder from there.

Although I wasn't scheduled for a break, I headed to the dressing room anyway. I needed to take a breath that wasn't scented with the sweet-smelling supposed artificial sex pheromones that the club pumped into the main area. Cesar claimed that it got everyone in the mood and made their wallets more loose. Personally, I never noticed a difference. I made money regardless of whether or not the club smelled like sex and cotton candy.

I took my place at the mirror again, turning so that I could study my tattoo. How the fuck had he done that? I looked closely, but it didn't appear to be red or puffy, so I didn't think it was infected. Besides, an infection shouldn't account for the design changing so fundamentally. Instead of a fallen creature haunted by her choices, I now had an avenging angel with eyes that burned hatred. It was a cool design… but it shouldn't be there!

The dressing room door slammed open behind me, and Benny and Diamond came in, Benny holding the limp form of one of the new girls. I think her name was Candy or something.

Her head lolled about as he placed her on the couch, and Diamond began slapping her cheeks. "Candy, Candy, wake up," Diamond hissed at her. "C'mon, bitch, you can't OD in here! Cesar will fire my ass if he finds out I hooked you up."

"What happened?" I asked, turning away from the mirror and its disturbing reflection.

"She was going on stage, and just passed the fuck out," Diamond said, sounding equal parts worried and disgusted. "I told her to go easy on the stuff. Stupid *puta*." She slapped the new girl harder, and the little blonde on the couch woke up with a gasp. Everyone in the room breathed a sigh of relief.

"I'll go on for her," I volunteered. "Keep Cesar from flipping his shit. Get her to drink some water or something, willya?"

Diamond nodded absently as the girl began to cry. "Why did you hit me?" Candy wailed softly, holding one hand to her cheek.

"I told you to go easy on that shit! You some kind of stupid or something? You're not even supposed to do it here!" Diamond said, nearly hissing her words in anger.

Candy began to cry harder. "I didn't do anything!" she whimpered. "It's still in my bag, Di, honest. I was just with that guy at Nine."

"Yeah? Then why is your nose bleeding like you got punched, little liar?" Di asked, slapping her again for good measure. Candy just continued to cry.

I left that drama behind and took my place behind the main stage curtain. Benny must have slipped out to tell the DJ, because next thing I heard, he was encouraging patrons to put their hands together and welcome me to the main stage.

This time, my music started with a rhythmic thumping and an eerie wailing noise, like a warped recording of a violin.

You let me violate you…

You let me desecrate you…

Yes, it was a classic, but it was a classic for a reason. I swept the curtain aside and prowled onto the stage like a hunting tiger. Thunder cracked overhead, nearly inaudible over the pounding beat of the song. The club was packed, doubly so than before, and we had to be getting close to capacity. I launched into my routine, my eyes aggressively looking for the clients' gaze. This song demanded it. One older man in the front row raised tired, hopeless eyes to mine.

His desire hit me like a tsunami, crashing over me and damn near rolling me back with it. I felt my aggression rise to the challenge, surging through my every movement. I was tighter, stronger, harder, and faster than ever before. Like Cambion had said, I drank the old man's need in, and I felt it ignite within me.

His faded blue eyes widened, and his face drained of color. A thin line of red began to trickle from his nose. I whirled around, breaking our gaze as I turned to the other side of the stage. There. A youngster this time, college age, judging by his baseball cap, his face like a shiny penny, and his entourage of four more guys just like him. He grinned at me and waved a folded dollar bill in invitation.

Inside my head I snarled at him. He thought to entice me? I was the hunter here, he merely prey. Prey has no power over the predator, the predator exists only to take. So I opened up my mind and I took. My hips ground lower and lower on the pole as I pulled his schoolboy desire in toward me in one long, pull. His smile faded slowly. That left him staring at me as if I were an impossibility too exquisite to be true. I arched backwards, pulling harder, and felt his last surrender as he gave me all he had to give. He, too, paled, and then slumped. His friends were too busy hooting and hollering to notice.

Up, again. I pirouetted on one platform shoe and grabbed hold of the pole with both hands. I kicked up into an inverted position, holding myself in place with my thigh muscles. I let go with my hands and ripped the sheer black shirt open, exposing my breasts in one violent movement.

The desire in the room crescendoed, coming at me from all directions. I closed my eyes and writhed under it, running my hands over my stomach, pulling in the need that pounded against every inch of my exposed skin.

When I opened my eyes, I saw Mr. Cambion sitting at his table, a smile on his lips, flames flickering in his eyes. I drew in a breath and faltered, sliding down the pole a good few inches before I caught myself.

What was I doing?

The song was about to end, and since my fall had brought me within reach of the floor, I put my hands down and did a walkover to dismount. I could still feel the need of the crowd pushing at me, begging me to take it and make it my own, but as I bent to retrieve my cash, I caught sight of the two still figures, one on either side of the stage.

I bent in front of the old man, nudged his arm with the toe of my shoe. "You okay?" I asked. I almost had to shout it over the noise of the crowd. They were cheering, clapping, chanting my name. The DJ had joined in over the loudspeaker, and the entire place felt balanced on the ragged edge of control.

The old man didn't move. Unnerved, I stepped back, turned to look at the boy. He, too, was pale as a sheet and when one of his friends bumped him, he fell backward in his chair.

Thin trails of blood ran from both eyes, his nose, his ears, and the corner of his mouth.

I clapped my own free hand over my mouth and fled back to the dressing room, chased by the sound of the crowd howling for my return.

Cesar was there, waiting for me backstage. He grabbed my arm and pulled me up against him. His mouth crushed down over mine, and his desire stabbed into me. I could feel what he wanted from me. He wanted me whimpering for him, aching for him the way I made him ache. He wanted to see me beaten, punished for treating him like he was nothing. He wanted to hurt me in so many ways…

I brought my knee up hard into his groin. Cesar gasped, and then rocked backward. I followed this up with a punch to his throat. His knees buckled and he fell in front of me. I wiped my mouth with the back of my hand and grabbed my bag from where I'd left it earlier. He'd messed up my lipstick.

"You think you're going to hurt me, Cesar?" I asked quietly, my voice the same seductive purr I used on the clients. "Oh no. I'm going to hurt you so much worse." Anger built inside me as I grabbed hold of his desire and pulled. Not the slow, steady building of pleasure that I'd done for the boy and the old man on the stage. No, I *ripped* his energy away in a move every bit as violent as what he'd planned for me. Cesar's face turned purple, and his eyes burst in his sockets as his nose and ears began to run freely with blood.

I screamed, half in anger and half in fear at what I'd just done. I whirled around and crashed through the door out to the main floor.

Into chaos.

The club had devolved into a full-on orgy of sex and violence. Dancers and patrons tangled up everywhere, need pulsing from all of them, battering at me to let it in. Two large men came toward me, their eyes blank, their faces slack with desire. I backed up, then turned and sprinted down the hallway to the champagne room. It wasn't empty, however, and the two dancers busily engaged with the man inside began to reach out to grab me.

I turned and fled again, finding the nearest door and plunging inside. It was the janitor's closet, and it was the only place in the club where someone's desire wasn't battering at my grieving, aching mind.

"Angel."

It was Cambion's voice, over the loudspeaker.

"Angel, my darling. Come out and play! You've done so well, sweetheart. You've made me very proud. With the energy pouring off of these fools, the breach will be fully opened. We will take our place beside our ancestors. Each of your new slaves will leave here and go home and ignite their families with the ember of your lust, and the resulting fire will burn forever! All of their life, all of their need and want will fuel us. See how powerful we have become? Come out, my queen!"

"No," I whispered in the dark, more to myself than anything. "I don't want to be your queen."

"I can help you," a voice said next to me. I stifled a scream as the Salesman from earlier flicked a lighter and illuminated his face. "I can tell you how to stop him. For a price."

"My lipstick?" I asked, half hysterical. He nodded, smiling gently. I fumbled for the bag that I still held, thanking all that was good when my fingers wrapped around the small cylindrical tube. "Take it," I said, holding it out. "Just tell me how to stop him, how to stop this."

The Salesman took the tube and opened it, taking a deep sniff of the distinctive vanilla scent of MAC lipsticks. Then he capped the tube and put it in his pocket. "The cambion is right. The people here have been infected. If you would stop this infection of need from spreading, you have to kill them all, without using your natural gifts of seduction."

"Kill them all? I can't... they didn't do anything wrong!"

He shrugged, nodding sympathetically. "Nevertheless, that is what you must do if you wish to stop the demons of lust from breaking through the barrier into our world. Real succubi and incubi would turn our entire planet into a chaotic, violent orgy of death, enough to make what's going on here look like a little kid's birthday party.

"I suggest fire, or..." he paused, and raised the lighter to the shelf next to us. On the shelf was an economy-sized bottle of Clorox bleach, and another economy-sized bottle of ammonia-based cleaner.

"Replace sex with cleansing death, Lola," he said. "It is not an easy choice, but it is the only way to stop your kinsman and the darkness that he represents from overwhelming the Earth."

I may not have graduated from high school, but that didn't mean that I hadn't aced AP chemistry as a junior. Ammonia and bleach equaled chlorine gas, which would be deadly to everyone in the vicinity. And with Cesar's pheromone misters in the HVAC ducts, the vicinity would be the entirety of the club.

"Will Cambion die, too?" I asked.

The Salesman nodded. "His body is as human as yours. You are related, after all. Your demon blood has lain dormant for a very, very long time. Ten thousand years, to be precise, when a common ancestor of yours was raped by an incubus. The child that resulted started the bloodlines that produced the two of you."

"All right," I said. "I'll do it." I didn't give a shit about a demon ancestor or any of that. I just knew that the wanting, the *needing* had to stop.

The Salesman nodded and let his light go out. I reached out, but my hand found nothing but the bottle of bleach. I was, once again, alone in the dark.

The orgy was in full swing, with Cambion sitting at the DJ both, watching it all with flames in his eyes. He was so busy pulling all the energy from the writhing mass of humanity that he didn't even notice me sneak from the janitor's closet back to the dressing room. I ignored Cesar's body and used a chair to get up to the HVAC grate on the wall. I opened it up, and found Cesar's makeshift pheromone delivery system. Basically, he'd rigged a bunch of misters to a homemade tank, and then positioned each of the misters behind the HVAC grates of every room in the club. But the tank itself he kept in the dressing room. I grabbed this and quickly disconnected it from the main hose. I dumped its stinking contents into the sink, wrinkling my nose at the intensified stench of candied sex. Then I carried the tank over to the HVAC grate and poured the bottle of bleach inside. I took a deep breath, held it, and then added the ammonia.

My eyes immediately began to burn, and my hands shook as I lifted the tank up and frantically began trying to screw the main hose into its receptacle. I might have slightly cross-threaded it, but to be honest, I didn't care. My eyes and chest were burning, and I had to get out of there. I stumbled, and then started toward the back door.

I got out, and ran for my car. Then I dropped down on the ground and began to cry. Deep, wrenching sobs tore at me as I thought about all the people I'd just killed. I sat and cried and waited for hours. Not a single one of them exited the building after me. Not one.

Out to the east, the sky over the Sandias began to turn gray. It was almost dawn. I decided that I'd best not be here when someone showed up and began to wonder why everyone inside was dead. I used my car door handle to pull myself up to my feet. I pulled my jeans and t-shirt out of my bag and got dressed there in the parking lot. As I pulled my shirt down over my ribs, I got a glimpse of my tattoo.

I had to check in the side mirror of my car, but it was true. The fallen angel was back to normal, her wings shading from purest white to inky black. Her face down, her arms crossed as she, too, wept for the choices she'd had to make.

Engraved

HAUMEA PUT THE FINAL TOUCHES ON ONE of her oldest clients, a large Caucasian man on the far side of middle-age. It was difficult to tell obscured as he was by so much startling body art. He lay on his back, naked and staring at the ceiling as if lost in thought. It had taken Haumea a great deal of care and effort to shave off her client's gray eyebrows and thick head of white hair without cutting any flesh or causing undue skin irritation.

He was the near completion of a body suit that covered his epidermis, including the skin under his fingernails and toenails, the surface of his lips, the visible sclera of his left eyeball, everything except for a small untouched patch of skin on his right shoulder blade, and she would soon attend to that.

The trickiest work yet she was now detailing upon the mass of long-healed but ugly scar tissue that covered the socket where his right eye used to be.

"Can't say this establishment is an improvement over your old home," he said.

"Well Carl," Haumea replied, using a liner to etch in a series of black dots, "you have to go where the work is, and that old farmhouse would have been a bit of an eyesore in current urban locales."

Carl grunted, "The only thing a city has in abundance is conflict, a lesson I've learned much too often."

"And what did this little altercation teach you, Carl?" Haumea asked as she shaded in the final swirl of a red and blue Celtic circle on the tortured flesh of the right side of his face.

"Only," Carl replied, continuing to stare blankly at the ceiling with his one good eye, "to choose my sleeping companions more wisely… and never nod off within easy reach of large stones."

"And this companion," Haumea said, "did you reciprocate her… gift?"

Chuckling, Carl raised his large, powerful looking right hand a few inches off the tattooing table and clenched it twice before dropping it down again, "I did indeed. Though *he* didn't have much time to appreciate it."

"Done," Haumea said, turning off her iron and stepping back to examine her work.

Carl sat up and looked at the huge mirror that covered a complete wall of the suite. Turning one way, and then the other, he quickly viewed the mass of tribal patterns, Celtic motifs, geometric shapes, sigils, symbols, and tiny figures that swarmed across face, neck, head, and ears. He stuck his tongue out for a moment and laughed at sight of the brightly colored and finely detailed donkey butt tattooed there.

"Are you ready to finish the job?" Haumea asked seriously.

Carl turned around and peered at her with his one good eye.

"This is really going to happen?" he asked, "No games, no stories, everything you told me over a hundred years ago is true. It's all coming to a head."

"Yes," Haumea nodded, "we had an agreement. I'm calling in all my tabs now. When I finish here, you will be the alpha point of the final tattoo."

"And you the omega," Carl whispered.

Haumea nodded, "I also have to pay the piper."

Carl took in a deep breath and let it out slowly, "The lord hates a coward," he said, and then lay down, face forward, upon the tattoo table.

"Haumea," Carl said, "what do *you* see when you look at my shoulder blade?"

Haumea stepped forward and traced the clean, uninked patch of skin on Carl's back with her right index finger. She then pulled her hand away and touched her own face for a moment.

"I'm the one person your special talent cannot affect, Carl," Haumea said sadly, "for when I accepted *this* gift, I was torn from the stream of fate. I live outside the realm of destiny."

"I never liked that guy," Carl said.

"You were always jealous of Johnny," Haumea said.

"For good reason," Carl replied.

Haumea dipped the needle of her iron into a rich purple, and then began freehanding an archane Aramaic symbol on Carl's shoulder blade.

Some time later Haumea and Carl exited the quick-room into the shop proper, barely able to find elbow-room in the now packed Mom's Bane. One dozen tattoo artists were inking clients at the same time, some doubling up on the tattoo tables, others just working on the floor itself.

"Carl," Haumea said, "I…"

"I've got a date with the North Pole," Carl said, "no time for chit chat. Goodbye Haumea," and Carl, wearing nothing but a pair of black shorts and red sandals strode into the crowd toward the front door.

A teenage Goth boy, wearing an ebony t-shirt sporting the words *Winona Forever*, jumped up from his seat near the exit as Carl approached.

"Wow," the kid shouted, "those are some awesome tats, man."

Carl paused for a moment and gave the kid the stink-eye, "I'll say it once, and once only… they're skin illustrations, not tattoos."

"Uh, yeah," the kid mumbled, "I hear you, man. Sorry."

Carl nodded and walked out of the shop.

"Well," Johnny said, "he didn't look too happy, kinda sap sap sappy!"

Haumea started, but just as quickly calmed down and turned to Johnny, and her eyes widened. The Salesman was in one of his manic stages. She'd witnessed them before, and they were quite frightening.

Johnny danced back and forth on his heels and the balls of his feet like some cartoon villain, bugging out his eyes and stretching his grin to a disturbing degree.

"You're pushing yourself too hard, Johnny," Haumea said, "can't you slow down?"

"No time, no time, no time," Johnny cackled, "gotta trade trade trade trade, that's how history's made! Ha ha ha ha ha ha ha."

Haumea swallowed nervously and just nodded her head, "We're on track, Johnny. I swear. Everything is going to plan."

"Oh, Haumea," Johnny laughed, "the strain, the strain strain strain strain strain. But Johnny is up to it, oh yesirreeeeee he is indeed, ha ha ha ha ha ha!"

"Johnny, I think I've spotted that guy following you," Haumea said, hoping to focus Johnny's attention, and for a few moments it seemed to work, as he immediately stopped dancing about, "a young guy, pale skin, average height, freckles. One moment I see him in the alley outside, the next in the prep lounge, and then poof he's gone. I didn't think anyone or anything but you could teleport through my barriers and protective spells."

"Oh he's a bad one alright, Haumea," Johnny said, "hard core, upper level, no holds barred batch of nastiness, my dear. Not one to mess with. The ultimate bane of existence."

"Stop scaring me, John. He's nothing you can't handle," Haumea said, "I've seen you rumble with a hell-god for Christ's sake."

"There are more things in heaven and earth, Haumea," Johnny said, "than even you have dreamt over the millennia. And on that note, I have a bar, pawn shop, and toy store I need to hit up for supplies. Toodles."

Haumea blinked her eyes and Johnny was gone. She chugged the last two cans of Red Bull in her fridge and was about to shout out for the next walk in when somebody tapped her on her shoulder.

She spun around and found herself face to face with the young stranger who she suspected of being Johnny's stalker.

"It's Haumea, right?" he asked, speaking softly with a deep baritone that somehow cut right through all the background noise, almost like he was simultaneously speaking in her mind, "my name is Prana, and I'm looking for somebody."

CHAPTER SIX

Cathedrals and Roses

by Vivian Caethe

Y
VEGNY REGRETTED MANY THINGS IN HIS life. Killing Sergei. What he had been forced to do to stay alive in prison. The person he never had a chance to be.

Tattoos covered his arms and torso, cathedrals and roses. The Russian prison system never showed kindness to the weak. His only means of survival had been to stand up to the hardest, the cruelest, the most fearsome within the confines of Vladimirsky Central. He could never be a businessman again, never live his life like a normal citizen. And that was before the tattoos.

He blinked and the world turned dark for a moment. For just a moment he could see what was to come. The world would burn and he was free just in time to see the end. Perhaps it was better to die a free man, but he doubted it.

Yvegny stepped from the bus and into the transit center that led to the streets of Moscow. He had no home and no friends remaining to help him. Even his brother had stopped writing years ago.

He started to put his hand in his pockets, but felt the weight of Sergei's ring in his right pants pocket. Flinching at the thought of the memory of touching his dead lover's hand, he rubbed his hands briskly to rid his skin of the cold sensation.

Agoraphobia weighed heavily on him, warring with the claustrophobia of a caged animal released into the wild. Weak-kneed, he pushed his way through the crowd to the street. Every man or woman who brushed against him made him flinch, made him feel as if he should reach for the shiv they had relieved him of before releasing him. Defenseless, he acted like prey and hated himself for it. Prey died, predators survived. Hadn't his years in Central taught him that? Not that anyone would survive what was to come.

Forcing his shoulders straight, he made his way through the families greeting their loved ones, the lovers meeting, the reunions and the joy. He had no joy, only the cold comfort of freedom after he had forgotten what it meant. The crowds parted around him, eyes leery on his tattoos. The sense of being watched, prevalent even in his years in the prison, followed him like an old friend. Ever since he had gone to Vladimirsky Central, he had felt the malevolent gaze of something on him. After so many years, he assumed it was his paranoia. The whispers in his sleep only confirmed his fears. Humanity was evil and he was the most evil of them all, forced to be to survive. If only he hadn't…

He tried to ignore the pain in his chest at the thought of what could have been… if he hadn't killed the only one who had known him for who he was and loved him anyway.

As he walked away from the terminal, his mind spun with the thoughts his new freedom had unleashed. He had spent so many years not thinking about life, or his past, that now it washed over him like a tide. He saw Sergei's face in the men he passed.

Yvegny's feet carried him to the Moskva River, but didn't let him rest. After so long being cooped up in the prison, he could walk for miles. Outrunning his memories, unleashed after so long imprisoned, could only work for so long. Perhaps if he walked fast enough, he could outrun the bleak future that the *drugiye* , the *other ones,* had revealed to him in his dreams. They came to him as the men he had slain, ghosts now sent to torment him.

Soul-weary, he paused by Gorky Park to watch how the lights of the amusement park played off the river. Gripping the wrought iron fence, he looked at the tattoos on his hands, blurred by twilight and tears. The cruelest thing the Russian prison system could have done to him was release him.

Shrieks and happy laughter coming from the amusement park came to him as if from a great distance, through the barrier of his heart and past. Nothing could touch him but the pain. He stared dully at the glimmering lights on the water. Sergei would be waiting for him in the afterlife, a vengeful ghost to meet him in Hell. He put his hand in his pocket, feeling the smooth curve of Sergei's ring.

As he turned the ring in his hand, he looked into the dark water. Imagining what it would be like didn't take much effort. He could climb the fence easily. Standing on the edge of the water, he would look up for one last time to see the stars come out. Then, falling forward slowly, he would wait for the water to embrace him, for his breath to run out. The hands of his victims would reach out to take his soul, Sergei, then the twelve men he had killed in prison. Sergei, Anatoly, Boris, Georgy, Dmitry, Ivan, Pavil, Maxim, Lev, Kirill, Eduard, Yury, Stanislav. Thirteen pairs of hands, ready to drag him to Hell.

Shuddering, he stepped from the fence and back onto the sidewalk.

"We all have our regrets," an amused voice spoke behind him. Yvegny spun, his fists raised. Heart pounding, he realized he hadn't heard the man approach. The man smiled, showing a gold tooth. "What would you do to get rid of yours?"

"Who the hell do you think you are?" Yvegny asked, ready to fight. No one had snuck up on him like that in years. Being free had cost him his edge. He could die here on the streets if he didn't keep it. *Don't trust Johnny*, Anatoly whispered in the back of his head. Anatoly had been his first victim in prison. Yvegny had strangled him until the light had gone out of his eyes. His sneer hadn't faded, even in death.

"Johnny the Salesman," the man's quirky smile glowed despite the shadow cast by his fedora. After a moment's pause, while Yvegny tried to combat the dissonance with the voice in his head, the man continued conversationally, "Folks throw bodies in that river to get rid of them, but you don't have any bricks, my friend."

Discomfited, Yvegny stared at the other man. This Johnny set his teeth on edge, as if he had bit on a piece of foil. After a few minutes, when the other man didn't drop his gaze, Yvegny asked, "What do you want?"

"You look like the kind of man who would be willing to make a trade."

"You don't have anything I want." Yvegny said. *You can't bring back Sergei or give me the past twenty years of my life back.*

"I can help you forget." Johnny said, his voice strangely compassionate after being so flippant earlier.

Yvegny looked down at his hands. "Nothing can do that."

"What if it could? What if the price was merely Sergei's ring?" Johnny leaned forward, showing teeth.

Before he could stop himself, Yvegny reached for the ring, to protect it from this man's avarice. His heart pounded at the thought of trading this man anything. *But what if*—he reached for a shiv, something to defend himself with. There was no way this man could have known about Sergei. No one in prison had even known his name, much less that Yvegny and he were lovers. Yvegny tensed, ready to fight.

Johnny smiled a secret, sad smile and held up his hands. "Never mind. Pretend I wasn't even here."

Yvegny blinked and the man was gone. "The hell—"

Sergei's ring in his pocket felt heavy and for a moment, he thought of throwing it into the river, of being done with it.

Reaching into his pocket, Yvegny gripped the ring tightly. *This is my penance, my memories of him.*

Phone books didn't exist anymore. With no way of looking up a hostel, Yvegny wandered the streets, wondering if the hundred rubles in his pocket would even be enough anymore to buy him a room. Nothing could buy him a restful night. Yet, as he walked, a growing desperation for even a moment of sleep grew within him, despite knowing what such sleep would bring. He had dreamt of the *drugiye* and the end of the world every night for the past twenty years. Being free wouldn't free him of them.

The city had changed in twenty years, had grown and mutated. Nothing looked familiar. He doubted even the old apartment complex where he had lived with Sergei still stood.

Morose and regretting more than just turning down the strange salesman, Yvegny rubbed his tattoos, feeling the itching deep within the scar tissue that had built up around the rough ink work. For a moment, he considered returning to the river, but he couldn't say whether it was to look for Johnny or to throw himself into the dark water.

As he walked by an alley, bright neon lights caught his attention. Curious despite himself, he walked down the garbage-strewn alleyway, finding it to be longer than he expected. After walking for at least fifty feet, he looked up at the red and yellow neon sign. The bright light didn't spell out anything in Cyrillic. Instead the tubes were shaped to look like a button with the holes off center. Frowning, he squinted and looked for any indication of what sort of business this might be. There were no windows, and no doors down the rest of the alley on either side.

Wondering why he was doing it, he looked at the door again. It appeared to be painted blue, but he couldn't really tell in the warm illumination. *If it's locked, I can just go on my way. And if it's not, what harm can it do?*

Doubts chorused in the back of his mind, and he waited for the *drugiye* to chime in. When they remained silent, curiosity took the best of him and he turned the handle.

Opening the door, he found the business was a tattoo parlor. *I've had enough of those for a lifetime,* he thought, ready to close the door and return to the night. He looked down at his hand on the door handle, seeing the fading blue and black ink. While in Vladimirsky Central, he had heard stories of the men who got out, of how they got new tattoos to celebrate their freedom, to cover up the memories they had inked into their arms and chests, gang members, trying to hide their affiliation, trying to make new lives for themselves.

How much would a new life cost? Before he could stop himself, he walked into the tattoo shop.

Bright lights lit the interior, illuminating flip boards on the walls, filled with flash. A counter barred the way to the back, manned by a short woman with pink hair and piercings that glimmered from the lights from the cabinet below her. Yvegny squinted and saw the tattoo machines displayed in the cabinet, each shining as if made of precious metal. A set of six barber chairs lined the right wall, while mirrors and obscure art covered the left. Past these, three massage tables jutted out from the walls. On one, a man leaned over a woman's back, the buzz of his tattoo machine filling the large room. Past the man and his customer, in the far back, doors stretched down a hallway presumably leading to smaller, private rooms.

"Can I help you?" the woman at the counter asked in accented Russian. She smiled like she wanted to stop his heart. *Wrong gender...* he thought wryly. He knew he was nothing to look at. Maybe she was just practicing.

"I..." he paused. Why did he want a cover up? It wouldn't get rid of the memories. *You'll never be free. You'll always be evil, just like everyone else,* the chorus of the men he had killed whispered. All but Sergei, always but Sergei. Despite his doubts, the words spilled from his mouth. "I was wondering what a cover up would cost."

The woman looked at him for a moment, assessing the ink on his hands that had bled out of the lines, blurring the edges of the roses. She glanced into the back of the shop, as if checking to see if they'd be overheard. "Why do you want to get rid of them?"

He opened his mouth, but couldn't find the words to express what he felt. Redemption sounded too impossible, as did forgiveness. This woman couldn't forgive him, and even if she did, it wouldn't mean anything. *Redemption is a lie. Humanity is damned.*

"Don't worry, babe. I get it," the woman said, as if she could hear his thoughts, as if she agreed with the *drugiye.* "You want to be free."

Unable to speak, he nodded, wanting nothing more than that in this moment. If he was free... The ghosts of the dead would plague him no more. The whispers would go away. The end of the world would come, but he could die in peace.

"Follow me," the woman said conspiratorially as lifted the end of the counter to let him through. "We'll fix you up."

Leading him past the sole client and the other tattoo artist, the woman led him to one of the rooms in the back. As he passed he saw the large man with the piercings and tattoos on his arms, creating a winged pattern on the woman's back. For a moment, he thought the wrought iron looking feathers moved, but then he shook his head and turned his attention to following the woman down the hallway.

When she opened the door and gestured for him to enter, he found a larger room with all the amenities denied him in his prison cell. A massage table jutted from the wall, with a tool cabinet next to it covered in stickers. A short, comfortable-looking stool waited on the other side of the massage table, next to the pedal that would operate the tattoo machine. On the opposite side of the room, near a door that appeared to lead to a bathroom, sat a small cot with a fridge next to it.

"Make yourself comfy, I still have to set up," the woman said. "My name's Lynette, what's yours?"

"Yvegny," he said, standing next to the door, folding his arms even thought the room wasn't cold. *You just want to forget? Erase everything? You know you can't do that. Evil can't be erased, it only grows and devours.* Dmitry and Boris whispered in stereo.

"You might as well get that off." Lynette nodded at him, indicating his shirt. "Let's see the damage."

Self-consciously, he took his shirt off. It had been a matter of pride, a matter of protection, to show his tattoos in Vladimirsky Central. Like flashing colors to warn off predators. But here, in the real world, it felt strange. Putting his shirt on a hook next to the door, he forced his arms to his sides as the woman gave him an appraising look.

"Well, it could be worse." Lynette pursed her lips. "It'll be tricky on some of them, the ink's set in pretty deep and bled into where it wasn't supposed to go. Those scars look like they won't help much either."

"If you can't do it…" Yvegny said, ready to grab his shirt and leave.

The woman put up a tattooed hand. "I didn't say it would be impossible, just difficult."

Looking at him for a long moment, she seemed to be reading the story in his tattoos. After the moment passed, she continued. "You've lived too many of those memories for too long to make this an easy process."

Yvegny found himself playing with the ring in his pocket, a nervous tic he didn't know he would regain. It had been his lifeline throughout his trial, but they had taken the ring away from him with everything else when he went to prison. He nearly slid it on his finger, but jerked his hand away. Folding his arms, he looked at the woman. "Let's get this over with."

"Sit down and get comfortable. This is going to take a while." Lynette said, adjusting the massage table to where he could sit in it with his back supported. Turning to the tool cabinet, she slid out drawers to pull needles and machines from it. Next she took out tiny cups and, looking at his arms, pulled out black, gray, and blue inks from the ink collection in the second to bottom drawer. Dripping the ink into the teaspoon sized cups she filled them to brimming.

He sat and rested his arm on the armrest. Watching with interest, he saw how carefully she attached the wires and tested her machines. The *bzzt bzzt bzzt* filled the air and he tensed despite himself. He had never been tattooed with a professional machine before; they weren't allowed in prisons for obvious reasons. He wondered for a moment how much it would hurt. Georgy laughed at his fear. *You'll never be free. The evil is within you. Let it out to fill the world.*

Shaking his head, he looked up at the ceiling. Instead of the white plaster he expected, the ceiling had been painted to look like a nebula. As he watched, he thought he almost saw the colors moving, as if the building breathed around him. With a shudder, he closed his eyes, then instantly regretted it. The visions that came to him in his dreams filled the darkness behind his eyes. Torment, burning cities, many-limbed *things* rushing to take over the world. Devastation and chaos.

And there, in the rubble, he saw the men. Twelve of the thirteen. Sergei, as usual, missing. Anatoly, his first prison murder. Boris and Georgy, the mobsters who had tried to kill him, thinking him weak. Dmitry, the guard who had tried to keep him from escaping. Ivan, Pavil, Maxim, thugs who he had killed because they were threats. Lev, Kirill, Eduard, and Yury had given offense by their sheer existence. Stanislav, who he'd killed just for fun after the man had tried to steal his food.

Yvegny mouthed the word, afraid to speak it. "No."

"No what?" Lynette asked, putting on blue nitrile gloves.

His eyes snapped open and he blinked rapidly. "Nothing."

"Ready?" She raised the tattoo machine.

Not trusting his voice, he nodded. She dipped the needles in the black ink and lowered her attention to his hand.

As the buzzing machine touched his hand, he forced himself not to flinch. Despite the immediate pain, he watched with fascination as the neat row of needles pulled the drop of ink and pushed it into his skin. From his years of tattooing himself, he knew the principles of how it worked, ink to needle, needle to skin, pain. But this was faster, so much faster than the painstaking process that had put the ink into his skin the first time. The machine buzzed like a bee, like a hummingbird, speed blurring the sound.

The pain became a constant and he leaned his head back, letting it wash over him. When Lynette paused to get more ink, or to wipe away the blood and plasma that oozed up through his punctured skin, it came as nearly a shock. Although she dampened the paper towel, the rough texture soon felt like sandpaper on his skin.

Curiosity got the better of him, and despite his half-formed determination not to look until it was done, he looked. Shocked, he nearly yanked his hand from her iron grip. "What are you doing?"

She paused, looking up at him as if from a trance. "We have to get rid of the old to make room for the new. The Sha'daa must become."

"The what?" he asked, dread building in his chest. He knew that word. How did he know that word? Hadn't the *drugiye* whispered it in his mind?

"Don't you worry your head." She smiled as if coming back to her senses. "Let's continue, shall we?"

Looking down at his hand, Yvegny still wasn't sure if he believed what he saw. Where she had used the black ink, the black ink of his tattoo had been removed, erased as if it hadn't ever been there. All those years in Central, not covered up... *erased.*

"Impossible."

"I can free you." Lynette met his gaze earnestly.

She's so young. He met her gaze for several moments. He already felt lighter and he knew that if he let this woman continue her work, he would be free of the burden he had acquired over the past twenty years. His sins would be expunged. But what was the price? There was always a price to magic. Every Russian knew this.

"Trust me." Her smile brightened. "I'm an expert."

Finally the pieces clicked into place. Fate would dictate his life from here on. He had not come across this place by accident. Fate had led him here for this sole purpose. The *drugiye's* whisper changed tone, nearly triumphant. *Who are you to deny fate?*

Despite himself, he hoped. It wouldn't absolve him of his sins, nothing could do that, but if he could free himself of that burden, if only for a moment...

"Continue."

Smiling, the woman dipped the needles in the ink.

As the hours passed, uncountable, and the ink disappeared from his skin, he found that if he closed his eyes, the dark world, the destroyed world had grown weaker. Yvegny found peace filling his heart, as if his burden eased with every inch of ink Lynette removed. He could close his eyes now, finding peace in the fading horror.

Tireless, Lynette worked as if possessed. Dip, buzz, buzz, wipe, dip buzz buzz. He lost himself in the rhythm, slowly growing to anticipate the pattern of her work.

Yvegny, stop this. The voice jerked him awake. Not the usual *drugiye*, the voice sounded like Sergei. After all these years, why would he speak?

"Shh," Lynette said, as if soothing him. She frowned, focusing on his upper arm where he had tattooed an elaborate cathedral, each spire representing five years of his incarceration.

He looked down and saw the roses gone along with the dots on his knuckles, one for each of the men he had killed. Lightened, he nearly laughed in relief. He would be free.

Looking up, he saw the nebula above him had disappeared. In its place was something dark, a vortex of barely discernable shapes. As he watched, nearing fear, the *drugiye* moved, peering out of the vortex to look at him with sneering gazes. He recognized them all and thought their names in litany, *Anatoly, Boris, Georgy, Dmitry, Ivan, Pavil, Maxim, Lev, Kirill, Eduard, Yury, Stanislav.* Only Sergei missing, his first sin.

"What is that?" he asked past the growing tightness in his throat.

"Oh nothing. *Our building* does stuff sometimes. It feeds, you know?"

With all the weirdness so far, he supposed one more weird thing wasn't too much to handle. "That's all from me? It's feeding on my tattoos?"

"Something like that." She smiled, but her expression looked more feral than reassuring.

Unsettled, he leaned back into the chair. Something churned deep within his stomach and it took him a few moments to identify it: the feeling he always got before he was going to be jumped. They were coming, the *drugiye*.

"Shh," Lynette said. "Relax, everything's going to be all right."

He looked at her. A difference lurked under her skin, as if something else was there, something strange and… evil. He blinked and it disappeared.

A new form of dread washed through him. *What if I'm dead at the bottom of the river? Or lying in a gutter, imagining all this? Will I never be free?*

Laughter filled his hearing and, startled, he looked at Lynette. She returned his gaze curiously, "Everything all right?"

"Fine," he said, his voice tight. The sense that danger loomed over him grew stronger. Tapping his left hand on the massage chair, he tried to ignore the memory of what had happened the last time he ignored this feeling. The memory came any way: lying on the floor of the dining hall, his face beaten to a pulp, his ribs kicked in, gurgling breaths through a broken face. They had patched him together in the infirmary, but only through a miracle.

Lynette finished his arm and moved to the tattoos on his chest, lowering the massage chair so that he lay on his back.

Inadvertently looking up again, he saw the vortex had grown darker, bending the light that radiated up to it. Something changed, something grew;

he closed his eyes. The city was gone, only the normal dark remained. He exhaled in relief. Nearly free, halfway there.

As she moved to his collarbone, the pain radiated through him like a buzzsaw on his nerves. He clenched his fists and tried to ignore it. A small price to pay.

For a moment, the thought crossed his mind that he didn't know what he would do when he was free. What could he do? Find a job? Find a lover? Build a new life? What skills did he have? And as far as he knew, it was still illegal to be gay in Russia. Nothing could have changed that quickly. He would have no happily ever after, but at least he could die in peace.

What about the rest of it? Yvegny wondered despite himself. The world had screwed him over, so he shouldn't care that it would end. But he couldn't disregard but the dread that the visions had engendered in him, even if he no longer saw them when he closed his eyes. *What was all that about?*

"You need a break?" Lynette asked.

"No, I'm fine," he said, surprised to find he didn't need food or water. He had gone hungry so long in prison that perhaps the stress of the tattoo, the constant radiating pain, had put his body into survival mode. His spine itched with the sensation of wrongness that filled the room. "Actually, I could use a break."

She wiped down the skin she had cleansed so far with a paper towel, then put ointment on it. In the wake of the ointment, his body healed itself, the blood and plasma flow stopping. All that remained was his aging skin. *When did I get old?*

"All right, if you need a snack, there's some in the fridge."

"Thanks." He stood up, wobbling. Catching his balance, he closed his eyes until the world stopped spinning.

"How long have we been in here?" he asked, getting a snack and a carton of orange juice from the fridge. He forced the bar down, washing the chemical taste away with the orange juice.

"About five hours," Lynette said. "But outside only a couple minutes have passed."

He nodded, accepting this new weirdness. "What is Sha'daa?"

"You'll find out." Her smile looked as if she was trying to be mysterious, but darkness lurked in her eyes at the mention.

Disturbed, he looked down at his arms and chest, seeing clean skin for the first time in twenty years. His first tattoo had gone, the one where they had held him down and forced the ink into his skin, trying to make him their bitch. Touching the space where it had been, he felt none of the scarring of that experience. Even the memory had distanced itself from his fear.

"What is the price?" he asked. "How much do I owe you?"

"Cover ups are free," she lied. He didn't know how he knew she was lying, but she had become increasingly strange over the past several hours. She no longer seemed to be the friendly and compassionate woman who had hit on him when he first arrived.

"I think I should leave."

"Lie down, Yvegny, you're almost free. Don't you want those gone?" she asked, nearly wheedling.

He looked up, finally able to make out some of the shapes in the vortex. Roses and a cathedral, dots, interspersed with the contorted faces of his victims. The *drugiye*.

"What are you releasing on this world?" he asked.

"The Sha'Daa must come." Lynette said, nearly intoning the words. "You will bring it here, your memories, your pain, your evil."

You are evil. The *drugiye* whispered in his head. *You chose to be that way, you cannot be redeemed. The only way you will be free is to unleash us on the world that threw you away.*

"I—" Yvegny paused. What did he care? The *drugiye* were right. But if that was the case, why bother with removing the tattoos anyway?

Lynette took his hand and led him to the massage chair. Guiding him to lie down, she looked at him. "Don't worry, it will all end soon. The entire world."

Flashes of memory, the world in tatters, his visions returned to him, but as he met Lynette's gaze, he realized he didn't care. *Let the world end.*

As the woman picked up the tattoo machine again and worked on the other side of his chest, he forced himself to watch the vortex. Things, the *drugiye*, pushed through, nearly into the world. Spiny limbs, lizard faces, monstrosities. And the *drugiye* who leered at him. *We will soon meet.*

The door bashed open and a woman rushed into the room. Yvegny stared at her in fascination. She had tattoos on her face, making her look like a colorful skull. Her top hat remained firmly planted on her head, despite her distress.

Johnny followed at a more leisurely pace, staring up at the ceiling with a frown. He met Yvegny's gaze and his frown deepened.

"Stop this!" the woman commanded. "Lynette, what are you doing?"

"The Sha'daa must come," Lynette murmured, as if half to herself.

"She's beyond our help. They've taken her." Johnny said, folding his arms.

"But how?" the woman said, then looked up. "How did they get past our protections?"

"He let them in, Haumea." Johnny pointed at Yvegny

"You!" the woman rounded on Yvegny. "Stop this, stop them."

Yvegny met her gaze, letting her see his despair, the end of his caring. "What do I care? I've killed everything I've ever loved. All I want to do is forget. Let me forget and then die."

The vortex swirling above their heads made a popping sound and one of the *drugiye's* arms came through. Yvegny tensed. Ivan's voice whispered, *This is what you wanted. This is the end of it all. You will be free soon enough.*

"We have to stop them," Haumea said. "I refuse to let Mom's Bane be the source of this madness."

"Then stop them." Johnny said insouciantly.

Haumea strode to the massage chair and tried to grasp Lynette's hand. The woman's hand went straight through the tattoo machine and the tattoo artist's hand. "What?"

"They're phase shifted." Johnny said. "Half in this world, half in the Sha'Daa. Only Yvegny can stop this. Your artist is too far gone."

Yvegny closed his eyes. Free. He could be free. Why did he feel… guilt? *Look at us,* the *drugiye* whispered. *See our glory, your world's future.*

Yvegny looked. The *drugiye* stared back at him. For a moment, Yvegny wondered who was the greater monster, these creatures that would destroy a world filled with evil, or him, the one who had murdered the only one who had ever loved him… the only one he had ever loved.

Sergei's face rose from the depths of his memory, blurred by time into just an impression. He thought he would remember his dead lover's face forever, but even in the past couple years, his memory had faded.

"Remember, Yvegny." Johnny whispered, as if able to read his thoughts.

Yvegny remembered the rage, the feeling of his hands around Sergei's neck, his surprise at how frail humans were, how frail his lover's life had been. He hadn't meant… the rage.

Tears came to his eyes, unbidden. He had tried too hard for redemption, but even this wouldn't work.

"You can still save the world, Yvegny. Redeem yourself."

The world is evil. Why should you bother? Wouldn't it be better for it to all go away? No more evil, no more prisons, no more sorrow.

"Stop." Yvegny said, grasping Lynette's hand. For several moments, she pushed against his grip, then stopped, her expression confused. "Stop and tell me the price."

"You know the price, Yvegny." Lynette said, her voice hollow. "You know you will bring the Sha'Daa, redemption and payment for your sins."

"Why me?" Yvegny asked.

Lynette shook her head, but Johnny spoke. "You probably already had a latent talent that they could use, then the murders made you susceptible to them. Years in prison wouldn't help either."

"They have been with me for years." Yvegny said to himself.

Sitting up, he pushed Lynette aside and reached into his pocket. Taking out Sergei's ring, he looked at the memory of his crime, of his downfall. The gold reflected the light of the vortex above him. The *drugiye* screeched as doubts cascaded through his mind. *There is no freedom, no redemption without us. Free yourself.*

The vortex, opened by the tattoos, by the memory and magic of his years in prison. He could take it back; he knew it would stop this… this Sha'daa. But why should he?

"What has the world ever done for me?" he whispered, half-expecting someone to answer.

He looked at Johnny, at Haumea, at Lynette, and then the creatures above him. They all wanted something from him, wanted to use him. The only person who hadn't wanted to was Sergei. Where was his lover? Why had he not joined the *drugiye* in his mind?

Clenching the ring in his hand, he wished fervently, for the first time in years, that his lover had fought back. That he had survived. But Sergei had let him do it, had died with compassion in his gaze, and understanding. It had made it all worse, the guilt, the sorrow, the understanding that he was evil, and irredeemable.

Sergei had believed in him, had loved him until the last moment. Had believed he wouldn't kill him, that their love would triumph. *What a fool.*

He wasn't sure if the thought was his or the voice of the *drugiye*.

Yvegny. He looked up, startled, hearing for the first time in twenty years the voice he had so yearned to hear. In the center of the vortex, Sergei stood like an icon, his face young and fresh. Yvegny's lover wore the dark bruises around his neck, remembered even in death.

"S... Sergei," Yvegny said, choking out the name. The words rose to his lips, but he couldn't speak them. *I'm sorry, I'm so sorry.*

Save me. Sergei reached toward him as the hands within the vortex pulled him back, away from Yvegny. Yvegny strained to take his hand despite knowing it was useless. Twenty years gone, Sergei could never be saved from Yvegny's deed.

Startled, Yvegny looked at his hand. Somehow he had put on the ring without knowing it. It fit his ring finger, even though Sergei's hands had been slimmer than Yvegny's.

He looked at Johnny, wondering why the man had wanted the ring. Would it have stopped this course of action, had he given it up for redemption? *Too late now,* he thought.

Save me. Sergei said, nearly disappeared into the vortex as the *drugiye* consumed him.

Redemption, isn't that what you wanted? Yvegny thought. *This is your chance, your one chance to fix everything.*

"Stop!" Lynette said, her voice a chorus with the *drugiye*. *One man can't stop us, not the end of the world. We are legion, we are unstoppable.*

Ignoring her and ignoring them, Yvegny closed his eyes. After taking a deep breath, he opened them and climbed on the massage chair. Ignoring everyone but Sergei drowning in the vortex in the ceiling, Yvegny prayed for someone else in the first time in years. *God, help me fix this.*

His arms were nearly too short to reach, but he strained and his finger touched the vortex with a jolt. Pain arced through him, worse than the tattoos, worse than the beatings he had received. He screamed and nearly jerked back.

Sergei reached toward him, his hand pale against the dark of the vortex.

"I'm sorry," Yvegny choked out, words he had not said then and had never thought to say. With supreme effort, he grasped Sergei's hand.

As they made the connection, the *drugiye* screamed. *NO.*

"Forgive me," Yvegny said, meeting Sergei's eyes. His lover's gaze filled with compassion and love, something Yvegny had not seen in years. Heart breaking, Yvegny reached his other hand out and shoved it into the vortex.

Screaming like a thousand insects, the *drugiye* fought against him. Jostled by them, he kept his grip on Sergei's hand as he drew the tattoos back into himself.

Every murder, every crime, every year marked by the tattoos came back to him. In the space of seconds and centuries in this timeless room, he relived them all. Bone crushing against bone, blood spurting out, dragged to solitary, left there for years, the feel of a knife through the ribs of a stranger, cruelty, survival. Screaming, he fought to keep his arm in the vortex as it shuddered and shrunk.

Gasping for breath, Yvegny collapsed to the floor hard, his body beaten and shattered by the force of the vortex. As he stared at the ceiling, he saw it collapse in on itself, as if the very building itself ate the remnants of the dark portal. Seconds passed and the ceiling went blank and white, empty of death and despair.

Johnny ran to him as Haumea went to her employee. The slap echoed in the room, and Yvegny closed his eyes. "Is it over?"

"It's never over," Johnny said grimly. "But for you, your part is complete. You did the right thing, Yvegny."

"They're quiet now," Yvegny said. "I can die in peace."

"You don't have to," Johnny said.

"There are no happy endings."

Standing on the edge of the Moskva River, Yvegny watched the morning sun rise over the water.

"What will you do now?" he asked Johnny.

"What I always do." Johnny gave him a quirked smile. "Trade and keep trading. My offer still stands."

Yvegny looked down at his hand. He hadn't taken off the ring, even after the night had passed. "No, I think... I can't now. Not with everything. I have to keep it all here, with me. If I don't... they could come back."

Staring at him for a few moments, Johnny finally nodded. "You would keep all that? Just to save the world?"

"Maybe. I need to see the world. To see what was worth saving. And if I forget..."

"Then it wouldn't be worth it." Johnny agreed.

"They'll come back, you know."

"I know." Johnny said, his expression suddenly weary.

"Call on me. If I can help..." Yvegny lost the words, and looked out over the river, trying to convey the sense of obligation he had gained. Sergei had given him a purpose. In that final moment, he had sensed his lover's forgiveness, and his penance. It wasn't to remain in the past, to wallow in his crimes, but to move on and to try to build a new life, despite the scars and tattoos. Or perhaps because of them.

He looked back and Johnny was gone.

The sun rose over the Moskva River and, for the first time in years, Yvegny felt at peace.

Ink Master

FOR FOUR HUNDRED YEARS HAUMEA perfected the sacred art of tattooing, the true art, first taught by the two sons of the God of Creation, Ta'aroa, to the very first Tufuga at the dawn of time. She mastered the fabrication of wood, tortoise shell, and shark bone rake needles and chisels, and the preparation of Kukui for the making of black ink.

Long after her parents, siblings, nephews, and nieces had succumbed to the ravages and final price of old age, long after her people assumed she was merely the great-great-great-granddaughter of that first Haumea, or more likely a namesake attributed to a series of orphaned women taken in by a line of cave witches carrying on an ancient tradition, she decided to leave Hawai'i.

It came to her in a dream, and so one morning she left her cave for the last time, looking not a day older than eighteen years of age, and she told the now mighty island nation of her vision, and many hundreds fell under her spell, and joined her on the high seas, in the most dangerous of migrations in the oral history of the people.

They spent weeks voyaging, losing many lives to accidents, storms, and sharks, but eventually they reached a large, lush, jungle island, that Haumea dubbed Rapa Nui.

Haumea's dream of a unified domain of peace was long in the making, but in two hundred years she'd founded and acted as high council to a trade empire comprising one thousand islands scattered over the central and southern Pacific Ocean, within a triangle whose points were New Zealand, Hawai'i, and Rapa Nui.

Hundreds then thousands of Haumea's tattoos became a unifying force among the people of the sea, and they marked the faces and arms of the mightiest and bravest of Polynesian seafarers, the hands of ambassadors, the faces of kings and queens, and the breasts of warriors.

But Haumea was not all-seeing, nor all-wise, and in an epic conflict that has long been stricken from oral Polynesian history, and never penned to parchment or paper, her two hundred year old trade empire was torn asunder by a vicious priesthood which sprung up secretly, well hidden from her notice, and they violently rejected her philosophies of peace to follow a series of battle gods, worshipped in the form of giant, hand carved statues on the rapidly deforested island of Rapa Nui.

In a handful of years, the vast ocean-spanning Polynesian union Haumea had spent decades building was disbanded, never to be reborn.

When the offspring of those ancient Hawai'ians who had followed her on that grand journey so many years ago finally succumbed to genocide and even cannibalism, she left Rapa Nui, abandoning her people, as she felt they had abandoned her, leaving the subregion of Oceana forever, to walk the earth in search of a new purpose for her seemingly endless life.

Loser

by Robby Hilliard

TONY JENKINS SAT DOWN AT THE BAR. IT was a hole in the wall called, The Closer, and had seen its heyday in the late '80s before the market crash of '89. Apparently it was meant to be a place for the good ol' boys of business to close deals in an atmosphere of liquid libations. That part of its past was long gone. Tony slung his backpack across the back of a bar stool, took out his cell phone, and put it in the outer pocket of the backpack. He was in no mood to talk to anyone until he had done something about this hangover. He then sat at the bar, put his elbows up on the wooden surface, and pressed the palms of his hands into his eyes. Red lines like lightning shot through his vision in synch with the pounding and throbbing of his head. The smell of stale beer and stale cigarettes permeated the dark interior and Tony felt his stomach churn.

"Fuck," he said out loud. "I need a beer."

The front of the bar was all large, glass plate windows and the bright afternoon light shone through giving everything a stark appearance. The interior was not designed to be seen by the light of day. The front door was propped open in an attempt to allow fresh air to replace the staleness inside, and the summer heat rolled in with it, causing Tony's t-shirt to stick to his back. He heard movement from the back of the bar, behind the counter, and looked up just as the bartender entered through a door that lead to the beer storage cooler.

"Well, well, well," the bartender said as he set the unopened case of beer on top of the metal coolers just below bar level. "I'm kind of surprised to see you in here today, what with how out of control you were last night." He smiled, only one side of his mouth curving up, the other half all business. "Need a little hair of the dog?"

"Yes," Tony said. "And what the fuck did I do? It's all kind of blur."

The bartender slid one of the metal coolers open, grabbed a beer bottle, and twisted off the cap in what appeared to be one seamless motion. He grabbed a beer coaster, placed it in front of Tony, and set the beer down. "You were funny, up to a point, joking about pick up lines and how stupid they were. Then you were going off about some kind of technique you'd heard about online in some kind of 'boy meets girl' pick up forum. You were talking about how abusive it was. And then, like an idiot, you started trying to use the technique."

Tony shook his head from side to side, picked up his beer, and took a deep swig.

The bartender began pulling beers out of the case and restocking the cooler as he spoke. "And that's where you fucked up. You started really pissing off some of the women who were in here last night and you wouldn't stop."

"Holy shit," Tony said. He ran both hands through his hair, the short, dark curls wrapping around his fingers briefly. "Negging."

"Yeah," the bartender said. "That's what you called it. Some kind of psychological manipulation thing."

"Ugh," Tony said. "It's pretty disgusting. You can find tons about it online."

The bartender gave a dry laugh. "Yeah, well, no need. You told us all about it last night. I'm surprised you didn't really get your ass kicked. You started hitting on girls right in front of their boyfriends. One girl even took your picture with her phone and said she was going to post it online labeling you as a sexual predator."

Tony winced, his shoulders physically hunching over. "Holy shit."

"Yeah," the bartender said. "Good luck on that front. Then you got off on a tangent about tattoos and tried to insist that women should touch yours."

"Wow," Tony said. He took another swig of beer. He set the beer down and glanced at the ink on the inside of his left forearm. It was a simple tattoo of a green plant that looked, at a glance, like marijuana, but not quite.

"Yeah," the bartender continued, "like I said. You were in rare form."

"Did I piss off any of the regulars?"

The bartender paused in his restocking and gave a full-throated laugh at this point. "Funny you should ask." He leaned forward placing both hands on the edges of the open cooler. "I wouldn't say you pissed anyone off at that point so much as you and Sheila grossed everybody out."

Tony's hands dropped to the bar and his head hung down between his arms. "Fuck."

Sheila was a regular, but not in the normal sense. Sure, she hung out in the place almost all the time, but she talked to herself. Not in a crazy way, but more in a "thinking out loud" sort of way. She was always going on about metaphysical things that had to do with spirits and other worlds, reeked of patchouli, and wore hippy clothing that might actually have been what she wore in the '60s. Thin as a rail and old enough to be Tony's grandmother, her skin was like leather. Generally she kept to herself though, so all the other regulars would just say hello to her and leave her alone. And she was known to carry a gun. Whenever a random gunshot was heard outside the bar, people would say, "must be Sheila."

"What did I do?" Tony asked.

"Well," the bartender said, obviously relishing this part of his tale, "it turns out that Sheila knew what the tattoo was before you told anyone."

"Mugwort," Tony said. "She knew what that was?"

The bartender glanced up towards the ceiling in an attempt at recall. "I think that is what she called it. And something else. She said something about 'the shadows' or 'shadda'. At least it sounded like that. She was trashed as usual. But not only did she know what it was, she had some kind of story about it being used to mark doorways and portals or something. Something about birthing or some such." The bartender stood up and made a dismissive wave with one of his hands as he spoke. "Whatever it was, it really got her going." He threw the now empty beer box on the floor behind the bar and lifted another to take its place. "Next thing I know you two are practically having sex right here at the bar. Had to kick both of you out."

"Mother fucker," Tony said.

"You said it, not me," the bartender replied.

Tony drained his beer and ordered another. A few other patrons entered and sat at tables while the two had been talking and the bartender made his way out behind the bar to take their orders.

"Nice ink," a man's voice said.

Tony turned to see who had spoken. The man was large, wearing a fedora, and despite the heat, a large trench coat. Tony couldn't make out his face, back lit as he was by the light coming in the front windows, except for the glint of a gold tooth as he spoke.

"Mugwort, yes?"

Tony squinted against the relatively bright light that outlined the man. "Do I know you?"

"Name is Johnny, and I know you, Tony Jenkins."

"Oh, fuck," Tony said. "Listen, uh, Johnny, I'm so sorry if I pissed you or your girlfriend off last night. I know it's no excuse, but Dude, I was trashed. I don't even remember meeting you or talking to you—"

"That's okay," Johnny said. He held out both hands in a palms down, "it's okay" pose. "We didn't talk last night. I'm just here to make you a deal."

Tony paused, momentarily caught off guard, "Uh, okay. I don't have any kind of cash on me, so if you need some kind of help or something, I don't know if I can really— hey! How the hell did you know my name if we've never met?"

Johnny pointed towards Tony's left forearm. "Your tattoo," he said. "Got it from a place called 'Mom's Bane, yes?"

Tony thought for a second. "Yeah."

"What I thought," Johnny said. "Look, here's the deal. Mom's Bane is a very special kind of tattoo parlor. The ink she uses has mystical properties and she doesn't give out tattoos to just anybody. If she gave you one, then you have a role to play in events that are happening right now." The man took a step closer to Tony and when he spoke again; his voice was slightly quieter so that only Tony could hear what he was saying. "The Sha'Daa is happening, and it's happening right now. The veil between this world and the next has collapsed. You play a role in preventing them from coming here."

Tony hadn't realized his mouth was hanging open. He closed his mouth with a snap, and looked around the bar to see if anyone else had heard what the man had said.

"So I'm here to make a trade," Johnny said. He reached inside his coat and pulled out a metallic cylinder with a hose of some kind attached to it, and set it on the counter next to Johnny's beer bottle.

The light from the front windows shone at steep angles across the bar and Tony could see that it was an aerosol can of some kind. He picked it up and read the label. It was an off brand of "fix-a-flat" to fix flat tires. Tony looked from the can to Johnny, and back to the can. "Uh, okay. I don't get it."

Johnny smiled, his gold tooth glinting in the light reflected back from the interior of the bar. "The subject of your tattoo, mugwort. It was used in ancient times to mark portals, yes?"

Tony nodded, his eyes transfixed on Johnny's gold tooth.

"That makes you a portal guardian," Johnny said, as if this should make sense.

"But, I still don't get it."

"You will, Tony. You will." Johnny took a step back and the atmosphere seemed to relax just a bit. "And now I need for you to give me something in return."

Tony stared at Johnny, in disbelief. He began to slowly turn his head away, towards the bar, his eyes staying fixed on Johnny's until the last second. Briefly he thought about giving Johnny the small pocketknife he kept in his back pocket. It wasn't very big or expensive and Tony ostensibly wore it to indicate that he was into climbing or rafting or some other cool thing. In reality, he most often used it to open mail and cut the plastic rings open on beer six packs. But then part of Tony's brain reasoned that if this Johnny fellow wasn't quite right in the head, and all evidence seemed to suggest that that might be the case, and he gave him a knife, he could be implicated in any crime the man might commit with said knife. Tony glanced around the bar, searching and finding nothing except his empty beer bottle and the beer cozy it sat on. Tony glanced quickly back at Johnny and then back at his beer bottle. He lifted the empty bottle and picked up the beer cozy by one corner. It was damp with moisture and flopped across his fingers, the thick cardboard like material going limp. Tony couldn't help but notice that his thumb covered the "C" of the bar's name and the side of the cozy that now faced Johnny just said, "loser".

Johnny reached out and took the cozy. "Nice doing business with you," he said.

Tony glanced at the can of fix-a-flat for a moment and then picked it up. It felt full. "I'm not so sure you are getting a fair trade. Now that I think about it," Tony said as he reached for his wallet and turned back towards Johnny. "I may have some cash—" Johnny was nowhere to be seen.

Three hours and five or six beers later the sun was gone along with Tony's hangover, dusk having settled outside. The light coming in the front windows of *The Closer* was, like Tony's memory of the evening before, much softer. The bar had slowly filled with regulars, many of whom gave Tony dirty looks and avoided saying anything, but a few who had actually laughed and bought Tony a beer. The can of fix-a-flat had remained on the bar as a conversation piece.

"So," the bartender said. "Are you just hanging out waiting on your girl-friend to show up?"

"What?" Tony said. "I don't have a girlfr—" then it dawned on him that the bartender was referring to Sheila. "Oh."

"Yeah," the bartender said. "She usually shows up just after sundown. You might want to settle up if you don't want to run into her tonight." He dropped Tony's bill on the bar in front of him.

"I think that's probably a good idea," Tony said. He pulled out his wallet and paid, making sure to leave a hefty tip. He put the can of fix-a-flat in his backpack, threw his backpack over one shoulder and made his way out the front door, onto the sidewalk. The warmth of the summer evening hit him in a pleasant wave and, combined with the alcohol he'd consumed, made his head swim. Even though the evening light was mild, Tony squinted at the stark contrast from the darkened interior of the bar.

"There he is, the asshole," a woman's voice said.

Startled, Tony spun around, not sure exactly what direction the voice was coming from.

"I knew if we waited here long enough the piece of shit would show up," the woman continued.

Tony eventually located the speaker and saw not only a young woman approaching him, her gait that of a marching soldier, but three rather large and athletic looking men in their early twenties. "I think we may need to have a conversation with Mr. Pick Up Artist."

The four of them made a box around Tony.

"Whoa!" Tony said. "Look, I think there has been some kind of mistake."

One of the men held a phone up in front of Tony's face. On the screen, Tony could plainly see a picture of him, his mouth open wide, caught in mid-word. Across the top the picture was the word, "Predator" in a bold font. Along the bottom was his name, misspelled, as "Tony Jakins." From the look of the surroundings in the background of the picture, it was obvious to Tony that the picture had been taken inside *The Closer*. From the amount of empty bottles and shot glasses in the picture, Tony was pretty sure it was taken last night.

"Look guys," Tony began. "And gals," he nodded towards the young woman. "I can explain."

One of the men grabbed Tony by the arm from behind and began to move Tony towards the nearest alley. "I'll bet you can. Why don't we step into my office."

Tony felt another pair of hands grab him as the three men shuffled him into the alley. The woman paused on the sidewalk, looking up and down the street, and then followed. The men kept going, pushing and shoving Tony as he feebly tried to drag his feet, until they reached the far end of the alley away from the road. At the end, the alley took a right turn behind the buildings. The men moved him just around the corner stopped.

The first punch took Tony's breath away and his legs tried to buckle. The fact that two of the men were holding him firmly by his upper arms was the only reason he didn't fall. The next punch caught the side of Tony's jaw as he slumped forward.

"Not in the face, you idiot," the woman said. "That'll just work against us if we get caught."

The man doing the punching glanced at the woman briefly as if he might say something. He hesitated as if he was considering saying something, but then turned back towards Tony. The next punch was in the gut, just below Tony's ribs on his left side.

The men let Tony fall to his knees. Tony wrapped one arm around his mid-section, the other feeling his jaw.

The girl squatted down in front of Tony.

"So, what do you have to say for yourself Mr..." she reached out to one of the men. The man hurriedly reached into the front pocket of his jeans and pulled out his phone. He activated the screen and handed it to the girl.

"Mr. Jankins," she continued. "How does it feel to be the victim, huh?"

Tony looked at the woman and, for a fleeting second, thought about correcting her concerning his last name. He immediately thought better of that.

"Look," Tony said. "I don't know who you are or how you got my picture, but I can assure you I'm no predator."

The woman spat in Tony's face. "Ha! Just like a Men's Rights Asshole. Nothing you ever do is ever wrong, is it?" She stood up, drew her leg back and kicked Tony in the chest.

Tony fell back against the legs of one of the men standing close behind him.

"I'm not in an MRA," Tony said. "I'm just as disgusted by those groups as anyone else is, I can assure you."

"Shut the fuck up unless she asks you a question," the punching guy said. He thrust his face towards Tony's, his features drawn up in an angry snarl, and drew one arm back and made a fist as if to strike.

Tony looked at him and his head shook with anger as he yelled. "She fucking did ask me a question you fucking idiot!"

The punching guy looked at the girl and then back at Tony. His face twisted even more and he growled through clenched teeth. He punched Tony in his chest, just left of the sternum, and Tony was pretty sure it would bruise deep into the bone.

"Mother fucker," Tony said. It came out as kind of a rasping hiss as he couldn't actually get much of a breath. When he could finally draw in some air, he felt a sharp pain just above his left lung.

"Don't even start that shit with me," the woman said. "Your photo was posted to a local network for women. The description has details of some of the things you said about psychologically manipulating women who have self-image issues and how to detect them. I'd say that's pretty predatory, wouldn't you?"

Tony looked up at the woman, as she spoke. Although she was clearly very angry, part of Tony's mind reasoned that she wasn't actually angry at him personally but instead at men who did what she described. And, because his picture had been posted to some network, she had no reason to think that he was any different. After what he had apparently done the night before had crossed some lines thanks to him being a drunken asshole, he couldn't really blame her now, could he?

"Listen," he began again. "If this is about last night, I can explain."

Punching guy drew back his arm for another strike and Tony flinched. Before the blow could launch, the girl put up a hand motioning him to stop. Or at least wait.

She looked at Tony for a brief second. "Talk."

Tony took a deep breath, winced at the pain, and began. "First off, I was drunk. So drunk that I don't actually recall everything I said and did last night."

The girl shook her head as if this was something she had heard before. Tony heard one or two of the men mutter things he couldn't quite make out but they all seemed to convey disbelief.

"Honest," Tony continued. "Look, you can ask the bartender. Yes, I was drunk and yes, apparently, I was being a real dick. But I wasn't actually trying to use any of the pick up techniques those guys talk about. I was trying to give examples of what they are and how they work!"

Tony's eyebrows rose as he spoke. He made sure to keep his eyes focused on the girl's face as he talked; searching for any sign that she might believe him.

The girl crossed her arms and set her jaw as if to say, "no, I'm not buying it." But at the same time, Tony got the impression that she was at least considering what he was saying.

"I think I started saying some of them out loud to people just to give examples of how stupid and obvious they were. And," Tony now hung his head for a second before looking back up, "I may have said some things to girls in passing who were unaware of the context of what I was saying."

He was quiet for a moment.

The girl tapped her foot and glanced away. She turned back to Tony and opened her mouth to speak when a loud, explosive bang was heard.

It took Tony a second to realize exactly what the sound was, but, as the concussive echoes bounced around the brick walls of the alley, it finally dawned on him that it was a gunshot.

Everyone of them jumped. Tony flinched again.

The girl changed whatever it was she was going to say to, "Fuck!"

The men all took slight crouches, their arms out at their sides as their heads spun up and down the alley way trying to determine just which direction it had come from.

"There!" one of the men shouted. "Some crazy bitch with a gun!"

The girl, in mid-reaction to the sound of the shouted direction stopped that reaction and instead reacted to what the young man had just said. "Hey, fuckwad. We don't use that word."

Punchy guy, the guy that had spoken, looked around at the girl. His face scrunched up in frustration and his fists reflexively balled up. He looked at Tony as if he wanted to punch him again and then looked back down the alley towards where the crazy woman was apparently standing. He shook his head in frustration and yelled, "Run!", and all four of them took off in the other direction.

Tony, still on his knees, leaned forward on one hand, the other still across his stomach. He looked back over his shoulder to see if he could figure out who it was that had saved him.

"Howdy, Lover," the woman said. Her voice was gravely with the hint of an alcohol induced slur. She stepped right up to him and stood looking down at him. It was Sheila. In one hand she held a very large, shiny revolver of some kind. In the other she held a large roll of duct tape. On her face was a maniacal smile that went perfectly with the glazed look in her eyes.

Tony's first reaction was relief, and he smiled in return. "Sheila," he said. "I never thought I'd be so happy to see you."

As soon as the words were out of his mouth, Tony knew he had said something wrong. In the chaos of the alley encounter, he had completely forgotten the role Sheila had played last night, not that Tony was really very sure of it himself. But, based on the description the bartender had given him earlier in the evening, at least one other time Tony had been very glad to see Sheila.

Sheila's smile disappeared. In its place, a grimace.

Tony's mind tried to formulate a response as Sheila drew her arm back.

"I guess you forgot about our date tonight, asshole."

Tony's vision filled for one brief instant with light, and then everything went black as the pistol struck him.

The throbbing pain in Tony's head woke him. The first thing he noticed was that he was wrapped in duct tape, around his chest and stomach, with his arms at his sides. He appeared to be in a wooden chair and, as he raised his head, he realized that he was situated in a large oval of lit candles.

Seated on the ground in front of him with her eyes closed and her legs crossed under her, was Sheila. She was rocking gently back and forth and it sounded to Tony as if she might be mumbling some kind of chant.

Tony took a second to look around him and all he could see were what appeared to be wood paneled walls lined with shelves, a table off to one side, and off to the other side was his back pack, lying on the floor.

"Where am I?" Tony asked.

Sheila stopped rocking and became quiet. She slowly opened her eyes. "In my cabin."

"How did I get here?"

Sheila looked at Tony like he was stupid. She looked down at herself and then back up at Tony. "I dragged you here. I'm stronger than I look."

Tony thought that over for a second.

"And," Sheila said, "now that you're awake, we can get this thing started." She sat up straighter and positioned her hands on her knees, palms up, in a yogic manner.

"Uh, excuse me," Tony asked. "What exactly is it that we are about to get started?" Strangely, in part of Tony's mind, he was hoping she would say something referring to a date. The fact that he was duct taped to a chair surrounded by a ring of lit candles conjured up images of witchcraft and human sacrifice. In light of that, he thought "date" might be the best option.

Sheila reached behind her and brought out a slender bottle of whisky, the kind people on the streets usually drank out of while keeping it 'hidden' in a paper bag. She unscrewed the top and took a deep swig.

"The Sha'Daa is happening. It's time to open the portal."

Tony sat dumbfounded. At first he didn't know what to say. Then he thought that whatever he said, this would be no time for attitude. The look in Sheila's eyes gave him the distinct impression that she was deadly serious, even if she was bat shit crazy.

"And what part do I play in this portal opening?" Tony asked.

Sheila wiped her mouth on her sleeve, screwed the cap back on the bottle, and returned it to some place behind her.

"You are the portal guardian, marked with the sign of the mugwort, Artemesia, the symbol of Artemis," she replied. As she spoke, she motioned vaguely towards Tony's arms under the duct tape. "You are here to insure the safe entry into this world of a superior being from another realm."

Tony's mind raced as he tried to think of some way to make sense of all of this.

"And just how is it that I am supposed to assist?"

Sheila looked away for a few seconds, and then back at Tony. "Do you not recall any of our conversation from last night?"

Tony knew that he didn't really remember anything at all. He recalled that the bartender had told him that he was excited about the fact that Sheila had recognized Tony's tattoo, but that was about it. Tony, on the other hand, couldn't really remember much on his own. As to the tattoo itself, Tony knew vaguely about Artemis and that she was a symbol for wilderness and some other things. It was just something that he had thought would be really 'cool' and outside the mainstream as far as he was concerned.

"I don't actually remember everything we discussed," Tony said. "If you gave me instructions as to what I'm supposed to do then I think I may need for you to repeat them."

Sheila appeared to think about that for a few seconds and then she shrugged her shoulders. "No matter," she said. "You are really just here to supply a life force. Otherwise I would have to give my own."

Life force. Tony's mind slid sideways just a little when she said that. It was probably a combination of the candlelights, the alcohol he had consumed earlier, and then the blow to the head. "I'm sorry, did you say, 'life force'? As in, giving my life force to bring some kind of creature into this world? Like I'm just food or something?"

Sheila nodded. "Exactly."

At that moment Tony recalled that Artemis, sister to Apollo, was also the goddess of fertility and midwives. The mugwort was invoked as a symbol of safe passage from the mother's womb into this world.

Holy fuck, Tony thought. *This is fucking crazy.*

"I see," he said. Tony was quiet for a moment. "Any chance I could get a swig of that whisky?"

Sheila seemed to consider this for a moment and then she shrugged as if to say, "why not." Instead, she said, "No. Why waste it? You'll be dead soon." She reached behind her, pulled the bottle out again and took another swig.

Sheila returned to the yoga like position and began her chanting and swaying.

Tony knew he had to do something quickly. He adjusted himself in the chair and, in doing so, was able to feel that his pocketknife was still in his back pocket. Slowly, he began to work his right hand closer to his back pocket, squirming every few seconds in an attempt to cover up the moment of his hand. Just a few more inches and he would be able to reach it.

Then it occurred to Tony that, since Sheila hadn't seen fit to remove his knife from his pocket, she might not mind loosening his arms and doing some of the work for him.

"Is there any chance I could get you to remove some of this duct tape on my arms? I mean, wouldn't it make sense to display the mugwort tattoo on my arm or something?"

Sheila slumped forward as if annoyed by yet another interruption. "Nonsense." She reached for the whisky again. "Nothing special about the tattoo other than to mark you as the portal guardian. That's how I knew you were the one I had to use instead of myself." She took a swig, and recapped the bottle. As she moved to return the whisky bottle behind her, the brown glass glinted in the candle light, and it reminded Tony of the glint of gold off Johnny's tooth earlier.

Again Sheila began to chant and sway.

Tony realized that what Johnny had been talking about was the same thing that crazy Sheila was talking about.

What the fuck did Johnny say? Something about preventing, not aiding.

Tony had to stop whatever it was that Sheila was about to do, if for no other reason than to get himself out of here and, from the sounds of it, save his own life. Tony looked to his side where his backpack lay. He'd have to reach over the candles to get to it, assuming he could cut himself free. But perhaps a quick 911 call would do the trick. At the moment, he couldn't think of anything else.

Tony continued to work his hand until he could feel the metal of the knife's casing against his fingertips. He wasn't sure what was about to happen but reasoned that if he could keep her talking, then it might delay whatever it was that she had in mind.

"So how long have you been preparing for this, uh, chadda thing anyway?"

"It's called, 'Sha'Daa,'" Sheila said. "Enough talking. Time for action. Now stop interrupting me." She straightened her posture again, and placed her arms on her knees, palms up. Slowly she began to rock back and forth. And slowly she began her mumbling chant.

Tony's fingers had begun to work the knife out of his pocket and now he was worried about dropping it when he got it out. He experimented with flexing against the duct tape and found that he would probably be able to twist just enough to actually begin cutting. How far he would be able to cut was unknown, but he saw no other option.

Cold air seemed to blow across Tony's face. For a moment he thought that perhaps a door had opened in the room. Looking around, he saw no indication from the candles that there was any kind of air movement. At the same time, at least to Tony's sense, it seemed that the air had somehow grown darker. Then he saw the green light.

At first, Tony thought he must be imagining things, as if he needed to dream up anything crazier than what was actually happening to him. But then he was sure. There was a green, almost fluorescent or electric neon green light coming out of Sheila's mouth. It glowed as if perhaps she had swallowed the liquid from one of those camping light sticks, her lips in stark outline. Then he noticed it had begun to emanate from the slits of her closed eyes as well.

Sheila's rocking began to become more extreme from side to side and her chanting was becoming louder. Although it still sounded like gibberish to Tony, he could have sworn that from time to time he heard the word, "Sha'Daa" being said.

There was no more time to be subtle. Tony tried to thrash in his chair. He tried to force his arms to one side, twisting them so his hand could get a better grip on the knife. He strained really hard against the glue of the duct tape and felt as if his own skin might be tearing but finally, he was able to grasp the knife. He thumbed the quick release button and felt the blade open.

At last, he thought.

The tip of the blade caught against the back of his pants and refused to open all the way.

"Fuck!" Tony screamed and strained again so hard he felt blood rushing to his head as veins popped out along his neck and duct tape tore at the skin on his arms.

Sheila seemed to respond to his yelling by raising her own voice, her eyes still closed, unaware of what Tony was doing.

Tony realized that the room had grown very cold and the darkness had become all consuming. In his mind he knew there was a ring of candles around them but he could only vaguely make out where they were. Instead, everything was bathed in bright, fluorescent green as Sheila opened her mouth wide and began to scream.

Tony heard as much as felt the blade lock into place. He gripped, twisted and strained again until he felt fibers in the duct tape begin to give. With each fiber he cut, the next became easier.

Sheila began to move. She struggled to get her legs unwound from beneath her and stand. She held her arms out wide and moaned and screamed even louder. Then she opened her eyes, and green light shone forth in beams.

Tony was bathed completely in the green. His skin chilled and, without knowing how, he sensed that there was someone, some *thing* else in the room with the two of them. And Tony had the distinct feeling that it was something that was trying to come out of Sheila.

With a final thrust of energy, Tony's arm broke free of the duct tape, just as Sheila began to step forward.

She was only about a foot away from Tony, her mouth and eyes seemingly aiming for his face as she began to lean forward for some kind of ghastly kiss.

Tony screamed and threw all of his weight to his right side, his arm thrust out in the direction where he had seen his backpack. He felt the chair begin to topple and then, just as he thought he would go over, it hung improbably balanced, neither moving towards falling nor returning to its original position. Tony tried to throw the weight of his head towards the side where his backpack was. Just as he knew that all hope was lost, he felt the balance begin to shift.

Tony felt Sheila's hands begin to touch his shoulders. Out of the corner of his eye, he saw only a blinding, green light.

And then he was down, sideways on the floor still duct taped to the chair. Hot candle wax had splashed across his face narrowly missing his eyes. His one free arm groped around in the darkness for his backpack.

Sheila, whose grasping hands had just missed their mark, turned towards him, and began to follow.

Tony thrashed wildly with his arm until he felt the backpack. He felt the top loop and, without any clear thought, thrust it towards his mouth, grasping the loop with his teeth. With his hand, he was then able to unzip the back pocket on the first try.

Sheila was lowering herself to her knees, her wailing moving towards becoming a high pitched keening sound.

Tony could feel her hands on his body as she began to crawl across him trying to get her face closer to his. For a fleeting moment of weird visual clarity, Tony could see that she might be trying to get her mouth to his mouth to allow whatever it was inside her, whatever it was that was producing the bright green light, to transfer to his body. Tony shuddered, then, as most of the contents of the pocket on his back pack spilled out, Tony distinctly felt his hand flail against his cell phone, sliding it across the floor and into the darkness.

Tony screamed even louder and beat against the backpack and the floor, his sanity beginning to leave him as his mind and vision turned red, black, and gray all blended with neon green.

Tony's flailing hand felt something round and metallic. It was the can of fix-a-flat. In Tony's mind he heard Johnny's voice as it said, "nice doing business with you."

Sheila was completely on top of Tony now and her hands were grasping at his face trying to turn his mouth towards hers.

Tony tried to resist but then felt the bones of her hands, skin rough like leather, as she delivered a vice like grip to his jaw.

Her mouth was open now, impossibly wide, and the neon green light was no longer just shining out of it. It seemed to be flowing as if there was some kind of energy rushing and gushing out.

Tony screamed and, with his single free hand brought the can of fix-a-flat to his mouth. Like a Hollywood soldier pulling the pin on a grenade Tony gripped the hose attached to the side of the can in his teeth and pulled the end near the bottom of the can free. It released with a resounding pop, the nozzle flopping up in front of his face. Without even thinking clearly, Tony used one finger to prop up the tiny hose and shoved it towards Sheila's mouth. He could see by the outlined silhouette of his hand holding the can that it was centered on her mouth, and then he pushed the release button on the top.

There was an abrupt gurgling sound and then a sudden change in the nature of the green light coming out of Sheila's mouth. It seemed as if the light had to navigate its way around something, and then the light was gone.

Sheila's forward motion stopped and her body jerked like a dog that has reached the end of its leash. Her eyes, no longer emitting green light, bulged out.

Tony kept his finger on the release button and tried to make sure that he kept the can in position in her mouth, the hose now shoved down Sheila's throat.

Sheila seemed to totter over Tony for a moment as foam continued to dispense, and then Tony heard her try to speak or make some kind of sound. She fell back, her hands grasping at her throat, the hose still stuck in her mouth snagging the can out of Tony's hand, but it was too late. The can had expended all of its contents, and they were now solidifying, sealing off Sheila's lungs.

Sheila thrashed for a minute or two before finally going still.

Tony's breathing was coming in ragged gulps, the pain from his earlier encounter in the alley finally making itself felt above the declining adrenaline in his body. The room began to brighten and the air began to warm as it occurred to Tony that whatever had been about to happen was no longer taking place. And then he realized that the room was getting very bright and warm and he smelled burning wood.

The circle of candles had caught Sheila's clothing on fire and spread to other things in the tiny room.

Tony's adrenaline immediately spiked again and this time he found no lack of energy. He found the knife and began cutting himself the rest of the way free from the chair. The interior of the room was almost entirely engulfed in flames by the time Tony made his way to the only door he saw in the room. He grasped the knob, turned it and felt the rush of cool summer evening air rush in.

The air also seemed to deliver new life the flames inside the cabin and there was a rushing roar as the flames instantly grew in strength. By the time Tony was thirty yards away and able to look back, the entire structure, a small ramshackle cabin, was on fire.

Tony slumped to the ground, his back against a tree, and watched as the conflagration burned through the night.

Saturation

T HE BALD, ELDERLY SAILOR WITHSTOOD the rush job as if the skin on his larger than normal forearms was made of granite. He was a tough-looking bastard, but still, Haumea knew she was inking deeper than normal, which always caused greater pain.

The old seafarer just chewed on his corncob pipe and stared off in no particular direction, lost in thought, perhaps dreaming about one of his many voyages as a commercial fisherman, or time spent as a longshoreman. His dark, sun-baked skin and wrinkles made him look to be easily on the far side of retirement age, but bulging muscles and a quick tongue showed he had the gumption and wits to keep doing his job.

"All done, Pops," Haumea said.

The sailorman sat up and perused each of his forearms.

"Mighty fine," Pops said with a raspy, froglike voice, and followed that up with a long appreciative whistle, "I loves it."

Haumea smiled. She'd given Pops the original black anchor tattoos many decades ago. He'd come back a few times over the years for simple touchups whenever the rich black had faded too much. But an hour ago he walked through the main entrance with his short but powerful bowed legs and made a special request. Pops still wanted the anchors touched up, but now requested a full array of blue and white ocean waves, and multicolored fish, whales, dolphins, mermaids, and seashells behind and all around them. And for being one of her oldest clients she was only too happy to comply.

They both walked out of the quick-room and gave each other a quick hug.

"You said you wanted the colors to jump out, Pops," Haumea said, "so I really doubled up on the saturation."

"Feels like the devil's pitchfork tenderized me arms," he said, "but it's worth it, my dear."

"A shame you have to leave," Haumea said, "I don't know when I'll see you again."

"It is not that life ashore is distasteful to me, Haumea," Pops said with a rough bow, "but life at sea is better."

And without another word Pops turned and pushed his way through the packed shop toward the front entrance.

"Crusty old coot," Johnny said.

Haumea turned to her right and smiled. A close look told her Johnny's manic spell had passed since his last visit.

"You're back," Haumea said, "so I assume the real world is still in one piece?"

"As your clock shows," Johnny said, "one day and two hours have passed since the Sha'Daa started."

Haumea glanced at her clock and did a doubletake.

"I'll be damned," Haumea said.

"For quite some time, princess," Johnny chuckled, "ever since we met, I believe."

Pops bumped into a large, red-skinned ogre pushing through the front door into the shop and gave it the stink-eye before heading out.

"Oh, what am I? Some kind of barnacle on the dinghy of life?" Pops said, "I tell you it's a violation for not having no exit which you can go into!"

Haumea leaned close to Johnny and spoke in a loud whisper to be heard over the background conversations and buzzing tattoo irons.

"I met your stalker, Johnny. He goes by the name of Prana," Haumea said, "can't say I liked the guy. Looked at me funny, like he could see right through me. I'm beginning to understand why you were avoiding him. Told me to tell you he wasn't on the warpath. Just wanted to talk to you. I sensed power, but not necessarily danger."

"I had the pleasure myself." Johnny replied.

"He caught up to you?" Haumea said, "I take he's not around to pester us any more, right?"

Johnny smiled, displaying his single gold tooth among a sea of nacreous white for a moment.

"Prana is the wild card in a rather flashy and *very* powerful deck, my dear," Johnny said solemnly, "and I'm speaking of a game that has even bigger stakes than the Sha'Daa. Believe it or not, he merely finds me an irritating curiosity, and doesn't seem to have much interest at all in the outcome of something as petty as a thousand hell portals all opening and promising the extinction of the entire human race."

"You didn't flatten him?" she asked.

"Maybe I'm conserving my strength," Johnny said, "or just following the advice of my favorite martial arts movie star, who said his personal life philosophy was *walk softly*."

"You're scaring me, Johnny," Haumea said, "I thought you were this solar system's big bad wolf."

"Coyote," Johnny said, "you're mixing up your myths, as usual. We still on schedule?"

"Yeah," Haumea said, "as long as nothing fucks with business, we should be able to create a decent surplus with hours to spare. How are..." Haumea turned back to Johnny and saw he was gone.

"Just like a man," she whispered, "if the world were a logical place, they would ride side-saddle."

The Nightwatch

by Richard Groller

"A hero is someone who has given his or her life to something bigger than oneself."—Joseph Campbell

Wow! There I was, buzzed to oblivion, and my crew had brought me to a tattoo parlor called Mom's Bane down a long ramshackle alley off of Liaoning St. Night Market in Taipei. I had always been treated like one of the guys, but this was the first time the team got me drunk *and* brought me to a tattoo parlor. Being an engineer of the female persuasion, I had the brains and chops for most anything, but this really caught me off balance. I was so drunk, I had no clue what to ask for, or if I even should. As my mind reeled I thought to myself, "Wow—what are you thinking? Late 40's, ex-military, yet you never got around to getting yourself a tattoo—Why now?" It had just never appealed to me, or maybe I just didn't care enough about anything that I would want it to be a permanent attachment to my body. Guess the real key was to be sufficiently drunk enough not to give a damn.

The tattoo artist before me was very beautiful and exotic but that skull tattoo was *way* too much for my tastes. However the designs and sigils and arcane symbols that abounded in Mom's Bane were intriguing and the spins were starting to kick in hard. I gazed into her imploring yet impenetrable eyes, said "Surprise me," and promptly passed out.

But not really. I was in that semi-conscious dream state before you crash completely, where you are no longer in control, but you are semi-aware of your surroundings. What I gathered from the conversations going on around me was that my tattoo artist's name was Haumea. She spoke absentmindedly to me in my quasi-conscious state, asking me rhetorically, "So haole, what are you doing here in Taipei?" I was helpless but to answer her wordlessly, my stream of consciousness no longer under my control.

I remember when I got the call to come to Taipei, I was eating bulgogi and kalbi at my favorite *katusa* mess in Yongsan, Korea. The ambiance was pure Cold War–corrugated metal Quonset hut, with concrete floors and space heaters, but the food was incredible. I went back to my cheap hotel, and finished my combat bottle of soju, but not before booking my flight for the next day.

Taipei is truly a city of contrasts: Wi-Fi and bamboo scaffolding; modern skyscrapers and large earthen ware kimchee pots on rooftops; sleek, silvery bullet trains and mangy dogs, scrounging for food and oozing blood.

Taipei always filled me with a sense of foreboding–the teeming masses and the stifling oppressiveness of the skyline. And a sense of dread when it comes to eating—the Chinese food was generally poor—no decent ingredients compared to the quality available in America. Viscous blue fuzzy goo dessert—nasty. Dim sum was passable for breakfast. I remember trying the local oysters and catching giardia. So sick for weeks. And that was in an American based hotel.

Winning the contract was the coup our new company needed. We were all ex-military working as defense contractors, and experimenting outside our comfort zone was proving to be viable and profitable. We were sub-contractors in South Korea, but when we got the word we had won the contract in Taipei, we were ecstatic. We only had a dozen folks, primarily doing system integration work. We are all dual-hatted at a minimum. I was working both systems engineering and marketing, so bringing in new contracts was a big deal—really the lifeblood of the company—no contracts, no money.

We were lucky—the living embodiment of the Chinese curse—"born in interesting times." Changes in foreign military sales procedures since the demise of the Soviet Union and the rise of the Internet made the processes less complex, and with the wars in the Middle East, surplus equipment that could be repurposed, upgraded, and resold to foreign governments relatively inexpensively. Imagination and innovation driven by necessity could create amazing new toys on the cheap, and so a handful of like-minded brethren in arms decided to break away from a larger defense contractor, found our own company, and chart our own path.

When the request for procurement came out from the ROC Ministry of National Defense for a replacement of their static electro-optic coastal surveillance imaging system, a holdover from the Cold War days, I figured "No guts, no glory," so we did not bid for a strict replacement. We bid a less expensive, more comprehensive system using totally different technology.

Being a former drone pilot, my proposal, "Nightwatch," was for a series of inexpensive drones to run in a racetrack around the island. Line of sight back to MND HQ and the airfield, so minimal architecture to maintain. Since infrastructure costs were negligible in comparison, we were able to offer a higher end payload. One that would cover DC to daylight, be reconfigurable on the fly, and be mostly autonomous, with an artificial intelligence based trip-wire system so the man could be out of the loop until an anomalous condition occurred.

Luckily this one of the Four Asian Tigers bit. We even came in on time and under budget. Now we maintain it. My crew was really jazzed since we just finished out first prime contract as a startup, and for an international customer, so I started a tradition of taking out the team at the beginning and the end of every deployment. One for luck, one in appreciation for a job well done.

That was years ago. My coup got me promoted to Director of Business Development. We were now on the map, using customizable, reusable off the shelf hardware and software in niche military markets.

This visit, I was there to negotiate some contract mods to build protective drones for the defense of the island nation. Think target invaders on the beaches using specialized munitions; our engineers were working on a two week installation and training schedule for my team of five engineers/field technicians, used in tandem with our surveillance systems.

I took up mountain climbing with Qixing Mountain right there in Taipei. Our party at the beginning of this deployment started out innocuously, but I sensed this time something was different.

I was staying at the Lai Lai Sheraton. I invited the crew there. The tab was celestial, but was worth it.

My crew had turned in for the night. I went upstairs to the penthouse bar for a nightcap before turning in. I ordered a double Gran Marnier and took in the view, taking my time to savor both. The only other Anglo in the place was a tall, gaunt gent in a black trench coat and fedora, who could have passed for a Dashiell Hammett gumshoe except for the gold tooth. He glided on over and said to me sotto voce "I have something you need."

I sized him up and down and said, "Beg pardon?" with my best look of bemusement.

He didn't miss a beat. "You're here on official business. Your plans will be—how should I put this—*interrupted*. I have something here that could make all the difference in the world, if you know what I mean."

He sauntered up to the bar closer to me, gave me a wink, looked at the bartender and said, "Three fingers of Glen Rothes, rocks, for me and my friend here."

I began to protest, "I have no idea what you are talking about. I am just a tourist."

"Yeah right. A tourist with a specialty in military electronics. So here is the deal—I wish to make a little trade with you. I have need of a portable direction finder set, one that costs less than a million bucks, like the one on your key chain. I wish to trade it for what is in my pocket—let's call it "your finger in the dike," What do you say?"

My corporate OPSEC briefing told me to walk away and report the incident immediately (in the back of my mind the Robot is screaming "Danger, Danger Will Robinson!") I countered with, "I'll bite—if you spring for another three fingers of scotch!"

His eyes sparkled as he exclaimed, "Done! Barkeep—leave the bottle!"

By now I was having second thoughts. My brown eyed daughter had given me the keychain as a joke when she was finally old enough to comprehend what I did for a living. When she gave me the little globe shaped keychain with a compass embedded into it—"a portable direction finder" as a gift, we had a great laugh, and I felt truly blessed. I really did not want to part with it.

But my new acquaintance began lining up shots of twelve-year-old scotch and I matched him drink for drink. Before I knew it, I was passed out. I awoke on the bed in my hotel room. My hair hurt. In my pocket, in lieu of the keychain, was a cork from a bottle of wine, specifically, from a bottle of Chateau Neuf du Pape 1961. A good year. I looked at the clock and realized I was late for my first meeting, so I stumbled into the shower, grabbed an old hangover cure of vitamin C, two ibuprofen and a Rolaids, washed it down with a cup of coffee, and painfully left to face the day.

Despite my head weighing a ton and my body feeling the worse for wear, that day proved to be uneventful, as did the rest of the deployment. Meetings went well, my engineers were at their professional best, no serious glitches. I even got in a couple of days of mountaineering. Good times don't always come so easily. The final systems acceptance test went off without a hitch and we finished early. The team was ready to celebrate. I joked, "You realize that it will be short night tonight, and not by *my* doing. I got the hairy eyeball, then explained, "Guys—it's the longest day of the year, the summer solstice." The gang groaned but wanted to prowl the night markets regardless, so who was I to refuse? Hanging out with the guys you pick up bad habits. Smoke like a chimney, drink like a fish, swear like a sailor. It's all part of being one of the boys, until you are ready to use feminine wiles, which puts them at a great disadvantage. It's all good. And the dude in the fedora was wrong–the job went off without an *interruption.*

Besides, it had been a long time since I went on a pub crawl.

I awoke bolt upright, frosty and hyperaware. The team was in a semi-circle in the back end of the parlor. Six pagers were going off simultaneously. It was surreal—I remembered that the outside of Mom's Bane was a blue door made from a single piece of wood, with arcane symbols carved all over it. You could *see* the sigils on the outside glowing so intensely that they were visible *inside.* "What the hell is going on?" I asked no one in particular. Haumea turned to me and blankly said "the Sha'Daa," and nothing more.

The glowing stopped and the door swung open. A hairy, seven-foot spider filled the doorway. I was aghast, eyes wide, thinking, no way, I'm not drunk enough to have DTs. I was utterly incapable of rational thought, though in a sudden moment of clarity, I remembered the gold toothed gentlemen's admonition, and the trinket in my pocket. It reared, and from its belly webbing sprayed inside, covering the closest patrons and freezing them in place. I was off to the side and out the arc of the webbing.

My military training kicked in. I leapt forward and I shoved the cork into the opening, and slammed it home with my fist. The spraying immediately stopped, but the spider drove its front legs into me and knocked me down. The spider's fangs hovered above my face as two of the tattoo artists came forward and each thrust a ji, a Chinese halberd with a spear head and two crescent blades on opposing sides of the spear head, into its body. The first thrust saved me from the bite. The second killed it. They pushed the body back out of the door, and closed it.

As I was given a hand up, I thought to myself, okay Toto, we are not in Kansas anymore. The tattoo artists brought out elaborate atomizers, which sprayed a purple mist that dissolved the webbing from the immobile patrons. My team had been hanging in the back and stepped forward, and I saw for the first time what they had done to them while they sat in their old style barber chairs. Each had a tattoo on his forehead and on the palms of his hands. They were sigils, actually more like Viking runes. I was like, okay this is either *One*

Step Beyond or maybe something out of anime. They *glowed*, and you could almost see the power emanate from around the tattoos.

The pagers never stopped buzzing, and we all finally checked them— it was ROC MND, recalling us to help with the equipment, which appeared to be giving false readings. Haumea looked at me and said, "The battle for mankind is beginning. You are warriors. Prepare yourselves."

"But who or what are we fighting?"

"The forces of evil from beyond the earth that come to enslave or destroy mankind, during the cosmic event known as the Sha'Daa. They are all the monsters and aliens you fear in your deepest nightmares. While you were unconscious, the Sha'Daa began in earnest. Your compatriots heard the requests of the others that came willing to fight and requesting to be armed. They all agreed they should do something, and we offered them the runes of protection. But the Sha'Daa is upon us now and there is no time to ponder. You must go and fight. We must stay and arm any defenders that come for aid. Answer the call of the MND. Your skills there, now that you know what you are up against, will be invaluable."

The trek back to the Ministry of National Defense was no fun. General panic engulfed the streets where ever folks had dared to venture outside. Why frickin' spiders? All sorts, all sizes, all full of surprises. Large ones webbing street entrances to catch the unsuspecting as they turn a corner. Armies of tiny spiders that dripped acid and left a trail of corrosive sludge in their wake. Jumping spiders bringing unseen death from far above.

We all would have felt better if we were armed with modern weaponry, but the folks at Mom's Bane were sort of old school. The men were each given a ji. I was given a Japanese naginata—a ko-naginata, to be precise, the one used by women. How nice of them. Though my crew's rune tattoos worked very well against any of the smaller threats. AND it was cool to watch! You could see the force field or magic or whatever it was emanate and pulse and envelop our arachnid foes. The jumping spiders just retreated from us whenever the forces were invoked. The small spiders withered on the spot. We avoided the larger ones by stealth. We figured along the way we could find some Guojun (National Defense Force) folks who might take pity and equip us.

Once we commandeered a working vehicle our small reconnaissance in force arrived at HQ in no time. We reported in and were expeditiously escorted to the situation room where our newly installed equipment was being reviled as useless. I apologized immediately and the team began to run diagnostics and adjust the settings. There were chaotic reports coming in from all over the island, but nothing made sense. There was no invasion force that was visible. No ships, no planes. The leadership was assuming terrorists using perhaps aerosol hallucinogenic drugs to create hysteria, but did not believe the reports of giant spiders.

We immediately began to recalibrate the equipment to look for new signatures. Taiwan has the largest number and density of high mountains in the world, with 286 mountain summits over 9,800 feet. Forget visual, concentrate of subtle infrared and thermal signatures. We were no longer looking for engine exhausts plumes. We were looking for biological signatures of spiders. I went online and did some quick research. Spiders are strict ectotherms—they are cold blooded and derive their body heat from their surroundings. I asked myself, "What would be the heat source for a spider running around at night?" They probably originated underground and were emerging from some fissures. Then it hit me. Volcanos. When I hiked Qixing—Seven Star Mountain—I had noticed hot springs and fumaroles. Could geothermal energy be warming the spiders? I told the crew to screen for low level thermal signatures but to target known areas with these geological traits. Soon, we had a map—four locations where there was the signature and movement, all coming down from the mountains. And the largest signature was above Taipei. We needed a coherent plan. It was time to talk to leadership.

Luckily, cell phone video from the streets, from civilians that stayed indoors, was pouring in. Leadership soon did not have to be won over. Tactics was another matter. Exterminators from all over the island were being mobilized to go after the small stuff. Napalm for large masses of spiders was deemed an effective way to go, with firefighters in tow to limit collateral damage to property where possible. Our sensors would guide the Air Force and Army where to drop steel on target. Hellfire missiles are effective against caves, and would do nicely to begin sealing up the fissures from which the spiders emerged, backed up by artillery and smart bombs. We had become the fire coordination center. Soon the flow of "thermal signatures" coming down from the mountains was down to a trickle. Three of the four ingress sites were collapsed. The reserves were called up, and the battle in the streets was becoming contained. But Qixing was resistant to closing. The more firepower that directed toward collapsing it, the more large spiders began to flow. Finally, it became a trickle and then stopped. And then all hell broke loose.

The top of the mountain collapsed in on itself. What emerged was a giant from a bad B-movie. A tarantula. Interesting thing about tarantulas—they have urticating hairs and they can use their back or legs to kick off and fling like a barbed nettle flechette. Some ROC F-16s flew in a close sortie and loosed missiles. Planes exploded and the missiles never reached target. After a few sorties, the remaining planes were pulled back.

The other large spiders on the ground, also had a new trick—they were huge black widows that ranged over a wide area and began covering the ground before them in spider silk. The tensile strength of spider silk is comparable to steel wire of the same thickness. And the density of steel is about six times that of silk, so silk is much stronger than steel wire of the same weight. What it didn't enmesh and immobilize it penetrated and killed. And then they walked on top of the ever expanding web and continued to expand it. And the tarantula was on the move, down the mountain with a growing entourage. Things did not look so good for Taipei.

The second I saw the tarantula I began to feel nauseous. It was hard to believe that in the heat of the battle, only a few hours had passed since we left Mom's Bane. I excused myself and ran to the rest room. I tossed my cookies and then sat down to relieve myself.

I looked down and said aloud, "Oh god, no! What have I done?" I caught the first glimpse of my tattoo.

I was black and blue. Not injured. My body was onyx black with aqua blue highlights. I pulled up my shirt. "Frickin' A," I muttered. My back was a shade of rust red. My entire body, except for my neck, face and hands was a massive bug tattoo. Jesus Christ, what would my daughter say?

I was rocked with another spasm. My body shuddered and I doubled over, while my head began to throb terribly. My mind's eye pictured me. I had a vision of myself, hovering aloft, and I knew what I could become. I knew that I could stand tall, spread my red wings and fly. And I knew I could sprout a new appendage, a very long stinger. And I instinctually knew my nemesis—the tarantula. My avatar was the spider wasp—in particular, Pepis formosa—the tarantula hawk.

The humor of the situation was not lost on me. I was a female drone pilot—the Women Airforce Service Pilots of World War II were called WASPs. Damn. One thing was for sure—Haumea had a terrific sense of irony.

I returned to the fire direction center and asked the crew if they felt the ROC troops they had trained were ready to take back over the operation.

Luckily, they had been riding side saddle with us since we began to do the recalibrations of the equipment, and once they saw the thermal images, and had their confidence restored that the equipment was top of the line and was not malfunctioning, they were eager to jump in. So we gladly obliged.

I went to request a transport helicopter for myself and the team to get in closer to the action, knowing that we could be put to better use now that their troops could run the equipment. We were refused. The ROC military was not going to accept responsibility for American civilian contractors getting killed trying to play hero.

Rather than try to explain that we had been *augmented* by our mysterious allies at Mom's Bane, we chose not to argue but to just leave. Undaunted, we retrieved the vehicle we abandoned when we drove to HQ, and decided to head up the mountain. Before we left HQ, we did manage to convince one of the ROC sergeants to let us sign out some side arms from the armory for self-protection. It took some cajoling, but eventually he came around. Pistols are way better than jis and a ko-naginata. But we kept those for backup.

We headed up the ridge road towards the approaching behemoth. We found a side road on an upslope that would allow us better visibility, and a more defensible position above the main road. We watched as the ever expanding perimeter of spider silk got closer and closer.

The team deployed out in a fan shape, and began to employ their runic force fields to slow the approach of the giant web spinners. Forward momentum slowed, then stopped, but the webbing began to rise in height, creating a wall of steel. That was actually a good thing, creating an ever-growing berm of spider steel between the approaching monsters and Taipei.

Suddenly, a large aggressive sun spider did a rapid end run around the left edge of the berm. The runic force fields did nothing to hold it back. Old habits of mind die hard. I emptied my clip and it kept coming. I slammed home another one, and then as one, the entire team delivered a hail of 9mm fire on the enormous hairy arthropod. The Taiwanese Beretta knock-offs were adequate to the task, though it was close. The sun spider collapsed, the prehensile claws of the creature landing inches from the feet of the leftmost crewmember. Any closer, and he would have been eviscerated. The men regrouped, and resumed directing their runic powers at the black widows, still holding position, but now scaling the walls and extending their webs even higher into the night sky.

I felt another wave of nausea and knew with a certainty it was time for me to act. I stripped down and saw the full effect of the full body tattoo, now glowing blue along the striped body highlights. I stretched out my arms, and stretched out with my senses. Wings enfolded in my back emerged glowing red like lava. From my loins sprang a two foot long stinger, full of deliciously painful venom. And the stinger point looked as sharp as diamond.

My legs elongated to maybe ten feet long, springing sharp hooks for grappling, other newer limbs appeared, also equipped with savage looking grapples. After the metamorphosis, my profile must have been twenty-five-feet across. I tested my wings and floated for a minute.

I heard a wolf whistles and catcalls of encouragement from the team, both impressed and possibly a little intimidated. I beat my wings harder, and was aloft. I arose rapidly along the wall, using it as a would-be shield, to protect me from projectiles should the tarantula see me. At the crest I stopped, and clinging to top of the wall, I could see my nemesis lumbering gracefully as only a spider can towards the mostly unsuspecting city below.

I accelerated for height, and feinted left, trying to circle around it. I then dove, figuring I could get in underneath it away from its barbed hairs. The legs on its left side reared and let fly. My only choice was to rise to avoid them. That's when the back let loose its barbs. I was above it and could not avoid them. I was impaled by multiple flechettes that collapsed my right wing. I spiraled downward, but onto the monster's back. I was now out of range for any more projectiles. My shattered wing burned like fire, but that only made me angrier. I embedded all my grappling limbs into its back, as deep and strong as I could, for I had no desire to be thrown. Then I felt the engorged stinger rising to strike. I was truly able to appreciate the masculine impetus, being a surrogate with a power that was not only violent and deadly, but carnal. The last thing I remember was driving home the point of my stinger again and again and *feeling* the tarantula's silent screams of agony. The rest, darkness.

With the sudden halt of the giant tarantula, the Nighthawk trainees reported a window of opportunity to the loitering ROC aircraft along the periphery of Taipei. A ROC bomber quickly raced in, and dropped two fuel-air explosive munitions above Taipei—one on the mountain crevasse that was the spider hordes point of origin to seal it, and one on the tarantula.

Thermobaric weapons cause considerably more destruction in confined spaces like tunnels and caves, and have more destructive power than any known explosive, except of course for nuclear weapons. The walls of steel web melted, but kept the damage channelized above the city. No one knows why the tarantula stopped its inexorable march on Taipei, but all in the war room whooped in grateful relief. The sergeant who provided the small arms to the American Nightwatch advisors reported that their last known position was in a vehicle headed up the ridge road. And the ROC trainees kept to their task, directing fire toward the ever-shrinking pool of available targets, hoping against hope that their American mentors were all right.

Tramp Stamp

HAUMEA FIRST MET JOHNNY THE SALESMAN, in one of his earlier incarnations, in a small cantina in Mexico City, Mexico, in 1839. It was nearing Midnight on November first, and the Day of the Dead celebration was into full swing. Candles, torches, and hanging oil lamps were lit everywhere, and colorful decorations gilded the front of every home and peppered the streets.

Stepping through the front doors of the *La Pesadilla de la Madre*, Benedict struck the pose of a handsome figure, tall and lean, wearing gray shirt and slacks, with dusty brown boots, a long tan leather duster, and a weathered ten-gallon hat. A mariachi band was playing in one corner. Benedict smiled, displaying a mouth full of bright white teeth with the single exception of a black gap in place of a missing left lateral incisor.

A peasant husband and wife near the front took notice of this and immediately crossed thumbs and index fingers in a ward to the evil eye before quickly exiting. Benedict closed his mouth and strode to the front bar counter. He caught the eye of a burly young bartender.

"La mujer que pinta Carne?" Benedict asked. The bartender frowned, so Benedict spoke again, "La femme qui peint flesh?" The bartender grunted and jerked his head to the left, toward some closed curtains. Benedict walked there in three long strides and peered into a small room, brightly lit by dozens of candles. Haumea now looked to be in her earliest twenties, having reached her full height, and as beautiful as ever.

"Just give me a few more minutes," Haumea said in Spanish without turning around, "I'm almost done with a month-long tattoo."

Benedict just stood there and admired her handiwork. Before Haumea laid a nude, bald man, with dark skin and covered from head to foot in Maori tattoos.

"You did all this?" Benedict asked.

"No," Haumea replied while tapping the final few ridge patterns across her client's lower lip, "the majority have been made over the years by my biggest competitor, an impressive island seer who unfortunately met his maker on his village's dinner plates, the price of drunkenly impregnating the Chief's unmarried virgin daughter."

Benedict took a step forward, "Interesting hieroglyphics. I don't think I've seen their like before."

"And you never will again. They are a complete theory of the heavens and the earth, and a mystical treatise on the art of attaining truth," Haumea said, "all of it an undecipherable puzzle, as the one and only riddle master is dead."

"And your job…" Benedict started.

"My job," Haumea said, "is to mark this predator of the sea as a child of Kokovoko, and to implant a vision in his flesh, and his mind, of his own great nobility, so that no matter how dire his life and health may become, he will never lose sight of his powerful sense of honor… and we're done."

Haumea's client sat up, and Benedict could see a small, shrunken head dangling from a leather cord around his neck. The client picked up a gunnysack, reached within, and pulled out a large, beautiful ivory sculpture of a tortoise carved from a Narwhale tusk.

"Thank you, Queequeg," Haumea said, accepting the payment with a bow.

Queequeg nodded, squinted for the briefest of moments at Benedict, and turned to depart through the curtains.

"Cuidado com este, senhora," Queequeg said in broken Portugese, "I sense the flames of Maui in him. He is one who seeks to spread fires of discontent," and the sailor left them to return to the open sea.

"An eccentric act," Benedict said, "and alarmingly perceptive."

"Have you been tattooed before, mister?"

"I'm here to make a deal, Haumea," Benedict said, "a trade."

"None now live who know that name," Haumea said, here eyes opening wide, "I abandoned it centuries ago."

"Your history is a tragic one indeed," Benedict said, "but I think you have reached the pinnacle of your current abilities… for the moment."

"And what is this to you?"

"I am Benedict the Trader, Haumea," he said, "and I am here to offer you a very special gift… for a price."

Haumea's eyes opened even wider, displaying their rich green irises to full effect, "I've heard of you," she said, "though you were known as Coyote in recent years, and many other names before that."

"Yes," Benedict said, "I must remember that you have been around… for a little while at least."

"I have all that I need, Trader," Haumea said, "there is nothing in your bag of tricks to dazzle me."

"Oh but what I offer you hold within yourself, Haumea," Benedict said, "I can free it, and put it within your full control, plied by your own skill, entering your very tattoos in a manner it never could before."

"No mortal or mere shaman can do this," Haumea spat.

"Whoever said I was a mortal or mere shaman?" Benedict asked, "the blood of Kohala flows through your veins, regenerates your cells making you nearly immortal, granting you unusual strength and speed, blessing you with impressive albeit limited scrying abilities and charms. But Haumea, you have much more to offer within you."

"What do you propose?"

"I will do for you what I have done for no other," Benedict said, "using your very special blood, I will tattoo every square inch of your exposed flesh. This will loosen all the latent, untapped power now surging in your blood, unshackling it for you to manage, and handle, and weave into the spells of your tattoos."

"And your price?"

"My trade?" Benedict asked, "why, only that between now and not too many years in the future you create a large, though finite number of very special tattoos, for a very special purpose."

"To help you fight your Sha'Daa?" Haumea asked.

This time it was Benedict's eyes that opened in surprise.

"I have listened to the whispers of the shadows," Haumea said, "and I know of your ages long and doomed campaign. Your so-called gift is as much a curse as it is a bargaining point. No, I think it will suit your purposes more than my own."

"You're refusing my trade?" Benedict asked.

"Not at all," Haumea said, "but what you will do to me is only one half of the full trade. I will allow it, and agree to your conditions, but you must balance this equation with your own separate payment."

Benedict frowned and slowly bit his lower lip.

"And what do you ask of me, one time daughter of the king of Hawai'i, and former high priestess of Rapa Nui?" Benedict asked, seeing that the appellations opened old and deep wounds in the tattoo artist's soul, but that she somehow managed to control her anger, once again impressing him.

"I ask that you become my lover for a full year, *Maui*," Haumea said.

"I have not gone by that name for many millennia," Benedict said.

"And I have never loved a god," Haumea replied.

"What you see standing before you," Benedict said, "has been my form for but a fraction of my existence. Perhaps I am not what you think I am, and thus, not so appealing."

"You are flesh and blood to the core," Haumea said, "this I know. This I sense. Regardless what grand and frightening powers are at your command."

"Yes," Benedict said, "though I am far more than you could ever imagine, I have been slaved to this body, this mortal shell of nerve endings, blood, and bone for over nine thousand years."

Haumea smiled, "then you are more human than anyone or anything that ever walked or now lives upon the Earth. Perhaps this is something you never stopped to consider."

Benedict hesitated for but a moment, then gave a quick nod.

"So be it. One full year. I promise nothing more than that," Benedict said, slowly removing his long duster, "my tattoos can take any form, Haumea," Benedict said, "and I will start with your face. Do you have a preference?"

Haumea glanced around her small parlor and her eyes fixed upon a small, colorful object on one of her shelves.

"That," she said and pointed.

Benedict reached out and picked up the little Dia de los Muertos sugar skull. The size of his fist, it was a beautiful skull-shaped candle, painted with a variety of decorative patterns and stripes.

"Theatrical," Benedict said, "and impressive. You surprise me."

"Then we have a deal, Benedicto," Haumea said.

"Yes," Benedict replied, and without further words Haumea stepped forward, reached up with her sinuous arms, pulled his unresisting head down, and pressed her desperately lonely and hungry immortal mouth against his.

Just Like an Angel

by Shebat Legion and Jordanne Fuller

ANGELA ANDERSON WAS NOT A PRETTY girl, nor an ugly girl. She existed someplace in between that is both, as well as neither. One didn't give her a second look, until she opened her mouth to sing.

Angela had the voice of an angel. Her voice climbed a full two octaves seamlessly and could hold the rapt attention of even the most tone-deaf listeners. Angela was a preacher's daughter, and her father gave her every solo in the church choir. Who could argue? It was a shame Angela did not resemble her angelic namesake—nor did she act the part.

It wasn't that Angela didn't take pride in her voice, she did.

"Too much pride is a downfall," her father would preach to his unhappy daughter.

"Plastic surgery," Angela would counter with a scowl.

Angela's voice, while lovely to her own ears, could not make up for the outward beauty she lacked.

"Please," Angela begged on her seventeenth birthday, "buy me a nose."

She received a lovely stationary set and a goat donated in her name to a Third World country instead—along with the rejoinder that true beauty came from within. She ended up tossing the stationary into her bedroom closet and kicking the door shut.

Angela sulked as she examined her nose, feeling trapped by its shape. "A goat? *Really?*"

Outside Angela's window, as the sky deepened to an alarming purple color, her inner thoughts turned a deeper shade of mauve. She posed in front of the mirror, observing herself with self-critical candor.

"You have no chin," she chided herself. "And your eyes are too small."

Angela stalked out of bed the next morning. She glanced outside her window where the ominous howling of unseasonable winds and deep sage coloured clouds mingled. The impending storm reflected her mood as she stumped down the stairs, shrouded in self-imposed gloom.

Her mother, Florence, dressed as always in smartly coordinated separates, eyed her daughter with visible distaste. "Good morning."

Angela, her hair tortured into curls that in no way complimented her surly expression, glowered at her mother. "Whatever."

Florence stood beside the kitchen island, where no breakfast made an appearance. "Smiling is good for the soul."

"I have no soul," Angela snapped at her mother.

From outside came the sound of rolling thunder.

Florence's voice held a slap, "You will go too far one of these days, young lady."

Angela grabbed an apple and stuffed it into her backpack. She glared at her mother and once again the house shook with thunder.

Florence continued to stare, her eyes a reflection of the tortured clouds that could be seen through the kitchen window.

"Why are you looking at me like that? What is wrong with you?"

"Just like an angel," Florence intoned. Her lips parted to speak, and a droplet of drool leaked from one corner of her mouth. "Just like an angel."

Angela shivered unexpectedly. "Mom?"

Her mother's eyes glittered with a hate so strong that it froze Angela. It was almost as if her mother wanted to . . . what?

Kill her?

Surely not.

"Better hurry, Angela. You will be late for school."

Angela looked at her mother uneasily and then glanced at the kitchen window, where the sky continued to darken. "It looks as if we are going to have, like, a hurricane or something. I don't think there is even going to be school today."

"There will be school," Florence replied.

"How do you know?" Angela argued. "Look at the sky."

"There will be school. Today of all days, there will be school. For you."

"Why are you acting so weird?" Angela wailed, but her mother walked out of the room without another word.

"What the hell?" Angela asked the empty kitchen and then stomped out of the house, slamming the door behind her. The sky threatened rain, if not worse, she'd probably end up getting drenched. Taking a deep breath, she ignored the sky and its rolling, green-tinged clouds.

While she waited at the bus stop, Angela pursed her lips and made an assortment of sounds to get her lips toned, tuned and warmed up.

If her voice was all that she had well, it was a good voice. Better, it was an amazing voice.

Everybody said so.

Nobody sang like her.

Nobody.

"Pride goeth before a fall," said an unknown voice as cold as ice and slick as oil.

Angela whirled around, but there was nobody there. She clutched her backpack defensively but when no monster made itself visible, she forced herself to relax. "You're hearing things, that's all. All great performers suffer from nerves. It was the trees."

It could have been, for as the wind continued to pick up, the trees swayed and groaned mournfully. Angela shivered and launched into *Ava Maria*. It was a pun of sorts, a jab at her nemesis, the bane of her existence, Maria—who could not hit the highest notes but possessed the beauty Angela desired. She closed her eyes and continued to sing from the soul she swore to her mother she didn't possess.

A pure and sustained note coaxed a ray of sunshine that struggled for purchase amidst the vibrantly hued clouds.

The school bus pulled neatly to the curb, its door opening with a wet squeak…like a rusty mouth inviting her to step inside.

As the bus pulled into its parking spot, Angela spotted Maria immediately. She was hard to miss, standing there in a yellow halter top and holding a bright pink sweater. Angela narrowed her eyes as she stomped down the metal stairs of the school bus and then gasped as Maria turned, raising her arms above her head and preening in front of the gaggle of girls that flocked around her, gawking and fawning.

There, upon Maria's back, were the outlines of two perfect, feathered wings. Angela's legs and arms moved of their own volition, her eyes as wild as the sky.

"Thank you!" Maria smiled as the other girls gushed. "Yes, I am lucky that my parents love tattoos. This is an early birthday present. They aren't done yet."

Done or not, they were beautiful.

"You *knew* I was going to get wings when I was old enough!" Angela screamed as she flew toward her rival.

The murmuring admirers quieted, shocked into silence.

"Angela, everyone's looking at you," Maria said.

"I don't care!" Angela bellowed, tears overflowing. "I *told* you I was going to get wings on my back. I am Angela. I *am* the angel. I *sing* like an angel. You know that! You know—"

"Yes," Maria interrupted. She crossed her arms and gave the hysterical Angela a sad and yet sour look. "You have told me. Wings. A nose. Boobs. You don't want to be you anymore. You want to be *me*."

"Or maybe she wants to be *more* than *like* you," one girl slyly insinuated, making kissing sounds. The other girls tittered.

Angela blushed angrily. "You just want all the attention for yourself." She snuffled back angry tears and stormed off to an accompaniment of jeers and giggles.

"I would give anything to look like you," Angela had told Maria once upon a time, when they had been friends and barely out of puberty. "You are so beautiful."

"Maybe. But I can't sing like you. You sing just like an angel."

"I would sing like a toad if it could mean that I would look like you."

"Oh, Angie," Maria had sighed. "Would you really?"

"Yes . . . or my mom. I would trade my stupid voice if I could look like either one of you."

Angela stalked in a huff toward her locker.

"I couldn't help but overhear," a deep, sly voice interrupted her thoughts.

Angela whipped around, startled. Before her stood a man in a felt fedora and a long black trench coat. He spoke again in a voice that sent a chill up her spine, as if an icy hand held it in its grasp.

"She stole your idea, did she?" His teeth flashed in a grin, a gold incisor glinting.

"Y-yeah," Angela managed. "Who are you?"

The man tipped his hat and gave a slight bow. He began to walk away and then stopped, turning slightly. "Be careful what you wish for." He gave a wink and added, "Ask for Haumea."

"Haumea?"

The man winked again and began to fade from view into the . . . crowd? What crowd?

"What?" Angela looked around, but the normally bustling school hallway was empty even though the bell had not yet sounded.

Unnerved and bewildered, Angela walked to her history class room, opened the door and walked into—

She screamed in surprise. No classroom this, but a dark alleyway instead. Somehow, she had walked into somewhere else. The flickering of a single light bulb hanging from a street lamp illuminated her pale and frightened face. A sign beckoned in the distance. Glowing green letters spelled out Mom's Bane as though da Vinci himself had learned the art of Graffiti and had risen from the dead to paint those words in neon. A dazed Angela walked toward the shining emerald sign and the store beneath it, and pushed the door open into what she hoped was a sanctuary.

Inside, as if in lying wait, appeared a walking skull; Angela backed into the closed door, yelping. The skull was attached to the woman who wore it etched upon her face, the colors wild and fervent, bold, and fierce. The woman mumbled, whether in greeting or something else, Angela did not know for sure. She cowered before the woman, trembling, her own face hidden in her hands.

The woman grunted again and Angela peered through her fingers. The woman's tattooed face, the lines of the skull etched in white, made her expression difficult to read. The woman crooked a finger and walked further into a spacious room to the back where a door waited.

"Where am I?"

The woman did not answer but pointed to where a sheet of paper lay, its very whiteness seeming a threat as it sat upon a sudden desk.

Angela eyed the woman as she sidled over to where the paper beckoned.

Mom's Bane.

Free Tattoo

Your choice.

Angela's lips moved as she read and then looked up, her eyes meeting those of the tattooed woman who stared back at her, beckoning once more with a finger.

"I don't understand." Angela's teeth chattered. "Did I win this? Where am I? Is this a dream? It's a dream, right?"

The woman shrugged; behind the tattoo her face appeared disinterested. She turned her back and began to walk away, but Angela cried, "sStop!"

The woman turned.

Angela thought furiously. "Uh . . . Haumea? I'm supposed to ask for someone named Haumea for a free tatoo."

The woman nodded.

Angela whispered, wetting her lips with her tongue, "Can I have wings?"

The woman nodded again.

"On my back. I want wings on my back," Angela earnestly explained. "I want big, beautiful, feathery wings."

The woman nodded and perhaps her face showed approval . . . and perhaps it did not.

"Wings," Angela insisted.

The tattooed woman nodded again and beckoned her to follow.

Time passed, but it passed either quickly or it slowed down, or perhaps it went sideways or even around and around in an endless circle. And there was pain, too—pain as the tattoo gun whirred and buzzed. There were strange sensations and another odd feeling of Time passing or going through her or leaving . . . but at last the sugar skull on the tattooed face creased in a smile from the one who wore it.

And it was done.

The tattoo was finished.

Angela stood up, legs shaking, and turned around, looking over her shoulder at her bared back revealed in the mirror behind her. Wings. Glorious wings. Angel wings. They were much better than Maria's wings . . . *far* better. They were so real looking, each feather etched separately and so concisely that one could almost imagine that feathers had been glued to the skin. The pain of it certainly made it feel as if they had been.

Angela's eyes met those of the woman, their eyes locking in the reflection of the mirror. "Thank you. Thank you! They are amazing!"

The woman only shrugged and walked away, leaving behind a beaming Angela.

"Just wait till Maria sees these. Her and her lame wings. Ha!" Angela's back began to ripple. She felt a spasm of pain and she winced. "Hey," she called out. "What do I do now?"

There came no answer.

"Am I supposed to keep a bandage on this? Isn't that what you are supposed to do?"

But there came neither answer nor explanation.

"I am going to wake up and all of this will be a dream," Angela addressed herself in the mirror. "But oh—these wings!"

Laughing under her breath, she walked toward the outer room and the door where she assumed she would exit into an alley. "Alleys and tattoo shops. Weird woman with a sugar skull on her face. Wings."

She pushed open the door and walked into her history class room, all eyes upon her startled face.

"You are late, Angela," the teacher said.

"S-sorry," she said as she walked toward her desk, only then noticing a sound of tittering that grew to raucous laughter as her classmates pointed at her.

Looking down, Angela saw she was naked.

From a desk toward the back of the classroom, Maria, oh-so perfect Maria, was the only one not laughing. She just stared at Angel with a mixture of horror and sympathy, took off her hoodie and approached her with it. To cover her, no doubt. To hide her.

To hide her wings.

Angela turned around, spreading her arms to each side. There was a silence in the classroom, as if a tap had been turned off. Too silent of a silence.

She turned again; arms still spread and faced the quiet room. "Wings," she said.

Maria stood before her, hoodie forgotten and trailing on the floor from a suddenly uncaring hand. "Like an angel," she said.

"Yes," Angela responded.

Her history teacher touched her back in wonder, which made her skin scream. "Yes, like an angel."

"Just like an angel," Maria said, and in her eyes there was a hint of *something*. Envy? No. Maria looked as if she wanted to . . . what?

Kill her?

Yes, that, certainly.

"Just like an angel," Maria hissed, and her nose began to bleed.

"Enough!" Angela yelled, pinching herself. "Wake up, Angela!"

She pinched and she pinched in that all-too quiet classroom, snatching Maria's discarded hoodie from the floor. She did her best to cover herself, modest in her terror as one by one, as if called upon by rote, each student took a turn to stand up at their desk, pointing at her and repeating the words, "Just like an angel."

"Enough!" Angela sobbed as she fled the room, half expecting to end up back in the alley. She ran as fast as she could, the pain in her back wrenching with every movement. She stopped only long enough to grab her band uniform from her locker before bolting out of the school and racing down the street toward her house. Block after block she ran, her breath whistling and sweat covering her brow. "Wake up!" She screamed as she ran. "Wake up!"

Angela raced up the driveway of home, yanking on the door knob which grudgingly opened, allowing her to enter. "Mom?" She shrieked as she ran toward her mother, who stood as if at attention, waiting.

"Mom. Mommy. I am having a nightmare. Help me!"

"Just like an angel," her mother whispered.

"Mom?" Angela all but shook her mother, but Florence did not or could not respond, offering her daughter only a blank stare. Blood began to trickle from the corners of her mouth.

"Mom?" Angela shrugged out of Maria's hoodie and held it to her mother's face. "Are you sick? What happened? Should I call 911?"

"Jus' like . . . an angel," her mother burbled, blood seeping faster, her pristine white shirt turning a bold color of crimson.

Angela ran to the phone, dialing for help—but the phone was dead, without dial tone or solution. She watched helplessly as her mother collapsed on to the floor, blood no longer trickling but now pouring from her mouth and soaking into the floor.

"Jus'...'ike ...angel," she gurgled.

Angela ran to the door in panic.

"I'm going for help, Mom. Mom! I'm going next door. Oh, my god. Oh, my god!" There came a sudden jolt of pain in her back that forced a moan from between Angela's lips. She wrenched open the door, only to find herself face to face with the man with the golden tooth, his hat set at a jaunty angle.

Angela screamed. "What did you do to me? This isn't a dream, is it? You did this to me!"

The man hitched his shoulders and gave a little twitch to his jacket. "What makes you say that?" he asked. "Who says I did this?"

"Who are you?" Angela whispered, looking over at her mother and then back again. "Are you the devil?"

"Naw," the man said as he pushed past her and strode into the room. "The name is Johnny."

"Well, whoever you are, my mom—my mother . . . she is . . . I don't *know* what is happening!" Angela wept as she rushed back to her mother's side. "I need help."

Johnny grinned and his tooth flashed.

"I need help!" Angela shouted. "Help me!"

"It could happen," said Johnny. He walked over to where Florence lay on the floor. She gave a sputtering gasp, and then there was a terrible silence. "Rather anticlimactic."

"Mom?" Angela screeched, patting her mother's cheeks. "Mom?"

"Deader than a doornail," Johnny said almost cheerfully. "Then again, dead people don't always stay dead, if you know what I mean." He looked at her with an expression of anticipation and winked.

"What are you?" Angela breathed in horror.

"Ya know, there was a moment…"

"What are you talking about?"

"There was a moment. There is always a moment."

"A moment? A moment *when?* What moment? What are you talking about?" Angela panted, holding her lifeless mother even as her back wailed in anguish.

"I heard you sing," Johnny explained.

"So?"

"The sun came out. It caught my attention."

"What?"

"Never mind, never mind." Johnny waved as if to brush his words away.

"I don't understand," Angela wept.

"And now you have wings, just like an angel. The whole package. Just what you requested."

"You sent me there! You told me to ask for Hama, Hauma, Haumea. Something. Someone. She did this. You did this!"

"It was your choice," Johnny pointed out.

"What does that have to do with my mom?" Angela demanded, leaping to her feet.

"Angels."

"What about angels?"

"Yeah, well, the thing about angels..."

Crack!

The pain sent Angela crashing to her knees.

Angela blubbered, "What about angels?"

"I fuckin' hate angels."

Angela's spine erupted in agony as the pressure on her shoulder blades crushed her into the floor.

"But they have their uses," Johnny grinned.

Her hand whipped to the spot where it hurt the most, regretting the motion instantly. She howled.

"Don't sound much like an angel, now. Do you?" Johnny pulled Angela off of the floor and propelled her outside of the house. "But you *do* sort of sound like one when you try, when you try real hard."

"What are you doing?"

"Fly," Johnny whispered.

Angela felt herself launched into the air, the skin of her back tearing and ripping. She shrieked like a bird . . . or perhaps even just like an angel.

She soared upwards, her wings bursting forth as she did, spreading out in an effort to catch her fall. She could feel each tendon as it strained, feathers ripping loose as she hurtled upward. She hunched her back, the new sensation of her wingspan allowing her to feel the loss of every feather.

Upwards, ever upwards she flew until the air thinned and she could feel a great hotness that at first smoldered and then burned away the tips of her remaining feathers. She screamed until she could scream no more and even then, she soared higher until she felt herself caught in sticky web that stretched across the shattered, verdant sky.

"What—is . . . this?" If it wasn't a voice that asked the question, it was something else, a dark something. A something that held her before it in its tight grip.

Eyes deadened with shock, Angela didn't even flinch as she heard Johnny's voice command her to sing.

She felt her defeated body being shaken violently as if by an oily hand.

"Sing, I said. Sing!"

Angela licked her dry lips and panted, hanging in mid-air with her wings ripped and useless.

"*Sing!*" Johnny commanded as her body was shaken again, bruised and buffeted.

Yes.

She would sing.

And then this horrible dream would be over and her mother would be alive again and Angela would never complain about her nose or the birthday goat or stationary—or even perfect Maria.

Angela opened her mouth . . . but not a single sound could she make.

"Come on," Johnny's voice urged. "Try!"

She opened her mouth and the smallest of croaks escaped.

The web that held her seemed to quake with laughter.

There was a silence, and then Johnny's voice condemned her

"Petty."

"No," Angela whispered.

"Useless."

"No."

Angela struggled but the strands held tightly, a pulsing, living thing that drained her not of blood, but of hopes and dreams.

"Sing!" Johnny roared.

Angela gave one last attempt and then bowed her head in defeat.

"No," she said soundlessly, mouthing the word. "No."

And down Angela went, wings bent and broken, useless feathered things that trailed behind her. Down and down and further down she fell until she lay weeping in the bathtub, what was left of her clothes in shreds. Her once beautiful wings hung wrapped around her like a tattered blanket.

"Angela," her father yelled as he ran into the bathroom. "Oh, dearest father in Heaven. Your mother. Your mother is . . . I thought you were. . . Oh, honey! Who was it? Who did this?" He sobbed as he held his daughter. She did her best not to scream from the pain of his touch.

"Who was it? Angela? Angela?"

"Wings," she whispered.

"Wings? What wings?"

Johnny adjusted his fedora against the abating winds. His golden tooth sparkled as he sneered over his shoulder at Angela's house. He spat on the ground. "Angels." He spat again. "Overrated." He shrugged in disappointment, tucked a fresh feather in his hat and continued walking beneath the red-streaked sky.

Kickin' It Into Third

TWENTY-FIVE TATTOO ARTISTS WERE sprawled all over Mom's Bane, creating a host of inkwork on the large crowd that was packed inside.

Haumea exited a quick-room with a solid looking, handsome young man with a two-day stubble of beard, shirtless, and sporting a large black cobra tattoo jutting up from under his pants' waistline to just a couple of inches under his chest. A black eye patch covered his left eye socket.

"We copacetic, trooper?" Haumea asked.

"Right on, sister," he said with a deep drawl, "A-number-one."

Haumea smiled as her client sauntered toward the exit in his gray combat slacks and boots.

"I heard he was dead," Johnny said.

"Not likely," Haumea replied and smirked, now more than used to Johnny's sudden teleportation surprises.

A loud explosion echoed in through the front entrance, rocking the shop and knocking down everyone not sitting onto the floor, with the exceptions of Haumea and Johnny. Haumea managed this minor miracle through sheer acrobatic talent where as Johnny appeared totally immune to the shockwave, as if it were just so much water splashing on his ankles.

"What the hell was that?" Haumea shouted.

"I would say," Johnny replied, "that the Sha'Daa has finally caught up to you, Haumea. Surely you didn't think your actions would go unnoticed by those dark things your wonderful, artistic creations are thwarting?"

Haumea strode to the front of the shop as quickly as she could, doing her best to avoid contact with the odd broken ankle and arm, or sprained neck. The massive oak door was in one piece, but the brick walks all displayed several stress fracture lines.

"Where…" Haumea started.

"That alleyway," Johnny said, "hell, that whole neighborhood in Gorky Park is gone."

"By gone, you mean," Haumea said.

"You know what I mean," Johnny said.

"The shop will be cycling that much more quickly between Harlem, New Orleans, Taipei, and Dublin," Haumea calculated.

"Tick tock," Johnny chided.

"We'll be ready," Haumea said, "assuming there's any world left to save in twelve hours."

"Haumea," a voice yelled from across the main tattoo floor, "we need more bandages."

"In the closet in the main bathroom," Haumea yelled back, "and there's extra adhesive tape behind the front desk."

She turned back to Johnny and he was of course gone.

"You always promised you could tame the dragon on my back," a female voice practically shouted to be heard over the barely controlled chaos of injured being attended to and two dozen tattooing irons going back into full swing.

Haumea spun around and found herself face to face with a thin, attractive, pale-skin woman of indeterminate age, wearing shiny black biker leathers. Her hair was carrot red and hung down to her shoulders.

"Only one thing can tame your dragon," Haumea said, "and that is a tiger. You need its brute strength to balance the ferocious wisdom of the saurian."

Haumea grabbed the woman's arm and half pulled her into one of the quick-rooms, "quickly, we don't have much time, Lisbeth."

CHAPTER TEN

What Manner of Fool?

by Christopher L. Smith

AUDREY WHIPPED AROUND TO FACE THE speaker, then took a small step back in surprise. It wasn't so much that he was strange or funny looking- just out of place. Audrey wiped her face in a futile gesture—the one hundred degree day had already caused her to soak her ACU pants and tee shirt. The sight of the stranger's large black trench coat and felt fedora made her feel even hotter.

"Excuse me?" she said.

The newcomer's voice was cool and calm, clearly enunciating his words. "I said, 'I have something you may need, Specialist Esperanza.'"

Audrey was again struck by the oddness of the newcomer. His speech rang with a tone of formality, as though he came from a different time.

"Oh really?" she said, "And what might that be, Sir?"

"This." He pulled a hand from the pocket of his coat, gently cradling what looked like a glass vial. "Ink—used by a brave and honest giant among men. One that freed a people."

"Ok, I'll bite. What in god's name would I need that for?"

"I'm quite sure an intelligent young lady such as yourself, could find an *application* for it." The strange man smiled, showing perfectly even and white teeth, with one exception.

Nice gold tooth, buddy. Going for the Bogart meets Superfly look, I guess, she thought. "Uh hunh. Sir, this is a military base." She made a sweeping gesture, indicating the whole of Fort Sam Houston. "The armed guards at the gate over there," she pointed, "and the standard issue beige buildings should have tipped you off. I don't know who you are, but civilians aren't allowed in this area. You need to leave, *Sir.*" Audrey crossed her arms and stood there sweating. *Just a skinny freak, probably won't cause any trouble.* She shrugged mentally. *But I could probably handle him if he did.* She glanced at the heavy monkey wrench next to the torn down transmission, and took what, she hoped, was a casual step in its direction.

"No need to worry about violence, Ms. Esperanza. I assure you, I have only your well being in mind." The gold tooth briefly caught the sun again as he smiled, then disappeared as his face took a more solemn appearance. "I have everyone's well being in mind."

Audrey raised an eyebrow, her eyes widening behind her shades. "Ok, weirdo, you're just about out of goodwill on my side." She hiked a thumb, punctuating each word with it. "Secure. Area. Get. Lost."

"I assure you, as soon as our business is completed, you will not see me again. May I inquire about your tattoo?"

Audrey was caught off guard. "What? Which one?"

"That one." The man pointed at her forearm. "It seems somewhat out of place, compared to the other."

Audrey glanced at the ink, grimacing at the memory. What should have been nothing more than simple, routine maintenance—a quick in and out job changing a timing belt on a Hummer—destroyed by the FNG hitting the starter when she was shoulder deep in the engine. It could have been a lot worse, given the circumstances, but as it was, she got off light with a long slash through her right forearm. A few inches more, and she would have mangled her hand. The resulting scar bisected her tat, leaving a jagged puckered line through the design.

Odd, I keep forgetting I have it until someone points it out. Or it starts itching, like earlier today. "Yeah, well, that one was a bad idea. Drunken night with the guys."

"What is in this vial has helped erase a tragic mistake."

"Whatever that means." Audrey shook her head in resignation. "Jesus man, you're nothing if not persistent. Alright, if I buy your crap, will you please leave? I got work to do here."

"You are under no obligation to purchase anything I offer, Specialist. That would violate the rules."

Audrey shook her head. "Whatever. How much? I only got a few bucks on me."

"You have exactly twenty-two dollars and sixteen cents. However, I am not interested in your money." He tilted the fedora back slightly. "That is, not your American money."

"Hunh? Wait, what?" *How did he know about that?*

"I understand you have a pouch with several coins in your possession."

"My dad's collection? You've got to be kidding." The pouch had the smallest denomination of coin from each country Audrey's dad had visited during his time in service. "Those things are practically worthless, less than a fraction of a penny each. I only keep them because they were his."

"And that is what makes them valuable, my dear." All traces of joviality had left his voice. "What is coming can be described as a crossroads. How much would you be willing to part with to give humanity an edge during a difficult struggle?"

"Dude, you're talking like someone that's been out in the heat too long."

"The temperature is nothing compared to what is approaching."

"Here," Audrey tossed the pouch to the freak, "If it gets rid of you faster, I'll take the deal." He caught it deftly and removed a single coin.

"And so the bargain is struck." He carefully placed the vial and coin purse in Audrey's open hand. "Good fortune, Specialist Esperanza." He walked away, only to stop and address her again. "May I ask about the other tattoo? It has a familiar style."

She turned slightly, giving the weirdo a better look at her left bicep. The tattoo looked like a typical rosary, however a large hand occupied the space that normally contained the cross. An open eye in the palm dominated the design, surrounded by swirls and scrollwork. "That's the Mal Ojo. Keeps the evil spirits away."

"Very nice. May I ask where you got it?"

Audrey shrugged. "Some dive in Nuevo Laredo a while back. Spooky Hawai'ian lady did the work."

"Ah, Haumea. She is very talented." The gold tooth winked in the bright sunlight. "May it serve you well, Specialist Esperanza."

Audrey took off her shades and wiped the sweat from her face, momentarily closing her eyes. When she opened them, the stranger was gone. "Dios te salve, Maria...Ok, Audrey, time to get done and out of this heat. You're seeing things." *Not to mention talking to yourself. Get a grip, girl.*

Audrey looked at the vial, shrugged, and put it in her ACU pocket.

Wait a sec, how did he know my name?

Audrey's apartment complex was low rent, to say the least. Home to many lower enlisted, it was cheap and run-down. The landlord knew he had a constant supply of mostly broke soldiers, desperate to live out of the confines—and restrictions—of Fort Sam, and kept things just barely tolerable. It didn't hurt that he had a city inspector in his pocket.

It was worth it though. Not having to deal with the barracks meant freedom from the twenty-four hour distractions of what was essentially a dorm room for young soldiers. It also meant she could keep her pistol and practice during off-duty hours.

Not that there had been many of those, lately. The Middle East, never known for its long-term stability, had been acting up again. The brass wanted everything ready to go at a moment's notice, so the work load had practically doubled over the last few months.

"Ugh." Audrey flopped on the couch, exhausted from the day's work. The room's AC, a welcome relief from the day's heat, gave her goose bumps as the sweat cooled. She sighed, closing her eyes and reveling in the sensation as a shiver ran through her body.

The moment was all too short, as the event manager on her phone chimed. *Oh for Christ's sake. Can't a girl get five minutes to herself?* Audrey sat up quickly. "Oh shit." She checked the phone as it chimed again. Drinks with Pete. "Dammit, that's tonight!"

Pete was nice, and even with the low grade headache and weariness, she didn't want to give him another rain check. And after only a few dates, she sure as hell wasn't going to invite him over here. Yet. Tonight was supposed to be the all-important third date, the one that set the pace for their relationship going forward.

She jumped off the couch, talking to herself as she moved into the bedroom. "Ok, five minutes to shower, ten to blow dry the hair," She checked her nails. "Oh good, the manicure is still in decent shape, just some grease under there…some tough chica, eh? Worried about your nails and what underwear to put on…the red silk ones, just in case…Now where the hell is my MAC Rebel lipstick?" She hopped on one foot, struggling to get her stubborn boot to come off. The phone rang.

"A la gran puta," she muttered, heading back to the couch. "An hour to get ready and now the damn thing rings," she punched the "accept" button. "Que quieres?"

"Whoa—Audrey?"

She sighed. "Hey, Doc. Sorry, late for a date. What's going on?"

Phillip Wohlrab, her battalion's combat medic, lived in the same complex. They had become friends shortly after she arrived on post, attending local gun shows and the range together. Doc's timing tonight, however, was lousy.

"Are you home?"

"Yeah, and trying to get ready."

"Looked outside?"

"Doc, I'm late. I don't have time for riddles."

"No, seriously, take a look."

Audrey moved to the third floor apartment's window, overlooking the courtyard below. The other three buildings framed in an open space containing a weed choked sand volleyball court and rusted out barbeque pits. Crappy as the equipment was, most nights there would be a group or two goofing off and cooking.

Tonight, though, a mass of about fifty had assembled. Mostly soldiers, but a few of the other tenants as well. Not just standing around, but ordered. They looked like a company in formation.

Doc's voice was low, "Weird, isn't it? So far as I can tell, they just started congregating a few minutes back."

Audrey scratched idly at her right arm. "Yeah, like some kind of flash mob. Oh my god, are those the Mulaney's?" she giggled. "I never would've guessed they were into that."

"Wow, I'm going to need something strong to get that picture out of my head. Laundry day just got waay more uncomfortable." Doc chuckled. "I don't think you can machine wash leather chaps and gimp masks, Mrs. Mulaney. They might be dry clean only.'"

"Yeah, I'll never look at them the same way again." The crowd suddenly snapped to attention, as if some unseen sergeant had barked orders. As one, they turned slowly to face Audrey's building. "Ok, that's creepy."

The headache that had been with her all day sent dull, throbbing waves of pain through her skull, into her shoulders, and down her right bicep. The itch became a flash of agony. She gasped, dropping the phone as she clutched her arm.

Doc's voice drifted up from the floor. "Audrey? Audrey! Hey, what happened?"

Clenching her jaw, Audrey picked up the phone. "Just dropped the damn thing," she said. "Sudden pain down my right side."

"Hang on, I'll be right there."

"Don't worry about—Oh!" Another wave of agony cut her off. "Ok, hurry."

His place was a floor up and down the hall. Less than a minute passed before there was a knock at Audrey's door.

"Audrey?" Doc's voice came through the heavy wood.

"Hang on, I'm coming." Audrey staggered to the door, gritting her teeth. It was coming more frequently, waves of pain rolling through her body. She threw the bolt and backed up.

"Holy shit," Doc said, coming in and closing the door behind him. "Lie down on the couch. Tell me where it hurts."

Audrey gasped as she lay down. "Head, right arm."

"Shit. Ok, there's a chance you could be having a mild heart attack." Doc opened his bag, pulling out a stethoscope. "I need you to pull up your shirt a little."

"No drinks first?"

"This is serious, Audrey. " Doc's face showed his concern. "If it makes you feel better, I'll close my eyes, but I need to examine you."

"Yeah, I know. Just trying to—*Oh!*" Audrey shut her eyes. "Do you hear that?"

"Auditory hallucinations aren't good," Doc muttered. He placed the 'scope on her sternum, eyes on his wristwatch.

"No, it's weird, like a whisper. And I swear it sounds like it's coming from right behind me."

"Uh, hunh. Not telling you to kill Lennon, is it?"

"No. More like 'Gather, Sha'Daa begins.'"

Doc looked her in the eye. "That mean anything to you?"

"No clue." The pain had subsided again. "I think I can walk now."

"Good." Doc said, packing up. "From what I can tell, you're ok to travel, but we need to get you to the hospital to be sure." He looked thoughtful, "Ambulance would be best, but we're only a few minutes from SAMMC. We could be there by the time the EMTs arrived here, and with that crowd outside, it might take them longer. C'mon, we'll take Das People's Kar."

Audrey sat up, nodding as she pulled down her tee. Then she stopped, taking a closer look at her friend. "Doc, are you wearing a skirt?"

A flush made its way up his neck and spread to his cheeks. "It's a kilt." He straightened to attention, standing tall. Well, as tall as he could—years of ruck marches with heavy packs had given him a slight slouch. "Her Majesty's Own Cameron Highlanders, Sergeant Phillip Wohlrab, reporting, ma'am."

"Um, okaaay?"

"Space: 1889." At her blank stare, he added, "Role Playing Game. I was heading over to a buddy's to play a few rounds tonight, and thought I'd look the part."

She had to admit, he did look impressive in the red jacket, blue kilt, and black hat. On his somewhat dumpy frame, the ensemble worked. "Ok, Sergeant, lead the way."

They made their way down the stairs, heading towards the covered parking slots. Audrey cast a quick glance over her shoulder towards the courtyard. The crowd had turned slightly, tracking her.

"That's really starting to bug me," she said. A fresh wave of pain assaulted her, stronger than the last. She sucked in air through her teeth and dropped to a knee, unable to speak.

"Almost there, Audrey," Doc wrapped an arm around her for support. "Come on, you can do it."

She forced herself to her feet and bit back a scream. Staggering, leaning heavily on Doc, she moved toward the car.

Das People's Kar was Doc's VW wagon. Silver, dusty, and a bit dinged up, it still ran like a dream. Doc opened the door, shoved the empty energy drink cans and fast food wrappers out of the way, and then helped her ease into the passenger's seat. He closed the door and ran around to the driver's side. A second later, the little wagon roared to life.

Audrey's arm was on fire, making her vision swim. She stared out the window as Doc navigated the streets that framed the fort, passing small shops and bars that relied on the constant influx of bored and desperate soldiers for their livelihood.

"Doc…" Audrey started.

"Yeah, I see it too. Thought I was seeing things, but too many people keep stopping and looking at us. What the hell is going on?" He turned down a side street. "How you doing?"

"I'm…better, actually," she said. "Hurt like hell a second ago, until you turned."

"Strange." Doc took another turn, heading towards the highway.

"Ow!" the pain returned with a vengeance, though not as bad as it had been. "Doc, stop the car."

"We can't—"

"Just stop, dammit!"

"Ok, ok." He pulled over, narrowly avoiding an old man coming down the sidewalk. The newcomer's speed, aided by the wheeled combat boots, caused his unbuttoned Hawai'ian shirt to flap behind him like some kind of Wahini superhero. The mohawk was unaffected.

"You bastard cultists! I know you got my gnomes, and I ain't stopping 'til I get 'em back!" he fired the shotgun he carried as he disappeared around a corner.

Doc shared a look with Audrey, "That's something you don't see every day."

"Turn around, and head the other way," Audrey said.

"No. We need to get you to the hospital. With everything else going on, we can't take chances."

"Just do it, Doc. I wanna test something."

"Fine, but then we head to SAMMC." He put the car in gear and pulled out.

As they approached the intersection, the pain faded. "Keep going that way. I don't hurt as bad."

They spent the next few minutes driving up and down the small streets around the base, using Audrey's pain to navigate. With every "correct" turn, it would recede, only to become more intense if they moved in the "wrong"direction. It disappeared completely as they passed a small strip center, returning at the end of the block.

"Pull in here," Audrey said, "I don't know what's going on, but this seems to be the place."

The building was run down— faded paint peeling from the cracked and pitted cinderblocks. Out of the ten slots, only a few were still in business, the other spaces plastered with 'For Lease' signs. Several had broken windows, and one had been completely boarded up. Doc parked at the back of the small lot.

Audrey's scarred tat began itching again. "Wait a minute, I've been here. There—'Skorpion Ink'." She held out her right arm. "It's where I got this."

"I've got a bad feeling," Doc said. "I really think we should get to the hospital."

"Yeah, let me just check something."

"Fine, but we go in prepared." Doc got out and moved to the rear of the VW, opened the rear hatch, and rummaged around. "Ah," he said, "Perfect."

Audrey came around to the back of the car and whistled. "Jesus, Doc. I knew you had a small arsenal, but…damn."

"Yes ma'am. Picked up a few things with my last check." He opened a case. "This is a Rossi Ranch Hand. Nice little lever gun, .357, decent at rifle ranges, devastating at pistol." He held up what looked like an Old West rifle that had been sawn off. He pulled out another case, large enough for at least two pistols. "Here, you take these, since they're closer to what you have."

Audrey opened the case and pulled out the Smith and Wesson .40, loaded the mag, and tucked it into her waist at the small of her back. The Sig went into the front pocket of her ACUs.

Doc picked up another pistol, loaded it, and tucked it away. "Ok, let's go." They made their way to the door of the tattoo parlor.

As they walked in, a shiver ran up Audrey's spine that had nothing to do with the AC. A strange sensation came from the Ojo tattoo on her left arm—a tingling feeling that, while not physically uncomfortable, made her uneasy.

The front of the parlor was empty, just a few chairs and a cash register. She walked through the curtain that led to the back, the metal rings rasping as they slid along the rod. The work room was empty, but looked as though it hadn't been used all day. The artist's station, with its leather bound chair and wheeled stool, were ready for a customer; the inks unused and neatly organized.

"Hello?" Audrey's voice echoed as it bounced off the tile and mirrors. "Anyone here?"

The tingling in her left arm increased, as though it was reacting to something in the air. In contrast, the itching from her scarred right arm had subsided. The whispers in her head, though, had come back stronger. *I am your Master. I am the Artist.* She blocked them out as best she could, trying to focus on her immediate surroundings.

Movement from the alcove at the rear of the room caught her attention. A man in a tank top and cargo shorts appeared to flow from the shadows, stopping a few paces away. Every inch of his exposed skin was covered in tattoos, making it difficult to tell what the original color might have been.

The images themselves seemed to be fluid, each individual piece flowing into and becoming part of the next—paradoxically appearing to contrast each other, yet still combining into a cohesive whole that was greater than the sum of its parts. Audrey found herself staring, then grimaced as a sharp pain shot through her right arm.

"Hello, my dear," the man said, his deep voice smooth and sinister, "I've been wondering what had happened to you."

"Excuse me?" Audrey took a small step back, keeping her hand close to the pocket of her ACU's. "What's that supposed to mean?"

"Simply that, out of all of my pieces, you are the only one that I've not been able to read fully." He gave a small shrug. "I could feel that you were near, but not the— ah— connection that we should have." His gaze shifted to her arm. "That explains it. You have damaged the canvas, deeply enough to affect the bond we share."

"Bond?" Audrey's head was spinning, the whispers in her mind surging forward with renewed intensity. *Sha'Daa approaches.*

"Oh yes, there is always a bond." The Artist continued, "My work is very intimate. A little of my blood mixed with the ink in your design, a little of yours mixed into mine." He extended his right arm, showing a smaller, but exact copy, of Audrey's design. "A most intimate art form, the tattoo. A piece of me forever etched into your body. Your ideas, my skill, combine to form a unique creation, one that will be a part of you until your end." He gave a slight smile. "Sad, really, that I must sacrifice my canvases for the Master."

Doc had been quiet throughout the exchange, but now spoke up. "What do you mean 'the Master?'"

"It is the time of the Sha'Daa," the Artist said, "The boundaries between our world and the Other are at their thinnest. My Master shall be summoned."

"I've heard enough." Doc leveled the Ranchhand. "Look, crazy freak guy, you've obviously lost it. We'll be leaving now. Audrey, shall we?"

"Oh, I think not, insignificant little man in a dress." The Artist gave another tight smile. "While you haven't felt the touch of my needle, your soul will be a welcome addition to the others."

"It's a kilt." Doc's finger slipped inside the guard, applying gentle pressure to the trigger. "Right. I think this is where I say, 'You and what army?'"

The Artist's smile grew. "Why, the one outside, simpleton."

Audrey turned slightly, using a mirror to check the front window. Faces, slack and lacking any sign of sentience, stared back through the painted glass. At least twenty people were approaching the front door of the shop, moving as if they were marionettes controlled by a skilled puppeteer.

"While this has been and interesting, and informative, distraction," The Artist continued, "I must insist you come with me. The Master awa—"

The Ranch Hand cut him off, deafening thunder bouncing around the tile and glass in the room. Audrey's ears, ringing from the first shot, barely picked up the sound of Doc working the lever before the next blast.

The Artist dropped as the .357 slugs tore into his chest, blood and tissue spraying into the air. Doc's mouth was moving, but Audrey couldn't make out the words. Doc grabbed her arm and hauled her towards the back of the shop. "…be a fire exit," he said.

Her ears still ringing, but functioning, Audrey followed his lead. A quick glance behind her confirmed that they were, in fact, being pursued. Slowly.

They hit the alarm bar on the fire door and entered the approaching dusk. One final look as they slammed the door showed the Artist stirring, attempting to rise to his feet. They ran for the car, Audrey praying that the horde of people under the Artist's influence were dependent on his guidance.

As they rounded the corner, she breathed a sigh of relief. The VW was in the clear. Doc fumbled with the keys, juggling the Ranch Hand as he tried to aim the remote and press the right button.

"Dammit!" the car began honking, headlights flashing, as they approached. He jammed his thumb onto the fob, silencing the alarm just as Audrey got to her door. She checked the group at the shop—less than half had entered, and the remaining people spun around at the sound of the alarm. Several started across the parking lot, shambling towards the car with a stiff, zombie-like gait.

Audrey grabbed the handle and yanked. Still locked. "Doc…"

"Sonofa-" the lock jumped up. "Got it!"

She wrenched the door open and jumped in. The Artist's minions, closer than she expected, were within several steps. "Let's get the fuck out of here!"

"Hell yeah!" Doc shouted as the engine roared to life, "that's some German engineering for you!" He threw the car into gear and floored it, narrowly avoiding the few people that had gotten within touching distance. The VW flew out of the parking lot and onto the main street.

"Where we going?" Doc's voice was calm, in sharp contrast to his white knuckles gripping the wheel. "Can't go home, not with the group there, unless you think they were all at the shop? I don't know what the fuck is going on, just that things have spiraled completely out of my range of experience." He addressed the car in front of him. "Oh, ok, so we'll just go really slowly, straddle the center line and block traffic. That's fine, no one needs to go anywhere, even though there is something really strange going on around here with guys that get up from gunshots and demons and *would you please be so kind as to get the ever living FUCK out of my way?*"

"Doc, get a grip." Audrey massaged her scarred arm. It itched again, becoming worse as they increased the distance between themselves and the shop. "We need to figure out what we're going to do about this."

"Cops?"

Audrey shook her head. "Don't think so. Half the crowd back there was in uniform, and the shop owner had several Fraternal Order of Police designs." She looked out the window. "Besides, we don't know how crazy it is everywhere else. Cops are going to be busy, if it's anything like it is here."

"Damn." Doc turned down a side street, checking the rearview to make sure they'd lost any pursuit. He pulled over. "So you're thinking we go up against this freak by ourselves?"

"Can't be sure who to trust at this point, and I get the feeling we don't have the time to interview potential teammates."

"Damn." He sat back and closed his eyes, rubbing his temples. "I've got about a hundred rounds of everything we'd need back there. I really don't want to go in guns blazing. Too many innocents, dragged into this just because they made a left instead of a right, you know?"

"Yeah."

"You realize this probably won't end well, right?" He turned to look at her.

"Yep."

"Scared?"

"Shitless."

"Me too." He shook his head. "Well, like the old saying goes, 'Courage is being scared to death…'"

"And saddling up anyway." Audrey gave him a grin. "Well, pardner, wanna go save the world?"

"Let's do this."

"Here. We're close." Audrey had used her tat to guide them to the Artist's location. The pain had increased as they had taken stock and loaded magazines, telling Audrey the Artist had moved away from the shop. She led them to the outskirts of a golf course, the trees along the perimeter shielding them from view.

They geared up, Audrey with pistols, Doc favoring the AK over the lever gun. He pulled out two radios and ear buds. "You ready?"

Audrey nodded, taking one of the radios. "I don't know what he's going to do, but try to get a clean shot. Aim for the head if you can. At the very least you might distract him at a critical point."

"Roger that. Be careful."

Audrey nodded, distracted. Something had been nagging at her since the tattoo parlor.

"What is it?"

"Something happened earlier today." *Jesus, had it only been this afternoon?* "Weird guy with a hat traded a coin from my dad's collection for this." She reached into her pocket and pulled out the vial of ink. "Hinted that this was pretty important."

"Fedora? Gold tooth?"

Audrey nodded. "Yeah, you see him too?"

"Yeah. Offered me an antique syringe for a couple of D20's. Actually, I have it here. Was going to take it to the game and show it off." He reached into the back seat and pulled out an old case, opening it to reveal a steel tube, polished and gleaming in the fading light. "It's a Down Brothers, made in the early 1900's. A classic."

"Tat boy there said something about my bond with him being broken because of my scar. I wonder…" Audrey studied the syringe. "Can you fill it with my ink?'

"Well, yeah, shouldn't be a problem." Doc took the vial and opened it, gently placing the needle inside. "Just pull back the plunger, and…Voilà."

The syringe had plenty of room for every drop. Audrey took it from him, held out her arm, and took a few deep breaths. "Okay, here goes nothing." She slowly inserted the tip into the design, applying gentle pressure to the plunger. "Just a little here," she said with a grimace. "Ow. And here…"

She quickly moved along the lines of the tattoo, injecting herself with small amounts of ink. The whispers in her head became faint, fading into the background of her thoughts.

"Seems to be helping." She shook the syringe. "About half of it left."

"I have an idea," Doc said, "Do you think you can get close to the freak?"

"Maybe. If he can't get a fix on me, I might have a chance."

"He stayed down for a bit after I shot him earlier. Unload a mag into him, and he might stay down longer. You said the ink helped break his control on you, right? What if you hit him with it? Maybe it'll let the others shake free, too."

Audrey looked thoughtful, then nodded. "Where should I inject him?"

"Contrary to the movies, going straight to the heart isn't done, and besides, you'd have to punch through his breast bone to do it. Too risky, you might break the needle. Go for the jugular." Doc tapped his neck. "If his heart's still beating, it'll take about ten seconds to get through his system, a little longer to reach his skin."

"Roger that."

"Look, Audrey, I respect you, but I think you should let me do this. I can get the needle right where it needs to be on the first try."

"No." She shook her head. "You're not the one he tried to control, Doc. I have to do this. For me. I know it's selfish, but I need this." She held up her left arm. "Besides, you saw how he flinched at this. Something tells me it might be our only protection against what he's trying to bring out. Not to mention, you're a better shot at long range. I need you watching my ass." She tucked the syringe into her ACUs and hefted the Glock. "Now, you ready to go be Big Damn Heroes?"

Doc's eyes widened slightly. "Marry me."

"Ha! Gotta buy me a drink first, lover boy."

"Only one?"

"After tonight, better make it several."

"Deal."

Audrey made her way carefully through the crowd. Strange, the people that were actively trying to capture her less than an hour ago were now ignoring her. They faced forward, focused on the Artist in his position in front of the congregation. It was eerily quiet, as though everyone had suddenly stopped breathing at that exact moment.

Audrey stopped as soon as she saw the Artist. He'd traded his street clothes for a heavy hooded robe and loincloth.

His low-voiced chant carried in the crowd's silence. "h'r 'wn b'l! Glasya-Labolas! Dyyn 'yyat h't qwm'n 'w h'rşn d'm pl'ak! 'yk p'árşl'ágn d'm qrbn 'w 'yr, Glasya-Labolas!"

"That sounds kinda like Hebrew or Aramaic." Doc said in her ear, "Whatever he's doing is some serious Old Testament shit."

The Artist repeated the chant, louder this time. Audrey used it to cover her whispered reply, "Can you take him down? Sounds like it's coming to a head."

"I don't have a clear shot. Relocating, wait one."

"Hurry, I'll try to get in a better position." She started working her way towards the edge of the mass of people, keeping the Artist in her line of sight. The front line of the crowd was about ten yards from the chanting sorcerer, close enough for her pistol, but just far enough to worry about missing. "Doc, I'm about as close as I can get without him seeing me. Are you in position?" No reply. "Doc? Dammit." Audrey drew the .40 and set her feet. The gang banger in front of her was her height, allowing her to aim over his shoulder at the now yelling Artist.

"!'yk p'árşl'ágn d'm qrbn 'w 'yr, Glasya-Labolas!" The Artist raised his ink-covered arms above his head, as though he was conducting an orchestra. Wisps of smoke rose from his fingertips, creeping towards the crowd like ephemeral snakes. Within seconds, they had reached the front row; those that they touched began shuddering, a bright mist rising from their eyes and mouths to join the cloud. As soon as it stopped, the person dropped to the ground, their mouth open in a silent scream, eyes wide.

Audrey squeezed the trigger just as a tendril reached the man in front of her, emptying her magazine into the Artist. He rocked back from the impact, bloody holes appearing in the front of his robe. Audrey dropped her mag and slammed another home, moving as she fired. In seconds, the slide locked back.

The Artist looked down at the bloody mess where his chest had been and sighed. "I really liked that robe." He looked up at Audrey. "And this is why I didn't put anything important there."

"Shit." Audrey struggled as two congregation members grabbed her arms. The life draining smoke parted as her escorts made their way forward, continuing on its deadly path after they passed. More and more people were dropping to the ground, the light from their bodies joining the others in a pulsing mist above the crowd.

"Ms. Esperanza, your futile gesture is noted. As you may have noticed, I am no longer bound to the strictly physical realm. This mortal shell has not been what you'd consider 'alive' in centuries." The wounds were closing as he spoke. "Now, if you'll excuse me, I have a summoning to complete." He raised his hands again.

The mist above the crowd coalesced as the remaining members of the congregation collapsed, forming a glowing, pulsing, ball. The Artist began chanting again, his voice rising and falling as he spoke.

Audrey could only hope that Doc was still out there, and his luck was holding.

The ball of life force sped towards the Artist, striking him in the chest, cutting off the chant mid-sentence. His face contorted in ecstasy as the glow from the life force diffused into his skin.

"Yes! Thank you my Master for—" he broke off, his features changing from joy to confusion. "Master? Why are—" He doubled over in pain, sinking to his knees.

"What's the matter, ink-slinger?" Audrey couldn't help but grin. "Not what you expected, asshole?"

The Artist's face began to contort, his mouth opening as rows of shark-like teeth erupted from his jaws. The robe on his back began moving, as though the skin underneath was struggling to keep something contained. Something that desperately wanted to be free.

Audrey started at a gunshot behind her, and felt a grip loosen. The body hit the ground as she pulled her arm free, a gaping hole in his forehead. The second goon landed next to the first, his face obliterated.

"Move, Audrey!" Doc's voice was strained, coming from behind her. "Get clear so I can get a shot!"

Audrey watched as the Artist's body convulsed, bent over, and became still. He raised his head slowly, all traces of the emerging nightmare gone.

In its place, the Artist's features had reverted to normal, but *different*. What could only be described as a beatific expression had replaced the former sadistic sneer. Yet for all the pious radiance, there was an undertone of deep cruelty. The look of someone that took religious joy in inflicting suffering.

Audrey shivered, her mind screaming at her to run. Doc stepped to her side.

"I'm not sure if I should pray, run, or try to do both at the same time," he said. "What about you?"

"Completely at a loss, Doc. Trying to keep a handle on my shit."

"Frankly, I'm just a bit disappointed that the end of the world comes, and I didn't cause it."

The Artist, or whatever had taken over his body, opened his eyes and looked at them.

"Kneel before me, servants. Show reverence for your Lord and Master."

Audrey traded a glance with Doc, then turned back. "And you are…?"

One thing she had learned, through years in the Army, and growing up on the South side— when faced with a threat, do whatever you could to throw off your opponent. Attack, confuse, misdirect. Show no weakness.

"Impudent harlot! Kneel before me or face my wrath!"

"Uh, hunh. Sorry, I'm not into submission."

The Artist gave her a cold stare, his formerly green eyes practically glowing with a golden light. "You defy Labolas? What manner of fool are you?"

"U.S. Army."

Labolas looked at Doc. "You. Control the woman. Force her to kneel."

Doc snorted. "You're kidding, right?"

"I shall not be disobeyed by a man in women's clothing!" Labolas took a step forward, closing the distance between himself and Doc, hands forming into claws.

"It's a fucking kilt!" Doc fired, the AK hurling bullets toward the demon as fast as he could pull the trigger.

Labolas was on him in a flash, grabbing the rifle and twisting it from Doc's grasp. Recovering quickly, the medic went for his pistols, but his efforts were in vain. The demon slammed his palm into Doc's chest, launching him backwards onto the fallen bodies.

Audrey drew her remaining pistol, only to have her arm go numb as Labolas struck, the power of his blow staggering her. The demon pressed his advantage, a well aimed kick taking her in the knee. She dropped, unable to stifle a cry of pain.

"You will kneel, human, whether you choose to or not." Labolas chuckled. "My brothers felt that free will elevated your race above ours. Idiots are they, to not see what pitiful, powerless creatures humans are. Pawns, to be used at our discretion. Father misplaced His faith in you." His eyes began to glow again as what felt like a vice squeezed Audrey's brain. "Submit, maggot, or be destroyed."

Gritting her teeth, Audrey reached into the pocket of her ACU's, left hand closing on the syringe. She recited her Grandmother's favorite prayer, the words barely above a whisper.

"Espíritu de nuestro Dios, Padre, Hijo y Espíritu Santo, Santísima Trinidad, descienda sobre mí." The tingling from her Mal Ojo tattoo became a pleasant warmth, spreading outward to her fingers and shoulder. Her voice found strength as she slowly stood up, ignoring the pain in her knee. "Alejar de mí toda las asignaciones demoníaco, el mal de ojo, y cualquier otros espíritus de la muerte y la oscuridad."

Labolas' eyes widened, the golden glow flickering as he took a small step back.

Audrey continued, a faint glow tickling the corner of her eye. "I command and bid all the powers who molest me—by the power of God Almighty, in the name of Jesus Christ our Savior—to leave me forever, and to be consigned into the everlasting lake of fire, that they may never again touch me or any other creature in the entire world"

The demon's head snapped back, as though her words had been delivered with a solid right cross. Audrey drew the syringe from her pocket, holding it alongside her thigh.

Labolas recovered and moved closer, grabbing her by the shoulders and lifting her off the ground."I will eat your soul, human." His face distorted, rows of teeth reappearing as his face elongated. "And I will savor it."

"In Christ's name, go fuck yourself." Audrey slammed the needle into the demon's neck, depressing the plunger. She hit the ground as the demon released her, the shock to her knee sending a new wave of pain and causing her to fall to the neatly manicured green.

Labolas staggered back, clawing at the antique hypodermic as he struggled to stay upright. Audrey watched as his skin became a spider web of black lines, backlit with the same glow the congregation's souls exhibited earlier. A strangled cry forced its way from his throat as he collapsed, the glow becoming brighter. She shielded her eyes.

Every soul the Artist had collected poured from the demon's mouth, a Roman candle of spiritual essence flying towards the heavens. The body began to age rapidly as she watched, going from a fit and healthy man in his 30's to a sunken, cadaverous mummy of indeterminate age with each escaping soul. As the last glowing green blob left him, the shriveled corpse collapsed into a pile of dust.

Doc struggled to his feet, groaning. "Well, there's only one thing I can say at a time like this,"

"Yeah?" Audrey gasped as she tried to stand up. Whatever the Mal Ojo had been doing for her had stopped with Labolas' disintegration. "What's that?"

"He chose poorly."

She laughed in spite of the pain. "Seriously? That's what popped into your head?

"Well, it seemed fitting."

"Do you think this is over? Did we do it?"

"Save the world, you mean?" Doc shrugged. "Dunno. Maybe. At least this small part of it." He helped her stand on the good leg, wrapping his arm around her waist for support. "C'mon. If you didn't need a hospital earlier, you definitely need one now."

"Fine." Audrey limped, leaning on Doc as they started towards the car. "Damn, looks like I stood Pete up." She smiled. "Guess you get to buy me those drinks, now."

"Injuries take priority over a good time."

"Killjoy."

Blowout

OVER THE CENTURIES, MOM'S BANE HAD many incarnations, from grass huts, to wood shacks, to stone sheds, to high-rise penthouses among others. Various men and women throughout the last couple of centuries, fated for greatness and celebrity status, came seeking her special talents and help, ink work that was purported to grant the wearer more than mere notoriety in the pages of tabloids, or tell-all unapproved biographies.

Among many of her private clientele were John Wilkes Booth, Teddy Roosevelt, Pretty Boy Floyd, Dorothy Parker, Elvis Presley, George Orwell, and the lists went on and on. Not all ended up being happy with her handiwork, and some even resented Haumea's influence upon their minds, jobs, and souls, but nevertheless, her ink *did* affect them, most often for their betterment.

Perhaps the one client she felt the most compassion for was the Aussie actor Heath Ledger. It was March of 2007 when he strode into Mom's Bane, its current resting place in a back alley in Melbourne, Australia. Even though partially disguised with worn tourist shorts and t-shirt, a month's growth of scraggy mustache and beard, and sporting red tinted John Lennon glasses, Haumea recognized his handsome face and dazzling smile almost immediately.

Heath's natural charm was infectious, and she soon found herself falling under his spell, and perhaps letting her guard down and not paying as much attention to her usually cautious conscience as she normally did.

Heath told Haumea in confidence that he was preparing for the biggest movie role of his career, that of a madman, a psychopath with a quirky sense of humor, and that he was having trouble capturing that perfect mindset. He said he needed something powerful, intense, and primal, and that she was his last hope.

Haumea spent a full day inking the entire bottom of his right foot. Heath had insisted it be on a portion of his body most would never see. When she was done he sat up on the tattooing table to admire the work. Vaguely reminiscent of Salvador Dali's The Face of War, Haumea's multi-colored tattoo sent shivers up Heath's spine the first time he viewed it.

"This is the true embodiment of madness… and evil," Heath said with his strong Perth accent, "its perfect."

But standing back and viewing it herself, Haumea felt a strong sense of foreboding, and thought that perhaps she had gone too far.

Heath stopped by the shop a few months later for the shortest of visits to tell her he was tearing up the film set with his performance and that he owed it all to her.

But all that Haumea kept thinking about were has final words just before he walked out of her shop for the last time, that he had trouble sleeping lately, being bothered by nightmares, and so she was not really surprised to hear he died from a prescription drug overdose on January 22, 2008.

Haumea cried for hours when Heath posthumously won the best supporting actor Oscar precisely thirteen months later.

Scorpion's Choice

by Leona R Wisoker

AROUND ME, MY BODY SLOWLY DIES. ONE *day, I will be freed, and all that is beautiful will be razed and shattered. This is the Way I have chosen: to be a part of that vast cycle of death and rebirth. Better philosophers than I have argued whether dark is necessary for light, demons necessary for angels, evil for good. I stopped caring many centuries ago. Now I simply accept: I am part of the destruction.*

This latest cycle, and my own imprisonment, began with a tattoo.

Jain was tall, and more lumpy than overweight; his flesh hung badly on crooked bones, and his green eyes were large and mismatched. *Masculine* was the default pronoun set used by most people, although in truth there were no visible distinctions either way, and Jain himself never said one way or another.

He worked at an unusual tattoo shop, *Rău-de-Bun*—informally, people called it "Bun's Place." It tended to attract peculiar clients. Many requested invisible tattoos, created with sesame oil or other unguents. At least once a week, he placed an ancient prayer on someone's tongue. He worked alone, although he did not own the shop. The owner was never seen by any client. Jain would not answer any questions on the matter, nor on what the name of the shop meant.

Clients ranged from rich to poor, mad to sane. There was no charge for the work. If they found their way to Jain's door, they were involved in Great Matters somewhere, and the tattoo was a vital part of their current mission. Jain never asked. It was why he was sent so much work. He did the work required with silent, unemotional dedication. He took no pictures of his work, showed no portfolio to the clients, rarely even drew preparatory sketches.

He never saw the same client twice; they simply never came back. A deposit appeared in his bank account every month that more than covered his meager living expenses. Jain did not wonder about this, did not concern himself with what happened beyond his door—and had, himself, no visible markings, piercings, or alterations at all. His body was littered with invisible spells and charms that he rarely thought about; they were just . . . there, and the memories of why he needed them were locked safely away.

He created the art that he loved more than anything else in the world. He ate indifferent meals, and he slept for unremarkable lengths of time, and that was enough. Until the day Johnny the Salesman came into *Rău-de-Bun* for the second time.

The tall Salesman, as before, was not alone. A bone-thin, twitchy girl with heroin rash across her face and inflamed marks along her arms lurked behind him, clearly reluctant to stand too close but just as afraid to step away from Johnny's implicit protection.

Jain studied the girl, trying to anticipate what she'd be asking for—or, more accurately, what Johnny would have primed her to ask for. Johnny stood still, four paces inside the doorway, looking around at the clean blue walls.

"You've redecorated," he observed. "Maybe *un-decorated* is a better term. What happened to all the art?"

"It was cluttering up the walls," Jain said.

In truth, he had come in one morning and found it all gone, with a note from the owner that it had been needed elsewhere. But that wasn't anything Johnny, or this odd girl, needed to know.

Johnny nodded and slanted a dry smirk at Jain, as though hearing what hadn't been said. "There's another mess coming up," he said. "Dana here is going to need some protection markings."

The girl shivered, hugging herself tightly, and stared at the bare walls as though remembering days trapped in an institution. Jain had seen that look before. It never boded well for the work coming out as intended.

"I have to run a blood test first," he said, directing the comment at the girl. "Shop policy." Because if things went bad and blood started flying everywhere, he damn well wanted to know what he'd just been splattered with. There were instant cures for almost everything—including some diseases normal doctors had never heard of before—in a special box under the counter, but most only worked within ten minutes of exposure.

"No," the girl said. Her voice was rough and shaky, but clear. "I ain't doing no fucking blood test. Fuck you. I'm out."

She turned and walked out of the shop. Johnny held out a hand a though to stop her, murmuring something as she went by; she ignored him and kept going.

The Salesman shrugged. "Well," he said, "I more or less expected that." He bowed and exited the premises.

Jain sighed, realizing that he was relieved. He'd had a lot of strange clients over the years, but this one felt like she might just have been more trouble than Jain could handle.

He crossed to the door and peered out through the smudged glass of the one-way window at the pair standing outside. The girl appeared to be yelling at Johnny, who listened without replying. After a few more moments, the girl turned and stormed off. Johnny made no effort to follow; he turned the other way, then paused, glanced at the shop window, and waved as though he saw Jain watching. Jain ducked back reflexively—the Salesman had a way of rattling him out of all sense—and when he looked again, Johnny was gone, the street empty.

Jain wiped sweat from the back of his neck and wondered, not for the first time, if he'd just had a visit from the shop's owner.

Johnny came back, without the girl, later that day. "There's a way around the blood tests," he said without preamble. "It requires you travel, though."

Jain shook his head at the last statement. "I don't travel," he said. "I don't leave this shop. Sorry, Johnny, you'll have to find someone else."

"You're the one I want. I'll make it worth your while."

"You can't," Jain said. "I have an agreement with the owner of this shop. I can't leave. I'm on call, every day, every hour. Breaching that even once—" He shook his head again, unwilling to offer more details. *Unable*, more accurately: there seemed to be a muddy spot where the information ought to be. He ignored the uneasy feeling, as he always did, and accepted the simple knowledge that the price was too high. "There's nothing you can offer to offset that price."

"I wouldn't be so sure," Johnny said with a dry smile. "I know the owner of the shop. I'll have a word with them. —*Would* you go, if given permission?"

Jain considered. He wasn't particularly surprised that Johnny knew the owner. The use of "them" instead of a gendered pronoun gave him pause; he'd often thought about doing that himself, but it seemed unnecessarily pretentious. Masculine default suited him well enough. "Yes," he said at last. "I want a guarantee of my personal safety if I'm going to forego the blood tests, though."

"Too broad," Johnny said. "Narrow it down. How about—I'll guarantee that any blood shed during the course of administering this particular tattoo will cause you no irreparable harm?"

"That's too narrow," Jain observed. "Take out *irreparable* and *this particular*."

Johnny frowned, apparently thinking that over, then shook his head. "There are variables I have no control over," he said. "I can't commit to that version. I can change the wording to 'any tattoo administered at this particular location'. That's as far as I can go. And before you say yea or nay, may I tell you the payment I had in mind?"

Jain pursed his lips and shrugged. "Go ahead," he said, "but I'm not optimistic that you'll have anything I'm all that interested in."

Johnny smiled and began speaking. Five minutes later, they shook hands on the deal and Jain went to pack for a trip to New York City.

This was when I became aware of, and intrigued by, the unrolling events. Johnny's offer hung dark and seductive, evoking a greed completely unrelated to material matters; his words hooked something deep inside Jain that cared little for physical comfort but fiercely craved connection with a very dangerous force.

What he offered did not even matter to me, at the time. It was the mere fact of the offer being voiced, and the intensity of Jain's reaction, that drew me to watch from that point on, and to look backwards to the chain of causation. I should have looked forward in preparation, as it turned out; my interest was my undoing.

Heat warped the air outside, air so thick that the diesel fumes seemed to glide in layers rather than flow in chaotic clouds. The shouts of street vendors were mired amidst the rumble of motors and the incessant, inevitable honking of impatient drivers. The air stank of stale pretzels, automobile exhaust, rotten pizza, and sweating humans.

Jain breathed it all in with increasing joy. He had stayed away from cities for many years because of this very reaction. It frightened him, how his chest loosened and his pulse sped up when faced with the morass of humanity. It should have repelled him, should have driven him away—his strict personal ethics abhorred violence of any sort, and cities were and always would be rife with an undercurrent of vileness. Instead—it excited him. Brought dark lights dancing at the edges of his vision. If he stayed too long, the protective glyphs on his skin would begin to itch, to burn—*to become visible*, said a small voice in the back of his mind, which he ignored. He would start seeing things—things that couldn't possibly be real.

Johnny had known. Somehow, Johnny had *known*.

The things you see in cities are real, he had said, *and I will tell you what they are.* He had said other words, but those had been the ones to catch Jain's interest. Jain hardly remembered anything else Johnny had said, in fact. He pressed through the crowd on the sidewalks, eager to get to the shop Johnny had described, heedless of his surroundings.

A hand shoved at him, a voice shouting "Hey, buddy, stop! Damn, you blind or something?"

Jain staggered sideways, refocusing on his surroundings, and recoiled a startled step; he'd almost walked across a body sprawled on the sidewalk. His grip tightened around the handle of his traveling kit.

"Sorry," he said, "Sorry—"

The man who'd yelled at him—a burly black man in a colorfully patterned shirt and cargo shorts—glared at him and offered a suggestion as to where Jain could stick his apology. "Fucking entitled white asshole," he finished.

Jain blinked, then shrugged and looked at the body again. It was a black woman, dressed in conservative business clothing; an odd outfit in this casually clad crowd. One of her sensible black pumps was missing. She lay face down, a trickle of blood making its way out from somewhere near her head. A briefcase rested near her feet: a sturdy black case with gold clasps and an odd symbol embossed in the top right corner of the visible side.

Jain looked up, looked around: there were no tall buildings near enough for the woman to have been thrown or jumped from. He glanced at the sullen crowd of onlookers: this felt like a wake, rather than an unexpected crime scene. No sirens sounded. Nobody was talking on their cell phones. The air hung thick and angry and silent. He finally asked, "What happened?"

The burly man shrugged, not taking his gaze from the body. "She got into something too big for her. Always told her she would. But it ain't your problem, is it? Go around, go away. We don't want you here."

"Has anyone called the—" Jain stopped at the look the big man shot him.

"You'd best not," the man said. "Now go away before something bad happens to you."

Jain felt an odd heat flush up his spine; his bewilderment edged towards anger. "Are you threatening me?"

"Stating a fact," the man said. "This is a bad time for outsiders to be parading around. Go back to the classy side of town."

"I have business here," Jain retorted.

The man rolled his eyes and waved a hand. "Sure, sure," he said. "Go on with your 'business', then, and get out of our neighborhood."

The heat climbed into Jain's face as he realized what the man was assuming. "I'm not here for drugs or whores," he said, caught between embarrassment and anger—*amusing*, the voice said in the back of his head, laughing. *This little creature is truly amusing. Thinking that I care about such things. . . .* Jain locked the voice back to silence and went on, "I'm a tattoo artist, and I'm on my way to meet a client."

The man's expression changed. "Tattoo artist?" he said. "You headed for Mom's Bane?"

"Yes."

The big man whistled sharply; heads turned. He waved over two equally large men, pointed to Jain, and said, "Get him to Mom's in one piece. Fast. And you—grab that briefcase up and take it along."

"What—" Jain began, glancing over his shoulder.

The man pointed at Jain, snapping his fingers impatiently. "Yeah, *you*, I'm talking to you, move it already! Get the case, get it back into Mom's, I sure as shit ain't touching it and the cops best not see it."

Jain edged forward, picked up the briefcase gingerly, and retreated in a near-leap. The two men—one dressed in shades of dun, the other in blue and black—grabbed his upper arms and hustled him through the crowd without a word. People moved out of the way.

"Ain't far," the man in dun clothing said once they were clear of the crowd. "You just keep up." He released Jain's arm, as did his companion. "We've got to watch for trouble. You keep moving."

"What's going on?" Jain said. Sweat slicked his grip on the two cases; he moved his fingers anxiously, trying to secure his hold on the increasingly slippery handles. A shivering excitement tickled down his spine, a dark glee completely at odds with his primary emotions.

"This is a bad time," the man in the blue shirt said. "We're all in danger. You shut up and keep moving." He had a gun in his hand now, a snub-nosed, nasty looking thing. Jain's pulse thudded harder, excitement flooding through his body.

"What's the danger?" he asked, tucking one case up under his other arm, wiping his hand dry, then retrieving the case. He repeated the sequence with the other case; juggling the motions made his step slow, but he managed to silence the slithering laughter in the back of his mind during the pause.

The man in dun snapped his fingers impatiently. "Shut up and keep moving." In his other hand, he held a length of metal that looked as though it had once been a bed frame strut. Silvery scratches formed a pattern too deliberate to be anything but writing, but they were trotting along too fast for Jain to make out further details.

Jain's arms itched, a burning sensation, like a tattoo needle drawing swiftly across his skin. He glanced at his forearms reflexively, but saw only his shirtsleeves; he'd chosen to wear a lightweight, long-sleeved shirt and black jeans, because even sweltering heat never bothered him. He could have worn a winter coat in this weather without trouble, but that would have drawn odd looks.

Now he wished he'd chosen a short sleeved shirt: his forearms bore powerful, invisible warding inscriptions from wrist to elbow. It was a bad sign that they were restless. He *remembered*, knowing it was a tiny fragment of a larger picture: he'd been told by the magician who'd set the marks in place that if he ever saw them emerge into visibility, he was in the presence of Death itself. Not that Death was necessarily coming for Jain, just then, the man had added, chuckling at his own words, but that it was nearby, and ready to take *someone*.

At least the sigils the magician had placed on the palms of his hands hadn't started burning. *That* would be the time to chuck everything and run. *How did I forget this?* Jain felt as though a gigantic maze were opening up in his head as he hurried through the overheated air; each step in the real world bumping him into the walls in his head, like a starving, blind mouse searching desperately for the treat it could sense near at hand.

He realized he was grinning—exhilarated—having more fun than he'd experienced in years. The men to either side of him exchanged grim headshakes, as though silently agreeing that Jain was a complete lunatic, and kept the pace too rapid for casual conversation.

The sun dimmed overhead. A hiss came from behind them. The men whirled, already aiming—already firing, before Jain could turn to see what was coming at them.

A scorpion, impossibly scaled—the size of a Clydesdale—rushed at them, tail raised high, almost mincing on its front legs in its eagerness to attack—

"Hey!" Fingers snapped by Jain's ear. "You gonna stand there staring at nothing? Come on, let's move!"

Jain blinked, stumbling sideways. The sun beat down, the air hung thick and still—no scorpion in sight, no gunfire taint in his nose. "What—" he said. "I thought—didn't you see?"

They scolded him back into motion, distinctly unhappy now, watching *him* as much as their surroundings, as though expecting him to attack them at any moment. The itching along his arms continued.

Black scorpion. That was an important symbol, one he used in many of his own custom designs. What did it mean that he was hallucinating a protective symbol trying to attack him?

Worlds overlap sometimes, the magician who'd placed the markings along Jain's arms and hands had said. *You may well be alive for one such event, if you are very fortunate.*

How had he forgotten that conversation? And—what had *happened* to that man? He remembered the nausea, the burring sound, the acidic pain of consecrated oils drilling into his skin; remembered the man's strange smile, his pale face wrinkled in concentration around that smirk. He'd muttered under his breath the entire time in a language Jain couldn't begin to comprehend. What had happened after he'd finished his work?

And why was he remembering this *now*, of all times? Memory gaps didn't matter. He had a client waiting, a promise to fill, a long delayed answer to hear.

They hurried past a line of parked cars. Jain glanced at the license plates as he went by—vanity plates always amused him—and stopped walking so abruptly he almost fell over. From the leftmost to rightmost car, the plates read:

TIME2 / RUN BOY / BLK SCRP / DKSHERE

The men began to curse at him; looked at the plates and fell silent, staring. "So you see it," Jain said hoarsely. "'Time to run boy, black scorpion, DK is here.'" What did DK stand for? *Demon king* came to mind; he dismissed that as absurd.

"That's not what they say," the man in dun said. "You're mad, if that's what you see."

"What do you see?" Jain asked.

Pointing at each car in turn, the man said, "Turn around, time's up, you're dead."

"Aw, hell no," the other man said. "You're both nuts. They're just a bunch of vanity plates about running. A bunch of exercise nuts parked here, that's all."

"There ain't no gym or running path near here," the man in dun said, looking around uneasily. "And why are we all seeing different plates?"

"Witchery," Jain muttered. He unbuttoned the cuffs of his sleeves and shoved the fabric back. A dark tracery of lines crisscrossed his forearms from inner wrist to the bend of each elbow: not the pattern he'd expected to see. It didn't even look like a design at all, more like a random scattering of markings without any real connection. A hot thrill raced through his body, and he realized that once more, he was grinning, baring his teeth like an animal in fact; on the verge of howling with laughter. He gagged briefly, shoving that bizarre ferocity back under control, and shivered as the heat faded to a moment of arctic chill.

The men looked at him and at one another with clear unease. "Fuck this," the man in dun said. "I'm gone." He turned and took two long-legged steps, clearly accelerating to run: as his foot came down again, something dark writhed *through* him, like a thick tentacle only partially solid. He screamed—a hoarse, choked sound—then fell apart as though his body had been passed through a gigantic, warped egg-slicer. His gun rattled to the ground.

Blood soaked the street, the nearest wall, splattered Jain's face. He breathed in the sweet-rot stench and couldn't help comparing the marks on his arms to the segments of corpse; they matched far too closely for coincidence.

His remaining escort retched, then grabbed Jain's elbow and hauled him roughly back into motion. "*Fucking run, asshole*," he said. "Up ahead, turn right, it's at the end of that alley. I'm on your back. *Go*."

Jain ran, very aware that his heart was pounding from excitement, not fear; swiping at the blood on his face—and occasionally, when his companion wasn't looking, licking the red from his hand.

Seeing him run was amusing. He ran with no grace and less comprehension of what had just happened. I found myself drawn into his story, into his moment of horrified shame—thinking he'd been the cause of the man's death, wondering about children and spouse and siblings—all irrelevant items, but powerful to one so very alone as Jain had always thought himself to be.

He didn't know, at that point, how many of his memories the "magician" had taken from him in exchange for protection. He believed many lies regarding the marks he carried on his body. He couldn't spot the holes in his own reasoning. I found him utterly fascinating.

It was far too late when I realized that very fascination was the product of a wonderfully crafted trap, set just for me.

Mom's Bane lay at the end of a dingy alley, blank walls to all sides as though the buildings themselves had turned away from seeing the shop. A neon sign glowed above the blue door, a slice of unnatural color in a gray world. The heat seemed to have been channeled into this narrow corridor, although the sun was blocked by the tall buildings; Jain and his remaining guard ran through a sauna and arrived at the door dripping with fear and heat sweat alike.

Johnny waited before the door, apparently unaffected by the ambient temperature: he still wore his signature long trenchcoat and hat, and his expression was grim. "Jain, wait here. You—go inside," he said, indicating Jain's escort. The man complied without hesitation, almost slamming through the door in his eagerness to reach shelter.

Jain stood, sweating, out of breath, watching the alley suspiciously. There had been no further attacks on their way here, but the marks on his arms hadn't faded, and he had a gritty, uneasy taste in the back of his mouth. "I'm here," he said, sullen. "Now what?"

"We're waiting on the client." Johnny looked at the case in Jain's hand. "Where did you get that?" Jain explained; Johnny's expression went from grim to sad. "Damn," he said. "If the lawyer's dead—put that on the ground. Face it away from you. Now—carefully, keep your hands as clear of it as you can—open it."

Jain set his traveling kit down on the ground, set the briefcase down some distance away, then popped the latches—it wasn't locked, which seemed odd. He jumped back as a mist rose into the air. His forearms burned, his hands began to itch; Johnny put a hand on his shoulder and drew him away from the case, and the discomfort faded.

"Damn," Johnny said again, watching the pale fog drift up and disperse into the air overhead. "There goes the contract. That means you're out a client, Jain. Sorry. She's dead." He sighed. "I'll still pay you what I agreed on, of course. It's not your fault this fell through."

Jain prodded the briefcase with one foot. It fell closed, latches rattling. "I'm beginning to think I should have worded our agreement differently," he said. "Almost getting killed on the way here wasn't part of my expectations, Johnny."

"You weren't in danger," Johnny said. He pointed at Jain's forearms. "Those are what drew the attention of the dark."

"The dark? Dark what?"

"Just the dark," Johnny said. "Saying its name out loud would draw it here again." He looked down the alley, then over his shoulder at the blue door. "I promised you answers. They won't make you happy, Jain. The truth never does."

"Can we go inside?" Jain said, scanning their surroundings nervously despite Johnny's assurance.

"Not yet," Johnny said. "You liked seeing that man die."

"—what?" Jain turned to face the tall Salesman, abruptly angry and defensive.

Johnny's chin dipped closer to his chest, his eyes half-closing. "It's those," he said, pointing at Jain's arms again. "You were tricked, a long time ago. Those aren't protective marks. They're a cage. They're keeping you in human form and holding you to human abilities. You're not human. You're a demon waiting for the Sha'Daa to free you."

Jain goggled at the Salesman. "You *what?*" he said; realized that was a completely incoherent response and tried again. "I what?" That was no better. He shook his head and finally managed, "You're *nuts.*"

Woven throughout his stammering, the dark glee rose, twisting his mouth into a snarl—or a smile—he couldn't tell. He turned his back on Johnny, breathing hard. *Sha'Daa.* It was an alien phrase, and yet, it wasn't: that one word had summoned an array of savage emotions that battered the inside of his skull like a beast fighting to escape. Some part of him knew what it meant. Some part of him *wanted* the violence he'd avoided for so long.

How long? The thought ghosted through his mind, then faded under Johnny's next words.

"You can break the cage and escape," Johnny said, inexorable. "You can join the dark out there." He pointed to the mouth of the alley. "There's no real reason you shouldn't, actually. I can't stop you. I won't even try. All you have to do is rip the marked skin from your arms and hands with your teeth. And— well, there is a binding spell on your tongue, I believe, so you'd have to flay that off with a special knife. That part might be unpleasant."

Jain looked down at his forearms. The lines had moved into a different configuration, taken on a distinctly reddish tint—now they looked like teeth, stained with blood. *I'm a demon.* Impossible. *Absurd.* And yet. . . .

Apparently seeing Jain's bewildered doubt, Johnny said, "You've been placing spells on humans to protect them from your own kind. You've been doing that for about two hundred years now."

Jain startled round, staring at the man. "I'm not even thirty!"

Johnny crossed his arms and met Jain's glare without flinching. "You're a lot older than that. You've served many masters. The most recent one put that cage on you, forcing you into human form and taking away your memories, because technology is making it harder to hide demons these days."

"Why are you telling me this!" Jain took a step forward, his hands clenched, half-raising one fist as though to strike the Salesman. A sense of hot betrayal stung his eyes. The magician had been a *friend*, by his memories— but Johnny didn't lie. He *couldn't.* Jain was *positive* on that point, although he couldn't have said why.

"Because it's the time of the Sha'Daa," Johnny said. "And I made a promise a long time ago that I'd give you this chance. I can give you your memories back. All of them. You'll be your true self again, and at that point you'll be able to set yourself free with ease."

"What do you want in trade?" Jain asked, sullen anger rounding his shoulders. "I know you wouldn't do this for free."

Johnny smiled. "You'll need that kit," he said, pointing at the case Jain had set down nearby, then motioned to the blue door. "Time to introduce you to Mom's Bane."

Of course I heard that conversation. Of course Johnny knew I'd heard it, although at the time that simply didn't occur to me. I thought he was rendered careless by his proximity to the legendary shop, thought he—he!—had made a mistake at last. I saw a traitor unmasked, and rage swept through me, further distorting my thinking. The creature I'd seen as human simpleton was the traitor I'd been searching for. I'd known that there had to be a demon working against me and mine—so many inexplicable defeats, so many unbreakable charms, all woven with far too much knowledge of demonic vulnerabilities.

Those spells could not have been created under duress. Jain had, for whatever insane reason, wanted *to defy his kin and deny us our rightful prey. I would remove his cage markings myself and devour him in retribution for his many offenses.*

They went into Mom's Bane, and I laughed at their presumption of safety. There is no place safe against me. I am destruction, darkness, and death incarnate, and no spell or barrier can keep me out forever.

As it turned out, I shouldn't have been thinking in terms of being kept out…

Heat prickled over Jain's entire body as he stepped into the tattoo shop, a sense of being swallowed by a gigantic beast. He paused, half-turned to leave again—a reflexive motion, a primal urge to flee—then caught himself and took three more deliberate steps into the parlor.

It was unremarkable, in layout and furnishings: old fashioned dentist chairs, clean wood floors, high ceiling, standard accessories and reference books arranged in the usual places. Three massage tables made Jain tilt his head in appreciation; he'd never thought about offering that option, but it *would* make back pieces much more comfortable for the client than his current setup.

Not that I'll be giving more tattoos, if Johnny's telling the truth—I'll be . . . free? He blinked as his vision went oddly blurry for a moment, then cleared. *Does the owner of my shop know? Is that why I've never met—them?*

The room was filled, every table, every chair occupied; Jain scanned the tattoos in progress, curious. There appeared to be no common thread; designs ranged from cartoonishly absurd to ornate. One gaunt young woman was having a grossly overweight, garishly colored version of Petunia Pig inked on her right bicep, while on one of the massage tables an intricate Japanese pattern was in progress.

Jain's eyes widened as he realized the one thing they all *did* have in common: not a single artist wore gloves or masks; not a single bottle of sterilizing solution was in evidence. He took a horrified step back. "What is this?" he exclaimed. "Are you all mad?"

"There's no danger of infection," a voice said from behind him.

Jain whirled, jumping back a step at the apparition before him: enormous black circles tattooed around her eyes, nose and cheeks inked with gashes—it took him a moment to recognize it as a sugar-skull pattern. He'd done one or two of those himself, but never as a literal full-face design—and never in such a stark, monochrome black.

She grinned at him, her black eyes lit with mischief. "Oops. Did I scare you?" Her accent was definitely Hawai'ian, as was her straight dark hair and facial bone structure. He couldn't speak to her skin tone, because every bit of visible skin was heavily inked.

He realized he was staring at her like a rabbit faced with a cobra; shook himself out of his paralysis and bowed to her. "I'm assuming you are the owner of this shop," he said.

"Yes." She looked at Johnny. "The girl isn't here yet."

"She's dead," Johnny said regretfully. "I had to go for the secondary deal."

"That's a shame," the woman said. She returned her attention to Jain. "My name is Haumea," she told him. "You would be Jain, yes? What's your preferred address, Jain?"

"I—what?"

"Male, female, neuter," she said. "How do you wish to be addressed?"

"Ah. Well—male, I suppose. I never really cared about that."

"Understandable, in your case," Haumea said.

Jain blinked, glanced at Johnny. "She—she knows about—?"

"What you are? Of course I do," Haumea said, laughing at him. "If I hadn't given permission for you to enter my shop, you'd have been destroyed on the threshold."

"Oh." Jain swallowed hard, looking up and around uneasily.

"You're safe, don't worry," Haumea said. "You're under my protection, and Johnny's, at the moment. Until you revert to your true form, at least; then I'll regretfully have to bounce your ass out of my shop."

"Give her your kit," Johnny said. "You won't need it any longer."

Jain's grip on the case handle tightened involuntarily. "What—why?"

"You won't be giving any more tattoos," Haumea said, her skull-stare sympathetic. Her expression felt like having Death incarnate pat his shoulder in pity. "It's the Sha'Daa, Jain. Once you rejoin the ranks of your fellows, your days of creating ink art are over." She paused. "I'll admit it's a shame," she added. "I've seen your work often. You're extremely talented. I'd thought about trying to hire you on here, in fact, but your—particular situation—made that inadvisable."

He opened his mouth, shut it again, at a complete loss for words. He'd been working as a tattoo artist for so long, the concept of not doing that any longer felt—*horrid*, in a word. Nausea ran through his stomach, and he put a hand to his mouth reflexively.

He looked around the room, taking in the tables, the chairs, the designs; smelling the acrid ink, the sweetness of incense drifting from somewhere nearby; hearing the humming of ink being driven into skin by automated needles. Two of the artists were using hand-needle techniques; their clients sat in stolid silence, wincing occasionally. He'd always preferred working in a quiet area, a room by himself—

Never give another tattoo. He swallowed hard, his eyes blurry again, and began to hand Haumea the case; then pulled it back before she could take it. "No," he said. "No. I can't do that. I can't give this up. Please. Johnny—help me." He turned to the tall Salesman pleadingly. "I don't want to be a demon again if it means I lose the ability to create art."

"You'll be able to," Haumea said quietly. "You just won't *want* to."

Jain bent his head, finally admitting that the blurriness was tears. "No," he said again. "I don't want to go back to not seeing—not caring—no. I can't do that."

Someone cried out across the room; someone else swore; as Jain looked up, startled, a flickering black line snaked through the air towards him. Blood pooled around segmented body parts, scattered across chair and floor.

Haumea shouted something in another language, her voice transformed to a booming roar. Jain stumbled back a step, putting his hands over his ears as his very brain seemed to rattle in his skull from the percussive sound. The black line fell to the floor as though slapped down by an unseen, crushing force; as it hit the puddles of blood, red splattered in all directions, causing more yells to erupt from clients and artists like. The black line stopped moving; everyone else, by that point, had scrambled clear and stood up against the walls of the shop, staring, glaring, trembling with shocked reaction.

The shop owner's gleamed with fury, all kindness gone; she could have been an aspect of some vengeful goddess. Jain flinched as she looked his way, half-raising a hand in useless ward. "You've brought death into my shop," she said. It took a moment for Jain to realize that comment hadn't been directed at him; Johnny bent his head in solemn apology.

"What?" Jain said, confused again—distracted, a moment later, by the scent of blood and pain. He looked at the blood dripping from the chair and fought the urge to go run a finger through it—a hand—to *lick it from his fingers*—his hands began to itch, to burn—

The sugar-skull visage, still glowing with volcanic rage, loomed before him as Haumea stepped into his line of sight. "The spell won't last long," she said. "Time to choose, Jain. If the dark gets you, you'll be ripped out of human form and become a demon again whether you want to or not. If you want to stay human, you have to bind it." She held up a large ball—almost the size of a basketball, but bound in smooth white leather. "Work fast," she told him, and tossed him the ball.

He caught it with one hand, cradling it against his chest to avoid dropping it; the shiver in his fingers told him the leather came from a sentient creature—probably human. He took one last look at Haumea's uncompromising glare, then scanned the black line on the floor, tracing it back to the point of entry; as he'd expected, the line trailed upward to a ceiling vent, wavering slightly as though the creature were fighting against the restraints.

Jain picked his way around the blood—not easy, as it was almost directly beneath the vent—and knelt, setting his case down. He opened it with one hand; cradled the ball in the crook of his right arm and began assembling his tools. As always, a floating calm swept over him, a joyous detachment from anything other than selecting the right needle, the right ink, the right design. This—this was worth living for. The pain in his hands increased, but somehow it didn't matter. He could ignore it. His hands remained steady.

Once he had his tools in place and the right design in mind—with his years, no, *centuries* of practice, it didn't take long at all—he carefully tucked the ball up beneath the intersection of line and floor. The ribbon of blackness gave, entirely tangible and buzzing with rage, draping across the rounded surface; he drew a breath and began.

One short line of red stitched across, then a longer line laid along the axis of the dark, intersecting the first in a crimson cross shape: the fastest and best design for binding an uncooperative subject. He could feel the vibration of the creature as it strained to escape. If it had chosen a form that produced sound, he suspected the screaming would have been deafening at best.

He set several more cross lines in place, moving the ball slightly between each one. When he finished the initial pass, the white leather was almost obscured with spiraling black lines, and the entire ball was trembling, rocking back and forth minutely on the floor. Very little darkness remained on the floor, and none now trailed from the vent above.

Jain changed ink and began the design: a distorted double sugar skull pattern, adorned with tiny black scorpions in place of flowers. Haumea, watching with her arms folded, gave an approving huff as the artwork formed. "Imitation," she said. Jain smiled and made no reply.

He drew open eyes on one side of the ball, closed eyes on the other; on the first, the mouth was shut, on the second, the mouth gaped open. The deliberate reversion touched every element of the design, from the ruined nose to the perfect, the lack of eyebrows to the bushy. Where one design had blue, the opposite had red; where there was black, the other design used a special, magic-imbued white ink—a *difficult* ink to work with, and one he wouldn't have used on any human being because of the toxins involved.

Last of all, at the top and base of the ball he placed the strongest binding symbols he knew of. Then he sat back, breathing deeply. *I am a servant, a vessel, a conduit; let the will of the divine move through me and place a seal of perfection upon this work.* It was the final prayer he recited to himself at the end of every piece. Sometimes he'd felt an internal warmth; sometimes, he'd seen a faint wave of color wash across the design and disappear. Most of the time, nothing happened.

This time, half the room exploded around him.

Bound into utter humiliation, my prison sealed by heartfelt prayer—holy words, said with true humility, from the mouth of a demon have unstoppable force—I coil, now, into endless Ouroboros loops, the darkness around me not of my own making. I have no idea what time has passed: hours, moments, years, centuries, I have no gauge, no fixed point from which to measure. I writhe in fury, my bitterness apocalyptic, and write this chronicle on the inside of my prison, in ancient sigils that burn wih brief light before disappearing and leaving me alone once more.

The world around me is scorched and raw—it must *be so, it is the only thought keeping me from utter madness. My brethren* must *have won the Sha'Daa, and they* will *find me, and they will free me. If not—if not—well, I am darkness incarnate. I will endure as my perishable prison disintegrates around me. I will endure. I will emerge, and all that is green and beautiful will be destroyed.*

I accept my place in the universe. I am destruction. I am patience itself, for destruction has no end and no beginning. My place is to wait, for as long as necessary; there will be a chance. There will be a time for me to emerge and wreak my fury upon the world once more, and next time I will not be so easily trapped.

The room wavered back into focus, streaks of red and iridescent white fading from Jain's vision little by little. The ringing in his ears took longer to ease, and every blink brought with it a nauseating wave of dizziness. Closing his eyes made it worse. He tried to breathe without gasping, felt his face with both hands to make sure it was still intact: the familiar lumps and rough patches reassured him that whatever had just happened, at least his face was no uglier than it had been.

As his hearing returned, a familiar, erratic buzzing sound replaced the tinnitus. Someone was creating a tattoo nearby, but there was no smell of ink being deployed. Inhaling carefully through his nose, he picked up a mixture of sesame and truffle oil: now *that* was a potent spell being inscribed.

He realized he was sitting in a sturdy chair backwards, shirt off. A tickling line swirled steadily across his back, looping like writing. The buzzing came from *behind* him. The tattoo was being placed on *his* body. He held still, knowing better than to risk disrupting a magical design, but said, "What are you doing?"

"Helping you," the artist said from behind him. "Hold still."

"I will. You're placing a spell on me without my consent, you know. That's not real safe, friend."

The swirling burr continued moving, unhesitating. "Safe is relative, at this point," the artist said. "Almost done. Are you going to turn a curse on me for this?"

"Depends on what the spell does," Jain said, closing his eyes cautiously, and was relieved to find no dizziness or nausea remained.

"Gives you extra protection," the artist said. "And control. —There." The buzzing stopped. "All done." A cloth patted across his back, blotting up oil and blood; a cold spritz of something wet—water mixed with an astringent, by the burning—came next, then another round of patting his skin dry. "You can get up now. Mind you go slow, in case you get dizzy."

"Thank you," Jain said with grave dignity, gripping the chair for balance as he rose to his feet. He turned to face the artist, who turned out to be a lanky person of indeterminate gender—long pale hair, thick pastel makeup, coarse features, large ear plugs and a jewel-encrusted nose ring, coupled with gender-neutral clothing and a voice that could have been either male or female. "Control over what? And protection *from* what?"

"It's the Sha'Daa," the artist said. He—*ze*, Jain corrected himself—began cleaning his tools and putting them back into the box. Jain took another, startled look at the case: it was *his* case, *his* tools the artist had used. He stiffened, irritated at the discourtesy, but before he could say anything the artist commented, "Sorry about using your stuff, man, but it made the spell more effective. I don't like using someone else's equipment, and I'd get rag mad if someone touched mine, so I get it if you're pissed." Ze looked up at Jain, shrugging, as ze closed the case.

"It's done, I suppose," Jain said with less than perfect courtesy, then looked around the room. They weren't in the main room of Mom's Bane; the walls here were a pale, unadorned blue, and the room measured maybe ten paces from one wall to another. The chair Jain had sat on was the only one in evidence, and the small table his kit rested on the only other furniture. One door led from the room, a softly glowing yellow rectangle with no evident knob or hinges. "Where are we?"

"Still in Mom's Bane," the artist said. "This is one of the special rooms. There was a lot of clean up to do out there, you know, and the shop had to move while that was getting sorted out, so Haumea told me to take you in here while I worked."

"...Move?"

"Yeah, it's the Sha'Daa, man. Haumea's trying to give as much help as she can. The shop's moving every twelve hours. You started out in Harlem, but you're in—uhm—" Ze paused and counted on zir fingers briefly, then said, "Taipei, should be."

"I'm *what*? Where? *What*?" Jain goggled at the artist.

"I don't make the rules, man. I just do the work I'm given. Speaking of which, you want to know about that spell, or what? You kind of ought to, I think."

"...Yes?" Jain said. It came out as a question, to his annoyance; he pulled his face into a more severe expression, trying to regain internal balance by displaying external ferocity. The artist seemed unfazed.

"Well, you're a demon, right?" ze said. "And you had those cage markers on you that kept you human against your will, right? And they were messing with your memories and stuff. So since you proved yourself—well, you about wrecked the shop doing it, but still, Haumea isn't *too* mad about that, it does happen, you know—anyway, you showed that you're not on *their* side in the

Sha'Daa. You're with us, with humans, with saving the world from oblitera-
tion. Right?"

Jain blinked hard, opened his mouth, shut it again, aware that he was
expressing a tired cliché with those motions and not caring. "...Right?" He
tried not to lilt it into a question this time, and completely failed.

"So the cage stuff is overwritten now. I did your arms earlier, while
you were unconscious," the artist said, pointing at Jain's forearms. "And your
hands, and your tongue. Those are all the ones I saw. Did I miss any?"

Jain turned his hands palm up, staring. A scarcely visible reddening of
the skin around a faint, looping silver line showed the placement of the new
spell. He moved his tongue gingerly; it was sore as well, but not nearly as much
as it should have been. "Over*written*?" he asked in utter disbelief. "You can't
just overwrite like that—it's not *possible*. I shouldn't even be able to *talk* if you
did my tongue!"

"It's a specialized process," the artist said, smirking a bit. "Uses a blessed
silver solution, holy fae blood, sanctified this and that. Don't need to go as
deep as most tats. It's my own specialty. I developed it, see, and not many
people have a delicate enough touch to learn it properly. I figure I could probably teach you, if you ever want to know. Assuming we all survive the coming
days, anyway."

"The what who how," Jain said, unable to think of anything more coherent
than that.

The artist laughed. "You're not caged anymore, is the point of the spell,"
ze said. "You're not blocked from your memories. It's all under your control
now. You're on your own. Nobody's forcing you to do or be anything at all.
If you want to change to a demon form, anytime, you can, then come back
to human form whenever. You want to remember stuff, you can remember
anything you want. But it's all in your past, you know? That's the protection
part. Remembering that stuff won't drag you down. That ugly stuff isn't *you*
anymore. It's a pretty big deal spell." Ze grinned, zis dark eyes glowing with
pride. "Took me a good long time to make that one work, tell you what. Got
me this job here at Mom's, in fact, when I showed Haumea this spell."

Jain gripped the back of the chair, blinking hard, trying to sort out the
sense in the flow of words. "I'm . . . I'm free?" he said, his voice hoarser than
he'd expected.

"Yep. Now, hey look, I don't want to be pushy here, man, but I have other
people to work on? It's the Sha'Daa. Every minute counts. There's a line like
you wouldn't *believe* out there."

"The Sha'Daa? Can *someone* please tell me what the—" Jain stopped as
memory broke free, rising into a 3-D, immersive wave of horror that swamped

him into silence. "Oh, god," he whispered, shutting his eyes as the carnage played out in his mind. "Oh . . . god. . . ."

He remembered:

He'd wanted to bring about the Sha'Daa once, a long time ago; had crossed the barrier with the help of ignorant, careless mortals, who'd then been quickly and easily ripped apart by way of reward. Had worked towards weakening the veil between worlds until a more savvy magician caught him in chains much harder to escape. But rather than forcing his captive to perform menial duties or wreak havoc on enemies, the magician had begun *teaching* Jain . . . patiently engaging in endless, frustrating conversations that began and ended with Jain screaming threats of death and retribution, week after month after year. Finally exhausted and bored enough to actually listen, Jain had begun learning. Reluctantly, argumentatively, resisting every step of the way . . . but *learning*, all the same, about human complexity. Good and bad, wicked and pure, the stories the magician told captured Jain's attention, interest, and, eventually, sympathy.

In under twenty human years, he'd begun his first attempts at art: clumsy, awkward sketches that slowly became more clever. At least one of his early works, in fact, now hung in a museum somewhere, credited to a human artist. He didn't mind.

His magician master had passed control of Jain to his best apprentice, and that apprentice, in time, to his apprentice, and so on throughout the centuries. On discovering tattoo art, Jain had been frustrated by the limitations imposed by his clawed hands; attempts to devise tools that worked for his particular grip had been less than ideal.

His master at the time, one of the most talented magicians Jain had ever worked with—better, even than his first master—had agreed to bind Jain into human form—

"Hey," the artist said, a bit impatiently now. "Like I said, there's a line. Do you mind doing the whole staring into space and drooling thing out in the main room, out of the way somewhere?"

Jain startled, then wiped at his mouth reflexively; he *had* been drooling. How embarrassing. He felt himself flush. "Thank you," he said. "I was just remembering."

"Yeah, I get that," the artist said. Ze pointed at the glowing door. "Just walk on through, man. You'll be back in the main room."

Jain picked up his case, took a step toward the door, then hesitated, half-turning to look at the artist. "Taipei?" he said. "Did you say I'm going to be in *Tapei*?"

"*Yes*," ze said, definitely impatient now. "Haumea has a ticket or something to get you back to your home, go talk to her. She's also got a clean shirt for you, yours was fucked up by the mess you left. Come on, man, *move* already, huh?"

Jain looked down at his black pants, noting the stiffened patches where blood had dried into the thick fabric. A few small tears littered one leg, but nothing so noticeable as to draw attention from passerby. "Okay," he said. "Hey—thanks. Uhm—I don't know your name—"

"You're welcome. Don't need to know my name, you just seriously need to *go*, man," the artist said, snapped his fingers, and pointed at the door commandingly.

"Okay, okay," Jain said, turning away, and walked through the door without looking back.

The main room looked almost the same as it had been on his initial arrival; one chair was missing, and a heavy scorch mark ran along the floor where he'd knelt to administer the tattoo. Every chair and table was filled, and two dozen people lounged against the walls, obviously waiting their turns with varying degrees of impatience and excitement. Johnny was nowhere in sight; neither was the man in the blue shirt who'd escorted him to Mom's Bane.

Haumea appeared at his elbow a moment later and handed him a loose gray shirt and a manila envelope. "Welcome to Tapei," she said. "I'm a bit busy just now, so I can't talk. There's a plane ticket and a passport in that envelope, and enough money to compensate you for various travel expenses. Johnny left you a letter, that's in there too." She paused, studying him critically for a moment, then shook her head. "If we survive this Sha'Daa, keep in touch, Jain. I may send work your way now and again."

He trapped the envelope between his knees and pulled on the shirt, then retrieved the envelope. "I'm sorry about the damages, Haumea," he said awkwardly. "I didn't intend—"

She waved a hand, dismissing the matter. "I've handled worse over the years," she said. "If I'd known you had a habit of *praying* after setting a design, I'd have put you into a secure room from the start." She grinned at him, a thoroughly unsettling expression on that sugar-skull face. "Go home, Jain," she told him. "You've done your part. Go rest, and enjoy what's left of the world in case it ends tomorrow."

He began to bow, then stopped, struck by a sudden question. "What happened to the—the ball?" he asked.

Haumea's smile widened. "It's somewhere very, very safe," she said. "Whatever happens in the next two days, that's one piece of hell that's staying locked up for eternity."

Jain couldn't help returning that wicked smile. "Good," he said. "Thank you, and—good luck, I suppose."

They exchanged grave bows. Jain took one last look around the busy shop, then walked out of Mom's Bane and into the busy streets of a foreign city.

The envelope held a mixture of currency, both U.S. and NT$; Jain bought a few touristy trinkets, sought out a few hard to source spell and ink ingredients in back alley shops, and made it onto the plane with moments to spare.

Settled comfortably into a first-class seat, sipping a surprisingly fine whiskey, he opened Johnny's letter; that envelope contained two pieces of paper. He read the letter. Read it again. Tossed back the remainder of his whiskey and read it a third time. Called for another drink—water, this time— and drank that down too. A fourth reading, and a look at the second paper, convinced him that he hadn't been imagining or misunderstanding:

> *Jain:*
>
> *Congratulations on earning your freedom. You've done more to save humanity, over the years, than anyone expected. This last effort was exceptional, and deserves a matching reward. Attached please find a copy of the title to Rău-de-Bun. It's all yours now. The bank account information and assorted other items you'll need to know about are in the safe at the shop.*
>
> *You're welcome to change the name of the shop, if you like; but by now you probably remember what it means, and understand why it was chosen. I do hope you keep it. I always found it very clever, myself, but perhaps I'm a bit egotistical in that regard, as I was the one to suggest the name.*
>
> *I never owned Rău-de-Bun, by the way; I know you've been wondering that for years now. I'm also not at liberty to disclose who the previous owner was. When they want you to know, they'll approach you themselves. Until then, I can only say that they are very proud of you, and completely trust you to continue the legacy they began with Rău-de-Bun.*
>
> *I hope that humanity wins this round of the Sha'Daa. If so, you'll no doubt see me again one day, as every victory is only a stalling tactic, not a comprehensive success. There will always be work to do, and you will always have clients coming to your chair.*
>
> *If humanity loses...well...it was a true pleasure working with you, and I suggest you kill yourself quickly, before your enraged former kin can get a hold of you.*
>
> *Sincerely,*
> *Johnny*

Jain folded the two pages—Johnny's letter and the title to the shop—with surprisingly steady hands and stowed them in his carry-on pack. The whiskey seemed to have had no effect at all, which didn't surprise him; he rarely got the least bit tipsy even on massive amounts of alcohol. Now he understood why: demons were immune to most human poisons.

He ordered another whiskey and sipped it slowly, staring out at the clouds and quietly appreciating the irony of his shop's name; he would keep it, he decided. It suited very well indeed.

Răderde-Bun, in Romanian, meant *Evil to Good*.

He could live with that. He could, most definitely, live with that.

INTERLUDE 11

Bodysuits and Canvasses

AN EXPLOSION OUTSIDE ROCKED MOM'S Bane harder then ever. Chunks of plaster fell from the ceiling and white dust kicked up everywhere, causing the dozens of artists and clients who had fallen to the floor to start coughing.

The overhead lights flickered several times before coming back on.

"It's okay," Haumea shouted, "that backup generator I installed last month just kicked on. We're tied to enough fuel to give us electricity for a full twenty-four hours. And just in case any of you idiots was having second thoughts, nobody, and I mean nobody leaves here without at least two wards inked on their skin. All bets are off for anyone suicidal enough to try this exit without real protection."

Stress fractures now ran across all the brick walls and tile floors.

"And if I'm not mistaken," Johnny said, having suddenly appeared out of nowhere, "the plumbing still works, probably the biggest miracle of all."

"Did anyone ever tell you that you're a regular Jonah," Haumea spat, "a real harbinger of doom?"

"Now, now," Johnny smiled, "don't shoot the messenger, sweetheart."

Johnny glanced toward the front door, two feet thick oak that now had a spider web of cracks running across the inner surface.

"First Moscow, then Taipei, next New Orleans, and now Dublin," Johnny said, "that's four football field size craters and several thousand lost human lives we're pretty much responsible for. Looks like your shop is anchored to Harlem for the next ten hours. It won't take the forces of evil too long to triangulate on this current location, hobbled as Mom's Bane is."

"Did you bring any good news?" Haumea shouted.

"Why yes," Johnny smiled, "with fourteen hours to go the Earth is holding strong and fighting the good fight. The planet has still got a million to one odds against actually surviving this madness, but if our little plan can be put into effect, they could increase to, oh, I dunno, ten to one odds?"

"I need to pull more clients into the quick-rooms," Haumea said in mild panic.

"And I've got a very important friend in a wheelchair to go pick up," Johnny smiled, "I'll be back in two shakes of a lamb's tail. And if you don't mind, maybe run a broom and mop across the floor a couple of times? This place is a mess."

Before Haumea could really let loose with a barrage, Johnny immediately disappeared, "Damn that man."

"Trouble in paradise, sugar-baby?" a deep female voice out loud, "Let me know if you need any advice."

Haumea glanced to her left where her apprentice, Maddy, was finishing up a traditional lighthouse on the right forearm of a recent Oxford grad who was dressed to the nines in a Brioni Vanquish II suit, the jacket slung across his knees, and the sleeve of his white silk shirt rolled up past the elbow. He was grimacing in pain and squeezing a green pussyball with his left hand as if his life depended on it.

The tattoo artist Maddy, somewhere in her thirties, was tall and shapely in that genetic lottery winner kind of way, with stunning eyes, high cheekbones, and a head of light brown hair that hung down to her shoulders. She was only wearing white sneakers, white gym shorts, and a khaki wife-beater, which allowed her to display a gorgeous Japanese style body suit from the neck down.

"I think I already know your opinion on assholes who tattoo a woman's entire body," Haumea said.

Maddy replied with a dark, dry chuckle and started swabbing her client's tat with Aquaphor in preparation for bandaging.

"Well that was different," Maddy smirked, "rumor has it you were a quite the willing recipient of that one's… ummm… attentions."

"Bitch," Haumea said.

"Whore," Maddy laughed.

"It still surprises me that you of all people," Haumea said, "decided to take up the craft."

Maddy finished with the clear bandage wrap, slapped her client on the ass and sent him on his way. He dropped the tennis ball he'd been cradling and made his way to the exit.

"The magazine covers weren't interested in me anymore," Maddy sighed, "not with this ornamentation, and, well, once I put all that madness behind me, looking in the mirror, I really grew to appreciate the art of it."

"One woman's enslavement nightmare," Haumea said.

"Another's career change," Maddy replied with a cackle.

"Listen, Maddy," Haumea said, "after my next client or two, I'm going to need a big favor, from both you and your rock-steady hands."

"What's up?"

"You any good at shaving heads?" Haumea asked.

"Oh, sugar-baby," Maddy said, "say it ain't so."

Haumea's only reply was a somber stare.

The Only Place To Go

by C.J. Henderson and Michael H. Hanson

"A man who has blown all his options can't afford the luxury of changing his ways. He has to capitalize on what-ever he has left, and he can't afford to admit-no matter how often he's reminded of it-that every day of his life takes him farther down a blind alley."
— *Hunter S. Thompson*

MARCUS PERRY WHEELED HIMSELF OUT of his doctor's office. A couple of medical technicians offered to push him, but he brushed them off with curt finality and rolled his unpowered wheelchair between the motorized sliding doors and down the clinic's front exit ramp. It took the usual efforts to lift himself and his folded wheelchair into his retrofitted handicap accessible van, which was not as difficult as some might surmise. Marcus had lost both of his lower legs in a car accident decades ago, and had ample upper body development to compensate for his lack of lower limb weight.

He slammed the door shut, strapped on his seatbelt, but did not put his key in the ignition. What was the point? He reached down under his seat and pulled out a small, holstered Glock 19. Marcus pulled out the clip and confirmed it held eight, nine-millimeter shells. All hollow point. He'd only need one of course.

Pancreatic cancer the doctor said. Advanced. The rest was a bit of a blur, suggestions of many new and hopeful treatments, pamphlets of support groups, thinly veiled promises of weeks, even months to put affairs into order. Marcus ignored it all. His own mother died less than a week after being diagnosed with the same killer two decades ago. She had been a tough old broad, a retired nurse and a hospice volunteer. She knew the routine loud and clear. Told the hospital staff to cut with the bullshit and just keep her filled to the hilt with morphine. It took just three days for dehydration to take her soul. She'd been sixty-eight years old.

Marcus was fifty-four, pushing fifty-five, divorced, no kids, no girlfriend, and lived alone. He hadn't seen his two sisters in years, all three living several states apart, and the two girls overly busy with their family lives. He'd filled out a will years ago, making one of his brother-in-laws, an accountant, the administrator of his estate, which didn't consist of much more than a used car, an apartment full of old furniture, and a few mostly worthless vintage posters.

Outside, a couple of bike enthusiasts rode by on some old, customized, Iron 883 Harleys. Marcus sighed. Just one more dream on he never got a chance at… not that the cancer ever ruined it. His lack of legs pretty much killed his wish to straddle a chopper one day.

Marcus raised the pistol toward the underside of his jaw.

"Hell of a thing, a bullet."

Marcus almost leaped out of his seat at the sudden unexpected voice. Sitting next to him, as if he just materialized out of nowhere into the locked van, a lanky man dressed in a black suit, trench coat, and fedora lounged in the right front passenger seat.

"Such a tiny thing, but filled with a whole bunch of promise."

"Mister," Marcus growled, "you sure picked the wrong man on the wrong day to rob."

"The name's Johnny," the creepy man of indeterminate age replied, "and I'm not here to rob you, just to make a trade."

Marcus instantly sensed the truth in the strange man's voiced, and quickly lowered his pistol, ashamed at his reaction.

"Sorry about that. You caught me at a bad time. Listen I'm not interested in any deals. How'd you get in my van, anyways?"

"Listen, Marcus," Johnny said, "I know about your problem."

Marcus squinted his eyes for a moment.

"Yeah? You some kind of hospice salesman? I'm not interested."

"No, nothing like that," Johnny said, "I'm more into trading options."

"Oh, I get it," Marcus smirked, "you're some cut rate Doctor Death, on the lookout for hard luck cases like me. Got yourself a big black pill to sell me for lots of cash, no questions asked? Well I ain't gonna pussy out like that. Now why don't you take a nice long walk and…."

"Your mom didn't pussy out either, did she Marcus?" Johnny asked.

Marcus gasped and his mouth grew dry. He clenched his teeth and trembled.

"I'm not offering anything for money, son," Johnny said, "and I can't promise you any miracle cures, though maybe, just maybe, you can help a lot of other people out with something just as dangerous as that nastiness growing inside you."

And what might that be? Marcus thought to himself.

"Merely," Johnny replied as if he could read thoughts, "that you let me pay for a tattoo in exchange for one really big favor."

Marcus screwed his eyebrows up tight and really looked at Johnny. Whatever this nutcase was cooking up, Marcus was netted.

"A tattoo of what?" Marcus asked.

As if on cue another two Harleys roared past the parked van and Johnny jerked his head and smiled towards them. For a brief moment a wide, bright white shark-like grin split the tall man's clean-cut angular face, and the gleam of a single shiny gold left lateral incisor flashed with reflected sunlight.

An hour later Marcus sat forward awkwardly in an antique tattooing chair at Mom's Bane, an odd tattoo shop at the end of a trash filled, rat infested back alley that was packed solid with all manner of weirdos and worse. It was like a cross between a tattoo convention and a freak show, with every square inch of the place taken up by tattoo artists and their clients. Also, the place looked like it had been hit by a quake of eight plus on the old Richter scale, and Marcus had his doubts about the stability of the walls and ceiling.

Following Johnny's directions earlier they barreled from Staten Island to Manhattan, and eventually down several poorly kept streets in Harlem.

The drive itself had quickly turned into a nightmare, as they barely managed to make their way through hastily built barricades throughout the streets of New York, manned by bloody and wounded civilians who looked like they had just fought WWIII hand to hand.

Hundreds of corpses lay sprawled everyone, not to mention pieces of things that Marcus didn't want to remember. They managed to skirt Central Park. Even from a couple blocks away it was obscured by dirt and debris in the air, as if a series of violent explosions had just occurred. Eventually they got to the shop and Johnny hustled Marcus quickly inside.

The Harley tattoo on Marcus's bulging left bicep was gorgeous. The detail was frightening and it looked to Marcus like it might just drive right off his arm. Fact was getting his first tattoo, especially one of a chopper, had been on his bucket list for years.

Guess I can check this baby off, and just under the wire, he thought, unconsciously patting his abdomen with his free hand.

Marcus's tattoo artist was a skinny, nearly emaciated woman, not much older than most teenagers, pale as an albino with a face and arms covered with painful looking piercings that displayed a wide variety of stainless steel studs and cheap jewelry. Her hair was a balled up mess of purple.

"So what's the catch?" Marcus looked up at Johnny, who was just exiting a side room with the shop's proprietor, a shapely and exotic woman with long black hair and a face completely covered with what Marcus quickly realized was a complex tattoo done up to resemble a sugar-skull mask.

"The catch is I have a mission for you," Johnny said.

"A mission," Marcus asked, "you shitting me?"

"A run," Johnny said, "I have a group of folks that needs to get from one place to another in the course of a day and a half. Time is running short, and the bikes are fueled up and ready to go."

"Bikes," Marcus practically shouted, "I don't have legs, Johnny."

"But you got a mind and a soul, Marcus," Johnny said, "and this friend of mine, he just woke up with a full-blown stroke, completely paralyzed him. Hell of a way for someone like him to go. Now, it breaks down like this. As crazy as this sounds, in exchange for that very special tattoo you just got, I can transport your very healthy soul into his broken nervous system, which will repair it and give him the strength to go on his trip. He thinks he's delivering an important package on a business trip, not to mention a friend some place for a very special occasion, but unbeknownst to this friend of mine and his pals, they will soon come in to possession of a powerful, uhhhhhh, talisman, that will help a great many innocent and helpless people if it can be delivered into the right hands."

"And me? What will this, uh, transporting do to me?" Marcus asked.

"You'll be there with him, feeling everything he feels, seeing and doing everything he does, just like you're there, two legs and all."

"Like virtual reality?"

"Even better," Johnny said.

"Who is this guy?" Marcus asked.

"Why he's you, Marcus," Johnny said, "In another nearby alternate dimension, a place where you never got your legs amputated, never got cancer. Unfortunately it's a place that has already suffered a minor incursion of something called the Sha'Daa, the mother of all apocalypses, something I'm trying to stop from happening right here, on this world."

"And this other me," Marcus replied, incredulous that he was actually buying this crazy story, "he's got a crew, or friends?"

"Let's just say," Johnny's mouth broke open into his most frightening grin yet, "he's got the ultimate group of buddies… real motorcycle baddies… a regular gang."

A flash of bright green light exploded from Marcus's Harley tattoo, filling his mind with pain so powerful he passed out…

…moments, or an eternity later, something turned on the lights, loud, not too distant screams of pain.

Mange, Burlap, and Fister were the first of us to take dirt naps that morning, but they would not be the last. Leading just a half-mile ahead of the main pack, barely five miles down old I-215, a screaming stab of Harley horns brought everyone to a fast halt—just not fast enough for all of us. Burlap's sawed-off shotgun and Fister's .45 both roared, but that weren't near enough to stop even one of the trio of scorpions—all of them black fast and the size of pickup trucks—from dragging our brothers off the highway and back to whatever holes they occupied down under the desert.

Our leader, Damn—and yes, that vile curse of fire and brimstone was really his first name—signaled the all clear with his right hand and that was that. We gave our fallen a roar of approval for their sacrifice and it was back on our way to Tijuana. After all, we all knew there was nothing more to be done there. Men don't fight shit like that. At best you survive it.

Besides, like Damn himself said, everything's gotta eat.

It had only been an hour and a half earlier we'd all been waiting snug as bugs for sunrise to make our start. Course, we was waiting on the real sunrise, not the deceptive, fifty mile distant glow from that pile of slag and concrete that was once old Los Angeles. Many an amateur nightrider had permanently lost their way mistakin' that radioactive eldritch beacon for dawn. Not to mention only a fool took a chopper out into darkness with nothing to detect Sha'Daa nasties but a rusty 91-watt headlight and two tired eyes.

Last night's storm had again changed the surrounding landscape. Almost all nine miles of the old State Highway 60 out of Fontana was ripped up or covered in sand. That first half hour was a slow-go, but you take what you get in life. It's not like we had much of a choice. We had a package to deliver, gold coin to be made, personal business, and nothing was going to stop us from reachin' the old Mexican border before the end of the day. We were running low on supplies at our main base camp and fact is we were all expendable for the greater good. Our marching orders were simple. Drugs and gold or don't come back.

I paralleled Damn for a while, takin' my turn bein' side man. No one mindin' riding point with Damn. You couldn't be safer. 'Sides, it was something to ride with him, to glance over and see him blazing along, grinning from ear to ear. Most of us Angels take our pleasures in the usual ways—booze or drugs or sex whenever they're available. And, it weren't that Damn would turn any of those down, but … well … it was just that, young as he was, he knew what life was all about.

It was if, to him, there was nothing that felt greater than the freedom of the road. The rush of a vibratin' hog between his legs, with nothing but endless highway stretchin' out in front of him, it just brought him alive. Anything else was just passin' time.

Durin' our point stretch, I saw Damn glance to his left for a moment, ponderin' a coyote path that led off eastward to the horizon. I knew he was thinking on the rumors we'd been hearin' lately that the Salt Lake and Albuquerque city-forts were startin' to venture outta their territories. We knew some minor trade had begun up northways 'round Seattle. This was gonna mean opportunity for anyone with balls and brains enough to take advantage of it. And it wasn't like our smuggling ventures couldn't do with some new arteries.

Still, that was the future whispering when we still had the present to deal with. While Damn and me were still on point, we reached Inferno Flats, that stretch of the old Inland Empire region of Southern California. Years earlier it started bein' reclaimed by the desert, the road surface slowly turnin' into a sea of potholes and worse road hazards.

As we rolled up to its edge, Damn split the pack in half—Bernardo leading fourteen of us over the footpath off the right shoulder of the highway, the rest following him up the opposite. A couple of hundred-foot-long, barrel-wide snakes, each painted with thick orange, black and tan bands, managed to pace us for close to nine miles before growing bored waiting for a chance to snag a straggler. A bounding deer caught their attention. One sight of that and they were off, tearin' out across the glassy sand after slower prey. It was slow going for us after that, but still we made almost ninety more minutes nonstop at twenty mph.

A little past midmorning we was hit by two tribes of cannibals. Mostly just naked savages, sportin' nothing more than stone clubs and sharpened brushwood, still they were more goddamned trouble than one would expect as Facial's chest was impaled by a long stake so hard he practically flew off his bike. But it was Bulldog what cued us to what was happenin'. His head did a leap offa his shoulders, tellin' the rest of us someone had strung neck high wire across the path. Still, Barney and Butcher were taken down by a pack of at least six of the starvin' maniacs who leapt outta what might as well have been nowhere, tearing 'em to blood and bone with their teeth right in front of us. Damn signalled a halt and hit. We half-circled and pulled our weapons, making quick work of about three dozen of the sick fucks with three short, careful barrages of gunfire. They needed the killin', but wastin' ammo ain't never an option.

At least, not on a day like that one. It seemed like every damned fuckin' thing life had to slam you with came at us. Even after we did our house cleanin' these two, four-foot-tall monstrosities erupted from some hidden hole and charged Damn. He was closest to 'em. The pair were something like people, but in the same way that oil is something like water. Foreheads and chins that sloped backwards, squishy, elongated skulls, curled yellow teeth, barrel-shaped rib cages, large kneecaps, and big hands that ended in short claws— Christ on a crutch, whether their deforms was the result of radiation fallout, plague mutation, breeding with Sha'Daa demons, or what was a question for someone who cared. Damn only knew the things were fast, strong, and looking to make him into an entrée. He unloaded a half clip from his Tec-9 at point blank range and practically cut the two grotesques in half.

When it seemed like the rats were gonna stay in their holes for a while, he searched for our brothers, but all we could find were their torsos. Heads and limbs had somehow been taken in the opening moments of the short battle. Damn stripped them of their colors and tied down the bloody leather vests on the back of his bike. Damned if we'd leave 'em for the savages. Soon as we were gone, we knew they'd be back for the rest. Eatin' our brothers as well as their own. Choke on 'em.

Five more miles of drag along and finally highway appeared again up out of the sand, with few enough potholes so we could charge up to thirty-five mph. Overhead, the sky swung back and forth from violet to fuchsia. There was ebony lines crossed through it, meanin' there was a storm—one a half day or so distant—startin' to form.

A couple of miles after that we spotted a dip in the road about half a mile ahead. It was Damn caught that first telltale glint of green. He extended his right arm in a rotating signal that told us to button up and floor it. Two minutes later Damn led us over the lip of a rise and down into a three mile-long valley crossing at full tilt. In seconds we were surrounded by thick, green mist. Everyone coughed, doin' their best to take as few breaths in as possible. We'd all slipped down our goggles, put on our leather gloves, and pulled bandannas up over our faces, but it was a far cry from the goddamned deep-sea diver's suit you needed to swim the mist without payin' the price.

It weren't more than a third the way across the valley's floor when the acid fog started eatin' away at whatever exposed skin a guy still had left uncovered. Everyone's lungs started burnin', our eyes goin' red, mouths frying no matter how hard you gritted your teeth. Damn, though, he just snarled and leaned even farther forward over his handlebars. Three times he almost lost it hittin' potholes we couldn't see, but somehow he managed to recover before wiping out and keep going.

A couple of times large, dark shapes, each as big as bears just shot across the highway in front of us. They were blurry as anything, but I thought for sure I counted at least eight furry legs at one of 'em, which was enough to make me think the best thing to do was stop thinkin' and focus on what little of the road I could see. Pretty sure it was what all of us were thinkin', that there weren't nothing to do but keep our burning eyes on Damn and hope he could guide us through.

After about two miles his engine started skipping, and it looked like his two-stroke was scary close to fallin' into vapor lock. If the engine died too soon, he might not have enough momentum to coast out of the fog. Worse, slowing down all of a sudden would make him a dangerous obstacle for all of us comin' up behind him.

But, once again we made it. Breakin' outta the valley, Damn cut his throttle and coasted to a halt like a quarter mile past the mist line. One at a time the rest of us glided up to join him—the rest of us only totaling twenty-one. We gave it a minute, but Gang Bang, Fat Ass, Stomper, and Bitch Tits never appeared.

It was a rough loss, and you could see Damn was shook. It had been his call to surf the green. True, the bloody were-fogs were transitory. We coulda sat our bikes on the other side and waited for a few hours and it probably would've gone clear. That tradeoff, though, could also have been a lot more fatal. I mean, just moving through the Inferno Flats was an open invitation for every kind of freak show to take it stab at you. Standin' still really made you a target, especially considerin' that if something did come at you, the only place to go was into the fog, which by then might be thicker.

No, nobody had a word to say over Damn's decision. The only one of us that ever doubted anything he did was Damn, himself. Which, really, is pretty much why we followed him. We all knew the score. The gang back home was bleeding and needed this haul real bad. Fuck.

"Move," Damn had finally yelled after it was clear the fog weren't gonna puke no one else outta its guts. He knew we didn't have no time to waste. It was nearin' noon by then, and we were barely half way to Tijuana. The goods we'd sworn to get there wasn't going to deliver itself.

Before long we could see the crosswind was pickin' up. The crap-filled jet winds always rocketing a couple of thousand feet overhead were starting to lower. A long ebony sickle-shaped formation looked to be slicing down between swirls of the boiling yellow clouds flecked with the sparkly purple motes that meant the end if they touched you. That told us we only had another four hours or so before it all hit the fan. It was going to be close.

Havin' clean road we roared it, screechin' out to make time. Being older than most of the others, I could remember back when we fuckin' ruled the skies, like it was all just another paved interstate system. Back before the Sha'Daa portal opened up and farted out all manner of nasty creatures and hell-beasts, and the military of every nuclear country on the planet panicked and started tossing nukes in a big bang that had leveled that beautiful world of ice cream and cigarettes, of rock and roll and air conditioning and running water—all the shit we didn't think twice about, all the goddamned miracles we flushed down the crapper—machines had flown in the sky.

Oh sure, I know how crazy it sounds, but it's true. Men once flew and hovered up above the world in clean, blue skies. They delivered goods, visited relatives, and went places just for fun. Oh yeah, and they fought wars. They painted the sky with blood and poison and fire and death. And finally, when that wasn't enough for them, they destroyed the forests and oceans and created the shithole we now all fight over.

They ushered in the age of winds, the horrible raging never-ending gales of fire, lightning and anything-that-ain't-nailed-down that knocked over the skyscrapers and ground down the mountains. That boiled the oceans and glassed the lakes, that killed off the bugs and birds and fish and pretty much everything green, leavin' those of us too damn stupid to die with a planet covered in monsters and pain, where every day was just another battle.

And, I have to admit it was probably all for the best. People had gotten so soft and stupid. They didn't deserve a decent world no more. Don't think I don't know what I'm sayin', either. Yeah, I was alive in the before, but I didn't do anything, didn't say anything about where we was headed. I sat back and lapped up the goodies and laughed as everything spun out of control, knowin' like the rest of the apes that the good times were never gonna end.

Well, they ended, hard, fast, and forever. And now, if a man out here in the free lands, far away from the city forts that still pumped out parts and hardware for good coin, wanted even one more breath he had to earn it. Every bite of food, every sip of water, you fought for it or you fuckin' died. Good. We got what we deserved. Everyone does in the end.

After about two hours of tearin' across the old I-15 and most of the way down I-805 S, we were scopin' for the exit of Via Rapida Jose Fimbres Moreno when we pulled around a tight bend and right into the middle of a party. We skidded to a halt as we eyeballed the gang ahead of us. Mostly they were sitting atop parked choppers, about sixty of them, forming a nasty looking gauntlet.

Another ten, twelve of them were off on the right shoulder pulling a train on four women, teenagers from the look of them. From the tension in Damn's shoulders, you could see he was thinkin' on burning rubber, and we were all for it, some wondering why he stopped us in the first place. Then, around nine bikes drove onto the road up ahead, effectively blocking any escape. Damn had spotted the trap before the rest of us. Killing his engine, he sat back and waited to see what the other gang intended on doin' next. They weren't long in showing us.

One of the partiers, a burly fellah with a large gut and a mess of carrot-colored hair made a big show of *suddenly* noticin' us, pullin' up his pants, and then takin' a casual stroll on over. Damn unsaddled, left his Tec-9 holstered on his bike, and just stood there next to it, arms akimbo.

"Name's Razor," the redhead croaked. "We're the Crows. Looks like you're outnumbered. So I guess you're gonna pay us a toll if you want to get out of here in one piece, eh?"

Damn continued to flash his best I-could-give-a-fuck-what-you-think look, without sayin' anything. This, as you might guess, didn't please Razor, who snarled and pointed a chubby index finger at Damn, spittin' his words—"This is Crow territory. You see the bird on my jacket? You get the big picture now, fuckhead?"

Damn glanced over Razor's shoulder to see the last of the other bad boys finishing up with the girls before tying up their arms and legs. The rest of the Crows just sat on their bikes expectantly. About a dozen of them had a free hand restin' outta sight meanin' some kind of weapon.

"Rat got your tongue," Razor asked, "or you just too busy trying not to piss your pants right now?"

This bit of wit got a chuckle from a couple dozen Crows on the sidelines. Us, our engines dead, kickstands down, we sat our bikes, not saying nothing, waiting for Damn to make the first move. Three of Razor's pukes had walked up to stand behind their leader, backin' his play to make their presence seem that much more threatening. Two of them were palming large wrenches, the third, what looked like a single-shot zip gun. All four took in the irons on Damn's jacket, the swastika on his right shoulder, the hammer and sickle on his left, and the upright middle finger over his right breast. None of them seemed too impressed with Damn's short, scruffy beard, or his attitude. When he remained silent, just waitin', Razor started losing it.

"You're beginnin' to piss me off, boy," Carrot-head shouted, "what the fuck club is stupid enough to tool around in my back yard? Who the fuck are you chickenshit losers anyway?"

Comin' forward, Razor took a step sideways to glance at the emblem on Damn's back. It took the Crow's leader a moment to focus on the image whose colors had mostly faded, stained as they were with blood and mud. When the carrot-headed asswipe's face went pale, Damn figured the punk had seen the skull and wings, and the look told him all he needed to know.

Stepping forward, Damn swung his long right arm in a tight arc. A foot and a half length of steel chain flew outta his sleeve, shattering Razor's skull, dropping him instantly. This signaled the rest of us to wade in. Leapin' off our bikes, we startin' poppin' off shots in every direction. Damn laid into Razor's bodyguards, snot-clownin' all three of them before they knew what hit 'em. A trio of explosions tore through the bikers ahead of us. The sound of the grenades made Damn smile. He loved it when the boys got creative.

It took him a couple of seconds to take out the two with the oversized plumber's tools. The third punk's hand was shaking so much his shot went wild, scoring a nasty but shallow gouge across Damn's right cheek, who promptly returned the favor with a kick to the bungler's groin, that followed by a rapid pounding of a steel-toed boot into the jagbag's head three times for good measure.

The dust-up was a good mix of gun and knives, eye gouging and neck snapping, and in just five minutes it was all over. Nine of us lay dead on the ground. But with seventy dead Crows scattered at our feet, it seemed like the kind of math we could live with. Damn just nodded, then wiped some of the excess gore off his face and flashed an evil smile to the rest of us. Most everybody smiled back. After all, if a thing was worth doin', it was worth doin' right.

Damn and the rest of us—four of the brotherhood double-saddling the young ladies we'd inherited a couple of hours earlier—raced as fast as we could that final run of ten miles. And man it was the weirdest stretch yet of this cursed trip.

Big, nasty fucking things, like the children of dragons raped by giant insects, came out of the sky and flew right at us. They was breathing some kinda green plasma from their mouths and noses and we knew if they caught us we were dead meat.

Just as the first of these Winnebago-sized mothers came down to strafe us a flash of blue light appeared overhead, striking it like a fist, knocking it loopy. The other things came in at us and it happened again and then again.

After a minute we realized that one of the chicks we picked up, a pale redhead not more than fifteen, was the cause of it. She had a fucking blue halo around her head that kept spitting light at the flying bastards and fighting them off. We just prayed she could keep it up for a few more miles.

We finally pulled up to the fortified battlement markin' the border crossing into the fort of Little Tijuana at the end of Blvd Las Lomas a couple hours later. The big storm had finally settled in and everything not nailed down was being sucked up into the sky and hauled off to wherever shit goes these days. Damn yelled twice beneath the deafening thunder reachin' down for us. Gettin' no response, he laid on his horn for a full thirty seconds.

"Business or pleasure," a voice yelled down from the wood parapets of the large stockade. Damn flipped a gloved hand in the direction of the biker closest to him, a scruffy but tough-looking, tow-headed teenager barely sixteen—the package we had had the pleasure to escort down from Fontana.

"Business," Damn yelled. "Plus our Elroy is here to become a man."

The figure above chuckled and shouted something unintelligible which apparently had the right effect, as the two huge gates began to swing inward.

"Business hours stop at sundown, and I can see you got women with you," the voice called back, a justifiable amount of suspicion running through it. "Why come here when you got all the gash you need?"

"Because shit, man, it's Tijuana," Damn called back. "First time a man gets laid, it's the only place to go."

We all cheered like maniacs, and a minute later Damn was leadin' us up a dusty side street to the front of a bunker-like saloon what almost looked like it was abandoned. A closer eyeballin' showed several half-naked women posing just inside the reinforced front door. Damn gave Elroy a nasty smile and shoved the boy forward to get the job done.

"Que pedo," a lovely female voice yelled, "here for a good time, Cabrón?"

Damn spun on his heel and balked at the sight of a short, beautiful, mocha-tanned senorita framed by a crumblin' adobe doorway on the other side of the street. A pale, jagged scar ran down the left side of her face that strangely enough only added an alluring fierceness to her already sultry visage.

"Maria," he shouted in surprise, "I heard you were dead."

"Not likely, citizen," the gal smirked, running a free hand over her ample supply of everything, "takes more than a band of cannibals to keep me out of commission. Looking good, Maldito."

That, of course, was all the foreplay Damn needed as he strode across the street, ignoring the fifty mph winds that were kickin' up the mother of all dust storms around us. Spinnin' her around, he shoved her into what couldn't have been more than a sliver of a room. After that, he slammed the steel door to the place shut and left the rest of us to do as we pleased.

We'd made it to Tijuana. It wasn't like we couldn't find something to do.

The next morning the storm finally died. Metal shutters were pulled up all around town while sun glare attacked the bloodshot eyes hiding behind them like a dog on a tree. Damn and the rest of us did our best to shovel down breakfast. Afterward we did a quick inventory on supplies while the acrid smell of burnt coffee filled the air around us. It was pretty easy to trade up considerin' we had the four teens the Crows had donated to our future welfare.

While Cookie was doin' those negotiations, Damn finished wiping the last bits of gore from the two prizes he'd taken off Razor the day before. There was a long thin SS dagger he slid into his right boot and a street chrome Zippo he pocketed in his stained blue jeans. He then held up his left hand, examining the gift Maria had given him this morning, a sterling silver pinkie ring, shaped like a coiled snake with red glass eyes. She did her best to convince him they were rubies, and he had played along with her little lie because, well ... why the fuck not? Wasn't like rubies were worth anything anymore.

Elroy was the only one of us that didn't have any duties. This was his trip. We'd all made it in our time. While everyone else worked gettin' ready to leave, he sat a few feet away from everything, stripped down to his waist, admiring two new black lightning bolt tattoos on his flexing right biceps. When the tattoo artist finished putting a small red scorpion on the left side of Bernardo's neck, Damn signaled the small Mexican over with a jerk of his head.

"Back of my right hand," Damn told him, "I want a red heart pierced by a dark blue knife."

"Si, Senor," the artist replied, taking in the four letters of Damn's name already inked on each knuckle. It took him just thirty seconds to set up his gear, a bastardized contraption that wedded an ancient foot-cranked Singer sewing machine with a customized pulley and gear driven tattoo gun.

At the same time, Bernardo pulled a needle out of his own kit and started working with a foot long stretch of black thread and the leather lanyard he always wore around his neck. With an ease I had to admire, he quickly sewed eleven blood-crusty ears to it, trophies of the rumble with the Crows.

"Spill it," Damn said over the loud clickity-clack of the ink machine, "how we looking?"

"Fucking brilliant," Bernardo laughed, "we got three bags of gold coins for the heroin, which should make the boss real happy. The rest is Christmas, a ton of loot we nabbed from that poser posse of one-percenter wannabees— fresh guns and ammo, not to mention two new Harleys, all the gas and oil we need for now, two kilos of black tar, five bricks of weed, and to top it all off, those four chicks we rescued should bring us some serious silver coin on the coastal slave market."

"Three chicks," came Maria's voice, correcting Bernardo, reminding him of the supplies we'd glommed up there in town, "the redhead stays with us. She carries the mark of Chalchiuhtlicue on her breast."

We all turned to look as Maria pulled back the girl's shirt to reveal a beautiful tattoo of a cross between a snake and a dragon-fly, or that's what it looked like to me.

"It is a sign," Maria went on, "Our priestess foresaw her coming. She will bring much good luck to our community."

While some of us laughed, Damn just nodded, remembering like we all did how this frail little chick had saved all our asses last night. You might think we'd have kept her for protection, but no, we Angels didn't hanker to the magics unleashed across the lands when The Sha'Daa broke through. Sure, we accepted any help folks wanted to give us, which wasn't often, but in the end we was all too superstitious to keep a witch like that long among us.

Bernardo nodded too, givin' her a comic bow, sayin';

"Why yes, *three* chicks." And then, quite uncharacteristically, young Elroy done shouted;

"*Plus* all the goddamned booze, cigars and whores a *man* can handle!"

This set off another round of laughter. Why not? He'd made the Tijuana run. He was as much of a man as anything on two legs in what was left of the world. Let him call himself a man. Worth about as much as rubies, I guess. Still, maybe I'm just gettin' cynical in my old age. Leanin' back, straightin' himself out, Bernardo gave our young Elroy a fist-pump and shouted back;

"Hey, screwed, blewed, and tattooed—not too fuckin' bad for such a hot run."

As we sat around the battered tables there in the cantina, I caught a look in Damn's eyes and I knew where his mind was. A dying preacher once told Damn he was barreling full-tilt down the road to damnation. I always know when he's thinkin' on that, because after, he always looks around himself and does the same thing. As his eyes passed over each one of us, you can just tell he knows that when he makes that trip, he will goddamn well not be makin' it alone.

Trust me, friend, it makes all the difference.

As the laughter died down some in response to Bernardo, Too-Long Belched;

"Fuckin' A, we definitely found paradise after crossing over to this side of the Inferno Flats."

"And tomorrow," Damn smiled, blessin' us with the voice of reason, "on our return trip, we get to do it all over again."

Silence filled the dusty cantina for maybe three heartbeats. Then all thirteen of us Hell's Angels broke out into loud, raucous, joyous laughter. Even in our rat's ass of a world, it was good to be alive.

And then a blast of pain exploded behind my eyes...

Marcus sat up wide-eyed. He was back in the Mom's Bane tattoo shop, but this time on one of the tattooing tables farther in the rear. A couple dozen people were all moving towards the front exit in barely controlled chaos and panic.

What immediately claimed his attention, however, was Haumea exiting one of the side tattoo rooms that were set up like apartments. She was no longer wearing her top hat. Her long hair had been shaved and the sugar-skull pattern on her face had been extended over and around her entire head. Also, she had stripped down to a black sports bra and bikini bottoms, putting most of her full body tattoo on display.

"What's happening?" Marcus shouted.

Stopping in her tracks, Haumea suddenly took notice of him and smiled.

"About time you woke up. It's the end game, sweet cheeks," Haumea laughed, "and the last of the pieces of this crazy puzzle are about to fall into place. Wanna join the front ranks, biker boy?"

Marcus frowned for a moment and then looked down at himself. He had two legs. He was dressed in worn, torn, dirty denim slacks, with faded leather chaps and jacket, with chains slung over his shoulders. He looked up to see his reflection. It was him, but more grizzled looking, and his hair a lot grayer than normal. Nasty old scars crisscrossed his chin, and his hands were large and calloused, and his teeth didn't look too good either. And for some reason, some crazy unknown reason, he knew that the cancer was no longer inside him.

"Yeah, sister," Marcus said as he slid off the table to land solidly onto his combat booted feet, "let's stomp some Sha'Daa ass."

Earth Veins

AUMEA, AND HER SHOP'S RECENT BIKER client Marcus, were the last two people to exit Mom's Bane. The remaining clients and artists had all been given their walking papers and were sprinting, leaping, dimension-hopping, and teleporting away in near blind panic. She had told them they had five minutes tops to clear the danger zone.

Haumea ran her right hand quickly over the top and back of her recently shaved and tattooed head. The power now circulating all across her body was exhilarating and nearly overpowering. She had not felt like this since that full year, long ago in Mexico, when Johnny had meticulously covered her with most of her tattoos. And now, centuries later, he had completed her body suit. This, though, was an even more alarming rush of sensations, as if the last piece to the puzzle of her soul had finally been fitted in place.

When she figured everyone had cleared ground zero, Haumea wrapped her right arm around Marcus's waist.

"Tighten up that sphincter, biker boy," Haumea smiled, "the bad guys are coming and it's time to ride."

The next moment they both flew straight up into the air, as fast as a rocket.

A half dozen creatures, moving so quickly that Marcus could only see their large, saurian forms as brown and green blurs, shot past them to converge on the alleyway that contained Mom's Bane.

Haumea and her companion were a full mile into the air when a horrendous explosion occurred beneath them. Marcus could barely hear Haumea's laughter with all the wind rushing by his ears. She began talking and he realized he was hearing her voice in his mind.

"*Rude awakening for our dragon pals back there,*" she thought, "*coming into proximity with my front door's Olmec headstones was like mixing sodium and water. I'm going to miss that place. She was my one true friend throughout the years.*"

"She?"

"*Mom's Bane was an ancient spirit, a powerful one whose life I saved many decades ago. She repaid me by making herself into my shop.*"

"So she just…"

"*Yeah. I didn't find out until twenty years ago she was permanently trapped in that form. She could change the look of her interior, colors, shapes, and so on, and transport herself between nexus points. But that was it. She could not become spirit again. We both knew Hina couldn't escape…*"

Marcus suddenly realized Haumea was crying, silently. He looked away from her until he sensed she had her composure again.

"*Where are we going?*" Marcus thought back at her, picking up on this new form of communication quickly.

"*Antarctica, buddy,*" Haumea replied, "*we're the other capstone to Johnny's grand plan.*"

"*Grand plan?*" Marcus asked.

"*Oh yeah,*" Haumea replied, "*the mother of all tattoos.*"

And on that cryptic phrase Haumea angled the direction of their flight southward, their speed increasing to a frightening degree. Marcus ducked his head against her side and clenched his eyes tightly shut against the burning chill of the air tearing at his skin and clothes.

An hour later Haumea's voice spoke once again in Marcus's mind, "*Look, it has started.*"

Marcus opened his eyes and saw it was now night. The sky was mostly clear and tens of thousands of stars filled the background. He realized they were several miles above the surface of the earth though the cold no longer bothered him.

"*Protective spell,*" Haumea said, "*you won't have to close your eyes any more either. Now, look down. We're roughly over the equator.*"

Though they were still moving southward at great speed the last bits of receding dusk allowed him to see the outlines of North, Central, and South America, but what really caught his attention were thin gold lines that started slowly appearing and forming back and forth across the continents, glowing brighter and brighter. In minutes, hundreds of miles were covered by this amber weblike pattern.

"*What's happening,*" Marcus shouted in his mind.

"*Thousands of tattoos,*" Haumea said, "*they're activating, reaching out, connecting to each other, becoming greater than what they were.*"

"*What are they becoming?*" Marcus asked.

"*Something beautiful,*" Haumea replied in his mind.

"*Care for a little company?*" a new voice entered their minds.

Both jerked their heads to the left to spot the young man-thing Haumea had met earlier, Prana, flying just a couple of feet away. He appeared to lay on his back, one hand under his head, with a big smile on his mischievous face. Haumea gritted her teeth and did her best to damp down on her terror. During their last few minutes together, when Johnny had completed her full body tattoo, he had told her all about Prana, how he was actually one of one thousand brothers, clones if you will, split off from a single unimaginably powerful being.

These Pranas had swarmed all over the Earth at the beginning of the Sha'Daa, not directly interfering with any of the many conflicts, but acting like scavengers, feeding upon the dying energies of all the hell-gods and hell-entities who lay dying after their failed attempts at conquest.

When each Prana had finished feasting it flew back to the heavens to join with its brethren, reforming back into what it had once been, but a super-being even more powerful than it had been before, a frightening thought as just a single one of the thousand Pranas was more powerful than dozens of hell-gods combined.

But *this* Prana, Johnny had told her, was different. He or it had achieved true autonomy, and no longer felt the need or desire to rejoin its former union, and only wished to follow its own will, its own destiny, one which hopefully did not hold ill will toward humanity.

"*I think I've figured out what you're planning, Haumea,*" Prana said, "*and I must say I am impressed. You are one brave little Hawai'ian woman. One crazy little Hawai'ian woman of course, but a brave one too.*"

"*Why are you here?*" Haumea replied.

"*Relax,*" Prana chuckled, "*I'm waiting things out until the true end-game. I've a feeling things are going to get really interesting during the last few hours of the Sha'Daa... that is, if your little plan works and you can put the beat-down on a few hundred nasty hell dimensions. If you fail, of course, I'd say the Earth is doomed. By the way, quite a hole in the ground you left back in Harlem, not to mention Moscow, Taipei, Nawlins, and Dublin.*"

Haumea licked her lips.

"*Have... have you seen Johnny lately?*"

"*Not for half a day,*" Prana shook his head, "*though I've been chasing that trickster to hell and back, if you don't mind the pun.*"

"*How was he doing?*" Haumea asked.

"*A bit worse for wear,*" Prana laughed, "*from what survivors told me.*"

"*What happened?*" Haumea asked.

"*Well for starters,*" Prana said, "*Johnny took on three hell-gods at the Triple-Six-Tavern, and don't interrupt, you know that place isn't on Earth so Johnny was free to strut his stuff. After that Johnny had to walk out of a molten holocaust in Dingle, Ireland. Seems he shared a really special moment with that pawn shop owner Ashley… but relax, Haumea, it was purely platonic, or as platonic as it gets when two fiery entities share their souls, and after this I followed up on several thousand more trades Johnny made and I still have not caught up with him.*"

"*You said you chased Johnny to hell and back,*" Haumea said.

"*You caught that, eh?*" Prana asked, "*well, seems Johnny got sucked into a hell dimension a number of years ago. I was curious how he eventually escaped and made it back to Earth in time for the Sha'Daa, so, well, I went to visit the place myself, warping time so I could see exactly how Johnny pulled it off.*"

"*And what happened?*" Marcus's thought emanations suddenly cut in.

"*One hell of an adventure, Marcus,*" Prana chuckled, "*but I'm out of time and need to be elsewhere. Who knows? Maybe we'll all survive to hear me tell you the epic tale. Or maybe not.*"

And on that note Prana disappeared, teleporting away to who knows where.

"*Holy crap,*" Marcus said, "*check it out.*"

Several miles away, an unusual looking ebony dirigible, shaped not unlike the front half of a great white shark, and easily a full five hundred meters in length, was rapidly accelerating upwards toward a lone but thick patch of cloud. In hot pursuit were a pack of several dozen bat-like creatures, each about twice the size of a human being.

"*Doesn't look good,*" Marcus said.

"*I'm sorry but we have no time to help them. Now hold on really tight, we need to get to the south geomagnetic pole fast.*"

And with those words they immediately sped up to an even greater velocity, until they broke the sound barrier, and beyond, with a loud sonic boom. The golden traceries below were moving steadily south at near the speed of sound, aching to catch up with the two flyers.

Haumea and Marcus rocketed earthward toward an empty and uninhabited stretch of Antarctic glacier. At the last moment Haumea slowed their descent so they touched down like a feather.

"Jesus, girl," Marcus said, "good thing I haven't eaten in a day. I woulda lost it out both holes."

"It's coming," Haumea shouted, "can you feel it?"

"Not sure I…" Marcus started, then stopped. The ground beneath them shook and he struggled to stand upright. The tremors reached a bearable peak, but did not subside.

"What's happening, Haumea?"

"They're converging on us from every direction," she said.

"What are?" Marcus asked.

"Ley lines," Haumea shouted, "we're the anchor for a hundred thousand ley lines, all filled with the power of thousands of tattoos I have made over the ages, activated and fed by the bravery, hope, and nobility of their wearers. People like you, Marcus. The real heroes of humanity."

"What do you want me to do?"

"Stand fifteen feet away from me, no, that direction," Haumea said, "you and your tattoo will deal with any overflow of the power I have to channel, directing it into the surrounding ice."

"Like a heatsink," Marcus said, "how do I activate it?"

"It will happen automatically," Haumea said, "as long as you stay conscious and keep standing. It might hurt, a lot. I can't guarantee you'll survive long being in such close proximity to such volatile energies. Nor myself for that matter."

Marcus smiled, "Haumea, the last two days have been the best of my life. It's all been worth it. I kinda wish I could see what all these ley lines look like from above before the shit hits the fan, though, you know, the final pattern and all."

"They're more than random lines of geometry, Marcus," Haumea shouted. "It's a vast spell, an ancient symbol of protection from my long lost people.,, and here it comes… now!"

Spinning around they could both see bright golden lines of light burning across the glacier towards them from all directions, within five miles, then three, then one.

Marcus turned to Haumea one last time and his jaw dropped. She had stripped completely nude, oblivious to the sub zero air as was he. Yet even more startling than her natural beauty was the fact that all of the hundreds of intricate tattoos Johnny the Salesman had inked on her skin were now glowing brightly, in a variety of wondrous, angelic colors, making her the most heavenly vision Marcus had ever witnessed.

Haumea looked up to the stars, "I don't know if you are still alive, Johnny. But I never stopped loving you."

As one thousand river-wide beams of blinding amber power simultaneously struck her naked tattooed body, and eternity lapped upon the shore of her soul, Haumea thought she heard a distant whisper reply.

"And I never stopped loving you…"

Appearing suddenly in orbit, far above the surface of the Earth, an enigmatic being of unimaginable power stared down upon the amazing glowing beams forming between tens of thousands of humans wearing magical tattoos and spread all across the planet.

In seconds the ley lines formed the shape of a gargantuan sea turtle spanning every continent, a glorious Honu, the ultimate guardian spirit, the Earth's own Aumakua.

In moments this living tattoo began closing and destroying hundreds of hell portals that had just completely opened during this last half day of The Sha'Daa.

"*Wow,*" Prana thought, "*even more beautiful than I imagined.*"

- THE END -

BIOGRAPHIES

HALO JANKOWSKI IS A TATTOO ARTIST AND a painter and has been tattooing for about eleven years after a year-long apprenticeship. He owns a tattoo studio and art gallery called Black Lotus Tattoos in Hanover, Maryland. Halo has dabbled in *many* mediums including airbrush, digital oil, tattooing and colored pencils. Most of his artistic inspiration has been passed down from his mother, both genetically and via her drive and *multi*-skilled personality.

Tattooing has given Halo an amazing insight into exactly what can be accomplished not only on human skin, but also from attaining an unconventional mental vision into the world around him. In most of his paintings, he has strived to give a *different* or *alternate* outlook on things that have inspired him, mainly fantasies: stories and folk tales he grew up with as a child, especially fairy tales because they allow him the rare opportunity to reattain a childlike imagination in adulthood.

Halo currently works primarily in the portrait style area of tattooing. He is quick to point out, however, that he can still make any of your wildest tattoo dreams come true. He loves to do freehand style tattoos, just taking markers and drawing you a one-of-a-kind custom piece directly on your skin before taking the needle to it. He also does custom auto airbrushing. Halo is an outstanding model for anyone looking for a "turn your life around for the better" approach. Halo beat the hell out of Cancer just shy of four years ago and was also a season-4 contestant of *Ink Master* on Spike TV!

You can see Halo's work and travel dates at www.tattoosbyhalo.com

TRENT ZELAZNY WAS BORN AND RAISED in Santa Fe, New Mexico. He has lived in California, Oregon, Arizona, and Florida. He currently roams around aimlessly. He's also a basketball fanatic.

Trent is also an American author of crime and horror fiction. His work includes *To Sleep Gently, Fractal Despondency, The Day the Leash Gave Way and Other Stories, Destination Unknown, Butterfly Potion, Too Late to Call Texas, People Person,* and *Voiceless.* His short story "The House of Happy Mayhem" received an honorable mention in *Best Horror of the Year 2009,* edited by Ellen Datlow.

Visit

SHADAA.COM

for all author biographies, the secret history of

this chilling franchise, and the inside

low-down on all the books in

Michael H. Hanson's

Sha'Daa™ series

(including those currently in the works)

and how you can order them.

The Sha'Daa is coming.

Are you ready?

MORE TITLES FROM MOONDREAM PRESS

Copper Dog Publishing LLC

OUR IMPRINTS

Pumpkin Hill Press

To find out more about our imprints
and our upcoming releases, visit our website:
www.CopperDogPublishing.com
or our Facebook page:
www.facebook.com/copperdogpublishing